TWO SONS
FROM
EGYPT

Book I: The Lion Awakes

TWO SONS
FROM
EGYPT

The Story of Thutmose III and Moses

R. S. SMITH

1603 Capitol Ave., Suite 310 Cheyenne, Wyoming USA 82001
1-888-980-6523 | admin@urlinkpublishing.com

URLink Print and Media is committed to excellence in the publishing industry.

Published in the United States of America
ISBN 978-1-64753-199-7 (Paperback)
ISBN 978-1-64753-200-0 (Digital)

Fiction
30.12.19

DEDICATION

This book is dedicated to the Hebrew people who, for centuries, not only fought for their land but for their right to exist. To the multitudes of Jews who lost their lives during numerous attempts at genocide, this author acknowledges and remembers the foundation on which the Jewish nation began.

Acknowledgements

Thank you to the many individuals who encouraged me during the years of researching and writing this book: to my family, especially my children, who put up with my hours of preoccupation; to friends, professors and peers for their suggestions and guidance. A special thanks to the curators of the Cairo Museum and New York Metropolitan Museum of Art for their help in locating specific archives; and to the many local libraries that ordered endless books for my perusal. Further, thank you to Dr. Bryant G. Wood and the Associates For Biblical Research; William H. Shea, Ph. D., former Professor of Old Testament, Andrews University, and Research Associate, Biblical Research Institute; and Grant R. Jeffrey, author and founder of Frontier Research Publications, Inc.

Finally, to those interested in the pursuit of truth: may you enjoy the journey back in time as you meet Moses and the characters surrounding him during the 18th dynasty of Egypt, even discovering who Moses was in the annals of ancient history.

CONTENTS

PART I

PART II

INTRODUCTION

Two of history's most influential characters were the Semitic slave leader, Moses, and the 18th dynasty conqueror, Pharaoh Thutmose III. To understand the importance of these two great men we must take a closer look at the ancient site of Jericho and Dr. Bryant G. Wood's rediscovery in the rubble of that ruin.

Dr. Wood re–evaluated the dates of the pottery originally excavated by John Garstang in the 1930's and found, true to Garstang's theory, the evidence indeed supports the city's conquest by the Hebrews (Habiru/Apiru) in the 1400's B.C.[1][2][3]

This discovery places Moses' birth not in the 1300's B.C. during the reign of Pharaoh Raamses (Ramases), as often assumed, but in the 1500's B.C., the 18th Dynasty

---

[1]   *The Pharaohs of the Bondage: The Israelite Slavery in Egypt*, Bryant G. Wood, (Akron, PA: Associates for Biblical Research, 2015) [DVD]

[2]   Douglas Petrovich, "Amenhotep II and the Historicity of the Exodus-Pharaoh," www.bibleseminary.academia.edu

[3]   *Correlating Biblical and Egyptian Chronology* and *Identifying the Early Israelites in the Egyptian Archaeological Record*, Dr. Douglas Petrovich, (Akron, PA: Associates for Biblical Research, 2015) [DVD]

of Egypt, contemporary with the greatest conqueror Egypt ever knew, Pharaoh Thutmose III.

Two Sons From Egypt portrays the struggle of these two personalities in the era preceding the Exodus. If Moses and Thutmose III lived together during the 18th Dynasty then we know the characters surrounding them at court and the events that shaped their destinies.

The Lion Awakes Trilogy begins with Moses' life in Egypt and the bondage of the Hebrews as told in *Two Sons From Egypt*. Book II, *Escape From Paradise*, portrays the plagues and the exodus from Egypt from both the Egyptian and Hebrew perspectives; and Book III, *The Crimson Cord*, tells of the conquest of Canaan and the story of Rahab, a prostitute, who joins the Hebrews and marries a Prince of Judah, privileged to be included in the ancestry of Christ.

The Lion Awakes Trilogy is based on recorded events and actual historical characters, though the spellings of the names have been modified for easier reading.

An archaeological discovery in an ancient tomb discloses even more of the characters in this otherwise untold tale, giving a clue as to who Moses may have been in Egyptian history.[4] While throughout this book he will be referred to as simply Moses, there is another name by which this man of destiny may have been known.

---

[4]   H. E. Winlock, "The Egyptian Expedition 1935-1936", The Metropolitan Museum of Art, 1937, p. 3-39.

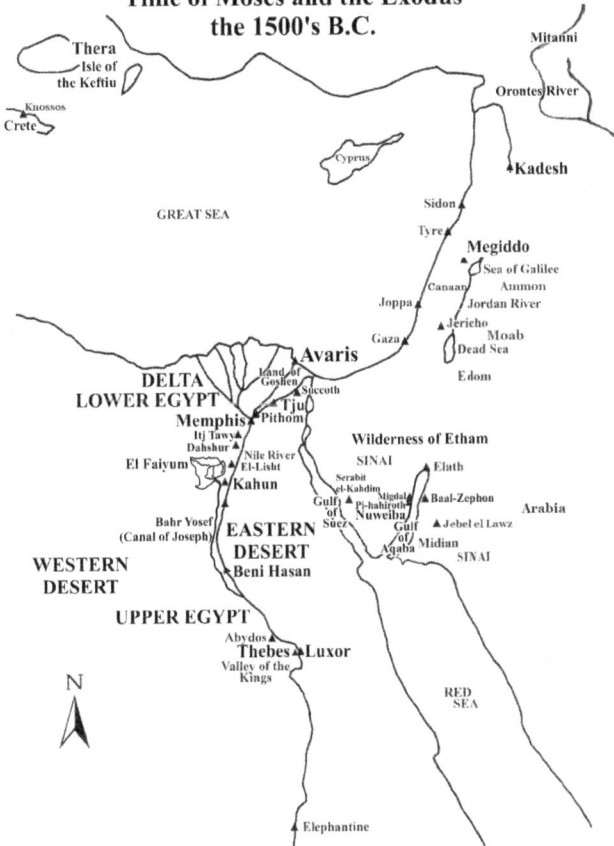

Map of Eygpt and the
Ancient Near East at the
Time of Moses and the Exodus
the 1500's B.C.

PROLOGUE

Ambrose Lansing blinked back the sweat that dripped down his brow and into his eyes. Wiping his face with a kerchief and stuffing it into his pocket, he stared into the gaping mouth of the tomb. "Find anything else?" he hollered.

William Hayes did not answer, instead Ambrose's own words echoed back from the dark cavern. He stood and rubbed the small of his back, turning from his perch atop the slope of Sheikh 'Abd el Kurneh to squint through the blinding light at the still lovely ruins of the temple of Deir el Bahri. At this height the temple appeared carved from the very mountain that rose behind it, a lasting tribute to Egypt's first female Pharaoh, Hatshepsut.

Even after all these years she was still an enigma. Yet one of her Officers puzzled him even more, his relation to the Pharaoh still unanswered.

He and Hayes had already excavated the man's first unused tomb that boasted the rare privilege of being hidden beneath the Pharaoh's temple court. His second was above the temple on the slopes of this same mountain, yet was never finished, nor was his body ever found as he had apparently fled Egypt, according to ancient texts, at 40 years of age.

While excavating his second tomb Hayes had discovered this secret cache dug into the cliff–side, offering the strangest piece of all to the puzzle of this man's life.

A light flickered in the mouth of the chasm. "Well, are you coming or not?" William's voice anxiously rose from the depths as if from the nether world.

Ambrose glanced a last time across the palm fringed Nile to the metropolis of Thebes, the glinting glass of modern buildings mixed with the crumbling spires and pylons of the ancient kingdom. The sight offered him a sense of comfort before succumbing to the cavern of the dead. Pushing his glasses onto his nose, he adjusted his knapsack and carefully climbed down the rickety ladder into the yawning depths below. Once on solid ground he peered about in the dusty silence, and involuntarily coughed, hearing his echo as if someone mocked him. He stood breathlessly still, waiting, fearing at any moment an unseen hand might reach from behind and latch onto his shoulder.

As his eyes adjusted to the blackness he could see the forms of two hired men working by torchlight over the remains of what Hayes believed to be the mother of the man in question. Ambrose joined them and took one of the torches.

They had found enough articles to identify the woman as Hatnufer. In fact, of all the mummies in this cache she alone boasted any amount of wealth, while claiming the unusually humble title of 'Mistress,' or 'Madam,' in modern terms. The folds of her flesh had dried to her bones like a wrinkled garment, evidence she had once been well fed and portly. While a bedraggled hair piece rested atop her sparse grey braids in what was surely the fashion of her day she was dressed in a mere loincloth, shown in ancient drawings to be the garb of slaves. In contrast, she was wrapped with linen from Pharaoh Hatshepsut's own store, having royal scarabs and jewelry scattered throughout the layers of cloth. Strangest of all was the coffin in which she lay, lined with a layer of pitch that had caused the linen to adhere to it like black glue.

Ambrose stepped near the sarcophagus and touched the bitumen. What could it mean? Had her son hoped to make her coffin water proof, taking literally his mother's voyage to the world of the dead?

He remembered a story he had heard as a boy, the tale of a Hebrew woman who had daubed a basket inside and out with pitch, setting it afloat on the Nile in order to save her infant son. Not so unlike the tale centuries earlier of Sargon of Akkad whose mother had set him afloat in a basket on the Euphrates. Had the first tale inspired the latter? Perhaps he thought that if bitumen had worked in this life, why not in the afterlife?

In another corner of the tomb Hayes labored over the Officer's father, Ramose, who also proved a puzzle as his disjointed skeleton appeared to have been unearthed from a previously muddy grave. Though the man had few possessions and no title whatever, he was honored to be buried here above Pharaoh's holy temple, and wrapped, as well, with linen from her royal store. He wore the same simple loincloth, and had long hair and a beard, the custom of Semites rather than Egyptians.

A worker motioned to them. "Look what these other mummies have borne, quite literally."

Ambrose hurried to his side, the light from his torch moving eerily along the wall as if a spirit hastened ahead of him. He shone the light on three other forms:

women whose dark braids and scanty garb matched that of the others, who also evidenced having been chipped from mud and gravel, but with one difference. Each was wrapped with an infant at her side.

Ambrose stared at the bodies while century's old dust swirled about his head. He coughed again, this time not even noticing the echoes that followed. "Hayes, you need to see this."

William shuffled toward the light as together they studied the find. The sight resurrected another memory from Ambrose's past.

Handing his torch to William he rummaged through his pack and took out a worn black book, an ancient relic in its own right passed on to him from his grandmother. He hastily thumbed through the pages to the book of Exodus, chapter one. Moving his finger down the text, he stopped at verse twenty two. Then he peered into the hollow eyes of the three women.

Moses as well had risen from the depths of slavery to a position in Pharaoh's court as an adopted son. He too had fled Egypt at 40 years of age, and had been akin to women who could easily have given their lives attempting to save their young from Pharaoh's henchmen.

Was there a connection? Might Moses and Senmut be one and the same?

Without moving his gaze, he slipped the book into his hip pocket, his eyes on the mummies. If only the dead could speak, what secrets would they tell?

The flame from his torch moved then flickered as if stirred by an unseen presence, as if the dead could read his thoughts and were about to speak.

PART I

"By faith Moses, when he was come to years
refused to be called the son of
Pharaoh's daughter...."
Hebrews 11:24

CHAPTER 1

Moses' fleet wound along the fluid avenue of the Nile, past silhouetted palms and villas, guided by a single star that clung to the horizon like a drop of dew as the wings of dawn slowly lifted.

Senmut Re Moses, son of the god Amon and Pharaoh Hatshepsut, stood at the prow of the foremost ship watching the pink and golden light usher in the rebirth of Ra from the body of Nut with the promise of sunrise. As the fleet rounded the bend, Thebes spread along the distant bank like a heap of geometric blocks and spires that grew until it filled the eastern desert.

He should have felt proud and impervious, having just signed a treaty with Egypt's greatest threat, the Keftiu from the Isle of Thera. Instead his heart felt heavy, though he stood regally, his body taut and tanned from weeks at sea. Everyone knew Egypt's enemies would not long abide Pharaoh Hatshepsut's peaceful policies. As heir, he was their only hope of strength and stability.

His voyage to Thera had been for that very purpose: to show his power as future Pharaoh while communicating a warning should the bounty of the Delta entice the Keftiu to notions of conquest as it had once done the Hyksos.

His eyes narrowed on the capital as the wind slapped the kilt against his legs. He purposefully kept his gaze from the western bank where the garrison ruins lay in mock silence amid the clutter of funerary temples from long dead Pharaohs, and where the cliffs of El Kurn rose behind it like an impregnable fortress, guarding the spirits of the royal dead and their treasures.

Instead, Moses squared his shoulders, his eyes eastward, reflecting the arc of sunlight as it crested behind the capital. He had seen the lush vegetation of the Delta, had experienced the blue–green expanse of the Great Sea, and had visited an island paradise whose technology defied Egypt's most learned scholars. Yet here at Thebes, glory of the Two Lands of Egypt, was where he longed to be.

The sun god seemed to agree as it smiled over Thebes, reaching across the land with arms of blinding light and embracing the beloved city. The white sails snapped above him and the falcon emblem writhed on its white linen as if to free itself as the wind tugged the ships to shore.

He could see the crowds already gathered on the bank, the Priests and choir leading the throngs in praise to Egypt's numerous gods. Soon, as evidenced by a colorful procession winding toward the river, the litters of Pharaoh Hatshepsut and her entourage would join them. Moses watched as the masses lifted their hands and voices in a thunderous cheer at sight of his fleet and the golden barque on which he stood. The High Priest prayed in the foreground while several web Priests swung censors of incense as if anticipating the arrival of a god.

Moses pushed all other thoughts aside and focused instead on the populace, Egypt's greatest asset. He had risked his life for them, facing the outrage of Egypt's enemies and the hostilities of a foreign court while entrusting himself to the gods' care. He had done it for these, the masses of Egypt. For Egypt was a people even more than it was a nation.

The sound of a trumpet pierced the air as Puseneb, High Priest of Amon, raised his hands in blessing. As if on cue, a web Priest opened a cage, letting loose a falcon, symbol of Egypt's heir safely returned. The creature flapped its wings, lifting high into the blue above the clamor and color of the crowds. Peering down at Moses with a haughty eye, it paused, mid–flight as if suspended, gliding in a slow arc above the ships.

Moses smiled, understanding a greater meaning in the moment, for he also soared toward the threshold of his destiny, having been caged in the shadow of Hatshepsut's reign for too many years. The time had come to free himself, as that falcon, and claim the title rightfully his. Neither he nor Egypt could wait any longer.

Spreading its wings, the bird opened its beak with a piercing squawk, circling higher and higher into the clear sky until eventually lost in the brilliance of the sun.

Far from the bustle of the palace and Avenue of Rams crowded with well–wishers, beyond the city gates and villas that marked the edge of the desert, a handful of ruffians romped with Prince Thutmose III, taking aim at their swiftly moving prey. The desert glowed with the morning sun as if afire beneath Ra's breath.

"After it!" Thutmose shouted, jerking the reins of his chariot this way and that in an effort to overtake the animal. His sturdy build appeared like the painted reliefs of his grandfather, Pharaoh Thutmose the Great, which decorated the walls of Karnak and halls of the palace.

Thutmose skidded to a stop amid a cloud of dust, his eyes on the target that had taken cover behind a sparse bush. The furry form could still be seen, panting hard as it attempted to become invisible. Thutmose stretched his bow with a well–muscled arm and let the arrow fly, penetrating the leafless shrub but missing the hare by a breath. It scampered from its hiding place as Thutmose pulled another arrow to the string, lengthening his reach and following the prey with a penetrating eye. Releasing his grip, the arrow whistled through the air and into its mark, fastening the rabbit to the ground where it momentarily wriggled as if to free itself, then stilled.

Thutmose grinned. "Got him!"

"Pierced as surely as a bloody Hyksos," Amenhab announced.

Thutmose stepped from his chariot. "I wish it were a Hyksos," he muttered. "I'll never have the chance for a real battle, not if Hatshepsut has her way."

Amenhab laughed, attempting to lighten his friend's mood. "I don't see why not? Pharaoh is far too taken with peacemaking to bother, and Moses can't defend every border. You may make a soldier yet, perhaps even General."

Thutmose snorted, trying to picture it, but could only see Moses at the head of Egypt's army and himself at the rear. He shook his head. "I doubt I'll ever have the privilege of real combat, unless we face our enemies in Egypt."

"With the borders as unsettled as they are, you may have your wish," Amenhab gravely answered.

Rekmire, dark skinned and wiry, perked his ear toward the river. "Do I hear trumpets?" He looked at Amenhab, his eyes wide. "Might Moses have returned?"

"By Amon!" Amenhab searched the distance, seeing a cluster of sails at port. Leaping to his chariot, he left a cloud of sand in his wake as he and Rekmire attempted to out–race each other to the river.

Thutmose stared after them, his gaze moving to the wide ribbon of blue and the foremost ship that reflected the sun as if Amon himself had entered Thebes.

"Moses," he whispered, his face impassable. If only he were heir instead, he knew what he would do with Egypt's power. He would march on the east as his grandfather had done, and in a series of swift campaigns, would push the Hyksos from the edge of the earth, exacting tribute from every Syrian city– state from Egypt to the Euphrates. He would sail to the Isle of Thera and take captive the beautiful women depicted on their vases, and would fill the temple of Karnak with treasures, buying the gods' blessings and his own eternity. Then, when Egypt had become the greatest nation on earth and he the mightiest warrior, he would rebuild the capital of Avaris in the Delta as his grandfather had done, creating a city to rival Thebes itself.

Thutmose clenched his teeth, his nostrils flared as he picked up the reins of his chariot, urging his horse to a run. Unlike Moses, however, born of royal and divine blood, his own was only half royal, and questionable at that. If he had not looked so much like his grandfather he doubted he would even have had the privilege of living at the palace, or watching Moses assume roles he could only dream of occupying.

Nefru held out a neatly manicured foot as her maid hurriedly applied henna to her toenails. Though impatient to see Moses, she was not willing to let a single detail of her toilet remain undone. Her younger sister could sleep the morning away if she wished, but Nefru intended to meet Moses in full regalia. At another sound of the trumpet Nefru bolted to her feet, nearly toppling the alabaster jar the servant held.

Ignoring her half painted feet, she ran to the balcony and leaned over the rail, straining for sight of him. Shading her eyes, she at last saw the royal fleet moored in harbor, their gleaming sails lifted like tiny pyramids against the blue, while the brown bodies of slaves, appearing like a steady trail of ants, unloaded goods and equipment at the docks. Nefru searched farther, seeing Moses and his Officers at the head of the parade of royal litters, already beginning their march up the Avenue of Rams and toward the palace.

Catching her breath, she hastened back to her room, ignoring the servant who followed her, and struck the metal gong to summon her steward.

Nefru's face reddened with a mixture of excitement and irritation. "Hurry, he'll soon be here!"

"My Lady, only now did any of us hear of the Prince's arrival."

Nefru had no time to reprimand. Seating herself once again she pointed her other foot, submitting to the experienced hands of her maid.

The Steward of the Royal Wardrobe entered with an armful of garments, holding them out as Nefru snatched at the gowns, tossing them in colorful piles about the room. Finally she hesitated over a blush of pink linen brought by way of a Syrian tradesman. Its gauze–like weave would reveal more than just the outline of her body.

"This will do," she retorted, succumbing to the deft hands of her maids. Color rose to her cheeks, complimented by the hue of the gown, as her eyes shone bright with expectancy.

Seated at the dressing table, a servant quickly applied kohl and malachite to accent her eyes, coloring her lips with a mixture of ochre and oil. The hairdresser entered with a dark wig perfectly prepared, and set it upon her head, taking care that every hair turned under until it appeared as uniform as a temple drawing. Placing a thin diadem about her brow, the maiden accented it with a fresh lotus that dramatically contrasted against the black wig.

Nefru stood and appraised herself in the bronze mirror, her bracelets and anklets tinkling like bells as she turned this way and that. She nodded approval as a servant splashed myrrh and aloes about her like the mists of morning. She must appear more stunning, more beautiful than any Keftiu maiden who might have stolen Moses' heart, for when he finally wore the crown she would stand at his side as his wife.

Nefru took a deep breath, attempting to quiet her heart while her servants one by one bowed from the room to await her in the hall, all but the Steward of the Royal Wardrobe who would follow. Slipping into her sandals, Nefru straightened her shoulders, following her entourage down the hall and through the palace. Though life as a Princess seemed an easy one, love was not, and she must be certain Moses' heart held room for no other.

South of Egypt's border in Kerma, capital of Kush Ta–Seti, 'Land of the Bow,' a hut glowed with light as a shaman performed the rite of sacrifice. He tossed a handful of incense into the fiery mouth of the idol and the flame flared, letting loose a billow of smoke like breath as the shaman waved his arms in an incantation. Still the icon stared unblinking above the fire, the smell of burning flesh mingling with the sweet incense.

The shaman called for the liver of the beast just sacrificed in order to read the future of the one who had requested the divination. He studied it then stared more closely, his mouth gaping. Stretching out his arms, he fell rigid and trance–like to the floor.

Tasha, daughter of the village chieftain, watched in horror from the shadows of the hut. Her hair fell in a cascade about her face, framing her features in the firelight while she stared at the image as if fearing it would speak. What had Ukuru read in the liver? What had he seen so terrible in her future?

Slowly the shaman forced himself from the dirt floor with dust clinging to him like a garment.

"Tasha," he whispered, "you must bring your father at once."

"What is it, Ukuru? I asked only that you tell me who I would marry." Her eyes fearfully held his.

"The gods have chosen to reveal more than just your destiny, little one." He paused, wondering if he dared disclose what he had seen, though he did not fully comprehend it himself.

Taking a deep breath, he closed his eyes in an attempt to remember every detail. "Two sons will arise from Egypt. One will sweep away the nations of the earth like shards of pottery from a table."

Tasha's mind raced. Egypt had done little in the form of aggression while ruled by their female Pharaoh, and every surrounding nation, including Kush, thought them easy prey. How could Egypt possibly strengthen itself now? And who were these 'sons'?

The shaman's eyes shot open as if sensing her disbelief. "I tell you I saw multitudes dead and more prisoners than Egypt can hold. A new Pharaoh will emerge who will change the face of the earth."

Tasha's eyes brimmed with tears. "Then Kerma will be destroyed?"

The shaman peered into the smoky darkness as if seeking the answer there. "After this new Pharaoh the second son will reappear, and with the help of a powerful god, will overcome the first."

A tear trickled down Tasha's cheek. "But what has this to do with me, and what of our people?"

"Your future, Tasha, is entwined in the destiny of one of these men. You will save the lives of your people as surely as he will save his."

Tasha's eyes formed a question, her lips quivering. "Am I to leave my people? Do you read no future for me here?"

Ukuru wistfully looked at her, wishing he could offer some comfort other than the truth. "I see you sailing north on an Egyptian vessel by which you will never return."

Tasha shook her head, covering her ears as she ran from the hut and over the stone path into the darkness of the jungle. She wished she had never entered the shaman's door. Her mother had warned her that knowing the future was too great a burden. She felt it now as if a weight hung about her neck so heavy she could hardly breathe. Why would she have to go away? She loved her family, her people, and her home. Her father would not allow it. He would incite the Madjai warriors to protect her.

But as soon as she thought the words she realized their futility. When had the shaman's visions not come true? If this new Pharaoh stormed their border as Ukuru predicted, Kush would have to relent or perish. Yet the holy man had said she would save her people. How? What could she possibly do?

Veering from the path she turned toward the river, falling onto the mossy bank and clinging to it as if weeping against her mother's bosom. The river seemed to cry with her as it coursed beyond the bank. Lifting her eyes to a blur of stars overhead, she prayed with all her heart that just this once the shaman's words would be proven wrong.

Hatshepsut tossed on her bed in the darkness, throwing off her coverlet and feeling for her sandals. Peering about the bedchamber, she saw only the shadow of the inlaid crown on a bust in the corner where she hung her jewels and the ankh she wore for protection. She stood, pacing the polished floor, remembering an incident thirty years earlier that haunted her still.

She was fifteen again and standing on the bank of the Wadi Tumilat, the Delta's easternmost branch of the Nile. The moon hung low, spilling silver onto the river and washing over the bulrushes at its edge as mists rose like mesh curtains.

Hatshepsut loved the outdoors, the feel of the grass between her toes and the wind against her bare skin, the movement of water as it rippled past her body like a silken garment. Her mother had called her a fish when she was young, and her father had built her a pool at the palace in Avaris so she might swim safely. She was not at the palace that night, however, but far from the capital at their summer palace near Pithom.

Hatshepsut had loosened the clasp about her hair, shaking her head as her hair spread like spun gold over her back and shoulders. Slipping off her garment, she dove into the water like a silver fish. She alone had visited their summer residence, leaving her mother at Avaris while her father, Pharaoh Thutmose, had gone on another of his campaigns, attempting to push the Hyksos farther east from Egypt's borders. His parting words ominously rang in her ears.

"Upon my return you will marry your half–brother, Thutmose II, and provide Egypt an heir."

Hatshepsut had found herself hoping her father never returned. She hated her half–brother and couldn't imagine him as her husband pawing over her. He did nothing but eat, drink and gawk at the naked dancers. She felt herself merely an ornament waiting to assure him his place on the throne. As sole surviving child of the Pharaoh and his Great Wife, Ahmose, she alone could bestow the right of rulership. But why had the gods given her such a detestable brother?

Hatshepsut stood in the frigid water, listening. Had she imagined it, or had she heard a cry?

A movement rustled the grass and she turned, instantly alert, aware that crocodiles were not uncommon in these waters. She backed a step toward shore, watching the reeds that formed a wall between her and the palace. Then she laughed aloud. It must have been the wind.

She was about to dive a second time when she heard it again, this time coming from the direction of the bulrushes. She searched them but saw nothing. Then she spied it, a dwarfed boat–like object moving among the grass until it emerged in full view...a laundry basket afloat on a moonlit path as if it had as much right to the river as a royal barge.

Hatshepsut smiled. It must have escaped a peasant doing laundry from one of the nearby slave villages. She sighed with relief as water dripped from her body, unaware until now how tense she had actually been. She was about to turn back when she stopped mid–step and blinked. Was she seeing correctly? It appeared the basket had shaken as if alive. She took a step closer, jumping back as it emitted a cry.

Hatshepsut gulped. A baby in a laundry basket?

She stood transfixed, contemplating the possibility when another cry rent the air as the basket continued toward her, guided by the gentle current of the wadi. Hatshepsut reached for it, the bitumen on the outside sticking to her fingers as she pushed it ashore. She wiped her hands on the grass then lifted the lid and peered inside with as much curiosity as if she were opening a gift.

"By Amon, a male infant!" Hatshepsut lifted the child from the wrappings, holding him up to have a better look.

She had heard of the plight of the Habiru in Goshen, of the 'purging' her father had ordered in the nearby slave villages, but had thought nothing of it as it hardly affected her. She hugged the wriggling baby to her breasts. Some at court had whispered that the edict meant death for all newborn Habiru males. The Habiru were distant kin of the hated Hyksos who her father feared might one day unite with Egypt's enemies and overthrow the kingdom as they had done centuries ago. But infants and children?

Hatshepsut shook her head in disbelief. Whatever role her father played in such a decree she could not believe he meant to harm innocent babies.

The infant curled his fist about her finger and she pressed it to her lips, snuggling him to her bossom to keep him warm. Her father's henchmen would not touch this one, she would see to that! This child, at least, would be spared.

Then she remembered her father's words. He had said she must marry to provide an heir, a son. Hadn't the gods provided, sending her a baby in a basket borne on the Nile? She laughed at the irony. The babe clutched at her as if communicating his own desire to be with her, but she knew what he really wanted. She must find a wet nurse from among his people, sure that there was at least one who would gladly keep silent just to know the child lived.

"Moses," she whispered the name, smiling down at him, "for I have drawn you from the waters of the river god Mo."

She laid him on the grassy bank then filled the basket with mud and rocks, sinking it in the wadi. Already a tale had begun to form in her mind: of Amon's gift to her, a royal yet divine son. Now she would not have to marry her step-brother but could rule Egypt in her own right, for the gods themselves had provided her an heir.

Hatshepsut sat up in her bed as the memories dimmed like the mists of morning, dissipating in the rising sun.

In spite of her insistence, her father had not believed her story, and upon their return from the summer palace had forced her to marry her sickly half-brother, Thutmose II. Thank the gods, after their father's death, her husband's rule had been brief and inconsequential, though he had sired a son, Thutmose III, by way of a comcubine, and had given her two daughters. Being young and capable,

Hatshepsut had stepped eagerly into the gap as Egypt's first significant female Pharaoh.

Yet Moses had remained hers, her miracle, her secret and her son who had grown into a stately Prince even now demanding his right to succeed her, a right surely the gods must question.

CHAPTER 2

Moses marched down the sunlit corridor, hardly noticing the flowers and waving banners for his benefit, nor the noblemen clustered in anticipation of his arrival. He was consumed with one thought: that he convince Pharaoh Hatshepsut and the council of Egypt's need for an army and of his own right to rule.

Far too long Egypt had abided Hatshepsut's peaceful policies, attempting to passively negotiate rather than prove the strength they had known during the reigns of previous Pharaohs. Too often Moses had watched the armies of their enemies build forces outside Egypt while Pharaoh balked at conscripting an army. The Two Lands of Egypt, north and south, could wait no longer, and neither would he.

Moses nodded at the guards who swung open the doors of the council chamber. Standing on the threshold, he peered into the shadowed room, his eyes taking a moment to adjust after the brightness of the colonnade.

"Greetings," a voice bellowed.

Moses recognized it as Puseneb's and clenched his jaw, for the High Priest hardly held the esteem his title deserved. Taking a deep breath, he entered, striding past the windowless walls that flickered with patches of lamplight beneath a ceiling lost in darkness. At the room's center around a long table sat Pharaoh and her Officers awaiting his arrival.

Puseneb motioned him to a seat. "Welcome, Moses. We look forward to news of your adventures in Thera and abroad."

Hatshepsut smiled, though her face appeared drawn and pale in the dim light, and Moses wondered if she had fallen ill during his absence. He dismissed the thought as more important matters weighed on his mind.

The High Priest opened with prayer, the drone of his voice making Moses restless. Puseneb sat to the right of Pharaoh, tending to dominate by his very presence. One could hardly miss him even in a crowd, not only for his bulk but for his tongue, for he rarely kept an opinion to himself, though he took care not to contradict the Pharaoh.

Beside him sat Tuty, the treasurer, and Nehisi, the seal bearer. Both had served on the council since before the death of the late Pharaoh Thutmose II, Hatshepsut's half–brother, and were now privileged to serve his Great Wife and Pharaoh in her own right. Moses had often seen the lanky pair walking the halls of the palace, discussing in private what they dared not say openly. They had a timidity Hatshepsut depended upon.

Ineni, elder advisor to three generations of Pharaohs, sat on Hatshepsut's left. He of all her confidants deserved the respect due his years, and Moses trusted his judgment above any other. Huddled against the walls on either side sat the scribes, cross–legged with their ink palettes on their knees, taking notes beneath the lamps.

Tuty stood and read from a lengthy scroll: "...The level of the Nile exceeds last year's height by 20 span, evidence of Amon's blessing; the tally of cattle is ongoing, with fifteen provinces reporting and an average growth of nearly a quarter; the corn seems sufficient until next season's yield, with 560,000 hekats of grain in Thebes alone."

Determination pulsed through Moses' temples, the angles of his face accentuated in the light. "That is all well and good, Tuty, but did you hear news from the northern provinces while I was away?"

The High Priest shot an inquiry to Pharaoh who raised a brow in nonchalance. "What news do you seek?" she asked.

Moses looked at Ineni then withdrew a papyrus from his satchel.

Puseneb brightened. "The treaty!"

"Not so," Moses corrected, "but a report from Governor Mitry of the Delta Province Nekheb with whom I visited upon my return. In it he tells of raids by the Hyksos on our easternmost villages and repeats a request he said he made months earlier for a border patrol."

Hatshepsut reddened. "How do these raids differ from the skirmishes that usually occur? The Hyksos have pecked away at our border for years without serious threat."

Moses met her gaze. "Only because your father subdued them during his own reign. Ever since you abandoned the Delta garrison they have repeatedly tested us, and I expect they will continue."

Hatshepsut fell silent while the High Priest stifled a laugh. "First this supposed emergency with the Keftiu at Thera, and now the Hyksos. Would you have us believe they also plan an invasion?

"It wasn't long ago they did just that, splitting Egypt in two and ruling the regions of the Delta with the help of the Habiru."

"The very reason we maintain the slavery of these Semites," Puseneb retorted, "so they won't join our enemies against us."

Moses' jaw flexed. "It's not the Habiru that concern me."

"I should think not." Puseneb's belly shook with a laugh. "Would you fear slaves who serve as meekly as lambs?"

"As meek as lambs and as strong as oxen." Moses impatiently rose. "But no, it's not the Habiru I fear, nor the Hyksos, nor even the Keftiu, but all our enemies combined. The Delta offers the best grazing land in Egypt, blessed with gardens and orchards throughout, a fertile plain in the midst of the Nile's tributaries. Why wouldn't it tempt our enemies? Without an army we as much as invite an invasion."

Moses peered about the table, leaning on it with well–muscled arms. "Egypt needs an army not to initiate war but to prevent one. We must arm the Delta or risk losing it." The room hushed with hardly the intake of a breath.

Hatshepsut uncomfortably shifted. "You just signed a treaty with our greatest threat. Everyone knows the strength of the Keftiu and the power of their navy. By your very signature you assured us —"

"Time, and under the guise of an army already in place. They basically signed the treaty on a bluff."

Puseneb jerked forward. "Then you believe this treaty only temporary?"

"At best. I'm sure they intend to test us. They know we haven't maintained our conquests in Syria since the reign of Thutmose I, and have heard, through tradesmen, of the weakened state of our borders. We are as ripe as fallen fruit."

Concern filled Ineni's eyes. "They aren't the only ones eyeing our borders." He avoided Hatshepsut's glare. "While you were away, Moses, we captured a spy from the Southlands of Kush Ta–Seti."

Puseneb glanced at Hatshepsut.

Ineni noted, "He had scouted the garrison ruins west of the river and was attempting to leave when we captured him."

A muscle worked in Moses' jaw. "Had he contacts within the city?"

"Not that we can tell. As far as we know he entered unaided, likely with a caravan of pilgrims for the Feast of Opet. We are holding him in the military compound west of the river, but he insists his Chief is prepared for war, and in his words, 'will prove his strength in our southernmost regions.'"

Moses' gaze narrowed. "The Isle of Elephantine. If the Kushites push as far north as the outpost they'll have a prize worth their efforts." His eyes burned like coals of fire. "An army, Hatshepsut, we must have an army. We can train here at Thebes, rebuilding the compound west of the river and dividing our forces. Half can sail north to the Delta while the rest sail for Kush. If we move quickly enough we can secure our southern fortress as well as our northern borders."

A heaviness settled about the room. Puseneb snorted. "At least Thebes lies in the safety of Egypt's center, thanks to Hatshepsut's foresight in moving the capital south. If an invasion does occur, we'll have plenty of time to arm ourselves."

Moses levelled his eyes at the small thinking Priest. "If it's your own neck you're worried about, think again, for war will eventually find its way here. Why do you think the scout was in our midst? We either arm ourselves now in the Delta and at Elephantine, or face our enemies in Thebes later."

Puseneb blinked but remained silent while the others hardly dared move.

Moses studied them, at last fixing his gaze on Hatshepsut. "Egypt needs an army, Your Majesty. I request permission to recruit and train as many men as possible, and in two weeks, to send half to Elephantine while I sail north with the rest to the garrison at Avaris. From there we will fan out across the Delta, protecting our coastal interests and the border villages nearest the eastern wilderness."

Hatshepsut heard nothing but 'the Delta.' The words jarred her like a physical blow. How could she send Moses where memories lay buried like corpses? She had managed all these years to keep him from the northern provinces, insisting he visit anywhere else on his excursions, and had even built him a summer palace south at Edfu. Then word had arrived of the Keftiu and their navy, and with hardly enough men to man his ships, Moses had sailed for the Isle of Thera. She had feared his passing through the Delta as much as she had feared the mission itself, but Moses had gone in spite of her pleas. Now he planned to build an army in that very place, training at the garrison only a day's ride from the villages of the Habiru.

Hatshepsut's hands shook as she sought an alternative. Absently she picked up the Gorvernor's scroll and scanned its contents. A 'patrol' was all he had requested...and a patrol was what he would have!

Clearing her throat she sat upright. "Governor Mitry has requested a patrol, and I agree that he shall have one." She handed the report to a scribe as if making the pronouncement final.

Moses incredulously eyed her. "Which is expected and long overdue, but what of an army?"

"The Governor knows the condition of his provinces better than we do," Hatshepsut countered. "If he had needed an army he would have asked for one."

"He didn't dare. He knows one doesn't exist."

"I don't maintain an army because I don't believe in war. A patrol will suffice."

Moses balked, "With two enemies at our throats? Do you hold so tightly to your policies you would risk the Delta merely to maintain them? Can't you see Egypt crumbles in your grasp?"

His words hung in the air like a dark omen while all eyes about the table stared at the two.

Ineni cleared his throat, daring to break the silence. "If you lead the northern patrol, Moses, who will lead the southern?"

Moses pursed his lips. "Ebny, our Kushite Ambassador, formerly a Madjai warrior and experienced in their ways of war. He is best suited to lead the southern campaign as he knows the customs and people."

Tension bristled between the two, and Hatshepsut lifted her chin. "You have risked enough, Moses, by sailing to Thera. I'll not have you endanger your life again, not when you plan to succeed me."

He lifted his eyes to hers, his face grim but challenging. "Then Amon has spoken concerning my coronation?"

Hatshepsut's lips tightened. "Not yet. Perhaps once our borders have stabilized the gods will —"

"Stop blaming the gods!" Moses' voice erupted like a pent–up volcano, his eyes ablaze. "When Hatshepsut? When will you crown me? A date, a time!" His lip cynically curled. "Surely now that I have returned victorious Amon will favor me." He pulled a second scroll from his satchel and slammed it onto the table. "This at risk of my life!"

Hatshepsut stared at the treaty, her face small in the shadows.

Yet Moses was past patience, past understanding. Who had heard of an heir in his thirties and not yet crowned?

"By the gods, Hatshepsut, what of my oronation?"

A tear streaked through the kohl about her eyes and quivered on her cheek. "I...I cannot speak for the gods, Moses. I cannot say. If Amon does not wish —"

"Or is it you who do not wish?"

Puseneb gasped while the others attempted to fade into the shadows, all but Ineni who gravely watched the Pharaoh.

Hatshepsut trembled, her eyes welling with tears. Amon had not allowed her any peace concerning Moses though she had wrestled with the notion these past months, even years. She knew he deserved the throne and Egypt him, but how could she defy the gods? How could she allow the deception of her own actions and Moses' past to continue? As much as she loved Moses, she feared the gods more.

"I am sorry, Moses." She shook her head. "We will talk of it after our borders have stabilized."

"If they stabilize," Moses reiterated, his chest heaving with conviction. He could not understand her reasoning nor did he care to. For more hung in the balance than his coronation. Though he could not force her to relinquish the crown, he could force the issue at hand. Egypt's future depended on it.

"I will lead the bulk of our forces north to the Delta where the risk is greatest, and equip Ebny and an advisor to sail south. It's the only move that makes sense."

Hatshepsut stiffened. She could not chance sending Moses to the Delta, let him rant and rave as he would. More than the threat of enemies outside their borders, she feared what he would find within them. She would leave the matter for now and would send someone else, anyone else, but who?

Faces flew before her as she grappled for an answer. Then at last she saw him, her late husband's son, Thutmose III, born of the concubine Isis, Moses' only real rival to the throne. Let Thutmose face the worst of Egypt's enemies in the north while Moses and Ebny sailed south. She would send Moses with his newly recruited army, ample arms, and the best of Egypt's fleet, while Thutmose sailed north with the patrol Governor Mitry had requested.

The buzz of voices continued as Moses and Ineni laid their plans before the council, but Hatshepsut did not hear them. What did it matter? Egypt did not need two armies any more than it needed two heirs. With Thutmose out of the way perhaps the gods would grant her peace concerning Moses.

Sunlight filtered through the garden where Princess Nefru fidgeted, the council doors plainly in view. How long would they imprison her beloved?

She glanced at the shadow clock then back to the doors, touching her toe to the lacquered stillness of the pond. An angel fish darted under the safety of a lotus.

"My, you are a shy one." She moved her toe in an arc across the water, sending the fish farther into the recesses. "Well then, I'll leave you alone and shower my affection on someone else, if he ever comes from his own hiding place."

Nefru heard the council doors open and glanced up to see Tuty and Nehisi emerge, their balding heads bent together in conversation while their robes billowed behind them as they continued down the hall. Puseneb's form filled the doorway next. Squinting into the sunlight as if surmising the hour, he entwined his plump fingers behind his back and waddled down the corridor, his rings glinting in the sunlight.

The next movement from that dark chamber took her breath away as Moses and Ineni stepped into the colonnade, talking in low tones. Her heart nearly stopped at sight of him, and then beat like a frantic bird.

She waved an arm. "Here, Moses, I'm here!"

The Prince paused as if weighing whether or not to acknowledge her. Exchanging a final word with Ineni, he strode toward the garden.

"Greetings, Nefru." He forced a smile, but his eyes followed Ineni down the hall.

Nefru tugged him to the bench, pretending to pout. "After all this time away and still you keep me waiting? Is there another, perhaps a Princess from the Isle of Thera, that has captured your affection?"

Moses studied her, then caught the playful glint in her eye, and laughed. "No, Nefru, you have nothing to fear." Though the Keftiu boasted magnificent buildings and possessed the greatest navy on earth, their morality fell far short of their accomplishments, even by Egyptian standards, obscuring any of their beauty. The memory sickened him still.

Nefru sighed, entwining her fingers in his. "Oh, Moses, when will we wed? I grow weary of waiting."

"I wish I knew." He peered into the distance. Both realized there could be no wedding without a coronation.

She cradled her head against his shoulder. "I prayed daily the gods would return you to my side, and here you are."

"You prayed for me, did you?" He smiled down at her, though his eyes remained grave. "I need all the prayers I can get."

A frown creased her brow as a breeze danced through her curls and her gauze-like garment. "Something troubles you, Moses. Is it the threat of war with Thera?" She knowingly paused. "Or mother?" She looped her arm through his. "She still hasn't named a coronation date, has she?"

Moses shook his head.

Nefru's cheeks flamed, certain she had found the source of his irritation. "She fears to give you the throne, I know it. Your policies differ too much from hers."

"True enough." He relived the last moments of the council, surprised Hatshepsut had given in at all to the notion of an army. Perhaps she at last realized the gravity of Egypt's situation.

"Mother can't hold to the throne forever," Nefru continued, encouraged by his agreement. "Everyone in the Two Lands awaits your coronation."

Moses grunted. "Do they?" He didn't have the heart to tell her of his latest commission. Instead, he gazed across the lawns and harbor to the desert of West Thebes. His grandfather had raised a garrison in that wasteland and Moses planned to repair it. Never again would an enemy find it empty.

"The Pharaoh proclaims peace, Nefru, but I balance, for peace is bought and maintained through strength."

Her eyes shone. "And you mean to bring about sucha balance?"

"I do."

Nefru lifted her chin. "Then I will stand beside you whether mother and all the gods choose otherwise."

Moses chuckled, her confidence awakening some small part of him. Upon his coronation as Pharaoh she would become his great wife. He studied the lure in her gaze, the dimple adorning her cheek, the sweetly rounded breasts visible through her garment.

Then he looked at her small hand in his, her eyes adoring. Would she never be more than his little sister? Though he must marry within the royal family, somehow he could not picture Nefru as his wife.

He pulled away, kissing her lightly on the forehead. "I must go, little one. I have something to attend to."

She sighed. "Will you always be busy? I suppose even once we are wed I will forever be making excuses for you, never on time for banquets and seeing your children only at a distance."

He laughed at the picture, but the sparkle died in his eyes. "It appears Amon has chosen to make me earn my crown. Whatever his reason, you will see little of me in the next few months."

He turned to the colonnade before she could press him further, taking the steps two at a time. "Keep praying for me, Nefru," he called over his shoulder. "Perhaps Amon will hear the pleadings of my little sister before he hears the request of his own son." He turned, and in a moment was lost amid the light and shadows of the colonnade.

Nefru sat breathless, savoring his touch on her arm, his lips on her forehead. Sighing, she rose and stood at the pool's edge, gazing at her reflection as if hoping to find him there, and rehearsing the words foremost in her thoughts.

"Oh, mother, can't you see we love each other? Grant him the throne if for no other reason than moments like these."

The sun beat on the romping party of boys as they followed their commander, Thutmose, whipping up sandstorm in their wake as they chased after him. They had managed again to slip away from the temple school and from the watchful eye of the Priest who had the unfortunate task of overseeing their studies. Though they were no doubt missed, there was little anyone could do to correct the situation.

Thutmose 'yaahed' his horse to a run, imagining himself at the head of an army of charioteers in wild pursuit of the Hyksos. Sunlight glinted off the dents in his chariot, turning it to gold and his headdress to the apparition of a helmet.

"After them!" His sword flashed in the air as he dashed between enemy ranks. He was bound for their leader and would not stop till he had plunged his blade to the hilt in Hyksos flesh.

His companions, confused about which direction to take, haphazardly wove about with their chariots, following his lead. They jabbed their swords this way and that, mercilessly stabbing imaginary enemies, though Thutmose had the only true sword among them, and most of the time they found themselves dodging his.

"To the wadi!" Thutmose shouted as he thrust his sword into the heart of a final victim. Signaling his cohorts, he raced toward the river, stirring a sand cloud behind him. His companions took up the cry, untangling their chariots and lifting their imaginary weapons into the air with a shout of victory before clattering after him.

Thutmose grinned over his shoulder, his teeth a slash of white against his tan. He let out a whoop of triumph as their chariots fell into line behind his. He would rather be in the wilderness any day, even if only pretending to be a soldier, than studying in that stuffy old temple under a Priest who appeared as ancient as the mummies of which he spoke.

He looked into the clear sky, imagining Amon Ra smiling down at him and his friends as they stirred a cloud of dust and commotion beneath it. But just in case the sun god didn't approve of this activity, he muttered a few lines from the Book of the Dead as he continued on his course. He reasoned it was far easier to worship the sun within actual view of the god than in a dank and dreary classroom, and he would tell the Priest so the next time he happened to attend.

CHAPTER 3

Moses' mare restlessly pranced as the Prince surveyed the former military compound west of Thebes. Even repaired it would not be nearly large enough to hold his new recruits. He turned from the sight to survey his troops as they marched in formation across the desert, a faceless throng with kilts as bright as their lance tips. Beneath the cliffs of El Kurn men aimed arrows at fixed targets, testing their skill against an imaginary enemy. Farther north a scatter of chariots wheeled in chaotic circles, enacting a battle.

Moses squinted beneath the sun. Though he had no space for horses or chariots on the few ships he had salvaged, they would prove useful in future campaigns when time allowed travel by land.

Ebny, the Kushite ambassador, rode toward him, his black bulk shiny with sweat and his white kilt contrasting against his dark skin. Though the late Pharaoh had promoted him to ambassador, he could still shoot a bow more accurately than most, and could outdistance any soldier with the lance. Moses regretted not being able to use him on his northern campaign, though he would prove invaluable in the southern.

"You summoned me, my Lord?"

Moses nodded, scanning the charioteers. "We may be wasting our efforts if all we do is win back the fort of Elephantine. What will keep the Kushites from attempting to retake the fortress once you and your troops leave?"

Ebny licked his lips. "We could station part of Egypt's army there permanently, my Lord. But can we spare the men? You'll need reinforcements in the north for your own campaign." He sobered. "Besides, fifteen hundred men may sound like a multitude, but the Kushites can gather twice that many in a matter of days."

Moses studied his distant troops who appeared, when marching side by side, like an advancing wall. "What advantage do we have over them?"

"Not many, my Lord. The Southlands are known as 'Ta–Seti,' 'Land of the Bow,' for good reason. We will need to place our own bowmen in the fore to meet force with force. If we move quickly we may be able to surprise them and retake the fortress, leaving behind enough men to guard our interests. I know of no advantage other than that."

"What of a treaty? If you could venture as far south as Kerma, their capital, we could offer them trade between ourselves, Syria, and perhaps even the Keftiu if need be, once we've enlarged our army."

Ebny wiped the sweat from his forehead. "They're not a people given to talk, my Lord. I don't know if a treaty would even be honored."

Moses took a deep breath. "Then do what you can, Ebny, but whatever you do, see that you secure our southern provinces."

"I'll do my best, my Lord." Ebny raised his eyes to Moses'. "I've not always worshipped the gods as I ought," he stumbled over the words, his face grim, "but perhaps Amon will smile on the venture of a humble soldier."

Moses nodded, his throat tight. "And on mine." He motioned to the compound. "Has the spy told us anything we can make use of?"

Ebny's teeth glistened with his grin. "Merely give the word, my Lord, and he will. I can wring water from a rock if allowed."

"Then do it," Moses answered. "Perhaps he will have more than insults to share with us."

Ebny dipped his head in a bow and turned his horse back to the garrison, stirring the dust in his wake.

Thutmose's heart pounded as he entered the royal audience room. Only once before had he seen the interior of this place. That was when his father had officially claimed Isis as his concubine, thereby admitting his son's parentage. Still Thutmose felt strangely out of place amidst the grandeur: the polished marble floor reflecting his form as he walked stiffly across it, the arched ceiling seeming to reach without measure into the heights of Ra's presence.

His palms were sweaty as he fixed his eyes on the throne, approaching with steps driven more by anxiety than purpose, his fists knotted at his sides. What could Pharaoh possibly want with him? What had he done now? He cringed at the possibilities, remembering how often he had skipped his temple studies.

"You are curious, no doubt, as to your summons?" Hatshepsut's voice filled the room as she peered down at him from the throne as a vulture would a mouse. He gulped as she continued. "There is word about the palace you seek a higher position, that you would be happier as a soldier than in the service of Amon."

Thutmose's face drained, his eyes widening. "Not so, Great One." He would gladly slit the throat of the instructor who had disclosed it.

"Hardly a wonder," the Pharaoh stated with a frown, "seeing you are more content to race about in the wilderness than to prepare the altars of Amon, and you, named after the god of learning."

Thutmose's jaw gaped, his lips quivering as he searched for an explanation, but Hatshepsut interrupted. "Therefore Thutmose, son of Isis and the late Pharaoh Thutmose II, you shall have your wish."

His mind whirled so that he nearly lost his balance.

"You are to proceed to the Delta at once, and there with a small number, will patrol the coastline and eastern border, reporting any sign of the Keftiu or Hyksos."

Thutmose's legs weakened. Had he heard her correctly?

She paused, measuring her words as she traced the ornate inlay on the throne's armrest. "It would be best if Moses did not know of this as he keeps busy enough with his own duties. I wouldn't want him to worry needlessly."

Thutmose attempted a reply but no sound came. A mission to the Delta? He could hardly believe it.

Pharaoh did not seem to notice his surprise. "This is a major promotion for one so young, and I expect you to take it seriously."

He nodded, babbling something incomprehensible which she took to be his agreement.

"Then it is settled. You will leave as soon as you can make ready a ship. There may be a salvageable vessel or two left from your father's fleet, though I wouldn't count on their condition. Moses has already repaired the best for his voyage to Thera, and will doubtless use them again in his southern campaign. However, make use of what remains. I will provide the supplies and weapons, and you the men. I should think a hundred or so more than sufficient. Promise them a soldier's wage, nothing more. Have you any questions?"

Thutmose beamed, his words erupting like a geyser. "I will gladly accept the mission, Your Highness, and will see to the men and ships, and —" Her eyes narrowed and he slowed his cadence to an uncertain rhythm. "I am sure I will find more than enough volunteers among my comrades here at Thebes."

She nodded. "Then it is done. I have a patrol and you a mission." She handed him a sealed scroll. "See that the High Priest signs this before nightfall. It allows your release from your temple duties and provides authorization before the Delta Governors."

Thutmose clutched the document in his fist, a rush of joy surging through him along with an overwhelming urge to shout. He opened his mouth to speak but she looked up sharply. "Well don't just stand there gawking, get to your task."

He took a step backward, unable to contain his ecstasy. "I shall be forever grateful, Your Highness, and will serve you unfailingly until death. You will not regret your decision, and I will do my utmost to fulfil your every desire, oh Pharaoh Hatshepsut Maat Ka Re, Splendid in Majesty, Lord of all the earth."

Her frown deepened, and fearing she would reverse the order altogether, he hastily bowed and spun on his heel, fleeing through the double doors and down the hall. His thoughts tumbled in riotous fashion as he hastened through the shadowy corridor. He, a commander and commissioned to the Delta?

Turning down the eastern wing, he broke into a run, pushing through the doors and into the waning sunlight toward the stables. At last he had his mission. All he needed now was the High Priest's signature.

Mounting his horse, he lashed it to a run, spraying dirt behind him as he sped from the palace yard toward Karnak. He would get this scroll signed by nightfall if he had to rouse that pompous Priest from his very bed.

Thutmose dismounted beneath the towering pylons outside the temple of Karnak as a wisp of smoke trailed into the purpling sky, evidence of the day's activities in the outer court. He hurried through the courtyard and into the silence of the temple proper where a few Priests still shuffled about, waving censors of incense to dispel the odors of the day and uttering final prayers before the disappearance of Ra's last rays.

Mumbling a few obligatory words before the image of Hathor, consort of Amon, Thutmose hurried through the shadowed sanctuary, turning down the western wing toward Puseneb's office. The treasured White House with its accumulated wealth and war trophies was also situated in this holy wing, accessible only to the highest officials.

Thutmose gulped. He was much more accustomed to the eastern wing with its scribal school, vast libraries, and numerous store rooms. He felt a quiver of apprehension, hardly noticing the blur of hieroglyphs along the wall as he passed. He knew, without even looking, that most depicted his grandfather, Thutmose I, smiting his enemies, or presenting treasures to the gods' house upon his return. Only a scattered few told of his father's exploits as the former Pharaoh had done little in the form of aggression. If Thutmose could choose, he preferred to be like his grandfather.

He neared the High Priest's office and softened his steps as if approaching the inner sanctum of the holy of holies. Taking a quavering breath, he announced himself at the door.

"Prince Thutmose III, Student Priest of the royal household, to see his Holiness, the High Priest Puseneb." His voice echoed as if in an empty tomb, making him feel all the more vulnerable.

At last the door creaked open emitting a slice of light through the darkness. The doorkeeper studied him with an indignant eye beneath an arched brow. "It is late and I am certain no one will see a Student Priest at this hour, especially not the High Priest Puseneb."

Thutmose's face fell. Then remembering the scroll, he thrust it through the doorway, royal seal upward. As if of its own accord, the door swung open and the doorkeeper bowed so low he nearly touched his head to the floor. "Come in, come in. Why didn't you say you had word from Her Majesty?" Irritation edged his voice as he ushered Thutmose into the outer office.

Thutmose was led through another set of doors to an inner office where Puseneb sat behind an expansive desk scattered with parchments, his head bent over the pile. He grunted at Thutmose's entrance but continued his work while the Prince gazed about in wonder at his surroundings.

Necklaces and headpieces decorated busts of long dead Pharaohs while foreign relics hung on the crowded walls. Gold overlay and colorful jewels sparkled on every object in sight, including the chair Puseneb sat on, Thutmose noted. Behind Puseneb's desk hundreds of parchments in separate cubicles filled an ebony cabinet etched in gold, the High Priest's private library, doubtless bearing the signatures of Egypt's highest officials and foreign emissaries. Thutmose's eyes widened. The High Priest's office represented a literal storehouse of its own.

"What is it Pharaoh wishes to inquire of me?" Puseneb asked, not lifting his head from his desk.

"My Lord, Your Holiness —" Thutmose stammered, not knowing where to begin.

Without looking up, the Priest held out a heavily jeweled hand, accepting the scroll. He broke the seal and scanned the document.

"'Commander of the Northern Border Patrol'? So it is soldiering you wish, do you?" He lifted his gaze, scrutinizing Thutmose until the youth squirmed. "You would throw away your temple training for this?"

"I, well, that is —"

"'Set your heart to being a Scribe that you may direct the whole earth,'" Puseneb quoted. "Have you forgotten your lessons so soon?"

Thutmose reddened, but the High Priest impatiently waved him to a chair. "I suppose I have no recourse but to sign. Yet if Hatshepsut had asked me I would certainly have told her what I think of the notion...And she with her policies of peace," he muttered.

He scowled, looking a last time at the document before lifting his reed pen in a flurry of signature. "Your grandfather wasn't much different than you, so taken with the ravages of war he could think of nothing else." Puseneb sat back, reflecting. "Nor have the temple coffers ever been as full. If you must be a warrior, see that you follow in his steps." He handed Thutmose the scroll.

Thutmose's thoughts collided and scattered, leaving him without the ability to concentrate on anything at all save the title: 'Commander of the Northern Border Patrol.' It sounded even more wonderful than he could have imagined.

"Thank you, Your Holiness." Thutmose swallowed, attempting to contain his excitement. "I would very much like to imitate my grandfather, to recapture the lands taken by the Hyksos and Syrians, and to push the Kushites back to the nether world where they belong."

Puseneb's lip curled. "As Commander of a mere border patrol you will likely never have that opportunity, nor would an Officer ever make General, as that is Pharaoh's duty."

Undaunted, Thutmose stiffly stood as if at attention. "I shall try to act worthy of the position, my Lord, as a soldier and as an educated man. You will not be disappointed."

Puseneb could have argued the educated point but did not. "Very well then, off with you, and Amon bless you whatever it is you do."

He waved the youth from his presence and Thutmose found himself once again in the outer hall with the heady realization of having just received permission to leave for the Delta. Leaping and emitting a war whoop, he raced down the empty corridor and back through the temple and courtyard, hardly noticing the absence of everyone save a few guards, nor the darkness that had fallen like a curtain over the light–speckled city.

Grinning, he jumped atop his horse and sped toward the poorer section of town near the river. He had much to do before morning, and even more to organize before sailing; but first to tell his comrades.

Tasha stood outside her hut long after her parents had gone to bed, staring into a canopy of constellations and musing over recent events. Months before her father had sent an Officer to Thebes to spy out the city. When his scout had not returned and upon hearing the shaman's prophecy, the chieftain had sent his best warriors north into Egypt. It had required little to take the fortress of Elephantine, and already his warriors planned to move as far north as Edfu.

Her father had insisted the shaman's vision merely a warning, believing the gods had granted them an opportunity to change their fate. And as easily as the warriors had taken Elephantine, it appeared he spoke truthfully. Yet fear of the prophecy still haunted Tasha.

She sighed as a breeze rustled through the trees about her. A chimp chattered somewhere deep in the jungle, answered by the high squeal of its mate, blending with the other night sounds to create a comfortable hum of activity. Behind it all she could hear the low song of the river as it lulled to sleep the villagers and creatures of the night. But Tasha was not among them, for questions plagued her like dreams even in her waking hours.

If she dared wonder again about her future, she had long since abandoned the notion, though three warriors had recently approached her father concerning marriage. He had refused them all, giving the excuse that she needed more time with her family before making a home of her own. In his heart did he also believe the shaman's prophecy, holding desperately to her lest the vision come to pass? Soon afterward he had summoned every warrior within reach to prepare for battle against Egypt.

Tasha forced the thoughts from her mind, inhaling the night air as if its familiar sweetness could dispel her fears. Her father had truthfully spoken, for she felt happy enough with her family. In fact, she could spend an entire lifetime enjoying the simple pleasures of meals about the fire, washing the brightly patterned clothes on rocks near the river, and collecting roots and fruit from the undergrowth with other girls her age. What did she care if they boasted of their future plans. When asked hers, she merely told them she had other desires and marriage was not a part of them. Aghast, they had whispered among themselves, but she didn't care. They had not experienced the horror of a shaman's prophecy.

Tasha shivered and wrapped her arms about herself. What if the shaman's words came true? How many of her people would die in an attempt to keep it from happening, and how could she possibly save them? Tears stung her eyes as she gazed into the night sky, her lips moving in a silent prayer to her god that the vision might not come to pass.

Thutmose jerked awake, blinded by the sun already high above the city. Throwing aside his sheet, he shoved his feet into his sandals, scolding himself for having overslept. How could he sleep when he had ships to scrounge and troops to summon? He had far too much to do, and all in a matter of days.

He paused and rubbed his eyes, smiling as he remembered the reactions of his friends the night before at hearing the news. His closest friend, Amenhab, had at first gawked, then laughed, then had danced about the room like a drunk monkey. Together they had planned and celebrated as if the night had no end.

Yet it had ended, and he had already slept away half a day of preparation. Dressing with all the care of a madman, he dashed from his chamber and into the corridor, nearly colliding with a servant coming from the opposite direction.

"Master Thutmose!" The servant hailed him as if fearing he would pass him by. "I was just on my way to summon you. Your mother requests your presence at once."

"I can't." Thutmose's face twisted to a grimace. His mother had a knack of asking for him at the worst of times.

"She called you an hour ago but —"

"I know, I was sleeping," Thutmose finished lamely, yawning at the mention of the words.

"Please, my Lord, a brief audience, nothing more. She says it is urgent."

It's always urgent," Thutmose grumbled, shoving his fingers through his hair and estimating the time he would lose if he complied. But seeing the pleading in the servant's eyes, obviously threatened with injury if he didn't accomplish the task, Thutmose relented. "All right, a brief audience, nothing more."

The servant's face lit with delight as he led Thutmose to Isis' apartment. Thutmose entered alone, finding her standing on her balcony with her back to him. She was overlooking the city, her body rigid and her head erect, and Thutmose knew at a glance she had heard. She could extract information from the speechless if given a chance, but must have had spies in his bedchamber to know this.

Hearing the door close, she turned like a lioness, throwing her hand to the sun. "It's already noon and finally you acknowledge my summons!"

"I overslept," he lamely mumbled.

"Expect it of a Thutmose, and leave it to you to keep me wondering all morning what you're up to. Yes, I've heard of your plans."

"Oh." He browsed through a bowl of fruit, picking a ripe fig.

Her eyes flashed. "I got word of your 'mission' long before you even rose from your bed."

"Really?" He asked, seating himself on her couch and concentrating on the fig. "What did you expect me to do, ask your permission?"

"Infidel!" She spat the word like a curse. "You'll find yourself at the end of a Hyksos' lance if you're not careful!"

"I'm going no matter what you say." He had to stop taking orders from women at some point or he would end up no better off than Moses. He reached for a date.

"Imbecile! Don't you see what she's up to?"

Thutmose glanced up as if daring her to continue.

The Pharaoh had her own network of spies, and even his mother's most loyal servants would not hide a blatant rebuke of Her Majesty.

She whispered hoarsely, "I know very well what she wants. She hopes to rid herself of the one rival who stands in her own son's way, the only one who could possibly take Moses' place on the throne. You!"

Thutmose laughed. "I'm no threat to Moses. Even if my father had named me heir, as you say, it makes no difference. Hatshepsut controls the throne and will have her way."

"Then why hasn't she crowned Moses?" Isis' eyes glinted like sapphires. "Guilt, that's why, and I pray the gods curse her more with it until she gives you what is rightfully yours."

"You and your curses," Thutmose laughed. "You would have made a better witch than Priestess."

Isis shrieked, raising her fists at him, but Thutmose glared at her and she stopped herself, pacing in a fit of rage. "Not only have her advisors and the council approved her plans but now the idiot Thutmose himself. In all your hours of sporting I've never seen you so apt to be killed."

She paused as if studying the effect of her words, then crumpled to a fit of weeping.

Thutmose awkwardly rose, not sure what he should do. He thought of bringing her a cool cloth but would just as soon have had someone else tend to her. "Shall I call a servant?"

"No." She looked up at him, her expression pathetic, her tears having smudged the kohl about her eyes into two black rings. Thutmose normally would have laughed at such a sight but she seemed too near hysteria.

She motioned him to her couch. "Please...sit by my side and tell me of your desire to serve as a Priest for our goddess, Hathor...of your hopes for advancement here at Thebes."

Thutmose shrewdly eyed her then pulled away. "I've decided and I'm going. I will leave for the Delta as soon as I can make ready my ships and gather my men, and I'll be the best Commander since my grandfather, you'll see." His words sliced through the distance already between them.

Isis moaned, lying back on her couch with her arms crossed over her chest in the manner of mummified Pharaohs. He studied her with indifference. She was as fit as she was phony, and he wasn't about to let her manipulate him into doing her bidding.

Reaching for another fig, he popped it into his mouth and turned to the door. "You'll be fine, mother, I'm sure."

"Me?" she shrieked, so that he almost swallowed the fig whole. "It's you I'm worried about. If they don't bury you your first hour in the Delta they'll bury me fearing it. Oh, Thutmose, I know this is not to be. You must stay and —"

"And what? Bend to the whims of a whining woman? Not me. I'm going, and in spite of what you say, I know why I'm being sent. If it's to spare her precious Moses, so be it, but she's wrong and so are you. I won't die at the end of a Hyksos lance or any other way, but like my grandfather, will make a name for myself in Egypt, in the lands of our enemies, and in all the earth, if the gods allow, and I'll fill the temple with treasures to prove it."

He opened the door, a gleam in his eye. "May Hathor bless you, mother, should you enter Paradise before me." Closing the door behind him, he felt the pleasure of having just won his first battle.

Not waiting for the guards to announce his arrival, Moses stormed through the entrance of Hatshepsut's audience room and found her standing before an open window studying the view west of the Nile.

Hatshepsut slowly turned toward him, motioning her attendants to leave, preferring to face his fury on her own.

She started to speak but Moses wasn't interested in conversation. "What have you done? How could you send Thutmose anywhere, let alone to the north, and with a mere hundred men, knowing all along I had planned to go?"

"Planned, but ignoring my decree at the council, if you remember?"

"Only too well."

She took a step toward him. "I am still Pharaoh, Moses, and my decision stands. In the long run it will prove best, and you can sail to Kush with Ebny instead."

"With my legions while Thutmose fights our greatest threat with a handful? Will you risk the entire Delta just to maintain your policies?" He searched her face but she remained impassive.

Moses shook his head, pacing. "What is it, Hatshepsut? What have I done to deserve this? No word, no warning, just the flick of a hand and all is changed?" He continued as if to himself. "I have paid my vows to the gods, never holding anything back, whether in offerings or worship, and have served you faithfully, even risking my life. Yet you treat me like an enemy."

Her eyes widened as if seeing a spirit, and she emphatically shook her head. "No, Moses. It is a small matter, a mere change of plans. I needed another Commander so I —"

"Ebny, your Kushite Ambassador, had agreed to attend to the southern campaign. He represents the perfect candidate, and was to leave in just two days." Moses' face constricted. "Why, Hatshepsut? First you keep me from the throne, and then you abandon the only recourse that makes sense."

Her lips quivered but she set them firmly. "I have decided, Moses, and that is final. I have ruled Egypt since my husband's death without your help, and will continue until —" The words caught in her throat, "until you take my place. Oh Moses," she broke, reaching for him, "I did it for Egypt, for you."

"How does it benefit Egypt to send a wild boar into an already unstable situation? He's more likely to provoke war than prevent one. He'll mangle any hopes of our maintaining the treaty."

Moses rubbed the back of his neck, struggling to control his tone. "If we lose the Delta we might as well forget the Southlands as there won't be an Egypt left to protect." He turned to her, desperation in his tone. "Thutmose can't be trusted to lead anything, let alone a patrol."

Hatshepsut raised her chin. "My decision stands. You will leave for Elephantine in two days, as planned."

Moses stared. "By the gods, Hatshepsut, you can't know what you're doing."

She bit her lip. "You forget your place, Moses. It is I whom the gods chose to name Pharaoh upon my husband's death. Egypt has known twelve years of peace in my reign and I plan to continue it."

Moses eyed her with contempt. "Until there is nothing left to rule." He started for the door but she clutched his arm.

"I did it for you, Moses, for us. I couldn't have you risk your life a second time."

He looked at her as one would a traitor.

A tear trickled down her cheek. "I know you don't understand now, but one day you will."

He pulled from her grasp and continued to the door, his resolve hardened, but she would not let him leave, not like this. "I had to protect you, Moses, to keep you from danger so that..."

He stopped, his hand on the door, listening to the words that tumbled forth in an effort to convince him.

"...So that upon your return you might wear the crown." She took a quavering breath. "I will plan a coronation to outdo all others. We will invite all of Egypt, north and south. The council will be relieved and Nefru jubilant, if I can keep her still until you return." She attempted a laugh, but it died on her lips.

Moses turned, studying her, his heart writhing. The words he had so longed to hear now sounded empty, even loathsome.

She implored, "You have earned the right, Moses, many times over. All of Egypt will rejoice."

Shaking his head, he turned his back to her, hiding his pain and leaving her standing in the doorway looking after him. As he rounded the corner of the royal wing he pushed her pathetic form from his mind, attempting to focus on Egypt's greatest need. Thutmose could not possibly stand against the ravages of the north with a hundred men.

The corridor seemed unusually silent as if the afternoon heat had driven even the attendants to escape it, but Moses knew better. No one cared to find themselves within earshot of a battle between the Pharaoh and her son. Only Moses' servant, Puemre, dutifully squatted in that sunlit space.

Moses motioned him and he scrambled to his feet. "Tell Ebny I need him at once; that plans have changed." Puemre nodded, his eyes bright as Moses continued. "Ebny is to sail for the Delta tonight with half our troops."

The servant's mouth gaped. "But my Lord, what of Kush? Ebny was our best choice for the southern campaign. He knows the customs and the people."

Moses steadied his voice, his face grim. "Just give him the message. And summon Ineni as we will need an experienced advisor."

Puemre dared one more question, his tone tremulous. "If Ebny sails north, my Lord, who will lead the southern campaign?"

Moses forced the words through clenched teeth. "That will apparently be my privilege."

CHAPTER 4

The crescent moon was still visible in a purple sky blushing with the promise of sunrise as Thutmose and his comrades climbed about the rigging, securing the sails. A row of bodies manned the oars on either side of the ship while the rest of the crew, taking shifts, slept below. The two rickety vessels had already spent several days struggling northward with the current and only now approached Abydos.

Thutmose shivered, glancing at the horizon and wishing the sun god would hurry and be born from the body of Nut to warm the earth once again. His flesh rose in bumps and he had to clench his teeth to keep them from chattering.

"Any sign of leaks?" He vigorously rubbed his arms to warm himself.

"We won't know until daylight." Rekmire had begun to resent Thutmose's airs and his insistence on their overzealous start.

"Run your hands over the hull," Thutmose ordered. "You ought to be able to feel any seepage."

"And slivers!" Amenhab cursed as he jerked his hand back, whipping it up and down.

Thutmose crossed his arms. "We need to make Abydos by noon, but we'll never do it if we sink first."

The crew patched the vessel as best they could, daubing pitch on any cracks they found, while hoping to be rescued with a call to breakfast. The reeds rustled about them, parting like a curtain as they passed near the shore, and sending a flock of ibis into the air. Soon the sun pierced the horizon in shards of light as villages materialized on the shore then diminished behind them.

Thutmose longed to see Abydos rise on the desert, first in a scatter of outlying villas and temples, then in the configuration of rooftops and pylons marking the city proper. He would visit the sacred burial grounds where pilgrims worshipped representatives of every god imaginable, from Sobek the crocodile god, to Apis the bull god, the city's main deity. Perhaps if he prayed to them all at once he could forgo the need to petition them separately. With so many gods looking out for his mission it would have to succeed.

Thutmose smiled beneath the sun as light shimmered over his body, melting the morning's chill. He glanced at his men, their former grumbling exchanged for a quiet servitude as they focused on getting the two rigs down–river.

Thutmose casually peered behind him, attempting to measure their progress, when a gleam on the river caught his eye. The brilliance grew as it reflected the sun's full glare, then parted and divided into three. Shading his eyes, Thutmose could barely see the outline of sails. Not one, but three ships followed his, and they appeared to be gaining. Who were they and what could it mean? Thutmose felt a sinking recognition. Moses!

Venom surged through his veins. "To the oars!" He signaled his second ship to follow. "They're after us!"

"It may be nothing of the sort," Amenhab countered. "Pharaoh often comes to Abydos to worship."

"In war vessels?" Rekmire frowned, pulling hard on his oar. "We'll never outrun them with these sorry ships."

"We can try." Thutmose scrutinized the river, his eyes locked on the gaining vessels. The foremost seemed to be filled with soldiers, the reflection of their armor making it seem as if Amon himself pursued them. "They're royal vessels all right, and appear weighted with as many men as they can hold." Thutmose snorted. "I should be so blessed."

"Wasn't Moses supposed to lead this mission?" Rekmire pulled hard again. "Perhaps he's carrying out his plans in spite of Pharaoh's decrees."

Thutmose nodded, his face grim. "We're about to be replaced. I knew it was too good to be true."

"But they can't." Amenhab's eyes flashed. "Hatshepsut herself appointed us."

"Do we look like an army that would scare the Hyksos into submission or keep the Keftiu at bay?"

Amenhab strained behind the oars. "Pharaoh can be as determined as Moses. Maybe even she saw the benefit of sending reinforcements."

Thutmose shook his head. "No. Ebny, Moses' Officer, is at the helm. Prepare to retire, men."

A glum silence settled over the tottering ships as the fleet approached, pulling alongside the two small vessels.

Ebny framed his mouth with his hands. "Commander Thutmose of the Northern Border Patrol!"

Thutmose braced himself, his heart pounding in his ears as Ebny continued. "Eight hundred men at your service, my Lord."

Thutmose lifted a brow. "Eight hundred what?"

"Soldiers commissioned by Moses to add to your forces."

Amenhab looked at Thutmose then back at Ebny, and burst into laughter.

"Haven't you come to replace us?" Thutmose asked.

"Not replace, my Lord," Ebny reiterated, "but to join. Would you have us follow your lead?"

Realization shot through Thutmose and he let out a whoop that sent another flock of ibis skyward. Three more ships and nearly a thousand more men! He felt dizzy with joy. A grin spread across his face, his chest swelling as he exchanged expressions of exhilaration with his men.

"I don't think we'll stop at Abydos after all," Thutmose exulted. "It appears the gods have already answered."

Thrusting a fist into the air, he ordered the fleet past Abydos and the sacred burial grounds, his two meagre ships leading vessels which appeared fashioned by the very gods as they made their way northward to the Delta.

Tasha heard the commotion and ran to the river's edge as three skiffs slid ashore with a horde of others furiously paddling behind them.

A warrior jumped to the bank, pointing down– river. "Egyptians! They've taken back Elephantine." He caught his breath, excitement nearly strangling him. "Now they sail here, toward Kerma." Doubling over, he panted while others leapt to the shore, confirming his tale.

Tasha's father glanced at his daughter then back at his men, concern etched on his brow. "How many ships?"

"Four, and who knows how many others will come."

Tasha shrank to the edge of the throng as if to escape the news.

"How many soldiers?" the chieftain queried.

"Hundreds, perhaps thousands."

A large man with a scar across his chest strode to the fore. "Not so many, my Lord. If all our warriors stand together we can outnumber them."

The chieftain peered northward as a crowd gathered about him.

"Rumbaya, send word to the southern villages. Tescumi, go north. The rest of you gather your weapons and meet me here by nightfall. We'll lay a trap for them they'll not soon forget."

"Father." The word caught in Tasha's throat and she ran to him, clinging as if to never let go.

He smoothed her hair, his voice gruff. "What are four vessels and some inexperienced Egyptians against the Madjai? We are stronger, we will win."

"What of the prophecy, father?" Her eyes glistened with unshed tears as she watched him.

He shook his head, unable to face the possibility. "Cursed be the vision! I'll not stand by and watch my people ravaged, my women violated."

"But the Shaman...."

"Speak no more of it! Go to the hut with your mother and keep the little ones inside. When I am finished with these Egyptians they'll bother us no longer."

Tasha froze. Would he risk his life and his men merely to keep the prophecy from coming to pass?

"If it means saving our people I'll go anywhere," she pleaded.

"Away with you!"

Tasha shook her head as if seeing the vision unfold, thousands dead and untold captives taken. Turning, she fled from the crowd whose spears pounded the earth and whose war whoops thundered like an encroaching storm.

Her feet hardly touched the ground as she ran to warn her mother, then to the fires of their neighbors to gather her siblings. Scooping her youngest brother into her arms, her sister in tow, she shoved them into the doorway of her hut. But instead of entering herself, she darted down the path toward the shaman's dwelling.

He had said she would save her people, but how? How could she spare them a fate that even now sped toward their shore?

The night was vibrant with noise as chimpanzees and other creatures chattered as if welcoming the Egyptians. Moses had hoped to make better time but the rapids had deterred him. The only way to prevent his ships from being splintered on the rocky falls was to tow them overland using every man possible. The fact the Kushites had not attempted an ambush so far only meant they were saving their strength for a more opportune time, and Moses feared that time had come.

"There it is, my Lord, Kerma, capital of Kush Ta–Seti, Land of the Bow." Ineni pointed to the city that gleamed like a gem through an entanglement of trees.

Moses peered into the undergrowth, sure an ambush awaited them. Yet he dared not leave without challenging the Kushites' aggression, though he hardly had enough men for a battle.

He turned to his Officer. "Menku, I want you and several guards to announce our arrival. Tell the Chieftain I bring an agreement of peace to assure the safety of both our nations, and in exchange, we will allow trade between ourselves and the nations beyond us. Offer these jewels as proof."

Menku stared at the basket of trinkets. "My Lord, what if he refuses?"

"Tell him Egypt's heir comes with an army to assure a peaceful settlement, and will meet with him before the night is through."

Menku swallowed hard, peering into the darkness. "My Lord, I fear an ambush."

Moses attempted reassurance. "We'll wait a few hours for your return, and then follow."

"And if I don't return?" Menku's eyes reflected the moon's glow.

Moses sobered, turning to the lights of Kerma. "If I establish a treaty, offering trade at a later date, I can assure the safety of our southern extremities until we have time to build enough of an army to support our claims. With gold such as the Southlands have available, trade could prove profitable."

Menku hesitated, but Moses laid a hand on his shoulder. "May the gods bless you and return you safely to us."

The Officer nodded, taking a deep breath and forcing his fear beneath a mask of resolve. Ordering a skiff lowered into the water, Menku and two soldiers climbed into the tottering vessel and rowed away into the night. Moses watched them disappear into the darkness until only the occasional splash of an oar could be heard. Eventually even that was lost to the hoots and howls of the jungle.

The moon slowly rose as Moses and his men waited. Once he thought he heard a cry, but dismissed it as that of a jackal. An hour passed, then two, with still no sign of Menku or the skiff.

Ineni approached. "My Lord, I fear Menku's fate. We should return to Thebes and await our northern army."

"What if the Kushites march before our return? I can't take that chance. We would lose all we have accomplished."

"Why not leave the majority of our men at Elephantine? They could keep the fortress secure."

Moses shook his head. "After this campaign we'll need every man available in the Delta. That means settling the matter of Kush first."

Ineni drew a breath. "Then perhaps we should move on Kerma at first light. We could divide the fleet, sending two vessels south of the city and the other two north, surrounding it."

"We haven't enough men to divide for any reason, and each is too valuable to waste." Moses' face clouded as he studied the darkness for a sign of his Officer. "On the other hand, being a god's son affords me a measure of protection others don't have."

"My Lord, your life is more valuable than any man's," Ineni protested.

"And risk more men? No," Moses shook his head. "If I approach the Chieftain now I may be able to secure a treaty before daybreak, before the Madjai have a chance to assess our numbers. We also have their spy, and can use him as leverage to secure an agreement." He turned to an Officer. "I want these ships lit until they appear twice as full. Give every man two torches, and see that you make enough noise to equal it."

Ineni's face paled. "I'll go with you, my Lord. I can speak enough of their language to get by."

"As can I."

The elder faltered. "But I could offer council. I have overseen many treaties in my years."

Moses watched him with concern. He hated to risk another life, especially Ineni's, but the elder had a point. He might need his advice. Moses nodded for a skiff and rower, and climbed into the vessel. Soon the same darkness enveloped him and Ineni that had swallowed Menku's party several hours earlier.

Tasha crouched in the hut beside her sister while her younger brother and a toddler huddled in the corner near their mother. Though she could not see them clearly, she could hear their breathing as even the little ones sensed the danger.

She had snatched a look at the war vessels in the harbor that were lit as if afire. So far only two small bands of the enemy had entered the village, each of them captured. Still Tasha felt uneasy. She wondered how many more men the ships held, and whether they aimed their arrows at her hut. With flaming arrows a bowmen could burn an entire village to the ground in a matter of hours. Tasha shuddered, hugging her knees to her chest.

The shaman ducked into her hut and glanced about, squatting near the door.

"Why are you here?" Tasha's mother hissed, her eyes large in the darkness.

The shaman ignored her, peering out through the tent flap to study the scene about the fire. "The Chieftain has captured the first Egyptians and sent them to the place of the dead. Now their Prince meets with your father." He turned to Tasha. "This is not what I envisioned."

Tasha edged closer for a better view. The younger Egyptian stood by the fire with an elder beside him, not nearly as menacing as she had imagined.

A confusion of voices rose in chaotic clamor but the chieftain raised his above the rest. "I want no treaty. Do what you like with your captive. Here is what I have done with mine." A warrior dragged several bodies into the light and dropped them in a heap before the fire. "The same will happen to you."

The Prince stood tall, his shoulders squared. "My troops will retaliate with force."

The chieftain clenched his fists. "Then we will break you like twigs. We are ready."

"We have many soldiers waiting in the harbor and more in the north. They will come to your land and you and your people will suffer," Moses answered.

Tasha scrambled to her feet, staring wide–eyed through the open door. The shaman looked at her and nodded. Her mother cried out, reaching for her but Tasha slipped through the doorway and toward the fire, stumbling as she ran, her legs weak and her body trembling.

The warriors jumped up and down before the flames as if restless for battle, their silhouetted shadows appearing like a single, multi–headed demon. Pounding the earth with their spears, their voices thundered as they leapt. A high pitched squeal began around the circle, growing until it drowned out the voice of the young Egyptian, making Tasha wonder if she hadn't entered the land of dreams.

Feeling faint, she pushed her way through the sweaty mob until she stood face to face with the Prince. Seeing her, the chieftain stopped his tirade and stared as Tasha bowed to the earth before the foreigner. All voices stilled as she spoke.

"I have a message for the light–skinned Prince, a word from the daughter of our Chief." She could feel the eyes of the warriors on her. "Though I am only one and my people many, there is no need for a battle or bloodshed." Her lips parted as if she found the words too terrible to speak. She glanced across the fire at her father, their eyes meeting. "I offer myself in their place."

Moses stood immobile, his brow furrowed in a question as he watched her.

The elder Egyptian nodded, his eyes bright before the firelight. "I believe, my Lord, this young woman presents a solution." He looked at Moses as if to convey an unspoken message. "An offer of marriage."

Moses stared.

Ineni stepped toward the fire. "It is customary, oh Chieftain, to make an alliance with neighboring nations by way of marriage between royal sons and daughters of other lands. If you will allow —"

"Noooo!" The chieftain's voice rose like that of a maimed animal and echoed through the night. Ineni cringed, stepping back into the shadows.

Moses took his place in the light, tendrils of hair clinging to his forehead and his torso glistening with sweat. "I have not yet married, great Chief. Your daughter will become my wife after my coronation. Until then she will be cared for in the palace by gifted servants. All of her needs will be met, and one day our children will revisit this land."

A woman screamed and ran toward the fire, falling at the chieftain's feet. A man followed, wearing the garb of a shaman. The chieftain's eyes blazed, his nostrils flared as his warriors crowded about, arguing in frantic tones.

Tasha raised her face, her cheeks streaked with tears. "I will go, father. I will sail north on the Egyptian vessel and will live in his house."

"No!" the chieftain cried again in anguish.

As if in answer, a voice rose in a chant, the warble of a shaman's prayer, and all fell silent. His words rang clear and strong as if spoken by another, promising peace if the Princess complied, and death if she did not.

No one doubted the shaman's vision now.

The chieftain angrily reached for his spear but a warrior held him back. Another dropped his weapon to the ground, and still another, until a mound of spears, lances and bows lay at the chieftain's feet.

The Prince touched Tasha's shoulder and she arose, hardly daring to look into his face. A child ran from the darkness with a bundle and pressed it into her arms, clinging to her waist, but Ineni hurried them along.

Tasha paused, glancing behind her at the fire, careful not to linger over the faces of her father and mother. Instead, she longingly looked at the shadow of huts, at the silhouette of jungle that emitted the night sounds she had grown so accustomed to hearing. She listened to the river as it sang past the village, and gazed into the star–lit sky arching above them. Then tearfully memorizing each detail, she turned to the river at the side of the Prince and away from her people forever.

The Delta port of Avaris appeared nearly empty as Thutmose scanned it, the three royal vessels that had joined his rising in stark contrast to the few others that occupied that space of blue, including his own two teetering relics. Egypt not only needed an army, it needed a navy.

A gull called overhead interrupting his thoughts, and Thutmose looked up to find Ebny studying him. It made him squirm to have someone watching over him as if keeping track of his every move.

Thutmose turned his gaze to the sea beyond the port. "I've been thinking, Ebny. You're an Officer in your own right and have been so long before I was commissioned." The black man raised his brow in response as Thutmose continued. "I would like to put you in charge of a unit here at Avaris. Someone needs to watch the port in case the Keftiu get any ideas."

Ebny eyed him, his voice deep and resonant. "With not even a thousand men, my Lord, do we have enough to divide and remain effective?"

"All Governor Mitri expected was a patrol, and instead he received," Thutmose grunted, waving his arm in an arc, "half an army. I'm asking you to keep the coast secure while I patrol the eastern border. By dividing we can better watch both fronts."

Ebny contemplated the notion. "How many men will you need?"

"We both need enough to make an impression. I could leave —"

"Six hundred?" Ebny interjected.

The black man had asked for better than half, but Thutmose would do just about anything to be out from under Ebny's watchful eye. "Five hundred and you have it."

Ebny's eyes narrowed. "I'll need slaves to repair the garrison."

Thutmose nodded. He could grant him slaves easily enough as the Delta had more than its share.

Thutmose mounted the horse the Governor had provided him, patting its muzzle. "Now, how about some dinner before we subject ourselves to the rigors of soldiering?" He motioned to an inn overlooking the port.

If you're taking the eastern border your hardships will be more than mine," Ebny answered, searching his face as if to determine his motive.

"Perhaps, but at least I'll have only one enemy to watch for." Thutmose smiled, more to himself than to Ebny, for with Moses' Officer out of the way he could command his men as he wished.

His horse restlessly pawed the earth, its dark mane lifting in the breeze as Thutmose nosed it toward the sea–beaten inn. He could hardly wait to reach the wilderness, and was even more jubilant to be free of Ebny's scrutiny. The next time the Hyksos stormed their border like a Hamsin wind he would be ready.

CHAPTER 5

A breeze fluttered the gauze curtains of Nefru's bedchamber and rustled the palms outside her balcony where pigeons cooed and distant geese squawked in patterned flight. Still Nefru did not waken.

Instead she saw Moses running toward her with outstretched arms.

"I've missed you so, dearest," he murmured, crushing her to his chest, his lips meeting hers. She could smell the scent of aloes on his neck as he swept her into his arms and carried her to his bedchamber. Laying her upon his bed, he traced her cheek with his finger. "My love is an overflowing cup. Drink deeply." His eyes reached into her soul as he pulled her body against his.

A trumpet pierced the air but Nefru did not stir. Instead, she nestled farther into the cushions, a smile on her lips.

Bending over her, he pressed his mouth against hers as....

The trumpet sounded again and Nefru's eyes flew open. Blinking, she let go of the cushions and sat upright. Had she only imagined it, or had a watchman announced the arrival of a fleet in the harbor?

Struggling into her robe, she ran to her balcony as a messenger galloped into the yard and a door swung open below her.

"A message for Her Majesty," the man shouted to the keeper of the door. "Prince Moses has arrived."

Moses! Nefru flew to her room as the Steward of the Royal Wardrobe entered. "Quickly! Prepare my bath and summon the attendants, and bring me the orchid gown. Take care with the pleats. All must be perfect for Moses' arrival."

Under the nimble hands of her attendants, Nefru hurriedly washed and dressed, her mind racing. The gods had once again returned Moses to her, Amon be praised! She would see her love at last.

Her cheeks flamed at the thought. It was as if the dream, so real only moments before, had suddenly sprung to life. She closed her eyes, the sweetness of him lingering, the rapture of his touch almost felt. But she had no time to daydream.

Her heart fluttered with excitement as she rushed through the ritual of her routine, eyeing herself in the bronze mirror atop her vanity. It was all she could do to sit still while the attendants worked over her, their hands deftly flying at their tasks as they tinted her nails and applied her make-up.

"More ochre on my cheeks," she commanded. Closing her eyes she drew a deep breath, attempting to quiet her thoughts while the servants obediently applied the brush, though her cheeks already flamed with color.

At last she stood transformed, the silken fabric of her gown slipping through her fingers like liquid. Moses would appreciate the feel of it, in spite of his rougher hands.

"Now the gold collar and jeweled sandals, and take care with my nails." She admiringly pointed her pink toes as an attendant slipped the dainty leather thongs onto her feet.

Another trumpet blast sent her dashing to the balcony, her pulse racing. Clutching the rail, she peered down the Avenue of Rams, barely able to make out a procession of litters and soldiers parading up the hill toward the palace.

Her breath caught in her throat but she gulped back her panic. She must calm herself or she would ruin the effect.

"The aloes," she ordered, whereupon an attendant reached for the jar. "No, the myrrh. I wore it when he last saw me. He'll remember."

The maid daubed the ointment on Nefru's arms and neck, placing a drop behind each ankle.

"More," Nefru commanded. She held out her wrists again as the servant reapplied the perfume.

A maid entered and approached Nefru. "Would my Lady wish to greet the Prince on her balcony or at the portico below?"

Nefru bit her lip. "The balcony first then the portico."

The girl bowed low as Nefru hastened to her balcony, smoothing her hair and pleats before bending over the rail. Then forgetting all else, she strained for sight of the royal entourage, joyously waving as they entered the palace yard. Would Moses notice her? Nefru breathlessly waited. Then, and as if at the gods' bidding, he turned her way and their eyes met.

She felt a rush of joy through her entire body. He had seen her. To the portico! She must be first to greet him.

Nefru swallowed, forcing herself to a regal gait, careful not to disturb her wig or the pleats that swung perfectly back into place with each step. A maiden led her down the stairs and through the near empty hallway to the palace entrance. The doors stood ajar, the space between them crowded with Officers and attendants.

"The Princess Nefru," an Officer announced as the crowd parted. At last Nefru stood facing the halted procession as if she alone greeted them, her body trembling with excitement.

Moses stepped from the foremost litter and Nefru held her breath, watching him as if seeing a god. Then forgetting her gown, her meticulous wig, the pleats that accentuated her waist and hips, forgetting all else but her desire for him, she ran to his arms, her face upturned, her lips awaiting his kiss. Hesitating only a moment, he embraced her, his flesh as warm as she had envisioned. However, instead of crushing her against him, he touched his lips to her forehead and gently released her.

"It is good to be back Nefru, to see Thebes, and you."

Nefru scarcely noticed his preoccupation. "I've dreamed of this moment so often," she breathed.

He smiled. "You have become a woman while I was away."

Her heartbeat quickened, her eyes dancing with pleasure.

A second litter stopped behind his and Ineni stepped out, opening the curtain for another to join him. From the shadows a slender figure emerged, a dark skinned woman, graceful yet hesitant, her large brown eyes taking in every detail of her surroundings. She turned to Moses, then to Nefru, watching them with a mixture of curiosity and trepidation. Lowering her eyes, she shyly stood before them in a brightly patterned skirt, her hair wrapped in a cloth, and a bundle clutched in her arms.

Nefru looked at Moses, trying not to laugh. "Is this another servant acquired on your journey?"

Moses studied his sister with troubled gaze. "Her name is Tasha, a Princess from Kush Ta–Seti." He paused, glancing at the Officers and attendants who would soon spread news of his accomplishments.

"It is customary, Nefru, when nations bind themselves by way of a treaty and in order to maintain peace —" He searched her face. "She is to become my second wife."

Nefru's features froze. She stared at Moses, then at the intruder.

"I had no choice," he offered.

Nefru heard nothing more. Looking at Moses with disbelief, she turned and fled through the throng and into the palace, her sandals clicking over the marble floor and echoing in the near empty hall. Bitterness scalded her eyes and tightened in her throat. How could he, knowing she had waited for him, knowing how she loved him?

Once in her bedchamber she threw herself onto her bed, not caring about her pleats or her wig, nor the malachite and kohl that ran down her face in streaks of green and black. How could the gods have allowed such a thing? She choked back the mention of their names. It was her mother's fault. If she had crowned Moses earlier they would already be wed and Moses would know he needed no other.

Several attendants hurried into the room, bending over her with concern, but Nefru did not heed them. Rage and humiliation screamed too loudly within her. She couldn't stand to live in the palace with that woman. She wouldn't! No one else must have Moses but herself.

Thutmose sat atop his horse scanning the dunes at the edge of the desert. Since his arrival he had seen the charred remains of several villages the Hyksos' had attacked, but had yet to catch sight of the enemy. These Semites travelled in nomadic bands easily losing themselves in the expanse of the desert. Perhaps they had heard of Egypt's newly recruited army through tradesmen and feared to approach the border.

It was even rumored some of the Syrian city–states had formed alliances with the Hyksos, and Thutmose tended to believe it. For years caravans had entered Egypt by Syria's coastal highway, the 'Way of the Sea,' yet the only caravan since his arrival had been from Gaza, the nearest Syrian stronghold east of the desert. Otherwise the border had remained quiet.

Thutmose's gaze pierced the eastern horizon while his horse restlessly pawed beneath him as if sensing his frustration. At this rate Ebny would experience the action of battle before he did. Perhaps he should have taken the coastal watch instead. Yet his grandfather had triumphed here in the east, claiming the land as far as the Euphrates River. If he could just win back one city–state he could teach Syria a lesson about making alliances with Egypt's enemies.

Turning his back to the desert, Thutmose nudged his horse over the dune that hid his small encampment. Smoke from a scatter of fires lifted into the sky, the aroma of roasting gazelle wafting toward him. The cooks and their aides dipped meal from large provender baskets into boiling pots, stirring the mix, while others turned meat on skewers over half a dozen fires. Clusters of men huddled about them, absorbed in idle conversation while they awaited the feast.

Amenhab sat nearby, leaning against his pack and whittling a crude idol, too preoccupied to lift his gaze. Thutmose dismounted near him, tethering his horse.

"A rider came through today," Amenhab noted, glancing up at him. "Said Ebny's gone to Memphis to get supplies and slaves for rebuilding the outpost at Avaris."

Thutmose joined Amenhab, warming himself near the fire. "Why tell us?" He didn't trust Ebny any more than Ebny trusted him.

"He wanted you to know he had appointed an Officer at Avaris in his place until his return." Amenhab studied Thutmose then continued whittling.

Thutmose mulled over the news. "That was it?"

"The messenger said Ebny would be gone for about a week and reported that there has been no sign of the Keftiu."

Thutmose cocked an eye at Amenhab then peered in the direction of Avaris. Was Ebny baiting him, or had his opportunity finally arrived? "When did he leave?"

"Yesterday at dawn."

"By Amon!" Thutmose turned to the others. "I want everyone to pack up and make sure your horses are well watered."

Amenhab abruptly stood, dropping his knife. "What in Amon's name?"

"We're breaking camp tonight after the evening meal."

"Whatever for?" Amenhab retrieved his knife, stuffing it and the crude idol into his sash.

"We're riding east to the first Syrian city–state we come to."

Amenhab crossed his arms, firmly planting his feet in the sand. "Where, in the name of Amon, is that?"

Thutmose smiled in spite of Amenhab's opposition. He had heard of the city from his grandfather and knew of its strategic importance. "The coastal city of Gaza, gateway to Syria."

Tasha stepped into the fragrant garden, escaping the clatter of servants and the chaos of the palace. Pharaoh had announced Moses would be crowned within the week, but the news did not excite Tasha as it had the rest of Thebes. Instead, it made her feel even more alone.

She walked down a petal–strewn path to a bench that faced a pool beneath a flowering almond tree. A bed of narcissus bloomed nearby, and overhead clusters of almond blossoms provided shade. Tasha sat on the bench and filled her lungs with the warm sweet air as sunlight filtered through the foliage above her, thick with fragrance.

It felt good to be outside after hours in her room interacting only with her tutor, Ineni. How she longed for the sounds of the jungle, the familiar huts of her village, the faces of those she loved, and the lulling sound of the river. Instead, Egypt's splendor overwhelmed her, its busyness alienated her, and everyone, but Ineni, treated her coldly.

She remembered in years past meeting newcomers to her village, girls whose clans had relocated during drought, or whose fathers sought a position in the Kushite army. She recalled the sadness in their eyes and her own indifference. She had been far too content with her own friends to care about them, but now she understood all too well.

At Thebes life sped by so quickly she felt lost amid the whirl of it. Buildings rose like contrived mountains, their surfaces polished and aloof, much like the people in them. Egypt's gods differed from hers, their language she could barely understand, and the people seemed far too preoccupied with position and appearance to be concerned about her.

What did she care of clothes and cosmetics when the ache inside her hurt so badly she could hardly breathe? Her father's cry as she had left the village re– echoed even here, heightening her pain and not letting her forget.

"Father," she whispered, rising to walk beneath an overhanging bough and leaning against the rough bark. "I miss you so." She gazed southward up the Nile as far as she could see, its glistening surface beckoning.

"Mother, Kasima, Tenero, Morisha, I miss you all." A tear slid down her cheek. Would she never see them again? Had the shaman been right? Would she never return?

A muscular figure rode into the yard and she caught her breath. Moses! The sun had burnished his body to bronze in the weeks since their arrival. Though his headdress obscured his face, he turned toward the garden as if sensing someone watching.

Tasha stepped behind the tree, clutching the rough bark, her heart racing. Had he seen her? She didn't know why but she feared it. He had been kind enough, but still she felt shy and awkward around him. She was thankful he had kept his word, allowing her to live in the palace in spite of the anger of the woman who had met them at their arrival.

Tasha had surmised the situation from the start: Nefru, the name as lovely the face, was also Moses' future wife. Yet the woman's outburst had set Moses on edge, and like a dagger, had driven her own sorrow deeper. Tasha had learned in that first meeting to keep her distance from the Princess, and to avoid ever coming between the two of them. Still she could not help but admire Moses, handsome and commanding, driven with a dedication few men possessed. She wondered what he felt for the beautiful Nefru.

Moses turned his back to her, stepping onto the portico and through the palace doors. Tasha let out her breath, her cheeks burning. Did something besides fear beat in her breast? Within days he would become her husband, yet the thought tormented her, for hers would be a marriage of necessity, merely the fulfilment of an obligation.

She swallowed as tears threatened to spill, and gazed instead across the manicured lawns and majestic city to the turquoise river. Would she ever find happiness here? Could she dare hope that Moses might one day love her?

The palace bustled with activity as servants hung wreathes and palm branches in preparation for the coming coronation. Colorful standards representing Egypt's provinces lined the hallways heralding the festivities of the week, the gold and white flag of Thebes standing out from the rest. Servants on ladders strung blue and white banners, the colors of the double crown of Upper and Lower Egypt, while others attached streamers in a rainbow of hues.

Moses watched the activity as if somehow detached from it. Ever since his return and Nefru's display he had kept to the garrison west of Thebes, not caring to provoke her again. More than concern about his future wives, he had a growing anxiety about the coronation itself, a fear lest fate should snatch it away from him. Keeping busy training his army kept him from contemplating the possibility.

Still, Hatshepsut had surprised him upon his return from Kush. Foregoing mention of his sending Ebny and half the army north, she had instead endorsed his one desire, allowing him to recruit an army of unlimited size. He had immediately sent word as far north as Abydos and south to Edfu, drawing upon the best archers and swordsmen in the regions. Yet Hatshepsut's sudden change puzzled him. Why allow him the privilege of building an army now when they both knew that once he wore the crown building an army would be his first objective.

Moses turned from the festive preparations to the quieter colonnade of the east wing, walled on one side with offices and rooms of state, and on the other with the royal garden. Sunlight filtered through the trees and across his path as he walked past the council chamber to the audience room. He could not bring himself to look into the garden, however, lest he find Nefru there. He thought he had glimpsed her earlier, but the bench beside the pool was empty, occupied only by a dancing pattern of sunlight and leaves. Perhaps he had imagined it.

Moses sighed. If only Nefru understood. Had she forgotten her own father's harem? Moses could hardly shun Tasha or refuse her marriage. After all, she was the key to keeping Kush from erupting into full–scale war. He dared not ignore her. In fact, in the weeks since his return he had seen her only in passing. Perhaps he should pay her a visit, but first the meeting to which he had been summoned.

Stepping through the double doors of the audience room, Moses put all other thoughts behind as he attempted to discover why Hatshepsut had summoned him. He hoped it due to some insignificant detail regarding the coronation.

Hatshepsut stood as he entered, appearing young and even beautiful from a distance. Her crown glistened in the light that streamed from the window, and her gown flowed about her delicate form like a cloud. Moses wondered at her fate of never having enjoyed a happy marriage.

She took his hands in hers. "Moses, at last you come from your duties. I have hardly seen you these past weeks, nor has anyone else."

If she referred to his distancing himself from Nefru, she did not press the point.

"How does the army prosper? Have you many new recruits?"

"We've more than tripled our size and continue to add soldiers daily." He paused, finding the words difficult to speak. "I am grateful."

She let out her breath. "Good. What of the garrison?"

He told of the repair and additions to the post; of plans to enlarge the prison compound should captives require additional space; and of his desire to construct a shrine for Amon so the soldiers could worship without having to cross the river to Thebes.

She nodded approval, but he noted an edge of hesitancy. "Then we shall see even less of you once this is done?" She glanced away, a winsome tone in her voice. "But if that is what pleases you."

"It does."

She turned, smiling too radiantly. "Then I have an announcement of my own, something I wish to share with you before I inform the council." She awaited his response, but receiving none, she continued. "I am awarding you a title, Moses, one you are more than worthy of in light of your recent successes," she paused for emphasis, her face aglow, "'General of the Forces of Amon.'"

Moses sharply eyed her, and she turned and strode to the window. She faltered. "Though you will naturally assume the title as Pharaoh, why not enjoy it now while preparing your troops?"

Moses remained grave, fear tightening his chest. Why the sudden interest in his army and why this title now when he would soon have it as Pharaoh? A shadow crept over his thoughts but he pushed it away, his jaw clenched. She dared not cancel the coronation now.

Hatshepsut forced a smile. "Doesn't it please you? I had hoped for at least a word of thanks." She searched his face, her manner over–pleasant but her eyes distraught. She turned back to the window, drawing a deep breath. "I will proclaim it at tomorrow's council, that is, if you accept."

"I accept," he answered, his limbs feeling as if they were made of stone. An unnamed heaviness weighed upon him, threatening to overcome him, but he would not allow it. He had too much to do to worry about trying to understand her.

Yet if she expected a joyous response she would be sorely disappointed, for he felt more wary than grateful and more burdened than relieved. Why summon him from the garrison to tell him now, when in a matter of days he would wear the crown?

Thutmose stared at the night sky through the open tent flap, picturing Gaza as he had seen it on their arrival, an impregnable city with walls too high to even consider scaling. He couldn't imagine how his grandfather had taken the stronghold years ago with an army, or how he himself could possibly do so with less than four hundred men? He closed his eyes, drifting into a fitful sleep and seeing in his dreams a repeat of his experiences these past days: a caravan of horses and soldiers, donkeys laden with baskets and baggage, plodding across an endless expanse of glaring desert. The waves of sand evolved to become an expansive sea with the city of Gaza, formidable and impregnable, rising up as if from its very midst.

Thutmose awakened the next morning to the welcomed smell of boiling lentils and salted meat. He rubbed his stiff neck, squinting into the sunlight as the aroma of breakfast wafted through the open tent flap. Peering outside, he could see the cook bent over a steaming pot, testing its contents with a spoon, while other pots simmered above a scatter of fires, their smoke filling the air with a pleasant haze. Lifting the lid of a three foot basket, the cook scooped another measure into the first pot, ordering an aide to stir it. Going to the next basket, he scooped a cup of grain and added it to the other mixtures.

Thutmose started with sudden realization, his eyes widening. He bolted to his feet and ran between the pots toward the cook. The man dropped his cup, spreading grain across the sand, his mouth agape with in silent exclamation.

"How many baskets do we have?" Thutmose demanded.

The cook took a step back as if fearing what his commander would do next. "Twenty some, my Lord."

Thutmose ran to the baskets, frantically counting each one to be sure. "Can they be emptied?"

The cook's eyes widened to match Thutmose's. "Not unless you want even your bedrolls filled with the stuff."

"Then do it! I want every basket empty by nightfall. We're about to give this Governor some booty of our own."

The sun worked its way across a brazen sky until once more it set in a flame of red behind the desert. The citizens of Gaza, aware the Egyptians were watching them, had kept their great wooden gates shut, not allowing traffic in or out of the city. Gaza specialized in the sale of purple dye made from the murex shellfish found along its beaches. Yet no business had transpired that day, though several vessels waited off their coast.

The next morning Thutmose and a small caravan of donkeys plodded toward the city.

A watchman hailed them from a high tower, speaking in Akkadian, the trade language of Syria. "What do you wish with us, Egyptian?"

Thutmose answered in Akkadian, one of the few lessons he had completed during his temple studies. "Gifts for the Governor in exchange for the promise that you will make no alliance with the Hyksos against us." He hid a smile behind an imploring tone.

"Alliance? Who told you we deal with the Hyksos?"

"It is common knowledge among tradesmen who enter Egypt," Thutmose answered.

The man bent to speak with his superior then turned back to Thutmose. "We don't deal with the Hyksos; and how do we know this isn't a trick?"

Thutmose nodded to the desert. "My soldiers await your response at our camp. We pray it is favorable." He lifted the lid of the first basket and scooped a handful of grain, letting it fall through his fingers.

The watchman conferred again then faced Thutmose, eyeing the baskets. "Since when does Egypt give booty?"

Thutmose opened a second basket of lentils and motioned to the rest. "A gift of peace from the good god, Maat Ka Re Hatshepsut, may she live forever. This we give in exchange for your word not to join with our enemies."

The watchman's eye, keen and calculating, moved over the breadth of desert to the dune that hid the Egyptian camp. He conferred once more then slowly nodded, whereupon the great wooden gates creaked open. A guard guided the caravan into the city, leaving Thutmose and his few men outside.

Thutmose waited, his heart pounding in his throat. Within moments he heard the whoop of an Egyptian and the clang of metal. At Thutmose's signal, a horde of Egyptians charged over the hill as the wooden gates swung open before them.

Thutmose dashed inside, watching the fray for an opening. His men shoved through the yawning gates, their swords flashing and their movements wild. A guard hurled a spear at Thutmose but he ducked, exposing an enemy behind him as the barb met its mark in the man's chest. Parrying to the right, Thutmose stabbed a soldier in the stomach, pushing him off his sword and crouching in preparation for the next, but before he could take aim, a war axe sailed through the air toward him. Thutmose dodged as the weapon gutted a Syrian at his side.

Another jumped from a stairway onto Thutmose's path, backing him toward the gate and attacking with his full weight. Their swords met with teeth–jarring force as the warrior pushed forward, meeting Thutmose in a hold that strained every sinew in his body. Thutmose threw the attacker back and waited like a lion ready to spring as the two circled each other, their eyes keen and their bodies taut.

The soldier lunged but Thutmose jumped out of his way. With a flash of his sword, he pierced the man under his ribs. Blood spurted from the wound as the soldier held his side, toppling to the ground and spilling a pool of blood beneath him.

Thutmose glanced up the stairs as a purple robe swung around a corner. He surmised it to be the Gorvernor's. Darting up the steps after him, Thutmose ducked into a darkened doorway and peered into the shadowy recess before stepping into the room. Slamming the door shut behind him, he found himself face to face with the Governor, his sword drawn. Thutmose readied his weapon, stepping about in a semi–circle until light from an upper window fell on him, illuminating his face.

The Gorvernor's jaw fell, his grip weakening. "By the gods, it's Thutmose the Great!"

The words so startled Thutmose he forgot to lunge. The Governor must have known his grandfather, and now associated him with the great Pharaoh?

Thutmose heard his voice as if it belonged to another. "Drop your sword and I'll not harm you."

The Governor paused, though his gaze never left Thutmose's face. "Let me live and we will pay you tribute."

"What about the Hyksos? Haven't you promised to join them?"

"Mere words," the Governor muttered, his chest heaving with fear.

"Where are your soldiers? Surely you have more than these?"

"We are a peaceful people, your Lordship, preferring trade to war."

"See that you remember that," Thutmose muttered.

"The ships in our harbor are proof," the Governor managed, "as they are waiting to purchase our dye and purple cloth."

Thutmose's lip curled in a sneer. "To help you keep your word I'll be returning to Egypt with your sons and daughters, human booty, so to speak, as a guarantee."

Outside they could hear the cheers of the Egyptian army amid the weeping of women as Thutmose's soldiers ravaged the city.

The Governor nodded with resignation, his sword clattering to the floor. Thutmose relaxed his grip on his own weapon, his chest heaving as sweat trickled down his brow. A grin broke across his face. So this was the taste of victory.

The symbol of the bull god leapt on the sails of the fleet from Thera as they approached the port of Avaris.

The Keftiu navigator nodded southeast and sneered. "Their main port. Intimidating, isn't it?"

Styrone grunted, hands on his hips, his hair pulled back in a tail with ringlets dangling on either side. His build was that of a bull jumper, one both men and women found attractive.

"Move in. I want them to see us. If they have any power they'll show it now." He peered at their near empty port where only a few ships bobbed. "By Minotaur, where's the navy their Prince boasted of?"

"There," the navigator pointed with a laugh. "Three old war vessels and some fishing boats. Gods! It looks as if the farthest two have been raised from the bottom of the sea."

Styrone laughed then studied the port with narrowed gaze. "There appears little to keep us from taking Avaris."

"Nothing except their supposed 'army,' if it even exists."

Styrone flexed as a smile crept over his face. "If it's anything like their navy, we'll swallow them like gnats." He paused. "Still, I want to know the extent of their strength before we disembark. It may be a trap and they are lying in wait for us."

"If not?"

"We move inland."

Styrone nodded toward the green shore. "We'll secure Avaris and the surrounding villages then send for the rest of our people. Once they arrive we could occupy as far south as Memphis." He self-assuredly nodded. "Bring us closer. I want a better look at the new capital of 'Santaurus.' Once we've taken the city and toppled their shrines, claiming them in honor of our bull god, we'll enslave the Egyptians along with the Semites they already hold captive, and rebuild the Delta for our own purposes. Then we'll push farther south until eventually both of the Two Lands are ours."

"Do you think Thera will last much longer?" the man anxiously watched his commander.

Styrone shook his head. "Perhaps a couple of years, but how can our people enjoy life when death hangs overhead like a monstrous god spewing ash and smoke?" He studied the sprawling city, the surrounding fields spread in every direction like an inviting blanket of green. No rumbling mountains jutted into the sky, nor black clouds threatened to rain grit and dust over their land. Instead, before them lay a pastoral peacefulness such as only the unsuspecting enjoy.

Ebny raced into the abandoned camp, whipping his horse in a circle. By Amon, where was Thutmose when he needed him?

He scanned the campsite, seeing nothing but the ashes of a dozen fires and a trail of hoof prints leading east. Alighting, he knelt and touched the hollows of the prints, then cursed. It wasn't enough for Thutmose to watch their borders. No, he had to raise a storm of trouble besides, and now of all times.

Ebny remounted, reining his horse, still hoping for a glimpse of the patrol, but saw nothing save an endless contour of desert and an occasional patch of brush. He gritted his teeth, showing an even row of white, his face grim. If he ever lived to get his hands on Thutmose....

But there was no time for that now. He only prayed Thutmose's absence didn't mean the Hyksos as well would soon be down their throats. In the meantime he had to get a message to Pharaoh, for the Keftiu lay in wait off the coast of Avaris, and as far as he knew, Thutmose and his patrol had deserted.

CHAPTER 6

Tasha stepped from the bath and wrapped herself in a robe, sitting at the vanity before her attendant.

"I think you'll look much better in a wig," the girl announced.

Tasha falteringly chose her words, using what little Egyptian she knew. "The days are hot and the wig heavy."

"Yes, and everyone in Egypt wears them. You should be no different, especially since you are to become a royal wife," the girl retorted.

"They are uncomfortable," Tasha managed. She liked her own hair, had an abundance of it, and couldn't see going to great lengths to feel top–heavy.

The maid threw up her hands. "Ineni says I am to fix you to look the part. Instead, you want to dress like a simple jungle —" She caught herself before finishing, but Tasha surmised the inference, the words stinging as surely as if a dart had pierced her.

The girl attempted a softer tone. "The wig will flatter you, and they are not as hot as they appear. You can take it off after the ceremony."

With that she motioned another servant who stood ready with the carefully arranged coiffure. Another brought? sandals and accessories, while a third held out a white gown edged in gold.

"Here you are." The girl shoved the gown at Tasha, picking up the discarded wrap she had previously worn and holding it at arm's length, unceremoniously disposing of it.

Tasha pretended not to notice, concentrating instead on the softness of the linen as it slipped over her breasts and hips to the floor. Unlike the heavier fabrics of Kush, its delicate weave allowed light to pass through, revealing the curves of her body. The gold detail shimmered over her shoulders and down her breasts as if she wore a finely braided necklace. She glanced into the bronze mirror, her face reflecting pleasure at her appearance.

The attendant prodded her to a chair, motioning the others to gather about and begin their duties. "Add extra henna for her nails and ochre for her lips so the color stands out against her dark skin."

"Skin as soft as a baby's," a servant cooed.

Though the words were the kindest Tasha had heard, the foremost attendant silenced the girl with a look. "Save your chatter. Right now we must prepare her for the opening ceremonies and later for the banquet. Then tomorrow we have to repeat the entire process for the coronation."

The second girl sighed. "And it will be the same every day until Moses decides what to do with her." She gave Tasha a quick glance and changed the subject. "Have you seen Nefru's gown? Fit for the bride of a god, and well it should be. She has ordered a headpiece from the treasure house, something her grandmother received years ago from Kush. Fitting under the circumstances, wouldn't you say?"

The girl nodded. "Has Nefru spoken with Moses since...the incident?" In her eagerness to exchange royal gossip the maid upset a bottle of henna, nearly spilling it on Tasha's gown.

The foremost attendant clicked her tongue in disgust. "Careful or you'll have us demoted to kitchen help." She turned to arrange Tasha's wig. "In answer to your question, yes, Nefru does speak, and frequently." Standing behind Tasha and looking in the mirror, she appraised the wig, adjusting it further. "She says she'll be glad to get this ceremony out of the way so she can have Moses to herself. She is planning a visit to Edfu afterward so she and Moses can relax without," the girl glanced at Tasha, "interference."

Tasha's face burned at the words and hot tears threatened to spill but she wiped them away, pretending aggravation from her eye make–up. She had learned more Egyptian than these servants realized, but preferred to feign ignorance rather than confront them.

Placing a final touch of ochre on Tasha's lips, the attendant clasped a collar about her neck and set a simple gold fillet on her head. "Isn't there a lotus or something to dress this up?"

"I'll see what I can find," a servant answered, and hurried from the room.

"Let me see." A maid stepped in front of Tasha to view their efforts and caught her breath, admiration surfacing in spite of her resolve. "Yes, she does look the part."

Footsteps sounded outside the door and with it a commanding voice. "Prince Moses to see his betrothed."

The girls gasped, looking about for a way of escape, and scurrying like frightened chicks out a back exit as Moses entered.

Tasha self–consciously arose, aware of the same urge to flee, but forced herself to stand and face him.

Her slender form framed in sheer white and gold caught Moses by surprise. Though her eyes momentarily held his, she looked away as he scanned her body, staring as if he had come upon a treasure more exquisite than any he had ever seen.

He found his voice. "I thought you would appreciate a visit before the ceremonies. After all, I hardly know you, and tomorrow you are —" he awkwardly paused, "to become my wife."

"Thank you, my Lord, you are kind." She slightly bowed, her breathing quickening as his eyes met hers.

The silence lengthened. Moses cleared his throat. "A gift for the occasion." He produced a small wooden box and self–consciously held it. "Somehow it doesn't seem appropriate. I'll see that an attendant brings something more suitable before the banquet."

He set the box on a nearby table and chuckled to himself. "I suppose I have been out in the field too long, for I haven't seen a woman in days, and never one more lovely."

It was almost an apology, and Tasha nodded in acknowledgement before looking away.

"If I had time I would take you for a walk in the garden or a ride up–river." He stopped, realizing her last boat ride had been the voyage from Kerma. He studied her, contemplating his words. "I wish the events of your arrival had been happier, for both of us. Perhaps once trade is established with the Southlands we could invite your family for a visit. I would like to get to know them under better circumstances."

Tasha winced and Moses chided himself for having mentioned it. Tears rimmed her eyes and he was sure he had caused them. He felt at a loss. "Is there anything I can get for you?"

She shook her head. "You are kind and I am grateful."

Moses turned to her balcony, studying the view of the city and wondering why he had not chosen a room for her overlooking the lawns and gardens, closer to his own. "I'm afraid I have neglected you these past weeks. I don't blame you for being unhappy."

Though her unhappiness had nothing to do with him, Tasha felt her resolve slipping. Pressing her hand to her mouth, she stifled silent sobs that shook her body, letting loose a flood of emotion.

Moses watched her, not sure what he should do. Normally he would have called an attendant or even a physician, but somehow he could not bring himself to leave her. He touched her hand then wrapped it in his own larger one, enfolding her in his arms. Her skin felt soft and alluring, her breasts firm against his chest. He brushed the back of her neck with his lips, attempting to quiet her heart as well as his own.

Neither spoke until she pulled away. "I — I am sorry for weeping, my Lord. I should be grateful for your kindness."

Moses could see the outline of her body beneath the gown and forced his eyes to hers. "Will I see you tonight at the banquet?"

"Yes, my Lord."

Their eyes met, desire surging through him like fire over straw. "You needn't address me in the manner of a servant. 'Moses' will do." He managed a smile, reluctantly turning to the door. Another day and she would be his. "Until this evening."

She nodded as he stepped from the room, closing the door almost reverently behind him.

At the sound of his leaving an attendant re–entered, shaken. She crept to Tasha's side, looking at her with a mixture of awe and trepidation. Opening the box the Prince had left, the maid lifted up two glittering ankh earrings inset with obsidian and turquoise, and a dainty bracelet to match. She put the earrings on Tasha and slipped the bracelet over her wrist. Then, with a last fleeting look at the Princess, she hastily bowed from the room.

Tasha hardly noticed, so absorbed with what had occurred. Seating herself at her vanity she relived the moments with Moses as if in a dream. Had he truly touched her, kissed her, tried to comfort her? Had he really offered her the happiness of seeing her family again? Somehow even that dimmed in light of his presence.

What was it she had seen in his eyes? Desire? Wonder? Her body warmed at the thought. Taking a deep breath, she attempted to quiet her heart as she awaited the summons to the ceremony. Moses would be there, and already she longed to see him.

Styrone, commander of the Keftiu navy, squinted, watching a large black man barking orders at a sparse troop of Egyptian soldiers.

Sunlight glanced off their swords and lance tips as they positioned themselves at the quay.

The navigator studied them then grunted. "Surely he doesn't expect to win a battle with that number?"

A smile spread across Styrone's face. "We can easily overpower them. Let's move out."

The fleet slowly slid toward shore, the carved dragons at their helms barring their teeth behind sinister smiles while their sails slapped above them in the wind.

Ebny and his men braced themselves. Except for the obvious odds against them, Ebny felt almost relieved to see the enemy move after having watched them offshore for more than a week.

His Officer glanced at him. "Any news of Thutmose?"

Ebny shook his head. "By the time Hatshepsut gets word and decides what to do we'll no longer be around to thank her."

"At least we have the afterlife to look forward to," his comrade offered.

"I'd rather go of the gods' choosing than my enemies'," Ebny noted, anxiously glancing eastward and cursing beneath his breath.

The Keftiu vessels dropped anchor a distance from shore, lowering smaller boats filled with soldiers into the water like infant spiders crawling from their mothers' backs. Ebny's muscles tensed as he tightened his grip on his lance, while his men lifted their bows and readied their weapons.

"Take aim as soon as they're within range," he ordered. "If we're lucky we can thin their ranks before they reach shore."

His eyes met those of a hefty Keftiu poised at the helm of the foremost ship, obviously their commander. The man lifted a shield and sword that appeared ablaze with reflected light. He flexed his muscles, glaring at Ebny as if daring him to personal combat. Ebny returned the look with his own fierce visage.

"I've chosen my opponent," Ebny muttered, widening his stance and balancing his lance in a meaty palm.

The Keftiu flashed a grin, his eyes bright with anticipation. Then his attention diverted beyond Ebny and farther up the avenue, a question on his face. His features, so self–assured only moments before, now widened with surprise.

Behind him Ebny heard the faint rumble of wheels, the neighing of horses, and the robust voices of chanting. He dared not turn to investigate nor did he allow the faintest hint of surprise to pass his countenance. Instead he challengingly held the Keftiu's gaze.

The enemy commander's eyes bore into his as if demanding an explanation but Ebny merely hardened his glare, the twitch of a neck muscle the only evidence of tension. Ebny listened as the sound of marching feet and rumbling wagons grew louder until lost beneath a multitude of voices that rose in triumphant chant to Amon. The confusion on the Keftiu's face reflected relief on Ebny's.

Styrone scanned the approaching army, estimating their strength and barking a command in the same instant. Thrusting an arm toward his fleet, he locked eyes with Ebny a last time before turning his back on the Delta and motioning the other skiffs to follow.

Only then did Ebny let out his breath, turning to view the sight for himself. Filling the highway from the quay through Avaris eastward, a caravan of carts and horses, prisoners and soldiers paraded the length of the avenue. Ebny's jaw dropped, seeing Thutmose at the head. The youth rode toward him, his face radiant with a grin.

"Thank the gods, you arrived!" Ebny exclaimed, his nostrils flared. "And none too soon." Thutmose deserved more than a few heated words but Ebny had no strength to voice them. He glanced at the rows of prisoners and cart–loads of wealth. "Where? How?"

"Gaza," Thutmose announced, beaming, "and wait until you hear how we did it!"

As the Keftiu ships faded into the waters of the Great Sea, Ebny surveyed the scene, listening to Thutmose's tale and attempting to count the carts and prisoners. He wished now he hadn't been so hasty in sending Pharaoh that message. He would feel more than a little ridiculous when this same 'deserter' marched into Thebes with booty and captives, a victorious conqueror.

Weary of endless ceremonies and her servants' constant attention to her coiffure and gown, Tasha had only one event left of the day: the evening banquet. Her attendants had insisted upon a flawless appearance and were still fussing over her when a package arrived from Moses.

Tasha unwrapped the gold foil with trembling fingers, finding inside a headdress more beautiful than any she could have imagined. Jewels of every color dangled from delicate chains while the exquisite crown lifted in a peak at the forehead. It looked like an adornment fit for a Queen, and she prayed it wasn't the crown Nefru had spoken of. An attendant carefully set it on Tasha's head before sending her to the banquet accompanied by an entourage of servants.

As Tasha entered the banqueting room it quieted to a whisper, her soft steps and the gentle swishing of her gown the only audible sound. The servants led her to the head table where Moses sat and their eyes met as she took her place at his right hand. Nefru, seated on his left, glared at her as a vulture would its prey, and Tasha couldn't help but notice the simple gold fillet encircling her wig. Turning, Nefru spoke in low tones to her mother and younger sister, casting a backward glance at Tasha for emphasis.

Moses did not notice, however, his attention captivated by Tasha. "The headpiece becomes you." He studied it with admiration then lowered his gaze to hers.

What did she see stirring in their depths? Passion? Desire too long restrained? She murmured her thankfulness then turned back to the entertainment, all too aware of his presence as she feigned interest in the dancers, watching them gyrate to the rhythm of the lyre and drums. The aroma of roasted duck and gazelle passed the table with dizzying frequency, while fresh servings of sweet breads, salads, fruit and wine were pressed on them until Tasha could not stand the sight of anything more.

Before the last course Moses leaned toward her and suggested a walk in the garden. Avoiding Nefru's venomous stare, Tasha accepted, grateful for an opportunity to leave the clamor and confusion of the banqueting hall.

Taking her arm, Moses guided her away from the tables of well–wishers to the garden while his personal lutenist followed, weaving a melody as light as the breeze that wafted about them outside the hall.

Tasha breathed deeply, grateful for the cooling caress of air that moved through her gown and brushed against her body. All at once she felt at ease, the darkness a soothing balm and the familiar scent of the river as heady as perfume on the moonlit night. They neared the elongated pool just off the patio, alive with reflected light from the hall and stars. On either side the walkway seemingly stretched into infinity, lined with lilies that beckoned with sweet fragrance. Moses led her down the shadowed path, leaving the lutenist at the pool, his music carried on the breeze like a larks trill.

"It is beautiful," Tasha murmured.

"So it is."

Tasha glanced up to find Moses watching her. She looked away, her breathing quickening. He touched her arm then enfolded her hand in his.

Walking slowly, they stared up at the star–lit sky. "You can see it tonight, the constellation of Orion destined to pursue his lover, Pleiades, throughout eternity," Moses murmured.

Tasha gazed up at the two clusters of stars so near each other. "Do they ever actually meet?"

Moses peered into her eyes, covering her hands with his. "I would like to think so." He nodded behind him. "This is where I played as a child, splashing about on hot afternoons and making a mess of the flowers. I haven't been here in years. I guess I've been too busy."

Tasha laughed. "It's hard to imagine with the pool so serene and peaceful."

"As you are." Moses hungrily eyed her. "I feel you belong here."

A strange delight welled within her, broken by boisterous laughter from the banqueting room. They resumed their walk while Moses spoke of his years at Thebes in the service of Her Majesty, and all he hoped to accomplish after his coronation. At mention of the word he stood still, his jaw tightening as he peered into the darkness, seemingly struggling with an inner foe. Tasha placed a comforting hand on his arm, whereupon he groaned and drew her to him in the shadows.

She could feel his breath against her forehead, then down her cheek and onto her neck. It was as if the spark of passion had burst into full flame. His lips found hers and lingered, then brushed her cheek and nestled in her hair.

"I didn't know I needed anyone," he whispered, "until now." He drew her closer, the silence lengthening.

But she did not answer, she couldn't. A struggle of her own filled her breast.

He loosened his arms, gazing down at her. "I realize we hardly know each other." The words hung in the air as if an apology. "Yet I can't deny how I feel."

She gazed into the night sky, hoping the air would cool her burning face. "In my village when a man wishes to marry he approaches the girl's father. If her father agrees, they decide on a price, and within days the ceremony begins. Often the girl does not even know the man and is rarely consulted." She looked up at Moses, her eyes glistening. "I always wondered if I would care for the man I married." She paused, a smile on her lips. "Now I know, for I do."

Moses moaned again, pressing his lips against hers and reveling in the softness of her skin, her body alive beneath his touch. Brushing her cheek with his lips, he tugged her to a bench as together they gazed into the night while Moses pointed out the various constellations, the stars seeming to hang so low they could touch them.

"Nefru had suggested a trip to Edfu after the ceremony, but it doesn't sound nearly as inviting as spending time with you." Moses studied her with longing. "Besides, I have others matters to occupy me." He took a deep breath, attempting nonchalance. "I suppose you've never been to the Delta."

She shook her head, finding it difficult to speak after the passion he had aroused.

"I will be needed there once we are wed." He paused. "The Keftiu and Hyksos both threaten our borders. I must join my army with that of the northern forces in case of an attack."

Tasha felt a pang of regret at mention of the words. "Then you will be gone?"

"Yes." His eyes held hers. "That is, unless you would join me." He closely watched her. "There is a palace at Avaris I could rebuild, and would send for you upon its completion."

She carefully chose her words. "You will move the capital to the north?" He nodded. Her thoughts lingered over the faces of her family and the villagers she had left behind. Avaris would take her even farther from them. Yet as much as she loved her people, she could not deny what she felt for Moses. She looked into his face, her eyes shining. "Then if you want me, I will go."

"Want you?" Moses pulled her to her feet. "I want you so badly I feel I will burst with longing." His gaze swept over her as he enveloped her in his arms, kissing her as if to never let go.

"Ahemmm." A servant cleared his throat and Moses pulled away, his eyes flashing at the intrusion. The man gulped. "The Lady Nefru requests your presence, my Lord. She says she must speak with you at once, that it is a matter of urgency."

Moses let go of Tasha, eyeing the man until he quaked. "Tell her to wait."

The servant swallowed. "My Lord, Pharaoh herself advised the meeting."

Moses' eyes bore into the servant's, his features hard. "Very well. See my future wife to her apartment and I will find out just how 'urgent' this really is."

The servant bowed low, leading Tasha down a seldom used path through the garden and toward the colonnade. Moses watched them go, the white of Tasha's robe swaying in the darkness until he could see her no more. How he longed for tomorrow's ceremonies to be over.

He glanced at the banqueting hall, hearing the methodical padding of sandals and clinking of bracelets as his sister materialized from the shadows. She approached him with the cold confidence of a lioness, her eyes glowing in the moonlight.

He waited until she had reached him, and seeing her face twist to a snarl, he spoke before she could unleash her sarcasm. "I won't be going to Edfu with you after all, Nefru. In fact, I will be relocating to the Delta as soon as I can prepare a ship."

Nefru's eyes flashed. "Why? To take a wife from the Keftiu and Hyksos, as well?" She glanced at the path where Tasha had just disappeared.

The lines of Moses' face deepened. "Hardly. This won't be a voyage of pleasure."

"Then what kind of voyage will it be?"

"Ask Thutmose, if you must know."

Nefru's brow pursed. "Did he send for you?"

"In a manner of speaking." Moses' jaw tightened, remembering Hatshepsut's reaction to the news that Thutmose had deserted. If the message was true, and he had never known Ebny to lie, the Delta needed him more than ever. "I'll be leaving with my recruits as soon as the coronation has ended."

"Will Tasha accompany you?"

"Going or staying is her decision." He hardened his visage, peering down at her. "What does it matter?"

Nefru's hand flashed across his face in the darkness, leaving its mark. "What matters is your choice of another over me!" Her lips whitened. "As for Tasha, once you take her as your wife I promise to make your lives as miserable as possible."

Moses grabbed Nefru's arm, his eyes narrowing. "Touch her and you'll regret it."

A smile sliced Nefru's face, her eyes dancing like tongues of fire. "Don't worry, Moses, I'll make sure your dark skinned bride lives to tell every detail of her torment. That way you will both feel her pain."

Moses squeezed Nefru's arm so tightly it took her breath away. "Harm her and you'll pay dearly! For once I am Pharaoh you can be sure I will have my way."

Nefru pulled free, rubbing her arm and watching him with disbelief. Then whirling, she disappeared into the shadows beyond the walkway.

The sun rose behind Thebes as if ushering in a god with golden brow against a clear azure sky. Moses, son of the god Amon and of Pharaoh Hatshepsut, strode down the palace steps between the parting throng and to his waiting chariot. He hardly heard as they called his name, nor noticed the dignitaries that had come from distant provinces solely for the event of his coronation. All he wanted was to get this ceremony over with so he could get on with his duties and the more pleasant affairs of his life.

Yet a nameless fear clutched at his throat making his breathing uneven and his head pound. Did the responsibilities he would face as Pharaoh already weigh on him? Or did a premonition crouch in the shadows like a demon waiting to attack?

The crowds cheered as he rode up the Avenue of Rams to the pylon entrance of the temple where he left his chariot, walking through the jubilant throng as if in a dream. Everywhere dignitaries and Priests crowded about while onlookers pressed into the courtyard, filling the sanctuary. Moses strode toward the shrine of Amon as officials in formal attire paid their respects in muttered blessings. Priests were everywhere, milling about as if in silent sanctum, or swinging incense censors and praying in a monotone. Web Priests in leopard skin garb stood like sentries between the Officers and the royal family, while the whispers of the crowd blended with the low hum of the choir sounding more like bees around a hive than the prelude to a coronation.

Moses searched the royal party for Tasha, seeing her at a distance behind Nefru. Fitting, he sardonically thought, but once wed she would never be second in his affection. He noticed Hatshepsut had not yet arrived and he wondered why, his chest tightening.

In spite of her absence Puseneb stepped before the altar and put on his most holy expression, a pious scowl somewhat lost in the folds of his face. The room stilled as he offered a prayer to Amon, while the Priests circled with swinging censors, adding thick sweet smoke to the already fetid air. That was Moses' cue. He stepped from the royal family to the center of the room, his skin glistening with a mixture of oil and sweat, and his head encircled with the serpent diadem he would soon exchange for the double crown.

He supposed Puseneb's prolongation of the ritual due more to Hatshepsut's absence than the High Priest's religiosity. What could be keeping her? Moses tried to slow his pounding heart, submerging his apprehension behind a rigid demeanor. At last Pharaoh arrived in her covered litter, and Puseneb, with an audible sigh, concluded his incantations.

Hatshepsut took her place beside Moses, appearing unsteady and pale. Had she fallen ill? Moses purposefully diverted his attention to Tasha where he found her ready smile comforting. Today she would be his, and though he could not allow desire to cloud his thinking, he looked forward to the comfort of her presence as he assumed the role of Pharaoh.

Puseneb called Moses and Hatshepsut to the raised dais before the god's shrine. Hatshepsut appeared frail and vulnerable beneath the double crown, and Moses chose to fix his gaze on the High Priest instead, his features grim and impenetrable.

Slowly and deliberately Hatshepsut turned to the masses, her voice clear, though her hands trembled. "This is a day we have long awaited...."

Moses took a deep breath, thankful it would soon be over.

"...a day the gods have proclaimed as holy." She avoided Moses' face as she continued. "So it is that I, Maat Ka Re Hatshepsut, do proclaim that until these wars at our borders have ended and we are at peace with our enemies...," her voice faltered, "Senmut Re Moses, General of the Armies of Amon, will reign with me as Regent on the throne of Egypt."

The room stilled then at once erupted with a multitude of exclamations.

"Regent?" Moses repeated the word like a curse.

Hatshepsut did not answer but, visibly shaken, muttered a few last words then called for her litter and disappeared through the throng.

Realization bolted through him as color drained from his face. So this was why she had named him General, allowing him to build an army. She had planned it all along! He clenched his fists. By the gods!

Moses glanced at Tasha, her disbelief mirroring his. Without a coronation there could be no marriage.

Tasha reached out to touch him as he brushed past her but he could not respond, instead he fled the gaping onlookers as if escaping an evil dream. Bodies blurred as he hastened to the outer court and to his chariot. Grasping the reins, he whipped his horse to action, riding through the cheering crowds who thought he had emerged as Pharaoh. He forced a path through the throngs and down the Avenue of Rams, but his way became blocked by a confusion of bodies. For some reason the mob ahead of him refused to part, and he looked more closely, realizing these were not Egyptians at all crowding his path, but men and women in chains whose attire he did not recognize.

Thutmose rode to his side, his face radiant and his chest heaving as though having run the distance himself. "Booty and captives from Gaza, my Lord. I have taken the city and have brought back gifts for Amon and the gods."

Moses attempted to make sense of his words: booty and captives? Then Thutmose had not deserted but had taken the Syrian stronghold of Gaza. The irony pierced him like a blade.

Oblivious to Moses' lack of response, Thutmose continued, "There is no need to worry, my Lord. The Keftiu have left our port, and the Delta remains secure under Ebny's command."

Moses shook his head, unable to assimilate the news, his body numb with the horror of what he had just experienced. Whipping his horse to a gallop, he left Thutmose behind, continuing past the curious gaze of the Syrians, past cartloads of booty and soldiers marching in ranks. Moses pressed toward the city gates, longing only for the solitude of the desert, his features fixed and his body rigid as if carved of stone.

Oh, that the earth would open up and cover him, that death would welcome him to the silence of a tomb. His worst fear had come to pass: the coronation had ended and he had not been crowned.

CHAPTER 7

Moses stood motionless under a blazing sun as he observed the new recruits Hatshepsut had personally added to his army. A group of them matched their strength against his regulars in pairs with wooden swords, their muscles glistening, while others practiced with blunt–ended lances and javelins, attempting to outdistance each other.

Moses wiped the sweat from his forehead, resting his hands on his hips. His hair clung to his face in ringlets, his eyes stinging with sweat as he studied his men. However, it was not the elements that occupied his thoughts so much as the maze of questions still hammering in his brain. Why had Hatshepsut done everything in her power to promote his authority, save crowning him? Did she selfishly hold to the throne to promote her own policies? Why then allow him an army and name him General? It didn't make sense. As the seed of Amon and the Pharaohs, no one else deserved the title. But why keep him from it? A knot of bitterness twisted inside him and with it the resolve to discover the answer no matter the cost.

With the wave of his arm, Moses ordered the recruits to their tents until the mid–day heat abated. Dousing a towel with water, he wiped the perspiration from his face and neck then poured himself a drink, and sat staring into the distance.

He remembered Thutmose's account of the events at Gaza and Avaris as if he had just spoken with him. With less than four hundred men the youth had approached the Syrian stronghold, and like an act of the gods, had emptied his provision baskets and gained entrance unawares into the city. Though deceitful and risky, like Moses' own bluffs at Thera and Kerma, it had worked. Thutmose had emerged a hero, carting captives and booty to Avaris where he had arrived just in time to confuse the Keftiu and save Ebny's army.

'It's as if the gods go before me!' Thutmose had exulted.

Moses' lip curled. Act of the gods? He took another drink. He could have boasted the same, having escaped Thera and Kerma by a ruse, but what of his coronation? Where were his gods then? Questions pounded in his brain until he became weary of thinking.

He stoically studied the desert as hoof beats sounded from the direction of the causeway. Moses turned to see a chariot and driver approaching.

"Greetings, Moses." Ineni stopped in front of his tent and dismounted, handing him a scroll with Hatshepsut's seal.

Moses glanced at it and tossed it onto the table, turning again to the desert.

"Pharaoh wishes to see you." Ineni searched Moses' face, the lines of his own brow furrowed more deeply than usual, evidence of his concern. "Perhaps she will tell you more if you approach her peaceably. She must have had a reason for what she did."

Ineni stopped himself before saying too much. Besides, Moses had not asked for his council, nor had the Prince returned to the capital since the day of his aborted coronation.

"So you think there's a reason why she has refused me?" Moses eyed the elder, but when Ineni did not answer he continued. "She awarded me the title of General, allowing me the privilege of building an army of unspecified size at this neglected garrison, and for what?" He met Ineni's gaze. "She knew all along she wouldn't crown me. She never intended to."

The elder started to speak but Moses turned his back to him, striding to the sharp shadowed edge of the canopy. "There's more to this puzzle." He crossed his arms, focusing on the compound at the far side of camp. "Hatshepsut never wanted me near the Delta, always insisting I spend my summers south at Edfu rather than go anywhere north of Thebes. She opposed my voyage to Thera and thwarted any plans of my leading an army to the Delta, even to the point of commissioning Thutmose in my place." He whirled. "She's hiding something, Ineni, I know it, and I'm determined to discover what it is."

Ineni met Moses' gaze with concern. Yes, he remembered the event only too well. It had happened while serving as advisor to Hatshepsut's father, Thutmose I. Word had arrived at Avaris of the birth of Pharaoh's grandson, 'born of the god Amon and the Princess Hatshepsut.' Yet Hatshepsut had never appeared pregnant, according to her stewards. The news had sparked a controversy, to be sure, but over the years, at Hatshepsut's insistence of its truth, the gossip had abated, known only to those too old to make it an issue or those confined to regions not frequented by royalty. Soon the topic faded from conversation altogether, dying, for the most part, with the former Pharaoh's administration. But it was a subject Hatshepsut had warned Ineni never to bring up.

The elder cleared his throat and nodded to the symmetrical rows of tents on the far side of the camp. "Right now, my Lord, your men need you. Why stir up the past?"

Moses' eyes shot at him and Ineni knew he had spoken too much.

"What does my past have to do with it?"

Moses studied him so intently Ineni faltered. "I mean, there must be an explanation. Perhaps if you approach Her Majesty —"

Moses' eyes narrowed. "What do you know of my past?"

The elder fell silent as his own questions resurrected themselves like flies over a carcass. "I — I cannot say, my Lord."

Moses knew him too well to be fooled. He gripped the elder's shoulders, his teeth clenched. "Tell me, Ineni. I must know! If our years together mean anything, tell me what it is."

The elder's hands trembled, his lips quivering as he shook his head, but Moses would not be dissuaded. He forced Ineni's eyes to his and waited. Finally the elder murmured, "Just before Hatshepsut's announcement of a divine and royal birth her father had condemned to death the male infants of the Habiru. Hatshepsut had been visiting the summer palace at Pithom near the slave villages when she had announced the news."

Moses' face drained, his eyes unseeing as a picture too repulsive to contemplate formed in his mind. Though he forced his lips to move, his thoughts remained locked in another time and place. "Which village?"

"She was staying at Pithom on the Wadi Tumilat in Goshen, near the slave village of Tju."

The temple store–room flickered to life under the lamp's glow, revealing a mountainous pile of gold and glinting objects.

Puseneb's eyes bugged as he studied the cache. Without moving his gaze he pointed to the various parts of the room. "Put the goblets and platters on the far shelf, and take care not to mar their designs. The articles of war can be stored in the next room for future use. As for the jewels," he involuntarily caught his breath, "I will care for them myself."

He picked up a ruby studded bracelet and laid it against his wrist, then, after admiring a necklace of lapis lazuli, he tucked the two into his sash. He held up a weighty amulet of gold and precious stones, mesmerized by the way it reflected the light. "I would never have believed it if I hadn't seen it myself."

Thutmose grinned. "Some of the jewels come from as far away as Mitanni and Punt, traded for goods from Gaza. Everything we took is accounted for, as I paid my men in human booty."

Puseneb did not bother to question, though Thutmose blushed at the memory. He hoped the size of his offering would appease the gods, considering the women he and his men had violated. Actually, he had only taken the choicest youths and a portion of young women, reasoning that taking at least one in every family would guarantee the city's generous and regular tribute. He intended to treat his prisoners well, and in fact, to train them in Egypt's ways.

"I have taken prisoners, Your Holiness, and wish to have them schooled."

"Schooled for what purpose?" Puseneb asked, though his eyes remained fixed on the amulet he held.

"They need knowledge of our customs and gods so we might one day return them to Gaza to govern under our authority, as was practiced during my grandfather's reign."

Puseneb frowned, turning from the jewels. "Are you suggesting we teach them here at Karnak, defiling our temple with heathen?"

Thutmose shrugged. "Why not? If we treat them well they will forget their ways and imitate ours, teaching their own people once they return."

Puseneb was about to argue the point but stopped himself. Thutmose had a knack for the unconventional. Yet strange as his notions were, they had certainly improved the status of the treasure house. He would not discount the idea just yet.

Thutmose continued, "I am sure Gaza's citizens will treat us with respect since we house their children, and will forego any notion of joining our enemies. Besides, education is another way of doing battle."

Puseneb snorted. "It will cost money for food and lodging, and who will look after them? They can't be trusted to roam about as they please. They might have a mind to take back these treasures with force." He clutched the amulet in his fat fist.

"True, it will cost at first, but I guarantee regular tribute from Syria in the meantime, and likely even once we return their offspring."

Puseneb stared. This boy's ideas hardly made sense. He turned back to the booty. Yet the gods had obviously blessed him with a measure of wisdom. "I want no part of it myself, and I don't want them here at my temple. I've too much to do with cataloguing and sorting all this." He squinted at the youth. "But if you're certain they won't retaliate, you may teach the best of them at the garrison across the river. However, they must be guarded at all times. I don't want them imitating your antics at Gaza and attempting to conquer Thebes."

"I'll see to it, my Lord." Thutmose smiled and started for the door, then momentarily turned back. "One more thing, Your Holiness. If you want more of this sort of plunder I'll need permission to march again, and with more men, for I hope to repeat Gaza's victory many times over."

"You will have to approach Moses on that account as he is General," Puseneb answered.

Thutmose shook his head. "Moses has refused all inquiries since the supposed coronation and has not been seen at the palace in weeks."

Puseneb's eyes glittered like gold as he turned his attention once more to the treasures. "Very well, I'll do all in my power to get you more men and anything else you might need. Just be sure to return all the plunder to Thebes. The gods can always use more booty."

A full moon lifted above Tasha as she nudged her horse from the ferry to the causeway west of the river, using a worn path through the reeds at the river's edge and crossing a soft strip of green that abruptly ended at the desert. Though Ineni had told her the location of the military compound, she didn't know if she could find Moses' tent among the others in the dark.

Once at the garrison she took a deep breath and dropped to the ground near the door of the foremost tent, the gold–fringed canopy reflecting the moonlight. Silently stepping to the open doorway, she saw the back of Moses as he hunched over a table, a goblet in his hand.

Tasha started to approach but something stopped her. Instead she watched as Moses lifted the goblet, draining it in a single swig, then hung his head and groaned. Tasha stood mesmerized as if seeing someone she didn't know. Even from behind she could detect the dejection in his form with his hair disheveled and his loincloth loosely tied about his waist.

She longed to comfort him and took a step forward, but he whirled about, his face hardened in the shadows and his eyes fierce.

"Who is it?" He clumsily groped for his sword, taking several staggering steps before stopping. "Tasha." She marveled he could speak her name with such reverence, but just as quickly his face convulsed to a sneer and he turned his back on her. "Why have you come? You shouldn't be here."

His tone sliced the air between them like a blade. What had happened to the man she loved?

She rested her hand on his arm and his flesh tightened beneath her touch. His tone softened. "You shouldn't have come. I don't want to see anyone, especially you." He shook his arm free and refilled his goblet.

She stood motionless, torn between pity and horror. "Moses." She laid her head against his back, wrapping her arms about him as if to summon back the man she had known.

A groan arose from deep inside him and with it a sob of desperation. He swept the goblet from the table and turned on her. "I told you I don't need anyone, least of all you!"

She shook her head in disbelief, her eyes filling with tears. How could he say such things? Her veil slipped to her shoulders and he stopped, watching her with such longing she stepped away from him as from a stranger.

He reached out and touched her cheek, tenderly unwrapping the veil without taking his eyes off her.

She trembled. "I love you, Moses. I had hoped we might wed in spite of the circumstances so we could enjoy a measure of happiness."

His face twisted. "Happiness? I will never know the word, I who thought myself a son of Amon."

He retrieved his goblet, filling it again, but she put her hand on his. "Please don't, Moses, you have had enough."

"I'll never have enough, never be able to keep the truth hidden beneath its depths." He tipped the goblet to his mouth then wiped a hand across his face, his eyes ablaze. "I might have had you as my wife but not now, not ever. If you only knew you'd not even want to marry me."

He stopped, suddenly struck by her beauty, his eyes hungrily roving over her. He touched her shoulder, her arm, then moaning, drew her to himself. Pressing his body against hers, he recklessly ran his hands over her back as he fumbled with the sash of her gown. He untied the sash allowing the garment to slip from her shoulders. It would have fallen to the ground had she not held it against her breasts.

"Not this way, Moses."

He wrenched the robe from her grasp and flung it across the room, his passion inflamed by his fury. Grabbing her, he pulled her toward him, but she cried out as if in pain and he drew back, startled, as she crouched naked before him, fear etched on her face.

His visage hardened and he pointed to the door. "Then go and never again approach me as a lover, for I swear, the next time I'll not stop myself."

Tears caught in her throat as she grabbed her garment and threw it about herself, tying the sash with trembling fingers. With a last glance back, she fled from the tent and mounted her horse, galloping down the causeway toward the river. Tears stung her eyes and ached in her throat as her gown billowed about her like a ghostly pall.

This wasn't the Moses she knew and loved. What had happened to him? She had lost him to something she couldn't see or understand, and like a phantom from the nether world, it had captured his heart.

Hatshepsut's breast fluttered with excitement as she waited in the palace garden for Moses' arrival. She had prepared his favorite meal, the aroma of roasted duck, fresh bread, and ripe fruit mingling in a savory mix in the warm afternoon air. A flawless table setting sparkled on the linen cloth, accentuated by a bowl of lilies and lotus blossoms. Today she wore no crown or uraeus, but had carefully chosen her attire, something informal to set Moses at ease yet elegant enough to flatter. She could hardly wait to see him.

Her heart had nearly risen to her throat when she had heard he wanted to speak with her. She had responded by messenger, suggesting lunch on the patio outside the banquet room, a feast for just the two of them. Wonderfully enough, he had accepted. She did not know for what purpose she owed this visit, but would have gladly agreed to anything if it would bridge the gulf between them.

A servant entered with a tray of sweet breads and she nodded to the table, lost in the whirl of her thoughts. Even the place of their luncheon held significance, for Moses had played in this very garden as a child, the pool at its center his escape from the afternoon heat. Hatshepsut avoided contemplating the most recent events, and instead imagined Moses as a youngster romping on the expansive lawn and making a mess of the flowers. How the servants had scolded. She chuckled at the memory.

All too soon he had outgrown his frolicking and had become a sober–eyed youth. As he developed so did his curiosity, his questions challenging even his tutors. Astronomy especially interested him, and there seemed no end to what he wished to explore. At last Hatshepsut agreed to a routine of temple studies and the basic trade of a scribe; then language, math and architecture, astronomy, and finally the rituals of the Priesthood were mastered.

The day had come when Moses had advanced to a place worthy of a position in her administration. Numerous lesser titles were awarded him, and he had proven so efficient at these tasks, Ineni had suggested something more challenging. Thus he was awarded the title 'Steward of Amon,' 'Overseer of the Works and Temple of the Gods,' and now 'General of the Armies of Amon,' and 'Regent.' He had never disappointed her in all he had set out to accomplish. Truly it seemed he was born of the gods.

A movement caught her eye and she looked up, seeing Moses standing in the doorway as if an apparition of Amon himself, perfect in form and appearance. He solemnly studied her, his features carefully molded, framed by hair that fell in waves about his forehead, his lean body hard beneath his tan. Yet she shuddered at the coldness in his eyes, an aloofness she had never seen before.

Attempting to ignore it, she breathed his name and held out her hand, but he made no response, and she awkwardly pointed to the table instead. "I thought we could enjoy lunch together in the garden, your favorite spot. Remember how you used to exasperate the nurses and splash about in the pool? You seemed more fish than boy."

She laughed but his features remained unmoved as he took the chair opposite her. "I've not come to discuss my past but my future." He asked a servant for wine. "I've a proposal to make as Regent." He pronounced the word deliberately then took a long draught from his goblet. "There is little need for my service as General since Thutmose and Ebny have the borders well in hand. According to Puseneb, Thutmose continues to effectively lead the army, and has even started schooling prisoners at the garrison. Why replace him? I can keep the title of General if you like, but I've no stomach for soldiering."

Hatshepsut smiled. She had always believed the same.

Moses lifted his eyes to hers, a subtle irony in them. "Instead, I would like to concentrate on perfecting my skills as an architect. I thought I might focus on building here at Thebes." He eyed her over his goblet. "I had hoped to begin with your temple."

Hatshepsut's face lit. "Why Moses, that would be wonderful! I don't know what to say."

He lifted his goblet for another drink. "I thought I would build it below the cliffs of El Kurn over the ruins of Amenhotep's run–down temple. The causeway is still useable, and the burial valley of the Gateway of the Kings is near. With the army relocated at Avaris, the garrison and tents could house the builders. I have even drawn up a plan."

He withdrew a scroll from his satchel but she did not look at it, her eyes on his. "Isn't that where you spoke of building your own temple one day? I am sure of it. Yet now you want to build mine there instead?"

He shrugged, avoiding her face. "There are other places I could build mine. Besides, your tomb could be dug in the valley on the opposite side of the mountain with a tunnel extending to your temple's holy of holies on the east side."

She quizzically watched him, not sure how to respond.

He unrolled the scroll. "This is where the causeway stands today." She followed his finger over the draft. "And here is where I propose to build your temple."

Hatshepsut gasped, her brow lifting. There, over her grandfather's insignificant ruins, stretched a tiered loveliness such as she had never seen. Several walled courts, each higher than the last, rose in a series of steps, the walkway flanked by sphinxes and myrrh trees. The sanctuary lay against the cliffs as if part of them, and an open peristyle roof allowed light to illumine the inner court.

Hatshepsut stammered. "Why it's unlike anything I've ever seen. Wherever did you get such an idea?"

"Inspired by my visit to Thera," Moses offered.

He awaited an answer and she looked up, her face radiant. "By all means, begin at once, and I will give you a title to match: 'Controller of All Construction Work of the Two Lands.'"

Moses set his jaw, his eyes moving to hers. "I'll send to Aswan for granite and sandstone, and will personally travel to Punt for myrrh trees to decorate the terraces."

Hatshepsut's smile faded as she contemplated the notion. A trip to Punt? Why, that could take more than a year. "Will you travel overland from here to Qasar on the Red Sea?"

Moses shook his head. "My other ships can travel overland if you like, but I will sail to the Delta. As General I should check on my army."

"You said Thutmose and Ebny have the borders well under control."

"Perhaps," Moses countered.

"Don't bother yourself with the army. Concentrate on building," Hatshepsut pressed.

"Then perhaps some recreation would suit me."

Hatshepsut enthusiastically nodded.

"Such as crocodile hunting along the Wadi Tumilat," Moses interjected.

Hatshepsut's face fell. She slowly raised her eyes to his. If he travelled along the Wadi Tumilat he would pass Pithom and the villages of the Habiru. Had he intended such? Why not travel overland with the rest of his ships? She wondered now at his motive.

He continued as if not noticing her concern. "The temple of Mentuhotep, which also stands in the way of your temple, tells of a trip made five hundred years ago to the land of Punt. I would very much like to make that visit myself, bringing back gold and ostrich feathers, myrrh trees and leopard skins such as the ancient Pharaoh inscribed."

Hatshepsut wondered how he could speak of the feat with as little emotion as he would a trip to Edfu. What did he hide? What lay behind his masked indifference?

She straightened. "It would be best if you sent someone else in your place so you could concentrate your efforts here at Thebes. You will need to coordinate the quarry work and prepare the land. It could take months, even years, to travel to Punt and back, especially by way of the Delta."

"I have weighed that." Moses ran his finger over the rim of his goblet. "In light of my recent," he paused, "disappointments, I believe time away from Thebes will benefit me. Meanwhile, I can concentrate on shifting my interests from military to architectural pursuits. I request a leave of two years."

The statement fell between them like a stone with only the occasional twitter of a bird breaking the silence. Hatshepsut's mind raced as she watched him. He had requested nothing of her since becoming regent, nor had he shown himself at the palace these past months, and she worried he had fallen into a darkened state, as Ineni had hinted. Yet here he sat interested in building her temple. Perhaps it was nothing more than the need to get away.

She studied the parchment again, enticed by the beauty of the edifice, and raised her eyes to his. "Very well, you may sail to Punt to gather gold and myrrh trees for my temple. It is a feat I will also commemorate on my own temple walls, but keep your focus, Moses." Her eyes bore into his as when he was a child and she had warned him of some danger. "You may take a fleet of trading vessels, most of which I will send overland to Qasar to await your arrival. However, Tuty and Nehisi will accompany you to the Delta."

He shot her a glance but she continued in explanation. "Ineni is too old for such ventures and would be more useful here at Thebes, overseeing the building preparations in your absence."

They furtively watched each other from across the table, each attempting to divine the other's thoughts. Moses clenched and unclenched his jaw. Did Hatshepsut suspect his motives? Clearly she intended Tuty and Nehisi to report to her. Determined to carry out his plans, he would find a way around even the eyes of these, her most trusted Officers.

Hatshepsut forced a smile. "I have always loved myrrh trees, and now to have a grove of them at my temple." She nodded to the platter of roasted duck but he shook his head, rising.

"Aren't you even going to eat?" She motioned to the buffet and laughed. "I certainly didn't plan all this for myself."

His voice barely rose above the breeze that rustled the grass and fluttered the tablecloth, carrying scents of succulent duck and fresh bread his way. "Not today, Hatshepsut. I have a crew to make ready and ships to prepare as I intend to leave before the week is through."

Hatshepsut started at the abruptness of his departure, then caught herself and attempted a smile. "Very well, Moses, I suppose I have no other choice but to enjoy this bounty myself."

He bowed from her presence and she watched him retreat up the wide steps and into the banqueting room, inwardly feeling anything but calm. What did he really plan to do in the Delta? It surely had nothing to do with a crocodile hunt. Already she was rehearsing what she would say to Tuty and Nehisi to convince them to watch him as closely as if she, herself, accompanied him.

Isis prostrated herself on the temple floor, her eyes swollen and her lips moving in a silent prayer to Hathor. How could Moses have handed Thutmose control of his army with no more experience than a student Priest? It didn't matter he had chanced success in one wild ruse. How like him to try to take a city with donkeys and grain baskets! And now he planned to march on all of Syria. She covered her face in despair. He would surely be killed!

Hatshepsut was behind this, she had to be. It fell all too perfectly into her schemes as she had always wanted to rid herself of Thutmose. Now, accompanied by a barely trained army, he would likely end up a casualty in battle or killed in one of his foolish schemes. Hatshepsut could then crown Moses without resistance.

The Priests had long since retired to their bedchambers or she would have demanded Puseneb intercede on her behalf. Instead, she was alone with the gods and her fears, begging protection for the only child they had granted her. She sniffed in the darkness and daubed her eyes, truly afraid for the first time in her life.

Isis mulled over recent events and the court gossip concerning Moses' announcement, not able to make sense of it herself. Moses' decision to build puzzled her as much as his handing the army over to Thutmose. Erecting a temple to Hatshepsut seemed an odd response to his obvious disappointment over the coronation. But a trip to Punt in her honor?

She shook her head. What had happened to the Egypt she had once known, the royalty whose actions she could predict and to some extent, manipulate? Nothing made sense anymore. To allow a mere youth to lead Egypt's army as if he were a General seemed unthinkable. With Moses no longer in control Thutmose could run rampant throughout Syria with his outrageous notions and impetuous ways. Someone had to give him orders in Moses' absence, but whom? Ebny? Puseneb? Hatshepsut? Surely not! No, instead he would be left to the wild imagination of his own schemes, digging an early grave for himself. What would become of her then?

A sob escaped her and Isis sniffed, the night unusually still and expectant. Then in the silence she heard the soft shuffle of footsteps and the command of a familiar voice. Hatshepsut! Isis' heart pounded in her breast. What was Pharaoh doing in the temple at this hour?

Isis crouched within the shadows of Hathor's curtained shrine holding her breath and listening. Hatshepsut paused before the incense altar, tossing a handful of powder onto the coals where it hissed and sizzled, sending sweet–smelling smoke throughout the expanse. Moving toward the shrine of Amon, the Queen prostrated herself before the god, murmuring a litany of prayers and petitions.

Isis leaned closer, positioning herself behind the curtain so she could better hear, but Hatshepsut no longer spoke, and Isis wondered as she listened if the Pharaoh had fallen asleep.

She began to grow tired and yawned, startled when Hatshepsut suddenly cried out. "Oh, Amon, if only...." Sobs muffled the words again as Isis strained to hear her. "I would never have kept him if I had known what would happen. I would rather have given him to someone else, anyone else, than risk your anger."

Isis' brow shot upward. By Osiris' beard, what was she speaking of?

"He was only an infant, innocent and worthy of life. Surely my righteousness in saving him merits the titles I have granted him. Bless him, I pray, and if you favor me, keep him from discovering...."

Isis leaned closer, her mind whirling. Did Hatshepsut speak of Moses?

"I won't crown him without your approval, oh god of all the earth. In exchange, I beg of you, protect him on his journey, and keep him from the slave villages of the Habiru and the truth of his birth."

Isis lost her balance at the words, grasping the curtain to keep from falling and holding her breath lest Pharaoh discover her. Instead, Hatshepsut quietly rose, pausing at the feet of Amon and whispering a final prayer before shuffling from the sanctuary and into the night.

Isis did not move, unable think of anything but the words still reverberating through her brain. Hatshepsut had clearly spoken of Moses, but what had she meant by 'the slave villages of the Habiru and the truth of his birth'?

A shiver crept up her spine and with it a deliriously delightful thought. Had Hatshepsut concealed a secret these many years terrible enough to keep Moses from the throne? Isis bit her lip and tasted blood. More importantly, might its revelation assure her own son a chance of acquiring it?

Chapter 8

Rekmire and Amenhab guarded the storeroom as casually as if they were awaiting the latrine, but stiffened to attention when Thutmose reappeared in the doorway. Glancing about, they each took an armload of goods from him while Thutmose struggled beneath an idol of Amon. Hadn't Pharaoh given him permission to outfit his troops? In so doing she as much as invited him to her supply room, he had reasoned.

Glancing up and down the hall, Rekmire whispered, "We'll never get away with this. How are we supposed to get this idol out of here without anyone noticing?"

Thutmose ignored him, nodding to the stretcher on the floor. "Now lay the stuff on it with the idol at the head then cover everything with this sheet."

The two carefully arranged the items on the stretcher, placing the idol at the top and covering it all with a length of linen.

Thutmose grinned. "That's how, the convenience of a 'fallen comrade.' Now take either end, you two, and let's get out of here."

"Why do we have to carry it?" Amenhab grumbled. "If we get caught it'll be our necks not yours."

"Only if Pharaoh finds out."

"Wonderful," Rekmire muttered, lifting the stretcher. They were about to leave when they heard the click of determined heels. Turning, Thutmose saw his mother approaching with the speed of a Hamsin storm, her eyes ablaze.

"Gods," he cursed. "How in Hades did she find me?"

The boys glanced at the stretcher then at the nearest doorway, concern etched on their brows, but there was no escape.

"Greetings mother. It's always a surprise to see you." Thutmose forced a smile.

Isis ignored the stretcher and turned to her son. "Greetings indeed! I've been trying to track you for days, ever since you arrived. Yet you've done nothing but ignore my summons, even though I've a matter of dire importance to share."

Thutmose scowled but obligingly waited while the boys lowered the stretcher to the floor. Though the lumps and bumps were in all the wrong places, the shape of a head at the top gave the form a semblance of mangled humanity.

Isis motioned the boys to her side. "I've made a discovery vital to Thutmose's future."

Thutmose's brow lifted in question, mirroring that of his comrades.

Satisfied, Isis continued. "I was at the Temple of Karnak late one night when —"

Thutmose groaned. "Not another of your visions?"

Amenhab suppressed his laughter, darting a knowing glance at Rekmire who hid his smirk behind a controlled countenance, crossing his arms and leaning casually against the wall.

Isis reared. "The most important news of your life and you make sport of me? By the blood of your grandfather, Thutmose, if your birthright means anything then listen to me." Rekmire and Amenhab changed their expressions to covert empathy and gave Thutmose a hearty jab.

Thutmose sobered of his own accord, wondering how she dared speak of his grandfather so lightly. This had better be good or he would show her some ire of his own, and his could better hers any day.

Isis took a deep breath and began again. "Late one night I happened to be worshipping Hathor at the Temple of Karnak, when from the shrine of Amon I overheard Hatshepsut praying. She said —" Isis pursed her brow, attempting to remember. "Oh, never mind her exact words. She was pleading with Amon to forgive her, hear this, for 'sparing Moses as an infant.'"

Thutmose shrugged, missing the significance of her revelation.

Isis leaned closer, her voice a harsh whisper. "She as much as confessed that Moses was not her son at all or Amon's, and did not deserve the crown." She straightened, meaningfully eyeing the boys. "She implied Moses was born a Habiru."

Thutmose's jaw fell, his eyes bugging.

Isis heaved a satisfied sigh. "So you can understand why —"

Thutmose uncontrollably sputtered then doubled over with laughter, while Amenhab and Rekmire glanced at each other, snorting in an effort to control their snickers but unable to do so. Finally Rekmire forced his composure enough to feign interest while Thutmose and Amenhab, shaking their heads, lifted the stretcher and carried it down the hall and out of sight.

"I tell you it happened just as I said," Isis insisted, indignantly glaring after the two. Turning to Rekmire, she pleaded, "Doesn't anyone have the sense to believe me?"

She met his gaze, but Rekmire shrugged, unwilling to commit himself.

"There's ample reward for the one who does," Isis stated, raising her full stature, "the title of Vizier, second highest position in Thutmose's kingdom, when he comes to power."

She had Rekmire's attention now.

"Thutmose's kingdom?" he reiterated.

"That's right. Before the former Pharaoh's death he pronounced our son the rightful heir. I had hoped my husband's words, may Hathor bless his Ka, would settle the matter. But Hatshepsut wouldn't hear of it, and usurped the throne after his death, naming Moses the heir instead. Now, by her own admission, Moses is unworthy of the title, and is, in fact, an impostor."

Rekmire keenly watched her. True or not, her story verged on treason, yet it piqued his interest.

"When you and Thutmose sail north with Egypt's army I will pay you well to fulfil a vow," she whispered.

"And what would you have me do?" The words slid from his mouth as smoothly as oil.

"You are to keep Moses' ships in sight and send news to me of what he does and where he goes. Note especially if he visits the villages of the Habiru." She paused as if her words carried the weight of the Book of the Dead.

Rekmire grunted. "What do you expect me to discover?"

"Why, the truth of his birth, of course."

"You're certain of what you heard?"

"I tell you I heard it myself in the very Temple of Karnak from Hatshepsut's own lips." Isis lifted her chin. "If you don't believe me I'll find someone who will."

"Oh, I'll do what you ask," Rekmire smiled, "whether I believe you or not, but I think you're wasting your time."

"Think what you like, but be sure I get my information. If you discover anything, anything at all, send word to me. You'll need to hurry though, as Moses has already left for the Delta."

Isis unclasped an amulet of Hathor from around her neck, handing it to him. "This will protect you on your venture. Return it to me once you have discovered the truth."

Rekmire smirked. "This is the payment I get?"

Isis reached into her sash and retrieved a pouch. "This and the position of Vizier in Thutmose's administration. I'm sure he'll reward you himself one day."

Rekmire closed his hand about the pouch, eyeing her as a snake would its supper. "I'll see what I can do."

"See you do better than that." Isis met his gaze with a meaningful glare, and turning on her heel, she marched down the empty hall.

Rekmire stared after her, absently weighing the pouch in his palm. If nothing else, he admired her cunning, finding it almost as keen as his own. He was certain of one thing, however: if anyone could discover the truth of Moses' birth, he could.

Tasha entered the polished grandeur of Karnak surrounded by the shrines and altars of the various gods and their consorts housed there. She knew she had to come, yet felt awkward and out of place. Her own idol stood on a stand in her apartment but it had not helped answer her prayers of late. Perhaps it had lost its effectiveness since leaving her homeland.

She glanced up at a row of slatted windows near the ceiling where dust filtered into the sanctuary on golden beams of light. The temple looked different today than it had the day of the coronation, perhaps due to its stillness and emptiness. Pillars stood like silent sentinels guarding the shrines of the gods, while the walls depicted endless stories of the Pharaohs' victories and the demise of their victims. She wondered if tales of her own country were inscribed there, but did not venture to look.

Instead she forced her eyes from the reliefs to Amon's gilded form as it stared down at her as if at an intruder. Fearfully she spilled a handful of incense over the glowing embers of the altar as she had seen others do, then stepped between the parted curtains, closing them behind her, and cautiously approached the dais. The curtained walls provided a measure of privacy from the prying eyes of the few Priests who milled about, but gave her little comfort as she faced the starkness of Egypt's favored deity.

Tasha dropped to her knees. "Oh Amon, god of Hatshepsut and Moses, I come to ask you a favor. I beg you to grant my petition on behalf of your son, Moses, who has worshipped you these many years."

She imploringly raised her eyes, tears forming in spite of her resolve. "I do not ask this for myself, for I want nothing but his happiness, but I ask it for him, for the son to whom you gave seed. Protect him on his voyage to Punt and return him safely to Thebes. Help him find happiness, and if I am honored to share his life, though I do not count myself worthy, I will not hesitate to call you my god."

Tasha lifted her tear–streaked face, watching the idol in its haughty stare and wondering if it had heard her, though she decided not to insult it by repeating herself. Rising, she bowed and quietly backed between the curtains, stepping lightly across the marble floor and through the sanctuary.

If praying to Amon would help, she would pray daily until Moses returned. She only hoped one day his heart would mend so he might rediscover the love he had awakened in her own.

Moses' ship coursed along the Nile accompanied by a cooking boat and servants' quarters. The rest of his fleet would bridge the desert overland from Thebes to Qasar and be waiting off the coast of the Red Sea to join him on his way south to Punt. Moses had taken this northern excursion in the guise of a recreational outing and would need, at some point, to prove his intentions.

He had already left behind the villas and spires of Memphis, and had reached the apex of the Nile where the river branched into seven tributaries most of which snaked through dense greenery and undergrowth toward the Great Sea. Moses chose the most easterly branch, the Wadi Tumilat, which flowed past Pithom and the slave villages of the Habiru in Goshen, eventually joining the Sea of Reeds, and by way of a canal, the Red Sea.

Though he had only just begun his journey with many more months ahead, the voyage to Punt did not concern him nearly as much as what he would find along the way.

He crossed his arms and called over his shoulder, "We'll be stopping in Goshen for a crocodile hunt. That's one creature I haven't had the privilege of hunting."

Tuty and Nehisi looked at each other aghast. "Here, in the wilds of the open marsh? We've nothing in sight but ruins and an occasional slave village?"

"We've already stopped twice," Nehisi reasoned, "first at Abydos, and then at Memphis. A third stop would merely delay us further." He and Tuty exchanged hopeful glances.

Even so, the ship continued up the wadi past various villas and the distant spires of what the Captain confirmed to be Pithom. Moses strapped a knife to his waist, motioning his servant, Puemre, to join him, then signaled the Captain to steer the vessel toward shore. Moses glanced at the ruins of an edifice near the northern bank that appeared much like the place Ineni had described to him, and thought it might be the summer palace where Hatshepsut had once lived.

"We'll dock here." Moses motioned the other two boats, ignoring the groans of his Officers. "Did you know there are more crocs in these waters than anywhere else in Egypt?" Even he sobered at the thought as he studied the murky depths, wondering how many Habiru infants had lost their lives here. "Tuty and Nehisi, you may accompany me on the hunt if you like."

"My Lord," Tuty stammered, "these — these creatures grow to enormous proportions and have powerful jaws."

"The very reason we should diminish their numbers," Moses stated. He ordered a plank thrown across the bulrushes to the bank as he and Puemre prepared to disembark. Tuty and Nehisi cowered on deck.

"Are you sure you won't join us?" Moses suppressed a smile.

Tuty placed a tremulous foot on the plank then quickly withdrew it. He glanced at Nehisi. "If it's all right with you, my Lord, we'll stay and watch the ships." He paused. "Just let us see the creature once you have caught it, if you would. Pharaoh will want to know of your exploits."

"Certainly," Moses answered. "Would you like to see it dead or alive?"

Nehisi gulped. "Dead will do just fine."

"Very well, but you don't know what you're missing."

"I'm sure we don't," Nehisi weakly replied as the two exchanged knowing glances. "May the gods grant you success, my Lord."

Moses smiled. Their reactions provided almost as much sport as the hunt itself.

Nehisi and Tuty continued to watch Moses and Puemre as the two disappeared among the dense foliage on the shore.

"What will we tell Her Majesty?" Nehisi asked.

"Exactly what she asked for: a record of his activities," Tuty answered, studying the rustling reeds surrounding their ship. "It's not his recreation she is concerned with, but whether or not he approaches the slave villages of the Habiru."

"A crocodile hunt," Nehisi muttered. "Barbaric! And to think, here in the north the Priests actually worship such creatures."

"Likely so they won't be eaten," Tuty noted.

The two exchanged wide–eyed glances, stricken with terror at the thought.

"Pull in the gangplank, will you?" Nehisi shuddered. "I'd like to take a nap without fear of becoming some beast's breakfast."

Moses struggled through waist–high grass toward the palace ruins, thoughtfully studying the structure. Something stirred in him at the sight of its limestone walls and columned porch. He seemed to remember it as if in a dream: an overgrown garden and orchard, a patio and steps leading to the river, and nearby a workman's cottage.

Ignoring the urge to enter, he peered eastward toward the outline of a village, the Habiru village of Tju. From a distance the strangely rounded huts appeared like a cluster of bee hives walled about by a brick enclosure. He took a resolute breath and turned to his servant.

"Puemre, I want you to go on that hunt and find us a crocodile, and under no condition are you to tell anyone I did not accompany you."

Puemre's eyes widened. "My Lord, do you mean to say that I am to —"

"Kill and gut a crocodile," Moses finished.

"But I — I couldn't possibly."

Moses' eyes bored into his. "If that carcass isn't lying on the palace steps by nightfall you'll be out here in the dark hunting it, and I guarantee you'll find one then."

Puemre gulped, taking the knife Moses handed him and nodding. He scanned the rustling grass as if expecting at any moment to see a long snouted beast emerge and pounce on him. He was so preoccupied, in fact, he didn't notice Moses had gone until he turned back and saw the empty space behind him, with no one else in sight.

Moses turned his steps to the village, the sounds of barking dogs and romping children drifting toward him as he approached it. It seemed almost serene as the morning sunlight filtered through a dusty haze, bathing the huts in its glow. But Moses was absorbed in thoughts of his own. If this was the Habiru village Ineni had spoken of, how would he find the woman's hut? Furthermore, he didn't speak a word of Habiru. He glanced beyond the village to the fields where rows of sun–baked slaves bent in monotonous movement, their white loincloths contrasted against their brown skin and the earth they labored over. These were the Habiru.

Moses turned from the sight, his stomach wrenching. Stepping past the guards and through the gates, he entered the village without being questioned, and gazed about. Everywhere dust and poverty bespoke an existence he had hardly imagined existed, and he wondered how he could expect to find anyone here.

A clucking chicken lifted its wings in protest as it skittered just out of reach of a toddler who waddled after it. From a darkened doorway an elderly woman stepped outside, wiping her hands on her skirt and called the youngster but he did not respond.

"Rueb," she called again, hobbling after him as the child smiled with glee, quickening his pace. The boy crossed Moses' path and without hesitating, Moses picked him up. The baby's smile faded to quiet curiosity, a finger in his mouth, as he studied the stranger who held him.

At sight of the Egyptian the woman cried out, fear shifting the wrinkles on her face. Falling at Moses' feet, she implored him in gibberish he could not understand, though alarm and desperation need no translation. She quieted only when Moses set the boy down beside her.

"Here you are." He reassuringly nodded, attempting a smile.

Instead of thanking him, the woman clutched the child to her bosom and scurried back to her hut, closing the door behind her. All around him the doors of numerous hovels closed just as firmly, though he could feel the eyes of the Habiru peering at him from dark windows as if everyone in the village was suddenly aware of the stranger in their midst.

Moses glanced about in frustration. Perhaps he shouldn't have come. He didn't belong here. He turned to leave when an elderly woman, still standing in her doorway, caught his attention. She watched him as if unable to move. He started toward her but she backed away into the shadows.

Moses slowed his pace. Even if he did find his mother, what would he say? What could he do? He neared the hut, pausing just outside the door to announce himself.

"Prince Senmut of the royal house," he announced, not waiting for her response before ducking into the shadowy recess.

The woman gasped somewhere in the darkness, and though Moses could see no one, he waited as the outline of objects took shape. Eventually he could see a few pieces of simple furniture and an elderly woman standing against an opposite wall. He could barely make out her features, though her eyes glistened with unshed tears.

She searched his face, her hair frayed, having escaped the braids draped over her shoulders. She took a step toward him, her hands working the worn cloth of her gown.

"Moses." She whispered his name as reverently as a prayer.

Something convulsed in him and he clenched his jaw, not allowing revulsion or wonder to consume him.

"Senmut Re Moses," he stated matter–of–factly as he watched her, hardly daring to breathe.

She shook her head, tears spilling in glistening streaks down her cheeks. A sob caught in her throat as she fell to the floor, bowing before him as if at the feet of a god. Moses let out his breath, a wave of relief washing over him. Perhaps this was not his mother after all but merely a former servant.

He gazed about the room, seeing a table and lamp in a corner and several straw mats for beds occupying the bulk of the floor. In another corner a chest bore the symbol of Apis, Egypt's bull god. Ignoring her, Moses strode to the chest and lifted the lid. Inside he found the utensils of a Priest: a censor, a laver, an assortment of knives and bowls, and some old scrolls.

"Aaron's," the woman whispered. "He is a Priest."

Moses glanced up. She knew Egyptian. "Where did you learn our tongue?"

The woman's lips trembled, struggling to form the words. "Years ago in Pithom, hired by the Princess Hatshepsut." She bowed her head in reverence at the name.

"Hatshepsut?" Moses spat the name with such force the woman glanced up in alarm. "How did you know her?"

"I —" The woman's voice faltered, her chin quavering as she met his gaze. "I nursed a child once long ago."

Moses' eyes widened in horror, refusing to believe. "The child's name?"

"Moses."

His mind whirled and his chest constricted so he could hardly breathe. Neither of them spoke as they watched each other: one dressed in Egypt's finery, his position evident in everything from the diadem on his head to the erectness of his shoulders; the other clothed in rags, her body stooped and worn, but her eyes shining with a secret too great to contain.

"Moses," she breathed his name again, shaking her head in wonder. "I never thought to see you."

Moses turned and groaned, his features twisting in agony. How could this be? Had Amon truly cursed him with such a fate? His head pounded with realization as the details of his past suddenly made sense: Hatshepsut's dread of the Delta; her husband's insistence on naming Thutmose III his heir; Moses' aborted coronation; and Hatshepsut's unreasonable fear of the gods. Now that same fear coursed through him, for he had falsely claimed Amon as his father, even to the point of expecting protection in death defying circumstances. Why had Amon spared him at Thera and again at Kush? Surely a Habiru and an impersonator deserved only the gods' wrath.

He turned his back to her. "Are there others? A husband? Sons or daughters?"

"I have a son and a daughter." Her voice shook, but dignity rang beneath her tone. "My husband is dead."

Moses swallowed, blinking back the significance of the words. "Your son, Aaron, is he here?"

"He serves as a Priest at the Temple of Apis near Pithom. He was called Senmen, and I Hatnufer."

Moses turned to her, a question on his face.

The woman lifted her chin. "Years ago the Princess Hatshepsut promised him schooling and me wages. I worked for her." She awkwardly paused. "Aaron was schooled as a Priest."

"Then he worships our gods?"

She straightened her shoulders. "He serves as a Web Priest but is faithful to our God, Yahovah."

"Your god?" Moses nearly laughed. "You mean you have only one?"

"We need only One."

Moses watched her with a mixture of curiosity and disgust. How could he be associated with a people who had only one god and whose god had allowed them to suffer these many years? Why had this god not combined his strength with others' to free his people and ease their burden? Did he have no power?

Moses took a last look at the surroundings, at the woman who watched him with bated breath, then stepped to the door.

"I will need a Priest for my voyage," he thought aloud, not looking back at her. "I will summon Aaron for the task, though it will mean several years of travel."

The woman enthusiastically nodded, following him. "He will go, and our God will go with you."

Moses flinched. Her eagerness grated him and the mention of her god only worsened the barb. He hardened his visage, refusing a backward glance, unable to associate himself with the pitiful sight. Striding through the village, he left her staring after him as he turned his steps toward the temple of Apis in Pithom.

Aaron pushed the broom over the wooden floor and toward the door, creating a cloud of dust that swirled upward in the beam of light shining through an open window. He averted his gaze eastward as he often did during the day, past fields lush with harvest and dotted with the bent bodies of Habiru, past travelers meandering to and from the city. Seeing the village of Tju in the distance reminded him again of his higher calling as a

Priest of Yahovah, and of the gathering about the well in the evenings when his duties at Pithom had ended. He would not have to wait long today as the sun was already beginning to drop near the western hills.

Aaron heaved a sigh and stroked the broom across the floor again, gathering the small pile for disposal. Opening the door, he brushed the dirt onto the road, and lifting his gaze, spied a stranger striding toward the temple.

Aaron's eyes widened and sweat beaded on his brow. The man was dressed in the finery of an Egyptian Officer. What could he possibly want at Pithom at the insignificant temple of Apis? Aaron's body stiffened. Had the officials heard of the Habiru's worship of Yahovah? Aaron had told his sister they should be more discreet.

He whispered a prayer and held his breath, hoping the Officer would pass him by altogether, but he did not. Instead the man stepped through the doorway, his eyes seeking Aaron's.

Aaron avoided his gaze, bowing so low his head nearly touched the floor as the official brushed past him into the small chapel. Trembling, Aaron clumsily rose and shoved the broom against a wall, gesturing toward the shrine of Apis.

"You grace our humble temple with your presence, my Lord." He started toward the shrine, praying he had rightly guessed the reason for the Egyptian's visit. "We have long awaited the honor of one such as yourself." Aaron bowed again then dipped his hands into the laver to wash, reaching for a towel. But the stranger shook his head, watching him with a mixture of curiosity and restraint.

The Egyptian cleared his throat. "I have not come to worship but to see you, Aaron."

Aaron gulped. The man knew his name.

135

"I have visited the village of Tju and understand you serve as a Priest of Apis, but that you also worship your own god, Yahovah."

Aaron clutched the towel, unable to move or breathe. So the Egyptians had found him out. Falling to the floor, he prostrated himself before the stranger. "My Lord, I beg you, have mercy. We meant no harm. Spare our lives, I pray."

The Egyptian watched in silence, a brow arched. "Rise, Habiru. I have not come to intrude upon your worship."

Aaron shakily arose, his eyes imploring. "Then why have you come, Great One?"

The Egyptian strode to the window, struggling to contain his emotions. "I am a Prince of Egypt and wish to employ you as my Priest." Pausing, he turned. "My name is Senmut Re Moses."

Aaron stepped back nearly stumbling. His jaw dropped. "Moses, Hatshepsut's son?"

Moses nodded, the words filling the gulf between them like an echo across a chasm.

Moses' eyes bore into Aaron's, his expression impassable. "Tomorrow I sail for Punt, land of the gods, to bring back treasures for Her Majesty's temple. It may be as long as two years before I return. My ship is moored near the abandoned palace at Pithom, and my fleet awaits me at Qasar on the Red Sea." He scrutinized the Habiru. "I will pay you well in gold, besides food and shelter, if you accompany me. I trust the terms are satisfactory?"

Aaron could not take his eyes from the man, not even noticing the uncustomary question a Prince had asked a Habiru. Instead, he breathed Moses' name as if unable to believe what was happening.

Moses turned to the door, his expression strained. "Under no condition are you to ever mention your race or the village you come from. As to your duties here, I will send word to your superiors of your service for the royal house."

Aaron tried to speak, shaking his head in disbelief, the implication of the request at last dawning. He followed Moses to the door. "Two years, my Lord. Am I to leave without returning to the village? I have a box of articles that would prove useful if —"

"You may tell your mother good–bye and gather your belongings." Moses stepped to the threshold. "Meet me west of the palace of Pithom just before nightfall. We sail at first light."

"As you wish, my Lord." Aaron bowed again, watching as Moses turned away from Pithom in the direction of the palace ruins near the wadi.

Aaron hesitated only a moment, and with a last look about the small room, he closed and locked the temple door, his feet flying over the dusty road toward the village of Tju. Moses had returned and had personally requested his presence. His heart beat as if it would escape his chest. What might this mean for him and his family, and what might it mean for the future of every Habiru?

Rekmire knit his brow as he pressed into the shadows of the cottage near the wadi. He had watched Moses' servant lure a gargantuan crocodile from the river into a rough–built enclosure. Then, while the animal enjoyed Puemre's lunch, the servant had jumped atop its back, and like a bull rider, had clung to the beast as it writhed and fought to free itself. Plunging a blade again and again into the crusty flesh, Puemre had at last dropped the creature. Giving way to exhaustion, he lay down in the dirt beside his prize as if they both needed a rest after the ordeal.

Finally, having caught his breath, Puemre had jumped up and danced a jig about the beast, similar to those who lost themselves in a frenzy of bull worship. Then, bleeding and gutting the animal, he had washed the carcass in the river and dragged it onto the palace steps where he sat down beside it, closing his eyes, as if the two were enjoying a leisurely afternoon nap.

Rekmire pursed his brow. A crocodile hunt? Where was Moses? At first he had thought the Prince was waiting a safe distance away, but he had not shown himself in several hours. In the meantime, Thutmose and his comrades were no doubt enjoying themselves in Bubastis by now, celebrating their position over Egypt's army, while he passed up women and feasting to watch the slaughter of a crocodile. Frustration flared in him. He was supposed to watch Moses not Puemre. What would Isis think? Never mind Isis, what would Thutmose make of his absence?

An eastward movement caught his eye and Rekmire stiffened. Moses! He watched Puemre scramble to his feet, going through the motions of the hunt as if he were a court jester. Moses nodded, studying the creature with approval. As the two conversed another figure approached, this time from the direction of the slave villages. He wore the garb of a web Priest and struggled beneath the weight of a wooden chest.

Moses greeted the man, introducing him to his servant, his words carrying to where Rekmire stood pressed against the cottage wall. "The Priest Aaron, trained in the service of Apis. He will accompany us on our journey and serve as my personal Priest and advisor."

Moses ordered Puemre ahead with the carcass, then walking past the hut where Rekmire hid, he spoke to the man. "Tell no one you are Habiru. You are a Priest of Apis, nothing more."

The man nodded, struggling beneath the box he carried as the two walked through waist high grass toward the waiting ships.

Rekmire's face contorted with a question, his breathing labored. A Habiru serving as Moses' Priest? He wrestled for a reasonable explanation but could think of none. He felt for the amulet about his neck and clutched it in his fist. He would send word to Isis at once. However senseless it seemed, he had a feeling he had witnessed something far more significant than even she had imagined possible.

CHAPTER 9

Rekmire entered the Inn of the Leopard at Bubastis, the city dedicated to the cat, and scanned the dimly lit room. The decor reflected the theme with sleek bodied panthers and leopards depicted on its walls, while attendants dressed in leopard skins. Rekmire at last spotted Thutmose and Amenhab sitting in a corner drinking beer and watching naked dancers with glazed eyes.

Thutmose glanced up as Rekmire approached, a scowl on his face. "So you fulfilled your promise to my mother, did you?"

Rekmire studied him before taking a seat, trying to sense the message behind his words. "Yes, and I believe I've found something that will satisfy her." He poured himself a mug of the dark brew.

"You're at last ready to serve your Commander? Or does Isis require you to chase after some other fool notion?"

Rekmire firmly set his mug on the table. "Isis may have a head full of sand, but if there's anything at all to her tale you stand to profit even more than the gods could imagine." He eyed Thutmose long and hard before taking a mouthful of beer.

Thutmose abruptly stood, toppling his chair. "Since when do my mother's orders over–ride mine?" His breath reeked and his words slurred into an almost unidentifiable jumble. "We're handed all of Egypt's army, and instead of gratitude you chase after the fantasies of a temple whore." He tipped his mug to his face, swiping an arm across his mouth. "Why in Amon's name, after all Moses has done for us, would you try to betray him?"

He took an unsteady step toward Rekmire, nearly collapsing as Amenhab reached for his arm, loosely draping it about his own neck. Together the two eyed Rekmire as they would have a traitor. Even Amenhab, who had more of his faculties than his commander, exuded disgust.

Rekmire opened his mouth to explain but Thutmose interrupted. "Habiru?" He spat the word. "You ought to know better." He attempted to turn his back on Rekmire but stumbled in the process, taking Amenhab with him as together they fell onto a nearby table.

Amenhab muttered an apology to the patrons, trying to right their mugs, and continued to the door, but Thutmose wouldn't let the matter drop. He turned and shouted a string of obscenities over his shoulder meant for Rekmire, but mistakenly directed to anyone within earshot.

Before a brawl erupted, Rekmire defended himself by blurting the truth of his find. "Moses stopped at Pithom near the slave village of Tju and has hired a Priest for his voyage to Punt, a Habiru."

Thutmose turned and stared, his eyes bloodshot and glassy. He sputtered, "A Habiru as a Priest? You're bewitched by an evil spell."

"I tell you it's true, I heard it myself, and Moses' steward, Puemre...." Rekmire slowed his words in anticipation of Thutmose's skepticism, "killed and gutted a crocodile."

Thutmose wrinkled his brow in derision. "Puemre killed a crocodile?"

Rekmire slowly nodded.

Thutmose sneered, his words thick with cynicism. "I don't know what you're trying to prove," he attempted to raise his full height, "but if I ever hear you spreading such tales again I'll feed you to the crocs myself." Cursing, he opened the door with Amenhab's help. "Killing a croc, by Hathor!"

Calling for their crew, the two stumbled out the door and toward their ships moored in the nearby wadi.

Rekmire swigged down the rest of his beer and followed with uncertain steps. Maybe he shouldn't have listened to that crazy concubine after all. Thutmose was right about her character, but if her tale held any truth at all, and he had a strange feeling it did, he wasn't about to miss his part in the scheme, nor the reward Isis had promised. More than that, he didn't want to miss the opportunity to prove Thutmose wrong.

Isis and Hatshepsut passed each other in the official wing, and except for a curt nod and mumbled acknowledgement, neither spoke nor looked at the other. Hatshepsut had been summoned to her audience room, and Isis had just received word a messenger had arrived from the Delta.

'Would she see him?' the steward had asked Isis. Would the sun rise and set in its daily circuit? 'Of course she would see him,' she had answered, 'in her apartment and at once.'

Her feet clicked the rhythm of her heartbeat. Had Rekmire found something out? She frowned, remembering

Thutmose's reaction. One day he would believe her, and when he did she would remind him of all she had suffered for him. Further, she would make sure he had a Vizier who she could trust would do her bidding.

Isis glanced behind her as Hatshepsut disappeared down the official wing. The Pharaoh had better enjoy her position while she could, for the day would soon come when she would grovel for the scraps at Isis' table.

Rounding the corner, Isis ascended the steps to the royal apartments, passing the rooms of Nefru and Tasha, and breathlessly entered the shadows of her own apartment. She soundlessly closed the door then turned and squinted into the semidarkness, unable to see anyone or anything, having previously drawn the thick drapes. What if Hatshepsut had found her out and a guard lurked in her room instead?

She heard a shuffle.

"Who's there?" Her breath caught in her throat as a faceless figure stepped forward.

"No need to know who I am, only that Rekmire sends his regards."

Who was this man and how could she be sure Rekmire had sent him?

As if in answer, he held out an object that caught a sliver of light. Isis took the cold metal ornament, tracing the pattern of Hathor with her fingers. The amulet! Her mind raced. "The message?"

"I am to tell you Moses did, indeed, stop in the Delta at a slave village, and has employed a Habiru as Priest for his journey to Punt."

Isis' jaw dropped. "A Habiru as Priest? Are you sure?"

"According to Rekmire."

Questions scrambled in her brain. Moses had stopped at a village of the Habiru and now a slave served him, but who and why? Though she couldn't make sense of it, this news was enough. Just as she thought, Moses had contacted the Habiru.

Dismissing the messenger with a coin in his palm, Isis whirled, pacing her dark chamber. Then, purposefully striding to her door, she marched into the blinding light of the open corridor. A matter of such importance could not wait until nightfall. She would meet with the High Priest at once. Perhaps together they could devise a plan to convince Thutmose of the truth.

While Isis hastened toward the nearest exit pondering Rekmire's message, Hatshepsut stood in her audience room, a hand on her mouth in horror. Before her lay a gigantic crocodile gutted and spread out on the floor as if enjoying an afternoon nap, as if, at any moment, it would thrash to life again.

"By Amon, who —"

The messenger gulped. "A message from Nehisi and Tuty, Your Majesty." He swallowed his own revulsion at the sight.

"I asked for a report," Hatshepsut flung a hand at the beast, "not a — a gutted carcass!" She shook her head in disbelief. "This is what they send me?"

"This, Your Majesty, and a message." He held out a papyrus with trembling hands.

Hatshepsut snatched it, eyeing him as if he had personally taken part in the scheme. Breaking the seal she scanned the document.

"So Moses killed the beast while staying at Pithom and offers this as proof of his activities."

The man blinked, not daring an answer.

Hatshepsut glared. "I should have known Moses was behind this. Such a display seems more his style than my officials'." She sharply looked up. "He made no move toward the slave villages of Goshen?"

"Apparently not," the messenger managed.

Hatshepsut scowled. "Then he stopped in the Delta to hunt...a crocodile?"

"It appears so, Your Majesty," the man lamely offered, his face paling beneath her scrutiny.

Hatshepsut reread the document, then abruptly stopped and read aloud. "...and has employed a Priest from the Temple of Apis to accompany him." She dropped her hands to her sides as if they were made of stone. "I know of only one Temple of Apis in Pithom and of only one Priest in its employ."

She stared into the space before her as a picture formed in her mind, her lips barely moving. "So he has found them at last."

"What in Hades?" Puseneb attempted to pull himself free from Isis' grasp but she continued to tug him down the hall of Karnak's east wing and toward a little used closest.

"In here," she whispered, "where Hatshepsut's spies won't find us."

"Spies? What spies? By Amon, this had better be good!" Puseneb jerked his arm free, still protesting as Isis pushed him into the closet and closed the door behind them.

She pressed her hand over his mouth but Puseneb shook her off, struggling to find the door and making enough noise to equal a pair of wrestling rhinos. "By Hathor, I've had enough!"

"Even if it means more gold than you could imagine?" Isis' eyes glittered like a viper's in the dark as she coiled her arm about his. "I have information even the gods will thank me for."

"Then speak before you suffocate us both."

Isis took a deep breath. "Several months ago while preparing for bed I was strangely burdened by a vision. I heard the god, Amon, of course, summon me to his temple."

"You're crazy," Puseneb muttered. "How could you have heard the god speak when I haven't even —" He stopped himself, clearing his throat as Isis continued.

"I did his bidding and entered the temple, kneeling before the shrine of Amon. After prayer I stopped to pay homage to Hathor when I heard Her Majesty enter, though she didn't see me. I couldn't help but overhear, for she profusely wept as she entreated Amon."

At mention of the Pharaoh Puseneb squirmed, finding the closet uncomfortably cramped and his clothes far too tight. He attempted to loosen his jeweled collar, aware of any number of duties he should be seeing to instead.

Isis' volume heightened. "She cried aloud to the god, begging for mercy for the sins she had committed."

Puseneb blanched, his chest heaving. "By Amon, this is nonsense! Open this door at once or I'll call the guards."

Isis threw herself against the door, her eyes wide in the darkness. "I tell you I heard it, and from her own lips. She admitted Moses is not her son at all but was rescued from death as an infant, that he is, in fact, Habiru."

The words reverberated in the silence of that small space until only the labored breathing of the two could be heard. Puseneb stared, his eyes the only visible part of his body. Habiru? Images flashed before him: of Hatshepsut continually prostrated before Amon's shrine; of her insistent offerings on Moses' behalf; of the recent scandal at the coronation; and now, of Moses' absence from Thebes.

Puseneb shook his head, his jowls wobbling. "This is absurd!"

He impatiently shoved her aside but Isis clung to him. "I tell you I heard it, and now a message from the Delta."

Puseneb held his breath as sweat beaded on his brow and trickled down his fleshy face.

"Moses has visited a Habiru village near Pithom and has summoned a slave as a Priest for his journey to Punt."

Puseneb reared. "A Habiru? But they worship another god altogether, a Yahoven or some such."

"He is not a Priest of the Habiru god but of our god, Apis."

Puseneb wrenched from her grasp. "You're mad. We have no Habiru Priests in our temples."

"I tell you there is, and Moses has taken him with him to Punt."

Puseneb found the door. "By Amon, Isis, if you ever mention such nonsense again, so help me I'll —"

Wiping the sweat from his forehead, he stepped from the closet and into the hall, muttering the rest beneath his breath. Without so much as looking back, he mustered his dignity, straightened his shoulders, and stepped purposefully down the eastern hall and out of sight.

A student Priest filling the lamps along the wall had witnessed the entire event from a distance. When Isis also stepped from the alcove the student gave a knowing nod. He had always thought Puseneb a man of appetite, but in a closet?

The young man waited until Isis brushed past him then turned to watch her shapely form diminish down the hall in the opposite direction. He smiled to himself. With recreation of this sort to look forward to, his future as a Priest didn't seem so bleak after all.

Nefru sat at her dressing table, a pout on her pretty lips. "I don't care if I am to become Moses' wife. What good will it do me?"

She picked up her mirror and scrutinized her make–up.

Meryet, her younger sister, leaned back on the couch, a dreamy look in her eyes. "I would care if I were you. Moses is as handsome as he is —"

"Distant." Nefru put in, straightening the lotus petals that lay against her dark wig. "He's halfway to Punt by now, and as far as I'm concerned that's as far as from here to the nether world." She restlessly rose. "Besides, when he is at home he pays me no attention at all. He's far too occupied with that jungle maid."

Meryet's brow knit disapprovingly. "You shouldn't speak of Tasha that way. Besides, when you do marry you'll be Moses' First Great Wife and Queen; she will merely be his second." Meryet closed her eyes. "I'd pass out on the spot if given the same chance, even to be second."

Nefru rose, her face clouded with anger. She opened the doors of her balcony with more than the usual force and was met with a blast of sweetness from the lilies and jasmine below, their perfume thick in the heat of the afternoon. "Not a chance. The position will be mine and only mine, if and when he is crowned."

Meryet turned onto her stomach, her chin on her hands. "Moses is heir so of course he will be crowned."

Nefru leaned over the balcony rail, seeing a young guard below whose dark body reflected the sun as if sculpted of bronze. She could not help but stare. "Moses may be gone for years. How can I possibly survive until then?"

The guard appeared taller than most, his legs rippling with strength and his muscular arms far too thick for the armband he wore. He glanced up at her and Nefru giggled.

"What is it?" Meryet scrambled from the couch to join her sister then stopped at sight of the man. "Why it's only a palace guard."

"Only a guard to you," Nefru said with conviction, shoving Meryet out of her way. "Haven't you anything better to do? I'm tired and want to rest."

"You'd like to rest alright, in the arms of a certain guard." Meryet tossed her head, her curls bobbing. "You know you're not to flirt with common staff."

"Of course." Nefru glared, strutting to the door with Meryet in tow. "Now go bother someone else. I'm hot and tired."

"There is no one else," Meryet objected.

Nefru opened the door just the same, ushering her sister into the hall. "Then go play in the pool or strike up a game of jackals with Ineni. Anything, just leave me alone."

Meryet knowingly eyed her before whirling on her heel and marching down the hall. Nefru sighed with relief, closing the door and hurrying back to the balcony, but the guard had disappeared. She searched the yard and portico but could see no sign of him. Hastening to her dressing table, she fumbled for her jar of aloes and reapplied another layer of ochre to her lips. Common or not, she intended to meet that guard in spite of Meryet's warning. Maybe even because of it.

Thutmose's grip tightened on the reins of his chariot as it rolled to a stop. He turned and scanned an army that filled the highway to Avaris, four abreast, as far as he could see. He studied a nearby field where a band of Habiru methodically bent over their labors, dipping shadoof buckets from the wadi and tipping them into irrigation ditches that streaked the land like silver strands among the green.

He eyed the slaves with disgust. Moses a Habiru? Impossible! These slaves mattered as little to Moses as they did to him. If Moses were to ever hand him the title of General his first order would be to revive the death penalty for newborn Habiru males as his grandfather had done. It only made sense, considering the army these Semites could muster if given the chance. If they ever joined with the Hyksos against Egypt they would be unstoppable, and the Habiru had reason enough to retaliate, considering their near four hundred years of bondage.

Thutmose turned eastward to the desert, his body tanned and his muscles hard. When he returned from his campaign he would approach Moses with the notion. Such an edict would not only rid the Delta of future risk, but should be enough to convince Isis once and for all of the stupidity of her delusions, for the order would come from Moses' own mouth.

Adjusting his war helmet, Thutmose addressed his troops. "This marks our first official campaign and I intend to make it count. Until we arrive at Gaza we will share water skins, so use them sparingly. After accepting tribute from the city, we will move north to Joppa. In the meantime, be on the lookout for sign of any Hyksos, and watch the rear guard. Amalekite bands also roam this desert and are known for surprise attacks."

Thutmose's words echoed down the ranks as his Officers passed the order to those who hadn't heard. Their weapons flashed beneath the sun as they lifted the standards of their various gods against a clear blue sky: Amon Ra, the revered sun god, dominated the forefront on a banner of blue; Apis, the bull god, and Horus, the all–seeing eye, were also held aloft in colorful repose.

Thutmose thrust his fist into the air. "Now go in the name of Amon, and may our gods prosper us!"

A cheer arose like the tumult of a wave drowning out all else. Whipping his horse to a gallop, Thutmose led his army eastward along the Highway of the Sea.

They soon left the greener stretches of the Delta, traded for a landscape of dunes lifting behind each other like waves on an endless sea of sand. The army had marched only a matter of hours over a seemingly infinite stretch when Thutmose stopped for a drink. The sun burned above them like a furnace while the ground reflected the heat in hazy waves, imprisoning them between the two. Allowing his infantry to catch up, he sat in the shade of a dune, surveying his ranks as they struggled to keep pace. Would his men even make it across the desert? He firmed his jaw, his features taut. He would allow nothing to deter him, no matter how it affected his men.

Amenhab rode up beside him and nodded, turning his attention to the men. "We'll have more casualties before war than after if we keep up this pace. The men need to rest."

Thutmose watched a soldier drop to his knees while two others hurried to his aid with a water skin. He glanced at Amenhab then nodded to the dunes farther east. "We'll give them another hour and see how they fare." He took a swig from his own water skin. "They're soft after months of inactivity but the desert will ready them soon enough."

Amenhab glanced at him askance. "Or kill them in the process. If we lose too many we'll have less chance of victory at Joppa, and the gods know we can't afford to lose. If these city–states unite against us we'll be the ones paying tribute." Thutmose threw him a dagger– like glare, but Amenhab continued under his breath, "And if the Hyksos ever get involved they'll not stop till they've won back the Delta."

The wind tugged at the sails of Moses' fleet as the ships moved over the Red Sea southward from the port of Qasar. Beyond the shore a ridge of rock lifted above the desert, changing color according to the position of the sun. At daybreak the peaks blazed orange and red as if afire; and by nightfall the shadows had lengthened adding streaks of grey, blue, and eventually purple. Periodically along the western shore a settlement materialized near the greenery of an oasis, connected by a trail that wound back to Qasar. On the far horizon a thin brown line marked the edge of the Sinai desert with unseen trails leading farther east to the mines of Serabit or the port of Elath.

Moses leaned over the ship's hull with Aaron at his side. The Priest had remained unusually silent thus far, doing merely what Moses had asked of him. Strangely enough, his tasks had yet to include any Priestly duties.

Moses turned to him. "The gods outdid themselves in creating this beauty." He attempted a smile, peering at Aaron as if to read his thoughts, then glanced away. "You don't believe in more than one god, do you?"

Aaron carefully chose his words. "It is to the One God we attribute all of creation: the earth, the sea, the sky, and all living creatures, including mankind."

Moses stiffened. He hardly cared to discuss the Habiru religion and had little respect for their god. What had their god done for them in their nearly four hundred years of captivity? He had saved one infant from slavery, but what was that compared to a multitude?

Moses changed the topic. "What is it like to serve as a Priest of Apis? Is it an occupation you would have chosen?"

Aaron watched a distant caravan stir the dust as it wound along the trail near the shore. "I guess I've never thought about it. Slaves don't have the opportunity to choose, we merely do what we are told. After so many years your dreams die and you forget others have them."

Moses reddened as the silence between them widened like a gulf.

Aaron mercifully bridged it. "I hear the Overseers at the mines of Serabit have allowed the Habiru to build a small temple to Yahovah." He focused on a point across the distant blue. "It would be a blessing if we were allowed the same privilege in the slave villages of Goshen."

Moses searched his face. "Would that please you?" He hesitated, not wanting to seem over eager. "Would your people serve more contentedly if they could worship their own god?"

Aaron nodded.

"A temple would cost little to build," Moses thought aloud.

"True enough," Aaron's gaze narrowed, "seeing my people are expert at building with brick, and labor for free."

Moses' delight splintered on the edge of Aaron's sarcasm and the two fell silent again, watching oases pass like rare blossoms on a lifeless shore as the shadows on the distant peaks lengthened. He hung his head. "It's no use, Aaron. We both know, don't we?"

Aaron took a quavering breath but maintained his bearing.

Moses studied him: the clean shaven skin where a beard ought to be; the shorter hair and white tunic, unlike the rustic dress of other Habiru; the deep–set eyes holding years of unspoken pain.

"What do we both know?" Aaron pressed, forcing Moses to speak the words.

Moses shook his head, his face lined with the struggle. "There is no sense ignoring it." He met his brother's gaze. "I want to make this voyage count, to make up in some way for the years we've lost."

Tears filled Aaron's eyes but he maintained his bearing. "Years meaning the years of our lives?" He paused, calculating. "I am now forty–four which makes you thirty–eight."

Recognition flashed across Moses' face as if hearing the words somehow confirmed their truth. Though tempted to allow the silence to lengthen, Moses would not give in to cowardice no matter how painful the subject, and Aaron had waited too long to let this moment pass.

"How old was I?" Moses murmured.

"An infant," Aaron smiled, "howling too loudly for us to hide you from Pharaoh's henchmen." His face fell at the memory. "So many died. Though I was only six years and too old to be a victim myself, I saw the others." He shook his head at the memory. "Some were our own relatives, not only babes but women who chose death rather than willingly give up their infants."

Tears rimmed Moses' eyes and he looked away across the sea, his voice husky. "How many?"

"Too many to count. Most were buried in shallow graves along the wadi or thrown to the crocodiles as 'living sacrifices.'"

"Didn't even one other Habiru my age survive?"

Aaron shook his head. "Not within the space of two years. Pharaoh had all the others killed. After Pharaoh's death and the coronation of his son, Thutmose II, Hatshepsut persuaded her husband to abolish the law, allowing a period of peace."

Moses surveyed the darkening water as if picturing the infants there. He looked away. "How did the family fare?"

"When Hatshepsut found you," Aaron glanced at Moses to be sure he should go on, "she moved our family to a cottage near the palace at Pithom and employed our mother as your nurse to care for you."

Moses felt his mind grow numb as Aaron spoke, hearing the tale as if it belonged to another. The task masters had forced their father to work the mud pits near Tju where he had labored until his death years later, never having given up hope of one day seeing his people freed. Their older sister, Miriam, was allowed to serve as a maid for their mother. In exchange for keeping the matter quiet, Hatshepsut promised to provide for the family and to educate Aaron in an honorable profession. When the former Pharaoh died, Hatshepsut and Thutmose II moved the royal family and capital south to Thebes. Moses' family never heard from him again...until now.

A hush fell between them as the account ended. Moses cleared his throat and tried to speak but could not, and gazed instead into the glowing embers of sunset, the pinks and golds reflected on the tops of the mountains and in the sea.

Aaron looked into his brother's face, his eyes glistening. "I had prayed for years to meet you, to speak with you even once."

Moses sardonically smiled. "It seems your god has answered."

"We all prayed, believing, as our father did, you might be the one to help free our people."

Moses shot him a puzzled look, not understanding his words and not wanting to. "I don't know how I could possibly help a multitude but I can better the life of one." He drew a deep breath. "What position would you like in Hatshepsut's administration when we return?" He emphasized the words, "Anything you choose."

Aaron paused, studying the distance then shook his head. "It is not my goal to accumulate titles, even if it means, as you believe, an honored status in the afterlife. I am content to serve as a Priest."

"Of Apis?" Moses smiled.

"No, of our own God, Yahovah."

The words stung but Moses ignored them. "You can worship whatever god you please, it matters little to me. Besides, Egypt always has room for another. Yet as Regent I have the power to greatly improve your status. Is there anything I can do for you, anything at all?"

Aaron stared into the water as it lapped against the sides of the ship, rhythmically rocking them in a gentle motion. He waited a long moment then looked up, purpose shining in his eyes. "There is one thing you can give me...."

Moses waited, hardly daring to breathe.

"...the brother I never had."

CHAPTER 10

Waves crashed like thunder over the rocks beneath Joppa. The city was surrounded on three sides by the rock and sandy shore, and on the other by the sea. Stirred by an unusually strong wind, the pungent scent of sea mixed with stinging bits of sand to become grit in the eyes and between the teeth. From his perch atop the wall the watchman searched the tempest with narrowed gaze as it tossed Joppa's fleet like scattered leaves. Seeing nothing out of place except the god's fury and the elements, he turned inland where farms and orchards could normally be seen, and squinted instead through a swirling cloud to be sure no trouble stirred there.

Shading his eyes, he attempted to peer through the haze, and rubbed them to be sure he was seeing correctly. By the gods, were those men or apparitions?

"Merdock!" The soldier below him on patrol broke his gait, lifting his face as the watchman waved an arm westward. "An army! Might it be —"

He hadn't even finished the words before the soldier sprang to action, closing the double gates and dropping the heavy bolt to secure them. Shouting to his subordinates, the man lifted his eyes, awaiting the watchman's verdict.

Word of Egypt's victory at Gaza had spread like fire over straw, and some of the city– states farther north had chosen to ally themselves with the Hyksos at Megiddo rather than risk facing Egypt alone. Joppa was not among them.

The watchman posed statue–like, praying for a space in the storm to clear. Then he saw it, an emblem high on a standard: the all–seeing eye of Horus.

"Egypt!" He expelled the word like a curse but the wind blew it back in his face.

Someone shouted it in the square below as the Governor bounded out the door of a high–class brothel, tying his robe as he hurried down the steps. He cupped a hand to his ear.

"Egypt!" The watchman repeated the word, pointing westward.

At once the courtyard erupted in a whirl of activity with the Governor shouting in the midst of the confusion. "Muster the forces, gather arms!"

Within moments an assortment of soldiers assembled in the open square, their movements frantic as they attempted to prepare themselves. Some readied their armor while others grappled with the reins of frightened horses, confused by the chaos and storm as they attempted formation.

"Send a runner to Megiddo to summon the Hyksos!" the Governor bellowed.

Echoing the command, an Officer shouted above the commotion. "A rider to Megiddo!" A soldier pulled back the reins of his steed in answer as the animal pawed the air.

"To the rear gate!" The Gorvernor's face purpled with exertion as he expelled the words. "The Hyksos are our only chance."

The rider's heel fell to the withers and the horse leapt forward just as a runner grabbed the reins, out of breath and struggling to keep hold. "It's no use, my Lord. The Egyptians have surrounded the city and blocked the gates. There is no way of escape."

The Governor's face froze. Slowly turning he looked into the faces of those about him hoping for better news, but saw only the frightened expressions of men who watched him with the same hopefulness. He knew of only one other recourse.

Going through the motions as if in a dream, he ordered his archers atop the wall and reinforcements posted at the gates. Yet he already knew what awaited them: legions of Egyptians aiming their bows and lances at his city with untold hundreds prepared to take their place as their commander prepared for a siege. The Egyptians would confiscate their grain, burn their hay, and raid the outlying farms that provided them sustenance. It was only a matter of time.

The Governor wiped the sweat from his forehead, his eyes large and his face somber. Without a rider to break through the entrapment the Hyksos would never know he needed their aid; and without the Hyksos, Joppa would fall.

Moses spotted the distant shoreline as a voice rang out from high on the mast. "Punt, land of the gods, due east!"

The five ships steered toward a sandy stretch of beach dotted with huts and shaded with clumps of palm trees. Already a colorful crowd was gathering, some bearing baskets, others balancing jugs atop their heads. In the distance an ornamental litter approached.

Moses glanced at Aaron, his eyes bright. "If the inscriptions on our temple ruins are correct we're about to see more luxury than you could possibly imagine."

Aaron raised a brow, unable to enjoy Moses' enthusiasm. "Being free to come and go as I please is luxury enough."

A cluster of scantily clad women waded from shore toward the boats, their breasts bobbing above the water.

Moses grinned and turned to his brother. "Do the Habiru have women like these?"

Aaron stared. "We have plenty, Pharaoh's decree saw to that, but I can't say ours are," he groped for words, "as eager."

Moses nodded over his shoulder, ordering the ships to disembark. Dropping into the knee–high water, he scanned his personal welcoming party. "It is just as the inscriptions promised: a paradise of unmatched hospitality."

A young woman reached his side and slid her arm through his while another tugged him toward shore through the gently lapping waves. Moses glanced back at Aaron to see him surrounded with the same sort of enthusiasm, though a frown remained fixed on his face.

Moses laughed. "You look like a pig about to be roasted. If you can't enjoy yourself in the land of the gods, where can you?" He wrapped an arm around each woman on either side of him. "As for me, I plan to forget Egypt and enjoy the scenery."

Aaron grunted, struggling to keep pace as the women pulled him toward the beach. Moses wondered if Aaron's reserve meant he already had a lover in the Delta, though he knew his brother hadn't married. He thought of Tasha but would not allow her memory to linger, for she could never be his, and these, for the moment, were.

A rotund Queen held up her hand in greeting, speaking sparse Egyptian. "You bless us with your presence, Egyptian. We have entertained many strangers over the years and but none in my lifetime from Egypt. It is our privilege to do so." She motioned to the feast already spread for them on the ground. "Come and eat."

Moses and Aaron settled themselves amidst a company of attentive females who filled their platters with fruit and other delectables. Moses chose a wedge of succulent yellow pulp with a prickly shell, and a slice with a thin orange rind that tasted similar to the melons of the Delta. The Queen seated herself before him amid her attendants.

Moses wiped his mouth, flashing a grin at the maiden still on his arm, and turned to the Queen. "To what do we owe this welcome?" He watched the Queen pick over her fruit with plump, pampered fingers.

"We have a record of Egyptians visiting our land years ago, bringing wealth, trading goods, and teaching us your tongue," she added as she delicately bit into a slice of fruit. "We had hoped for more permanent trade with nations such as yours, but so far only a few have ventured the distance."

Moses managed a smile as he dipped his roll into a bowl of broth. "It is truly an adventure and well worth the journey. Your hospitality is unsurpassed."

He glanced at Aaron who seemed more intent on filling his mouth than his eyes. "Yet my purpose is not for adventure but to honor our Pharaoh and her temple. I have brought exquisite goods which I hope to exchange for," he pursed his lips, "myrrh and gum trees to grace her terraces, perhaps leopard skins, and —"

"Gold?" The Queen laid her platter aside, rising with help. "Come." She pointed to a stuccoed temple not far from shore. "Though I cannot reveal our source, I believe what we have will impress you."

Moses nodded, shedding the arms of the women and following the Queen up a grassy knoll. The temple hardly lived up to its title, being a simple edifice with a thatched roof. Once inside, however, past the temple proper, the Queen ushered him through the doors of a treasury holding more raw gold and jewels than he had ever seen in one place.

Moses laughed. "Where? How?"

The Queen smiled and shook her head. "Where it comes from does not matter, you need only know we have an ample supply. Perhaps one day your nation will believe us significant enough to add us to their trading route. Until then," she closed the door again, "we will remain a novelty, if not a legend."

"Once I wear the crown you can be sure we will trade with you often."

The Queen brightened. "I would be honored, Prince of Egypt." She led them from the room. "We have more than this to show you, or are you weary from your journey?"

"Not too tired to feel impressed. Rest assured I'll do all in my power to make this voyage worthwhile for both of us."

She smiled, leading them out into the sunlight. "Your word is good enough. Come, if you have finished feasting I will show you to your hut."

Tasha stirred in the darkness, the images vivid in her sleep. A hand reached toward her and she recognized it as her father's, smoothing her hair as she clung to him on the grassy bank of the river. She looked up at him with tears in her eyes, but her father was no longer there. Instead, Moses caressed her, whispering his love. She closed her eyes only to open them again and find herself in the arms of another. Shadows obscured his features but she could feel his breath on her face as his burley arms tightened about her, holding her captive in his grasp. She cried out, struggling to free herself but he merely strengthened his hold.

"Moses, help me!"

Tasha's eyes shot open, her face damp with perspiration. She had dreamed it again. Fear clung to her as she pushed tendrils of hair from her face. This same dream had haunted her several nights in a row. Rising, she forced the picture from her mind, lengthening the wick on the lamp and wrapping her arms about herself, though the heat from the previous day lingered.

What did it mean, and why this same dream? Ever since Moses left she had dreaded nightfall. She rubbed her forehead. Was it because of her last memory of Moses at the garrison? Were his the arms of her attacker?

She shook her head at the thought, her hair tumbling in a cascade about her face and shoulders. No, she refused to believe it. Moses would never harm her.

Tears sprang to her eyes and all at once the room seemed close and oppressive. She rose and opened the doors of her balcony, inhaling the sweet night air and attempting to push the darkness from her mind. Turning to the sky, she marveled at the lights scattered like sand across the black expanse. Might Moses be looking up at this same sky, charting his travel by the stars?

The thought brought a pang of longing and she started to close the doors. Then she saw them, Orion and Pleiades, the star–lit lovers locked in eternal pursuit, ever struggling to unite but never actually touching.

Her features constricted, every doubt and longing rushing to the surface. Was this her and Moses' plight? Would they never know love again?

"Oh Moses, why are the nights so endless and why do I despair of them so?"

Then, as if in answer to her heart, she knew: it was because she did not share them with the one she loved.

Moses awakened with a start, unwrapping himself from the sleepy embrace of the woman at his side. His dream seemed to linger like a spirit, yet he had not seen the Puntite woman in his sleep, but Tasha.

He abruptly arose, fastening his kilt and slipping on his armbands. How long had he enjoyed this paradise? Weeks, months? What seemed such a short visit only hours before now felt like a lifetime.

He had to get back to Thebes, not only to deposit his cargo but to see his loved ones...to see Tasha. Might her father have already retaliated because of his broken vow, or worse, have taken her back to Kush?

His mind raced at the thought, and just as quickly another loomed before him: a glimpse of Thutmose at the head of Egypt's army with a sea of soldiers at his command.

Moses anxiously paced. Why had he entrusted his men to the likes of that rebel, and how much damage had Thutmose done in his absence? Moses' pulse quickened.

He raked his fingers through his hair, thinking of his real mother and sister in the Delta. His real mother? Did he actually consider a Habiru his mother? He stepped from the hut and gazed up at the stars. Yes, Jochebed had risked much for his welfare and deserved acknowledgement for all she had suffered. Perhaps he could spare her and his sister the ravages of slavery, assuring them a measure of peace in their remaining years.

Moses pursed his lips in thought. He could do more, he could provide his deceased father and closest relatives a burial, assuring them an afterlife with the gods.

"Aaron." He shook his brother awake. The woman at Aaron's side complacently rolled out of the way. "We're leaving today."

Aaron's eyes opened. He looked first at his brother, then at the woman with whom he had grown accustomed to sharing his bed.

Moses tugged him to his feet. "Come, I've had my fill of Punt."

"It took you this long to decide?" Agitation edged Aaron's voice, though he reluctantly left the woman.

Moses gathered his belongings. "First we must return to Goshen. I don't know how much longer our mother will last." He met Aaron's gaze. "I want her and Miriam to accompany us back to Thebes."

"What will Nehisi and Tuty say?"

"Let them say what they like. I can always use more slaves. What does it matter where they come from?"

Aaron overlooked the implication, fear for Moses taking precedence over all else. "What if someone discovers the truth?"

Moses shook his head, shoving articles into a satchel. Knowing his family suffered without his help seemed far worse than the possibility of discovery.

A second trumpet blasted above the commotion of the crowds at the port of Thebes. Women stood on tiptoe while men, too eager to abide protocol, blocked their way. Children, rambunctious with excitement, scrambled underfoot, eating sweet breads and fruit sold by the vendors, while banners waved above them like snatches of a rainbow.

In the foreground members of the royal household watched with reserved expectancy, some sitting in curtained litters, others in chairs while servants fanned them with flabella. Word had arrived earlier in the day by rider from Abydos that Moses' fleet was approaching, having sailed by way of the Delta. The crowd pressed as near the river's edge as they dared, each hoping for a glimpse of the god's son in his gilded barque.

At last the ships came into view, so burdened with goods and trees they appeared like miniature islands slowly approaching the port of Thebes.

Tasha shaded her eyes, straining for sight of Moses. Amon had answered her prayers, returning Moses safely to her. She placed a hand over her breast to quiet her pounding heart as a breeze stirred in her hair and rustled her robe.

In that moment she saw him. Did she imagine it, or had he looked her way? Her breath caught with delight, and though she felt Nefru's glare on her, she could not hide the truth that beat in her breast and shone in her eyes. She loved Moses as much as he had once loved her.

Nefru lifted her chin, her cheeks flaming at the possibility of Tasha and Moses reuniting. She remembered all too well his return from the Southlands and her first glimpse of the dark skinned woman. She would never forgive Tasha for coming between them. Perhaps now, after two years away, he would realize the folly of his former desires. With outward calm Nefru straightened her pleats and smoothed her wig, but not only for Moses' benefit, but for the Officers who were also in attendance. She had learned from experience not to place all her hopes in one man. Besides, as Queen she could have consorts of her own, and she knew of several, including a certain palace guard, who would die for the opportunity.

Not far from Nefru, Hatshepsut anxiously watched the ships. In Moses' absence she had forgotten the weight of her dark secret. Now at sight of him it burdened her with even greater intensity. Who had he discovered in the Delta and what of this Priest from the temple of Apis? Her stomach churned as she searched the vessels. She might have averted this trip altogether had the gods granted her peace concerning her son's coronation. Son? The word seemed strangely out of place. Did she even have a son? Yes, a son who was Habiru.

Her temples throbbed at the admission and she swooned in the heat of her carrier. Two attendants rushed to her side but she waved them away, catching a welcomed breeze through the open curtain and drinking in the vision of Moses at the helm of his ship. It was as if she were watching a god, his form as regal as any of Egypt's deities. In spite of his birth the gods had blessed him. Surely Amon would award him his place on Egypt's throne now that he had successfully returned.

Puseneb hovered near Pharaoh, his eyes glittering like jewels as he watched the ships approach the port. A monkey dangled from a high mast excitedly chattering, while a caged leopard paced in its cubicle, searching the shore as if to pick out its prey. Puseneb moved his gaze to the ships' cargo, his attention captured by an assortment of bulging baskets. Eager to have the first look, he pressed through the throng toward the dock, inadvertently brushing past Isis without greeting.

The consort sniffed, her eyes narrowed in concentration as she intently studied the fleet. It was not Moses she searched for but the Habiru Rekmire had mentioned. Another movement caught her eye and she fastened her gaze like the fangs of a viper on two women, a younger and an older one. Her heart nearly stopped. Their dress and braided hair appeared unlike any drawings of Puntite women. Could it be? Her eyes darted to Moses, bright with interest. Had he dared bring his secret to Thebes?

Moses scanned the shore, his heart in his throat and his body taut. He thought he had seen Tasha but now could not be sure, and searched the throng again, this time taking in the dark stare of Isis. Moving past her he found Nefru, and finally Tasha, her hair flowing about her face like a dark veil, her skin vivid next to her white gown.

Moses feasted on the sight. She appeared even more lovely than he had remembered. Strange, but the thought of her brought him no pain, only longing. Their eyes met and he held her gaze, his face softening. Then, in a flash of memory he envisioned their last meeting, his unrestrained passion, and her dismay as she clutched her robe to her bosom. Shame consumed him and instead he turned his attention to the dock as the ships pulled ashore.

Hatshepsut stepped up the gangplank, her back rigid and her delicate features hard, as if her face had turned to granite. Maintaining her poise, she stiffly held out her hands in greeting and he kissed the back of them, only their coolness revealing the turmoil that stirred within her.

"It has been two long years since you left us, Moses." She attempted a smile but her eyes were lined with concern.

"And the gods have blessed, returning me with more bounty than either of us could have imagined. It is good to be back, Hatshepsut." Moses smiled in return with no trace of the bitterness she had expected.

She nodded, searching the space behind him. "Then tell me what this 'Land of the gods' was like and what you have brought me? Is it as wondrous as the temple reliefs portrayed?"

Moses remembered the young women who had shared his bed and he averted his gaze, adjusting a stack of bundles at his side. "It was all that and more, but will never equal Thebes." He scanned the shore, seeing Tasha's litter weave through the crowd in the direction of the palace.

He glanced back at Hatshepsut, her expression frozen in dismay as she stared past him at a Priest who had stepped from behind a stack of goods, checking off items on a scroll.

Aware of the discovery, Moses nodded over his shoulder. "Aaron, bring us the list. I want you to personally present them to Pharaoh."

Aaron bowed low, reading from the scroll as Hatshepsut listened in silence, the words hardly penetrating her thoughts. So Moses had found his brother. The man did not appear at all like the child she remembered. Her eyes moved to Moses and back to Aaron. Yet she could see a resemblance, even a dignity she had not expected.

Moses studied her, his face grim. "I initiated another venture as well," he moved toward two women who stood behind Aaron, "an investment in human goods, so to speak."

Several of the crew wrestled past them with myrrh trees, awkwardly lumbering down the gangplank toward Puseneb who waited with his scribe, also tallying the goods, while others hoisted bundles and baskets on their shoulders, forming a human chain.

Yet Hatshepsut's attention remained fixed, her lips barely moving. "Where are they from?"

Moses' eyes bore into hers, their depths intensifying. "The village of Tju near Pithom. They are Habiru."

Hatshepsut's flesh grew cold. The plump older woman avoided her eyes while the younger paid masked obeisance. Both wore braids and the dress of slaves, but Hatshepsut recognized them at once. The younger appeared much like the elder had when she had met her years ago.

Hatshepsut took a quavering breath, turning to Moses who stood with his arms crossed, his bearing hardened and his expression impenetrable.

She shook her head. "Very well, Moses. They are in your keeping now," her eyes met his, "but take care. I wouldn't want anything to happen to them or to you. Even a Pharaoh has enemies."

Moses nodded, all too aware of her implication. He watched her go, his gaze instinctively moving to the shore and falling on Isis' litter. The curtain momentarily opened in his direction, though he could not see even a shadow of a form within the dark interior.

Turning to Aaron, he spoke in low tones. "We will proceed to the palace at once where I will make arrangements for your lodging. Warn Jochebed and Miriam not to speak to anyone other than myself, and under no circumstance are you to reveal who you really are."

Isis and Puseneb stood within Amon's vast treasure house in Karnak, a mountain of gold and goods heaped on the floor while baskets and bundles lined the walls. Puseneb bent over the pile with his voluminous backside to her, sorting through the artifacts while attempting to count the gold rings Moses had added to the lot. He paid Isis no attention at all save an occasional grunt, just as easily due to his position as to any agreement on his part.

Still Isis continued to address what appeared to be half a body. "I tell you I'm certain of it. Ask them. They're Habiru as surely as you're Egyptian."

"Humph." Puseneb rose with a groan, placing a wide palm on the small of his back. Though he had lost count of the number of rings long ago, clearly the amount Moses had entrusted to his keeping exceeded anything the treasured White House had ever received. He sighed with the same satisfaction he would have upon finishing a huge meal, and hobbled to the door.

Isis followed, talking to him in low, conspiratorial tones as Puseneb stepped from the room. Ignoring her, he ordered the double doors secured and bolted behind them, then looked up and down the hall in either direction, and motioned the guards to resume their posts, satisfied no one lurked about to try to gain access.

Isis continued, undaunted, "I tell you the Priest is Habiru. Why wouldn't the others be?"

"Why should they be and what does it matter?"

"It matters a great deal. It proves Moses' identity."

"How? We all use slaves. What do I care where they come from?" Puseneb turned and waddled down the hall in the direction of his office with Isis in pursuit.

"If Moses has lied about his birth then why...."

Puseneb waved her away as one would a pesky fly. "I've no time for such prattle. Go bother someone else and leave the royal family to me." Isis started to argue but Puseneb stiffened his neck. "If Amon is satisfied with them, so am I."

Quickening his pace, he left her standing in Karnak's darkening western wing, an expression of bewilderment on her face. How could she hope to win the throne for her son if she couldn't even get Puseneb to listen to the truth?

Thutmose turned in his chariot, his gaze narrowed in the darkness as he surveyed the scene behind him, having just returned to the Delta. Several rows of captives trudged by torchlight, most of them men, though a few choice women were also roped among them. Weary after the siege at Joppa, his troops trudged on either side of their captives, providing a human barrier, with an occasional ox–drawn cart breaking the monotony.

Thutmose barked an order and pulled off the road, watching as Rekmire rode ahead to lead the entourage to the garrison near Avaris. The compound would seem like paradise after what he and his army had endured, and he could hardly wait to find his bed. First, however, he must deposit this booty, human and otherwise.

"Move!" Rekmire's voice barely carried above the multitude of tramping feet that resounded through the night like the steady pounding of surf. "Faster, and keep those lines even."

The echo of hoof beats sounded as a rider approached them from the opposite direction. The man's horse snorted from exertion as it entered the circle of torchlight, its flanks frothing.

"A message from Thebes, my Lord," the rider matter–of–factly stated, dismounting before Thutmose and handing him a scroll.

Thutmose came to a stop and unsealed the scroll, leaning toward the light. Hardly surprised, he found it was from Isis. He read a few lines then looked up, knotting the parchment in his fist and tossing it to the ground. "What do I care whether Moses has slaves in his keeping from Tju or anywhere else?"

The messenger's eyes widened as if seeing Thutmose for the first time. "I only did as she ordered, my Lord."

"Next time take care whose orders you obey. Moses could have your head for this," Thutmose growled, galloping in an arc ahead of the army and back onto the road.

Rekmire stared after him, retrieving the document with his sword and stuffing it into his sash. There was no need to read it to determine who had sent it or what it pertained to. His gaze pierced the darkness in the direction of the rider, though he could no more see the man than the road beneath his feet. Yet a resolve grew within him as surely as the night air filled his nostrils. Thutmose would discover the truth soon enough, and what better time than with Egypt's army at his command?

CHAPTER 11

Sweat trickled down Moses' neck and under his jeweled collar as he studied the plans for Hatshepsut's temple.

"A jug of wine from the cellars," he blurted, noticing Jochebed's heavy footsteps as she shuffled to the door to do his bidding. Though serving in the palace was preferable to life in a slave village, she also suffered from the heat since coming from the cooler regions of Delta.

Feeling a pang of regret, Moses rose to stop her, nearly toppling his chair in the process. He hurried into the hall but she had already gone. Frustrated, he returned to his desk attempting to concentrate on his revision of the temple plans, a change necessary because Hatshepsut had insisted on incorporating additional items from Punt into her funerary temple.

The official ground–breaking had already occurred and the foundation was laid. Even now materials were being gathered in the south at Aswan where slaves worked the quarries, sending massive blocks of sandstone up the Nile. Thousands labored at the task, measuring lines and pounding wooden stakes into the rock at precise locations. The quarrymen would swell the wood with water causing the rock crack, whereupon the workmen would lift out great squares of sandstone, transporting them overland to the waiting barges then up the Nile to West Thebes.

Moses uncomfortably shifted. Just thinking about working outside in this heat made him sweat, and picturing the Egyptians forcing slaves to do so bothered him more than he cared to admit.

Jochebed returned with the jug, her face flushed from exertion. She had not even stepped through the door when Moses stood, lifting the sweating flask from her hands and filling a goblet with the cool liquid, but instead of tipping it to his mouth, he ordered her to a couch and placed the cup in her trembling hands.

She looked aghast, shaking her head and pushing it back towards him. "No, you drink."

He studied her face, her eyes glazed with exhaustion, her crimson cheeks framed by tendrils of grey that clung to her forehead.

"For you," he whispered, kneeling before her as he would have a child. Tipping the liquid to her lips, he watched with satisfaction as she drank. She closed her eyes, nodding a thank you then lifted her gaze to his. Tears filled her eyes as she whispered words he did not understand, though they seemed to reach through the shadows of his memory into his very soul. His vision blurred and he stood once again, pouring himself a drink and turning his back to her.

"I wish it didn't have to be this way, with you serving me." He groped for words, his voice husky. "Perhaps one day things will be different."

She smiled and shook her head, tears spilling down her cheeks. "I am happy. I prayed you would come and Yahovah has answered."

Moses studied her, overwhelmed by her tenderness. He had known motherly love from Hatshepsut, albeit tempestuous at times, but this was different. It was as if Jochebed gave all she had and still possessed an abundance from some secret store. Had she always loved him so?

The thought unnerved him. Unable to meet her gaze, he turned to his balcony and finished his drink. "You may go now. I have nothing more for you to do."

She hesitated a moment before she left. "I am thankful to Yahovah to be here. It is enough to serve you again."

Moses nodded as she made her way to the door, not allowing himself to turn about until he heard it close behind her. When finally alone, something deep within him wrenched and broke. Clutching the table, he hung his head and wept, not for who he was nor for what he had suffered, but for the woman whose love for him had endured nearly forty years.

Tasha stepped from the banqueting room and into the garden still fresh with morning dew. She searched the walkway in hopes of finding Moses as she had not spoken with him since his return, and the thought of him so near made her loneliness that much more acute. If only she could speak to him and mend the pain of their past.

She caught her breath. There in the distance he stood as if an apparition, his face ruddy with boyish enthusiasm and his actions overly self-conscious. Kneeling near the pool he plucked a lotus blossom and shook the water from its petals. Had he seen her? Did he wait for her to approach? Instead of looking at her, however, he turned to a young woman who stepped from behind a hedge.

Tasha stared in dismay.

"A flower to emphasize your beauty," he said, his voice low and reverent.

The woman blushed and held the blossom to her face, breathing its sweetness. Moses took the flower and slipped it above her ear and the woman smiled, her thick braids dangling over her shoulders.

Tasha recognized her as one of the slaves Moses had brought back from his voyage. Her throat tightened. So Moses had a mistress, and a slave at that.

"You are a vision, Miriam," he whispered.

A sob escaped Tasha's lips and Moses glanced back at her, surprise then agony crossing his face.

She froze as their eyes met, neither moving as each studied the other.

Didn't he care? Hadn't their moments together meant anything? Feeling the sting of betrayal, Tasha turned, fleeing across the garden, past beds of narcissus and lilies, beneath the boughs of an almond tree, and up the seldom–used path to her apartment. Her heart pounded and her breath came in gasps. Though she dared not look behind her, she was sure she could feel his eyes on her still.

Isis' servant stood outside Hatshepsut's audience room meticulously dusting and re–dusting the already polished doors, all the while listening to a battle raging within.

Moses paced the floor, his tone demanding. "I tell you I want them freed, all of them. There's no reason to keep them in my care. You know the truth of their being here as much as I do."

Hatshepsut's voice dropped to a hoarse whisper. "I can't go about freeing slaves. Someone will suspect, if they don't already."

Moses ignored her. "They deserve their freedom. It should have been given to them years ago."

"Why? So they could stir up the rest of the Habiru? No, they'll have a comfortable enough life here at Thebes, even as slaves, and will want for nothing. If you like, they may do little or no labor; it doesn't matter to me, as long as they keep their past to themselves."

Moses forced steadiness into his tone. "Aaron is practically free already, educated as a Priest and able to read and write Egyptian."

"But he is not Egyptian."

"Nor am I." Moses forced the words through clenched teeth.

Hatshepsut paused, an uncomfortable silence between them. "You are my son."

"And they are my family." His words reverberated throughout the room. He began pacing again, his footsteps heavy. "All I ask is for a proper burial for my father and the dead I have brought with me, and freedom for the three in my care."

"Freedom from what?" Hatshepsut's eyes locked with his. "For years I paid them wages, even took them from the confines of their slave camp, and where did they go when I left them? Back to the filth of slavery. They want it that way, Moses. Leave them be."

Moses shook his head. "I can't believe they would return of their own will."

"Well they did." Hatshepsut's lip curled. "I think in some strange way they're actually proud of who they are." She lifted her eyes with resolve. "Forget them, Moses."

"Then forget me." He turned his back to her, gathering the documents he had brought for her signature and strode to the door.

"Moses!" Her voice sounded thin and desperate. "If it matters so much," she dropped her tone to a whisper, "I'll see they are freed." She paused as if already feeling the weight of her words. "But I fear repercussions."

Moses turned to her. "I fear nothing. The fact the gods know is shame enough. My real father? Not a god at all but the lowest of men, a slave chipped from a muddy grave in a brick pit."

Hatshepsut's voice caught in her throat. "You should have left it alone, Moses."

"Then you should have left me alone."

His footsteps neared the door and Isis' servant jerked to one side as Moses stormed through the doors and down the hall. The girl stared after him, her eyes wide and her mind racing. With quaking fingers she clutched her rag then turned up the eastern wing toward Isis' apartment. The former concubine would pay well for this information, though the girl could hardly believe herself what she had overheard.

Hatshepsut's temple gleamed like the brilliance of Ra spread beneath the cliffs of El Kurn as if carved from the very mountain. A series of courtyards, each lower than the other, dropped from the sanctuary like receding steps eventually met by the causeway stretching like a welcoming path to the banks of the Nile.

Moses eyed the structure, turning to his sketch and readjusting his notes. The sun beat on his back, intensifying its glare on his bronzed flesh and forming sharp shadows beneath his face as he eyed the sketch with furrowed brow.

"Aaron." He turned to the Priest who stood between him and Ineni. "What do you think of the columns about the sanctuary?"

Aaron studied the pillars, unaware of Ineni's discomfort at Moses asking the opinion of a Habiru. The elder had already surmised the Priest's identity, and felt torn between revulsion and fear.

Aaron pursed his lips. "They're graceful and slender, unlike any I've ever seen."

Moses nodded. "Good. We'll keep them. I copied the design from a temple in Thera. Ineni, tell the sculptors to continue their work according to the sketches already given them."

Ineni searched Moses' face, glancing at Aaron then back again.

Moses steadied his gaze. "Is there something you wish to say?"

Ineni slightly bowed. "No, my Lord." He averted his eyes. "I will relay the message."

"See that you do." Moses watched him with irritation. "And have Puemre bring us refreshments. This heat is oppressive."

Concern stirred in Aaron's eyes as he watched the elder stride toward the tents at the edge of the work site. "My being here bothers him, doesn't it?"

"It hardly matters." Moses changed the subject, pointing to the overhanging cliffs where, in a secret cache, they had just buried their father and several relatives. It was the young women and their infants who died at the time of his own birth that affected him most, though he didn't even know their names. When he had learned of their deaths he had insisted on bringing them as well, feeling a kinship in all they had suffered, and preferring to imagine them enjoying an afterlife instead.

Moses pushed the memory from his mind. "As soon as the temple is completed I'll begin work on my own tomb there in the cliffs above our father's grave where I can watch over our loved ones for eternity.

Aaron glanced at the cliffs encircling Pharaoh's temple. "Have you drawn any plans?"

Moses studied the place as if attempting to visualize it. "I'll carve an open peristyle courtyard, and inside a shrine and crypt. It will be simple, as Hatshepsut has spoken of something more elaborate for me elsewhere."

"The Egyptians certainly place a lot of emphasis on death. Our practice is to stress the present as we believe eternity is contingent on our actions in this life."

Moses stiffened. "We believe the same. If an Officer dies poor, he remains so for eternity. If he dies rich he is just as wealthy in paradise, even if acquired in the final moments of his life."

"Do your gods care only for material wealth and position? What of moral obligation?"

"You should know the answer yourself having studied in Egypt's temples. We believe in fairness and equity, and consequences for wrong behavior."

Aaron nodded. "Yet those with enough power and position can buy their righteousness, as if the gods look the other way for some while standing in judgment of those too poor to afford the same. Your gods judge unfairly."

Moses took a measured breath. "It is true some are blessed while others are not as fortunate, but it is the gods' choosing not mine." He threw his brother a warning glance. "Be thankful for your freedom, Aaron, and the fact you have the status to enjoy it. Eternity lasts much longer than a lifetime." That said, Moses turned to the temple with quick steps. "We should view the improvements of the sanctuary."

Aaron nodded, hurrying to keep pace as they approached the lower courtyard.

Moses referred to the sketch as they walked. "We will plant myrrh trees here on either side, interspersed with sphinx replicas of the Pharaoh."

Aaron fell into step beside him as sweat ran in rivulets down his face and neck. The heat of this desert made even the slave villages of the Delta seem like paradise.

"I've planned for several shrines near the open court," Moses continued, "a library and some store rooms. Behind that, across from Hatshepsut's tunneled tomb, we will carve out a holy of holies from the mountain where only a privileged few will enter." Moses' face lit with a smile. "You and I will check it before and after its completion: the 'privileged few.'"

Aaron nodded, trudging after him up the wide steps to the higher courtyard as Puemre hurried to catch up to them with a tray. The servant seemed to lose ground until Aaron paused on the steps to await him. Aaron took the jug and poured himself and Moses a drink, handing it back to Puemre.

Moses studied his brother as the servant headed back to camp. "Does it bother you to have others serve you?"

Aaron shrugged. "I suppose someone has to do it. At least he is paid wages."

"Are you suggesting we pay the Habiru wages?" Moses laughed aloud at the thought.

"It's not payment they want."

"Then you believe we should free them?" Moses shook his head before Aaron could answer. "Not even I would like to see they damage they could do if given the chance."

Aaron took a sip of the cool wine. "Do you actually think the Habiru would attempt retaliation or try to take the Delta? It's their own land in Canaan they want, not Egypt's."

Moses lifted his goblet to his lips. "Still, I wouldn't chance it. Besides, they do us more good in bondage than freed."

"Us?" Aaron's eyes flashed. "Who do you mean by 'us'?"

Moses snorted. "Why us Egyptians, of course."

"Do you consider me and the rest of our family Egyptians?" Aaron's eyes narrowed to meet his brother's.

Moses stared. "Isn't that what you wanted, the freedom to be like other men?"

"Men or Egyptians?"

Moses grimaced. "Aren't you even grateful for all Hatshepsut has done for you?"

"Hatshepsut, yes. Egypt, no. You forget our father would still be alive except for the Egyptians."

Moses' brow knit. "And where would I be if not for Hatshepsut?"

Aaron keenly eyed him. "In the belly of some beast at Pharaoh's decree."

Moses shook his head then finished his drink. "Come, we've time enough to debate when your head has cleared and your newfound freedom hasn't blinded you to a bit of gratitude."

Turning, he made his way across the uppermost courtyard and into the welcomed shadows of the sanctuary while Aaron followed with slow and deliberate steps, absorbed in thoughts of his own.

The heat of the day had finally begun to abate when Moses and his entourage returned to the palace. He had just changed his clothes and refreshed himself when a servant entered, gasping for breath.

"It's the Mistress Jochebed —"

Moses sprang to his feet. "What is it? What happened?"

"She had a bad spell and is asking for you."

Moses ran from his room. "Summon the physicians and High Priest!"

"It's been done, my Lord. They're on their way."

Moses covered the distance to her apartment in less time than it took to walk the length of his room.

"It's this damnable heat," he muttered as he burst through her door. She laid on her couch, an attendant nearby.

"Moshe," she whispered in Habiru, slowly reaching her hand out to him.

"Mother." He took it and knelt beside her. Realizing who was watching, he waved the servants from the room, his eyes never leaving his mother's face. "Send in the physicians as soon as they arrive," he added as they closed the door.

Moses pressed Jochebed's hand to his lips. "Are you in pain?"

She attempted a smiled. "I can manage now that you are here." She took a quavering breath then winced, tightening her grip. "My heart has endured much over the years."

"Too much." Moses searched her face. "But those years are behind you now. You can at last enjoy the riches of Egypt and a life of ease."

She shifted. "If I had wanted riches and ease I could have had it." She managed a smiled. "I wanted only you, Moses, and now you are here."

Moses clenched his teeth against his fears, taking in every detail of her countenance. "Then you shall have me always."

She groaned, waiting for the pain to subside before continuing. "You don't know how I prayed to see you, how I waited for even a glimpse of you. When you finally returned to our village I was overwhelmed with joy. To live near you again is too wonderful to believe." She gasped for breath.

"Damned physicians," Moses breathed. "Have they feet of stone?" He tightened his grip. "As soon as they arrive —"

Jochebed shook her head. "I want only you, Moses," her eyes softened, "and Aaron and Miriam."

The words no sooner left her lips than Moses shouted a command to the servants outside the door. "Bring Aaron and Miriam." He turned back to her, his face twisted with anxiety. "The physicians and High Priest will soon be here. Puseneb will assure you a blessing of the gods. He knows every ritual on record."

Jochebed coughed and the spasm wracked her body. Once she had caught her breath, she continued. "I am blessed to know the only true God, Yahovah, and He is enough."

Moses' eyes widened with fear. "Don't say such things. You may incite the gods' wrath and endanger your status in the afterlife."

"Anger gods made of stone fashioned by your own artisans?" She managed a chuckle. "That would be a wonder." Her face constricted and she gripped his hand, pulling him closer. "There is only One God, Moses," her voice dropped to a whisper, "the One who watched over you as a baby on the Nile, and guided a basket to the arms of a Princess." She took a labored breath. "Only Yahovah could have accomplished such a feat."

Moses watched her with a mixture of consternation and fear as she smiled up at him, a tear making its way down her weathered cheek.

An announcement sounded at the door, and Miriam and Aaron hurried to her side. Puseneb and two court physicians bustled into the room behind them but Moses never moved. Instead he cradled the beloved hand as if only the two of them remained in the chamber.

A physician approached the bed, feeling Jochebed's forehead then checking her wrist. His brow furrowed and he rummaged through his bag, picking out a vial.

Unstopping it, he tipped it to her mouth then stepped back to confer with the other physician.

Moses anxiously watched her, hoping for sign of improvement, but instead she seemed driven with desperation. Clutching his hand, she searched his face. "Worship only Yahovah, Moses, for it was He who spared you as an infant." She gasped. "He has a purpose for you, I know it. Your father knew it."

Determination so surged through her that she raised herself partway from the couch, looking into his eyes as if to exact his promise, but Moses could only stammer in response, saying he would surely add this god to the rest if she wished. His words slowed their cadence then ceased altogether as she closed her eyes and slumped back on the couch.

Moses stared in disbelief. The physicians hurried to her side, attempting to revive her, but to no avail. Instead, she remained as still and peaceful as if she slept.

How could she be gone? How could he have had her so briefly only to be snatched away again? Anger flared through him at this god of hers. If he were so powerful why had he allowed her to die? And why now when she had just received her freedom?

Moses put his hands on his head, overwhelmed with his loss. The room blurred with activity as Miriam threw herself atop the body, uncontrollably weeping. The physicians stepped to one side as Puseneb approached to minister the last rites, but Aaron pre–empted.

Lifting his hands with conviction, the young Priest's words rang throughout the room: "Oh great Yahovah, God of our fathers, of Abraham, Isaac, and Jacob...."

"Jacob," Puemre repeated in recognition. 'Ben Jacob,' meaning 'Son of Jacob,' was a Habiru recorded in the ancient annals as Vizier over northern Egypt during the reign of the Hyksos. Rumor had it his body lay in a sarcophagus somewhere among the slaves in Goshen.

"We offer this, the spirit of our mother, Jochebed, for Your acceptance into Paradise," Aaron continued. "She has lived her life for Your purpose, giving up the enticements of this life for the glory of the next. Receive her, we pray, and may we, when we come to our end, be found worthy to stand with her among the faithful, having fulfilled the desire of Your heart." Aaron's voice dropped to a whisper. "In the name of Yahovah."

Puseneb's face blanched as he stared at the trio, fixing his eyes on Moses with growing realization. He looked at Moses' Priest, then at the young slave woman by his side, and finally at the deceased slave who peacefully lay in their midst, oblivious to the stir she had caused.

"By Amon!" Puseneb cursed. Turning, he shoved his way through the crowded doorway and down the hall as the two physicians, in a quandary as to what to do next, hurried after him.

"Don't you wish to administer the last rites, my Lord, before we prepare the body?"

Puseneb continued his flight, his robe billowing behind him. "Didn't you see what happened? Didn't you hear him?"

Their faces wrinkled in question. "My Lord, we —" But Puseneb neither slowed nor acknowledged them.

Rounding the corridor in the direction of Isis' apartment, he threw the words over his shoulder, his voice echoing behind him in the near empty hall. "Do what you like with the dead. My concern is with the living."

The cliffs of El Kurn lit with the colors of sunset, reflecting pinks and golds onto Hatshepsut's funerary temple which had just been the site of Jochebed's funeral. Dwarfed by the grandeur, a group of mourners gathered on one of the outer courts, bearing gifts for the recently deceased slave to be carried up the mountainside and deposited in a secret cache beneath the site of Moses' future tomb.

Isis, the first of the royal party to leave, watched with Puseneb from the ferry, making their way back to Thebes across a river that glistened with fragments of light like scattered diamonds.

Her eyelids drooped, heavy with unspoken knowledge, as she leaned toward him. "Did you see where Moses was going to bury her?"

Puseneb nodded. "In a crypt up the mountainside just above Hatshepsut's temple."

"Below the site of his own tomb, the same place he buried the others." Isis' eyes bore into his. "Now do you believe me?"

The High Priest scanned the cliffs. "I would never have thought it possible, but I do now."

"And what do you intend to do about it? Will you let a Habiru sit on the throne, rule our people, overtake our land?" The water rhythmically lapped against the ferry as Isis awaited his response.

Puseneb shook his head, allowing his gaze to drift down–river in the direction of the Delta. "Egypt needs its rightful heir."

"My own son, Thutmose III."

Puseneb did not answer, keenly eyeing the funerary party that appeared at a distance like ants carrying crumbs from a banquet as they trailed toward the mountain.

"And what of Moses?"

Puseneb looked at her, his expression stony. "Leave Moses to me." Turning to the tranquility of the river, he filled the silence with his own thoughts.

Isis persisted. "Hatshepsut is the one who brought him here. It's her fault he's even alive, and now look at them. If they have their way they'll free every Habiru in Goshen."

Puseneb nodded, stunned by recent events and the actions he must now take. "Send word to Thutmose, a messenger we can trust. Tell him to return to the capital at once, that I — that we have an urgent matter to discuss with him."

Isis' eyes brightened. "With pleasure. What of Hatshepsut and her impostor son?"

Puseneb turned to study the miniature party making its way up the mountainside with Jochebed's funerary articles in tow. "All in good time, Isis, all in good time. Right now what happens to Egypt matters more than what happens to them."

Thutmose sat in the garrison compound with one leg flung across the table, his chair precariously tipped backward. He toyed with the papyrus he had just received from Thebes. So now even Puseneb believed Isis' tale. She had finally convinced him. Well he didn't buy it, nor had he time for such fables. What did he care of Isis' schemes? He had only one desire: to lead Egypt's army in conquest, a privilege Moses himself had handed him.

Since weather would not permit him to campaign year around, he would march as soon as the flood waters crested, knowing the months of Akhet would soon give way to the season of Peret with less snow in Syria to contend with. Megiddo would prove a challenge enough without having to battle the elements, especially if a combined army of Hyksos and Syrians awaited him.

Thutmose watched Rekmire and Ebny as they played jackals in a corner, their intensity evident even in a game.

"I hate to break up a contest between two so equally matched, but have a look at this, Rekmire." He placed the papyrus before his Officer who casually picked it up, his countenance changing to one of wary acknowledgment.

Thutmose strode to the window. "I know it's early and spring hasn't yet arrived, but I hope to march east within the month, reaching the central mountains as soon as the snow melts."

"Megiddo?" Rekmire lifted his eyes from the parchment.

Thutmose nodded, standing at the window and surveying an infinite stretch of green. "I'll have to go around the mountains to get to the stronghold as it is well situated."

Rekmire peered at him as if calculating the possibilities. "If you take the northern route they'll hear of it by way of their scouts and be waiting for you. If you go south, you'll likely encounter the same."

"I'll take my chances. I can't sit here and wait for them to come to us."

Ebny studied him. "Why not? Our borders are secure enough. Perhaps it's time we merely maintain them."

Thutmose threw him a heated look. "I'll say when we march and when we don't. The gods aren't complaining nor the High Priest and his ever–widening belly." He frowned and turned back to the window, staring again at fields where sheep and cattle grazed.

Rekmire motioned to the papyrus. "Very well, then I'll go to Thebes in your place. We need to transport the captives and booty from our last campaign anyway. I'll take them to Karnak and meet with the High Priest on your behalf, a liaison of sorts."

Thutmose sneered. "You'd like that, wouldn't you? Then you could conspire again with my mother. I always thought you stronger and more discerning than to believe such tales." He peered eastward out the window, hoping the lush greenery would calm him as he attempted to calculate the weather he would encounter in Syria. "If you're willing to waste your time I won't stop you, but if Puseneb is angry because I haven't come, tell him I plan to conquer an even bigger prize this next campaign. I can't imagine him complaining."

Rekmire rolled the papyrus between his hands. "Perhaps he has something better in mind for you than commanding an army, perhaps a nation?"

Thutmose snorted then glanced at Ebny, realizing the impact of Rekmire's words, but it was too late. Already the black man appeared uncomfortably alert. Thutmose reddened with rage at Rekmire's carelessness. If word got out of Isis' intentions it could cost him his career, or worse.

Thutmose grunted. "Nonsense. Women's gossip and nothing more." He purposefully turned to the black man. "However, I've something in mind for you, Ebny. I want you to accompany me on my next campaign. I need a strong arm to aid in the battle against Megiddo. I think you would prove useful."

Ebny watched him with masked suspicion. Rising, he strode to the door, fear pulsing through his veins and pounding in his temples. "If Moses doesn't need me, my Lord, I will consider accompanying you."

"Moses is the one who sent you to me in the first place."

"Very well, my Lord, I will go." Tension widened between the two as each watched the other, neither speaking. If rebellion was afoot, Ebny owed it to Pharaoh to get word to her. "May I go, my Lord?"

Thutmose warily nodded, his eyes boring into the black man's. He would have Ebny closely watched, making sure nothing came of this conversation. His eyes narrowed. If need be, he would find a way to permanently silence him.

CHAPTER 12

Hatshepsut accepted the basket of fruit with a nod, dismissing the messenger who had come by way of one of Thutmose's ships. Surely this was not a gift from her stepson? She laughed aloud at the notion as she had never known him to give a gift, especially to her. If he did, whatever he gave would be suspect.

She lifted the cloth and picked through the fruit: melons, dates, pomegranates, and figs, among an assortment of others. She started to set the basket aside when she noticed a small scroll hidden at the bottom of the basket. Strange, but it bore Ebny's insignia. Had this come from him? Her heartbeat quickened as she opened and scanned the message.

Ebny had indeed sent it, relaying news of Rekmire's return to Thebes to meet with Puseneb regarding Thutmose's future.

Thutmose's future? Hatshepsut's hand shook as she clutched the scroll. Had Puseneb discovered her and Moses' secret? When and how? Might Amon himself have revealed it? Her breath caught in her throat. But even if the god had not, enough indiscretions had occurred so as to alert even the most unimaginative to the possibility that something was amiss. At Moses' insistence she had allowed three Habiru to live in the palace, granting them their freedom. She had lavished gifts from her own funerary store on Moses' deceased relatives, allowing them burial in West Thebes within sight of her holy temple so they might enjoy an afterlife. She had granted Aaron and his sister the right to worship their Habiru god, giving permission for a small temple to be built to Yahovah in the slave village of Tju.

Hatshepsut covered her face with her hands. What had she done? Had she already overstepped the bounds of her eternal destiny, incurring the gods' wrath? Her stomach churned and she felt light headed. She could almost see Amon's countenance, furious and accusing, as he pronounced her doom. Would she lose eternity in exchange for the kindness shown to slaves?

As if in a vision she pictured the misty morning forty years ago when she first held Moses in her arms, tiny and vulnerable. Her father had doubtless surmised the truth as he had soon afterward insisted she marry her stepbrother to provide Egypt a 'legitimate' heir. The venture, however, had proven fruitless as she had never borne a son, nor did happiness come of her marriage except in the eventual death of her husband and her own right to rule.

Would Amon take the throne from her now, or worse, demand the lives of her and her children? She clutched her stomach at the thought as nausea overtook her. She had not meant to anger Amon, only to do what she must for Moses and herself. Was mercy shown to slaves such a crime? If so, she had already lost eternity, and all of her efforts to appease the gods were pointless.

Hatshepsut slowly turned, viewing the grandeur of her audience room, the ornate furnishings and gilded throne on the dais. Did her inheritance, her blood, her name, mean nothing? Perhaps it did not.

If Amon had already abandoned her, she must take matters into her own hands. She had only one option left that would assure her survival and that of her loved ones, but she must act at once.

An eerie glow encircled Rekmire and Puseneb as they huddled about the table, a single lamp in their midst. The light from the flame danced and gyrated, making grotesque caricatures of their shadows on the walls.

Puseneb rose, throwing up his hands in exasperation. "Then what will it take to convince him? Must I personally travel to the Delta and bring Thutmose back?"

Rekmire shook his head, his face white in the lamplight and his eyes deep hollows. "It would do no good, my Lord. Right now he marches somewhere between the wilderness east of the Delta and the mountains of Megiddo, only this time he faces the combined Hyksos and Syrian confederation."

"Confederation?" Puseneb spat the word as if it were a curse. "Likely a rumor." The High Priest lowered his voice. "If he must fight let him do so as Pharaoh, not as a puppet soldier under Hatshepsut's command. But first he must come to Thebes to be crowned."

"This campaign is crucial, my Lord," Rekmire reasoned, "whether or not a confederation exists. Thutmose has never fought the Hyksos, and they are a formidable foe. He must face them at Megiddo and win, making an example of them before all of Syria."

"Curse his campaigns! If Thutmose can't answer the summons of his own High Priest...." Puseneb broke off in a mutter of obscenities that made even Rekmire squirm. The Priest abruptly stood, pacing. "Something is afoot, I can feel it. Hatshepsut hasn't visited the temple in days nor has she called for me, though I inquire regularly as to her well–being. Still she gives me only platitudes: 'The Pharaoh is unattainable,' or 'Her Majesty is indisposed.' Gods of the Underworld! What does 'unattainable' and 'indisposed' mean? Is she ill, stricken with some disease? Have the gods wreaked their own vengeance? Why in the name of Amon won't she answer me?"

Rekmire shrugged. "Perhaps she knows of your scheme."

Puseneb turned, open mouthed, and stared at the youth. "Knows? How? From whom?" Possibilities paraded before him until a vision of Amon himself formed in his mind. Had the god warned her? All Pharaohs alleged divinity and communication with the divine, yet he had always thought it mere propaganda. Now he wasn't so sure. Might she have a connection with Amon he knew nothing about? After all, she was of royal seed. Perhaps the gods favored her in spite of her sins.

He shook the thought from his head. Impossible! Even if she were divine, to jeopardize Egypt for the sake of slaves was unforgivable, and to place a slave on Egypt's throne was blasphemy. Nonsense! He waved a hand at the notion. Let the gods sort it out in the afterlife, he needn't concern himself. What mattered was Egypt's future. In the impetuosity of youth Hatshepsut had misjudged, bringing an accursed Habiru into the palace and proclaiming him heir. As High Priest, he had the right, no, the duty, to end this, or the gods themselves would hold him accountable.

Puseneb drew a deep breath, raising himself his full stocky height and levelling his eyes on Rekmire. "You tell Thutmose that if he doesn't return to Thebes immediately

I'll conjure up so many spirits of the dead in judgment of him that even his royal blood won't win him a hope of eternity! I'll call down so many curses on his head he'll wish...."

Rekmire rose, backing away. "I'll get him here, Your Holiness, don't worry." He pushed a blank papyrus across the table. "Just sign this and leave the message to me."

Puseneb scrutinized Rekmire above the wafting flame, the light casting an ominous glow on the youth's features. What could this ruffian do that he himself could not? Did he have some secret power bestowed him by the gods?

The High Priest considered the notion then grunted. Foolery! When even a lowly mortal appeared divine something was wrong with one's religion.

He pursed his lips, eyeing the blank papyrus, and picked up a reed pen. With more fervor than necessary, he scrawled his name in oversized fashion, shoving the document back to Rekmire and eyeing him. "If you're able to rouse that rebel and return him to Thebes I'll pay you well from my own store."

Rekmire stared at him then shook his head, feeling a rare benevolence. "I already stand to gain should Thutmose come to the throne, but if I ever need a favor I'll let you know."

Puseneb let out his breath, thankful his meagre percentage of the god's store would remain untouched in spite of his generous offer.

The receding Nile in the months of Peret seemed to accentuate the afternoon heat as it weighed upon the inhabitants of Thebes. Even the birds and bugs knew better than to venture forth, all but two youthful figures who stretched out upon the green as if it were an inviting carpet, and a third who kept undetected watch within the shadows of the palace.

Nefru pulled from the young man's embrace and arose, giggling and running across the lawn. Her admirer, still in the uniform of a guard, darted a glance about the courtyard before pursuing. He easily bridged the distance with his lanky form, pulling her into his arms and pressing his mouth against hers.

Nefru's breath caught. She had not meant to entice him, only to flirt. What would Moses say? She tried to break free but could not, and instead gave way to the passion pulsating through her body.

Isis purposefully strode across the yard to them and cleared her throat. "Young man, I see you are closely observing the royalty today." Cynicism curdled her tone and her eyes intensified. "I should let Pharaoh know of your 'loyalties' to the royal house."

The man drew back, his panting changing to gulps of fear. "Your Ladyship, I —" at a loss of words, he glanced at Nefru who indignantly smoothed her gown, "that is, we —"

"On the other hand," Isis straightened her posture, meaningfully eyeing the girl, "I might be merciful if the two of you promise not to let this happen again."

Nefru lifted her chin. "I won't be bullied by a has–been concubine. I'll see who I want when I want, and without your permission."

"Not if you plan to provide Egypt an heir." Isis glowered at her, dismissing the man with a flick of her wrist, whereupon he hastily tripped across the yard and out of sight. "By Osiris' beard, a palace guard? Surely even you understand the need for discretion."

Nefru sighed as if her mother herself reprimanded. "There's nothing else to do in this boring place. Besides, who are you to tell me so?"

Isis' eyes blazed. "The mother of Egypt's future Pharaoh."

Nefru's jaw dropped, her eyes bulging with disbelief. "You're talking treason. You're saying your son Thutmose —"

"— deserves the throne, and so he does, and he's the only one who does." Isis' eyes narrowed with the conviction of a cobra, her tone fierce. "Have you any idea who Moses really is?"

Nefru tried to speak but Isis plunged ahead as if her life depended on it, for truly it did. "Moses, if you were but to observe, has fallen from the gods' favor. Why? Because he does not deserve the crown." She took a step closer and whispered with conviction, "He is not of divine blood at all, or even royal seed."

Nefru's jaw dropped but she willed her lips to move. "That's a lie. Mother herself —"

"— has continually lied concerning his birth." Isis' muscles tightened as if ready to spring. "Do you know who he buried near his tomb? Who occupies the most obscure caskets ever laid on the sacred soil of West Thebes?" Isis paused for emphasis. "Habiru, all of them: the woman Jochebed, his mother; Amram, his father, dug from the brick pits near Tju. The others, women and infants who lost their lives nearly forty years ago at Pharaoh's decree. I spoke with the embalmers myself. This is the heritage he brings to the throne and to your offspring."

Nefru shook her head, searching the ominous face before her. "You're lying." She groped for words. "You've always hated Moses, always wanted Thutmose to rule.

Well you'll not have my help, and by the blood of the Pharaohs, I'll not stand here and listen."

Isis' scowled. Had she misjudged the girl? If so, she dared not turn back now. Reaching out, she clutched Nefru's arm. "Thutmose is the rightful heir, his exploits prove it. Even the gods know it. Whether or not you believe it doesn't matter. The gods will never allow Moses to rule. Whatever you feel for him is futile." Isis lunged for her final ploy. "If you aim to be Queen it will not be at Moses' side but at Thutmose's. Beware you don't waste precious royal seed in the meantime on palace guards. Save it for the future Pharaoh's bed."

Nefru's nostrils flared as she pulled her arm free, whirling and hastening back across the lawn. Isis held her breath, watching her go, the swing of her body and arch in her back, even the toss of her head all noted by Isis' shrewd stare. Yet Nefru did not turn toward the official wing as Isis feared, but toward her own chamber, affording a backward glance that told Isis everything she needed to know. For the girl had a lust of her own for the throne and a craving for power. Greed and self-indulgence beat in that young breast as surely as it did in her own, and would eventually turn the girl's head. Thutmose may not be Nefru's first choice for a husband, but if he provided an avenue to the throne, he would be her best.

Moses stood in the garden outside the banqueting hall watching Tasha as if beholding a vision. He marveled she had come here at all considering the pain of their last encounter and the intimate moments formerly shared in this place. He took a hesitant step forward and Tasha looked up, dismay marring her delicate features.

Her mind raced yet her limbs refused to move. Willing her body to obey, she turned from Moses and walked toward the grove of almond trees.

Moses' pace quickened. "Tasha, wait! I must speak with you."

She slowed her steps as Moses bridged the distance, and lightly touched her shoulders. "Tasha, I — you don't understand."

She stifled a cry as he turned her toward him, lifting her chin to meet his gaze. Tears swam in her eyes and he bent to kiss them away, enfolding her in his arms. She trembled in his embrace. Then, giving way, she clung to him, weeping.

"Tasha." He smoothed her hair, reveling in the warmth of her body, her skin soft beneath his touch. Passion surged through him and he reached down to kiss her but she shook her head.

"I can understand sharing you with Nefru, for she is of royal seed, but a slave? Am I not better than a Habiru?"

Moses' features constricted, his gaze becoming as cold as stone. He let her go. "If you are better than a slave then you are too good for me." He looked away, forcing himself to say the words, "I myself am Habiru."

Tasha's eyes widened as Moses continued. "Years ago Hatshepsut adopted me as an infant. The other woman you saw is my sister, Miriam; Aaron is my brother; and Jochebed was my mother. We buried our parents and relatives above Hatshepsut's temple and below my tomb to provide them an afterlife."

Tasha stared, shaking her head in disbelief.

"Now you know why I grieved as I did, why I gave the army to Thutmose, and why I brought these Habiru back to Thebes. They are more mine than Hatshepsut could ever be. Though I would never choose to love a slave as I love you, it is all I deserve."

Tears swam in Tasha's eyes as she flung her arms about him, nestling her head on his chest. "Oh, Moses, if I had only known I would have told you it doesn't matter. It doesn't change who you are. You are still Moses to me."

He didn't answer, he couldn't. Her unexpected love had proven greater than his pain, breaking the walls he had built around his heart and rekindling a longing he hadn't thought possible. Moaning, he enfolded her in his embrace, kissing her with a passion neither had yet experienced.

"I love you, Tasha, more than I'll ever be able to express."

She closed her eyes, shutting out everything but this moment. "You are all I want, Moses, the only man I'll ever love. I don't care who you are or where you are from. I'll love you as long as I live."

Moses tenderly studied her, then, glancing behind them at the still empty garden, he swept her into his arms, carrying her down a seldom used path toward the flowering boughs of an almond tree and the seclusion their love required.

In the shadows of the colonnade a figure stirred. Nefru stepped into the light as Moses and Tasha vanished, hatred coursing through her body like fire through a dry field. Her pulse raced and her temples throbbed. She no longer cared who she hurt, or whether or not Isis' tale proved true. If it aided in Moses' and Tasha's destruction it was good enough for her.

Thutmose jerked the reins of his chariot, clattering to a stop beneath the majestic heights of the Syrian mountains. Cedars lifted on either side, free of winter's snow, while patches of white still clung to the upper clefts, contrasting against the rocky steep. Like irregular pyramids of the gods' making, the mountains crowded against each other with only a narrow gorge between. Miles beyond them, unseen behind this mountain impasse, lay the fortress of Megiddo, prize of Syria and base of the confederation.

Thutmose turned to Amenhab. "We'll camp here for the night in the cover of these mountains."

Amenhab nodded, passing the order along the ranks to the rest of Egypt's army. The men moved quickly, setting up camp even as Amenhab spoke, welcoming the chance to stop and rest.

Thutmose motioned Amenhab, dropping his voice in the darkness. "When was Ebny last seen?"

"This morning, my Lord, heading toward the western fork of the highway in the guise of a tradesman. I sent a scout to find out what became of him."

"Good."

Amenhab leaned across his horse, his brow pursed. "Do you actually think Ebny will return? You gave him an unusually risky mission."

Thutmose grunted, looking at his Officer with less than the usual solicitude. "Scouting is always risky, but the information he gains could save our hides. If the confederation involves only several city–states we can easily overcome them, but if more have joined we will have to wait until next year to take Megiddo."

Amenhab peered into the darkness. "Perhaps we should concentrate our efforts on a smaller prize such as one of the coastal city–states father east."

Thutmose stepped from his chariot and handed the reins to a servant. "No. Better to strike now before the confederation has a chance to grow in numbers and confidence. Surprise is always the best tactic."

"...If they haven't already heard of our arrival," Amenhab answered, dismounting and taking his pack from his horse.

Thutmose ignored the comment and signaled his Officers to break for camp. By nightfall a circle of fires blazed before a silhouette of tents, appearing like a miniature range beneath the backdrop of loftier peaks. Thutmose and Amenhab sat silently near a fire as they finished their evening meal.

Suddenly a rider broke through the encampment alighting before Thutmose, his face stark in the firelight and his countenance solemn, encouraging silence. "Ebny's been taken, my Lord. I got as close as I dared without being seen. They have a confederation all right, as the men who captured him had the garb of both Syrians and Hyksos. I can't say how many city– states they represent, but more than a few."

Caught between thanksgiving and guilt, Thutmose asked, "And you're sure Ebny's been captured?"

The man nodded.

Thutmose smiled. "You've done well and will be rewarded."

The messenger muttered his thanks, continuing as forthrightly as he dared. "I wouldn't suggest an attack, my Lord. Their camp is spread outside the fortress of Megiddo like a second city. There's little hope of winning against an army of that size, and no hope of saving Ebny."

Thutmose poked the fire with a stick, watching the embers burst against the night. "I suppose the risk could prove insurmountable as we're not prepared to meet all of Syria." He glanced at Amenhab, his features impassive and his eyes holding little regret. "On the other hand, the cities of Tyre and Sidon would prove easy prey, especially if their armies await us at Megiddo."

Concern shadowed Amenhab's face. "And if they don't?"

"We'll fight them anyway. Without the help of the coalition we can easily win, likely making it back before the Hyksos even know we have come."

"They'll have scouts of their own in the mountains."

"I'll take that chance." Thutmose tossed the stick onto the fire. "I doubt they move from the safety of Megiddo."

"Perhaps," Amenhab muttered, his face somber in the firelight. "Do you think Ebny will talk?"

Thutmose shook his head, a smile flitting across his face then vanishing. "Not now."

Ebny trudged ahead of the Syrian guard, prodded by a sword toward an auspicious looking tent. He touched his hand to his mouth where blood trickled, his body stiff and aching after being subdued by the sentries at the entrance to the valley. He had been taken as a spy, in spite of his garb, something he suspected Thutmose had set him up for. Still, just in case he escaped this place, he noted the tents spread out beneath the standards of half a dozen city–states, housing the various armies outside the towering walls of Megiddo. He glanced back across the valley to the foot of the mountains and saw the far plain was empty, but before he could study it further the guards shoved him inside one of the tents.

He squinted in the half–light, his eyes focusing on a massive form in the shadows.

A guard pushed Ebny forward where he barely stopped himself from colliding with the bulk of a man. "Found him travelling south along the highway," the guard said. "Looks like he is from Kush Ta–Seti, but I have my doubts. He may be an Egyptian spy."

Ebny understood the conversation in Akkadian but forced his eyes to a nondescript stare.

"Speak!" A huge Hyksos stepped forward, raising a thick hand and slamming it across Ebny's face. The blow would have sent most men sprawling, but Ebny took the force from the shoulders up, his feet rooted to the ground.

The Hyksos barked a message and a youth scurried from the tent toward Megiddo to summon the Governor.

Ebny assumed the man to be the confederate leader. The Hyksos cursed, pacing before Ebny like an enraged lion, his broad shoulders further enlarged by layers of animal skins that hung about him like trophies. "I said speak or you'll wish you had!"

He struck the other side of Ebny's face, but the black man met the leader's scowl with a fierceness of his own. The Hyksos shook his head, his hair bushing about his grizzled countenance. He motioned a gangly youth who had just entered with a slate.

The boy nodded and took a faltering step toward the captive. He briefly paused before speaking in Akkadian. "Where do you come from? Who sent you, and why were you travelling to Megiddo?"

Ebny stiffened, lifting his chin, his eyes defiant.

The interpreter glanced at the Hyksos, took a deep breath and began again in Egyptian. "Are you party with the Egyptians? Tell us and we will spare your life."

Ebny watched him with feigned ignorance. If only he hadn't gotten close enough to be captured. Yet Thutmose had known the risks when he sent him. He also knew it wasn't in Ebny's make–up to betray loyalties, not as a Madjai as he had once been, or as an Egyptian Officer, no matter how absurd the orders nor how desperate his plight.

He closed his eyes as the tirade continued, trying to picture himself anywhere but in the enemy camp. A view of Thebes formed in his mind: the tranquil river with a scatter of ships and skiffs afloat on the glittering surface; the majestic skyline of buildings and pylons rising into the blue; and the faces of his friends and associates as he remembered them. He wondered if his message had made it past Thutmose's scouts to Pharaoh Hatshepsut. He could only pray it had.

The Hyksos grabbed him by the shoulders, his face inches from Ebny's. "Tell me or die, black man!"

Ebny's eyes fell on the glinting edge of a blade on a nearby table as the man roughly released him.

"Take him to the prison compound. I have other ways of getting my information."

Ebny willed his muscles to relax, and in so doing the guards instinctively loosened their grip.

The Governor poked his head through the tent flap. "Is there an army on its way? Has he revealed anything?"

The Hyksos raised his full height, shaking his shaggy head. "Not yet, but he will."

The Governor eyed the prisoner, slowly nodding while searching the face of the Hyksos. "If he is in Egypt's employ they will not be far from here. Perhaps we should divide our armies, sending half north and the other half south to wait at either entrance to the valley."

The Hyksos shook his head. "No. To divide our strength on any account would mean being only half as strong. Besides, we can't leave the city vulnerable. We're better off here until Thutmose shows. He's not the kind to resist a challenge, and Megiddo is a prize he'll want to add to his conquests."

The Governor stammered, "It's early in the season. Maybe the Egyptians aren't even here yet. Why not send out scouts to be sure?"

"We have scouts at both entrances, and if the Egyptians are out there they'll soon be seen." The Hyksos glared at his captive. "As for me, I'll find out by other means."

The Hyksos reached for him but Ebny lunged for the knife, plunging it deep into his own gut. The leader caught him as Ebny fell at his feet, inadvertently pushing the knife farther into Ebny's oozing belly. He turned Ebny over and retrieved the blade but it was too late. Blood ran from the black man's stomach, creating a pool about him on the ground where he lay.

Ebny managed a weak smile, a hint of triumph in his eyes before he sagged lifeless in the arms of his captor.

The Hyksos stared in disbelief, unable to speak.

"So much for finding out any news," the Governor muttered, taking an unsteady breath. "What if he was only a tradesman after all?"

The Hyksos stood and shook his head, his eyes fixed on the motionless form. "Would he have sacrificed his life so readily? No, he was a spy alright, who knew he had only one way of keeping the information to himself."

The Governor anxiously watched the Hyksos. "What do we do now?"

The Hyksos' features remained expressionless. "They've likely only just heard of our confederation from spies such as this one. Knowing Thutmose, he'll want to be prepared, which could mean we won't see him until next spring."

The Governor studied the open stare of the black man as if willing him to reveal his secrets. "Then I suppose we're better off where we are. Let Thutmose think us easy prey, even cowardly."

The Hyksos nodded. "In the meantime we'll convince the city–states of Kadesh and Mitanni to join us, increasing our numbers enough to assure us victory when the Egyptians do arrive. With an army of that size we could even march on the Delta and win."

The Governor looked uneasy. The Hyksos had coveted the Delta ever since the Egyptians had forced them from Egypt years before. Yet conquering Egypt would never be his goal, though keeping Megiddo was.

"What if Thutmose marches on some of the city–states in the meantime?"

The Hyksos frowned. "If he is even here." Firmly setting his jaw, he stepped over the body and toward the door. "Sooner or later he'll have to face us in battle, and when he does he'll find an army even greater than he bargained for."

Nefru stood near Isis' door, pretending to admire a bouquet of irises while glancing down the hall as if waiting for someone. Attempting a natural stance, she soon heard the pad of sandals and glanced up to see Tasha, nearly toppling the vase in the process as she watched her step lightly down the hall toward her apartment. Nefru scowled after her, wishing she could do the girl physical harm, but her mission with Isis would be effective enough.

She let out an exasperated breath, resuming her vigil.

Soon the brisk clip of heels sounded and she looked up to see Isis approaching as if the gods themselves pursued her. The former concubine frowned in Nefru's direction then hurried past to her own apartment.

"Wait!" Nefru dropped her voice to a whisper. "A word with you, if I may?"

Isis paused, wondering whether or not to accommodate the girl, but curtly nodded toward her door. Nefru stepped through the opening and gazed about in wonder.

The consorts' room was filled with ornate artefacts, many of them acquired as gifts during her years as a Priestess. Most were of non–Egyptian origin given by way of appreciative tradesmen with whom, Nefru had heard, she had shared her feminine talents. Articles from every country imaginable hung on her walls or stood on pedestals, adding to the international flair of her decor.

Isis dropped to her couch, kicking off her sandals and lifting her feet to the table. Arching a well-groomed brow in Nefru's direction was an invitation for the girl to speak.

"I have thought about our conversation and," Nefru faltered, "I believe you are right." She cleared her throat. "There may indeed be something strange about Moses. I recently overheard a conversation I am sure will interest you."

Isis straightened, her eyes glittering like black beads.

Nefru traced the design on an ornate table as if gaining strength from it. "I —" She glanced up, hardly daring to meet Isis' stare. "I overheard my mother speaking of a coronation, of crowning Moses as Pharaoh."

Isis caught her breath, nearly strangling at the disclosure, but swallowed hard instead.

Nefru continued, "She was speaking with Ineni and they agreed Moses should rule in spite of 'the circumstances,' whatever that means."

"When?" Isis blurted so sharply Nefru jumped.

"I — I don't know." The Princess glanced at the door as if considering an escape.

Isis stood, approaching Nefru, her eyes intent. "A date, a place!"

"On the occasion of my mother's Jubilee two months from now at the Temple of Karnak. They have yet to approach Moses with the notion."

A smile crept over Isis' face. Her web of informants had considerably improved, seeing she knew of the scheme before Moses.

She patted Nefru's hand, her voice as smooth as oil. "May our goddess bless you, Nefru, for your 'loyalty' to Egypt. Should you discover anything else, a date, a time, I would be most grateful, and will reward you accordingly."

Nefru smiled with relief as Isis strode toward the door, opening it in a graceful arc. "If you ever wish to 'council' again, you are most welcome." Her blood red lips curved upward.

Nefru nodded, stepping into the hallway.

"Do come again," Isis dropped her voice, heavy with meaning, "and be sure you bring more 'news.'"

Isis carefully closed the door, listening for Nefru's fading steps before bustling through her chamber, cursing the name of Moses, and calling for a scribe. A young man entered.

"A message," Isis' voice shook with emotion, "to Thutmose at Avaris. Tell him —" she paused, biting her lower lip in concentration, "tell him I have fallen ill and wish to see him before I die."

The scribe looked her up and down as if assessing her health for himself before continuing.

"Tell him he stands to inherit much," she paused, measuring her words, "but I wish to personally bequeath it to him before my death. Signed, his adoring mother, Isis."

The scribe raised a brow in question but Isis sealed the note and handed it back to him as he hurried out the door with the weighty task of finding a messenger to deliver it.

Isis took a satisfied breath. If her own summons would not rouse the rebel, perhaps greed would.

Hatshepsut stood statue–like before her open window, not turning even when Moses entered. Knowing who it was, she nodded to the spires of Karnak. "As a child my one aim was to please the gods, and I have never wavered from that goal. Regretfully, after all these years, I feel no closer to winning their favor than I did at the start. It seems a futile struggle." She turned to Moses, her countenance drawn. "I suppose I must accept the fact and enjoy what little I have left of life, for I cannot be certain of the afterlife."

Moses' jaw tightened. "You are of royal lineage, Hatshepsut. The blood of gods and Pharaohs flows through your veins. Surely, if anyone pleases them, you do."

She smiled, shaking her head. "I'm not so sure any more. There is little I have done that meets their standards. I have come to believe that all men, even Pharaohs, are finite and cannot hope to attain perfection in this lifetime."

Moses strode to where she stood, his eyes on the view beyond her window. He could see the city sprawled below the palace, the limestone of the official buildings and mud brick of the lower caste hovels all appearing the same brilliant white beneath the sun. He straightened. "But you did not call me here to council you concerning the gods. Why did you summon me?"

She squarely faced him, her voice expressionless. "I have decided the best recourse is to crown you."

Moses' eyes shot toward her. He started to speak but the words would not come.

She sighed. "I know what you must think. I never planned to go my own way, to force my will on the people or the gods." Her eyes misted. "Yet we stand to lose too much if we don't act. If the gods won't come to our aid, we must do so ourselves."

Moses' eyes narrowed. "Would you have me rule without Amon's blessing?"

Hatshepsut paced the length of the room, her voice measured as if having rehearsed the words. "We can't afford to wait. Egypt languishes under my rule, even I can see it. We need a new Pharaoh, Moses, we need you."

"A Habiru?" He laughed beneath his breath. "Even I think it unreasonable. No one would approve if they knew."

"But they don't." The words resounded in the silence as the two of them watched each other.

Moses shook his head. "The gods know and that is enough for me. I would rather die than go against them."

"Then you may have your wish." Hatshepsut walked to the table and picked up a small scroll, handing it to him. "Even now Thutmose plots with Puseneb to take the throne. If word gets out of who you really are and what we have done —" She let the words fall into the space between them.

Moses scanned the document. "You think Thutmose would take the throne by force?"

"He has the strength of the army behind him, and now apparently the Priesthood, which is all he needs."

Moses studied her. "You're suggesting we thwart his actions to save ourselves?"

"Yes, and those we love, including your family and Tasha. Our lives aren't the only ones in danger."

Moses shook his head. "Thutmose is far too grateful for all I have done for him to harm us, nor would he go against my direct command."

"When did you last see him?"

Moses sobered. "Over two years ago." His voice sounded husky in the silence. He perceptively eyed her. "What is it you propose?"

Hatshepsut resumed pacing. "We will plan my Jubilee after the months of Shemu have blessed us with harvest and the Nile has begun to rise, as we will need time to prepare. After a simple coronation I will hand all matters of state to you." She nodded, sighing. "I know our policies differ, but even I realize the need for balance. Perhaps Egypt will experience peace because of it during your reign."

"What of Thutmose?"

"You must remove him at once and place the army under Ebny's care. You can't trust your rival with our most powerful force."

"And the Priesthood?"

"If you continue to maintain the flow of tribute from the city–states already conquered, Puseneb will switch loyalties easily enough. He is enticed by Thutmose's booty, nothing more."

Moses nodded. "I should have known better than to give Thutmose the army." He gripped the scroll in his fist.

"Yes, the time has come. We can't leave it any longer."

Moses set the scroll aside, his face grim. "Then I accept your proposal, but only so I can assure the safety of those I love. Not for you, or Egypt, or any other reason." He watched her a long moment then turned to leave.

Hatshepsut stood transfixed, staring after him long after Moses had gone, and wondering what had become of the one she had groomed to be Pharaoh.

CHAPTER 13

Rekmire sat outside the garrison near the embers of a dying fire, evidence of several days' vigil, and took a last swig of beer, glancing at the waning sunlight before tossing what was left of the fetid liquid onto the ashes. Where was Thutmose anyway?

He scanned the highway leading from Avaris to the desert. The season of harvest was nearly passed and the Nile would soon rise again in the months of Akhet. Thutmose should have returned from Megiddo long ago. Had his campaign soured?

Rekmire threw his cup near the charred heap of ashes and mounted his horse. If Thutmose had met with disaster the repercussions would be worse than damning. Kicking his horse to a gallop, he headed for the border. Perhaps he would meet a tradesman near the border who had heard news.

He passed a field where slaves still dug in the earth for vegetables while others fastened bulging baskets of leeks, onions, and garlic onto the sides of donkeys to be carted away for market. The pungent aroma made him long for a home–cooked meal as he continued up the highway. He had hoped to find a clue as to Thutmose's whereabouts, but saw only an occasional Overseer and band of Habiru trudging back to their villages. He passed an orchard, the trees still heavy with fruit as they mingled their sweet scent with dust and earth.

The sun dipped lower until he could barely make out the road beneath his horse's hooves. Then he heard it: the faint strain of singing and the pounding of feet as if the earth itself had a heartbeat. He whipped his horse to a run and topped a knoll. There before him lay a sea of soldiers with carts and captives in their midst, standards aloft, and Thutmose at the fore.

Rekmire galloped to meet them, unable to conceal his relief. "Greetings, Commander. I see you've made another killing in Syria."

Thutmose grunted, his eyes dull and his face drawn. "Tyre and Sidon, if you can count them a prize. We didn't dare approach Megiddo as it's crawling with coalition armies." He met Rekmire's gaze. "We lost a scout to them."

"Ebny?"

Thutmose said nothing, his silence admission of the fact. Behind him his army marched to a familiar rhythm, embellishing the words to fit the occasion:

"I have given to thee might and victory against
all countries, I have set thy fame, even the fear
of thee, in all lands, Thy terror as far as the
four pillars of heaven...."

Rekmire glanced over his shoulder, speaking above the tumult. "Then the Hyksos have a confederacy of armies?"

Thutmose nodded.

"I thought as much." Before the conversation could turn to next year's campaign, Rekmire produced a scroll, handing it to him. "A request from Puseneb."

"What now?" Thutmose read only a few lines before tossing the parchment to the floor of his chariot. "I've too many other concerns."

"Such as women?" Rekmire glanced behind Thutmose at the wench in his chariot.

"Daughter of the Governor of Tyre," Thutmose noted. "She had heard so much about me she as much as asked to be taken." He grinned. "I've a mind to marry her as well as violate her."

Rekmire's eyes widened. "Marry her? But you can't."

Thutmose arched a brow. "You're telling me who I can and cannot marry?"

"No, my Lord, but you're a Prince of royal blood."

"— and deserve an assortment of wives," Thutmose added with finality.

Rekmire swallowed and nodded, plunging ahead in spite of Thutmose's tone. "Speaking of which, my Lord, Puseneb has organized a celebration in your honor." They topped the hill, the silhouette of the garrison barely visible in the distance. "He requires — or asks — that you accompany me to Thebes for the festivities."

"What has that to do with my acquiring wives?"

"Nothing, except," Rekmire paused, grasping for an answer, "I'm sure there will be more than an ample supply of women at the capital."

Thutmose eyed him askance. "As there usually is. To whom do I owe this 'honor'?"

"Puseneb, my Lord."

Thutmose scooped up the document and handed it to an attendant. "A celebration in honor of my victories?"

"And now Tyre and Sidon. All the more reason to pay you homage."

"It's unlike Puseneb to concern himself with anyone else's success when he could be counting the gold acquired at their expense."

"I tell you it's true." Rekmire's voice lifted in desperation. They stopped before the garrison and a figure emerged from the shadows. Rekmire recognized him as Isis' messenger and felt a sinking sensation. The man's eyes gleamed as he handed Thutmose a scroll.

Thutmose eyed Rekmire as he stepped from his chariot. "Two messages in one day?" Breaking the seal, he leaned toward the last rays of Ra then turned to Rekmire. "First a celebration in my honor, then a deathbed summons? What matter is so urgent as to employ the wit of my mother and the High Priest to summon me?"

He handed the second message to his attendant and started toward his quarters. "I've had enough orders for one day. Bring the girl once she has bathed."

He walked to a basin and washed his face and hands, throwing the words over his shoulder. "I'll go, Rekmire, but not for their reasons. When even your closest Officer joins in the scheme it's time to get to the bottom of the matter."

Hatshepsut faced her advisors as if standing her ground against a pack of wild boars. "I'm sure a procession to Abydos will not be necessary."

Nehisi glanced at Tuty and stammered. "Surely a brief journey to Abydos would not —"

"I've decided and that's final. As it is, we have had to wait until after the months of harvest, and already the floods of Akhet have begun to rise."

Moses stepped through the doorway, followed by his servant, Puemre who carried a tray. He surveyed the scene with interest.

Tuty shook his head. "If finances concern you, Your Majesty, worry no more, for Thutmose swells the treasure house with enough wealth to fund several coronations."

Hatshepsut stiffened. "Two months from today I will begin my Jubilee. When it concludes Moses will wear the crown, and I will not tolerate further delays." She scowled. "Whose idea was this trip anyway, Puseneb's?"

Her Officers looked at each other aghast. "No, Your Majesty. We merely thought it customary."

"Think again! Simple and direct is how I want the ceremony, and I won't leave Thebes for any reason."

When they had gone Hatshepsut glanced at Moses. "I can't have a moment's peace without every Officer in my employ annoying me with needless details." She pressed her hand against her forehead. "Even two months seems like an eternity when any day Thutmose could return, and only the gods know what would happen then."

Moses motioned to Puemre who set the tray on a table and left them alone. Moses waited until his servant had gone. "Thutmose is probably still in Syria, if even alive, and Puseneb has said nothing to contradict your announcement of the coronation."

Hatshepsut paced. "That's what bothers me. He always has something to say, but lately even at the council he just sits and stares as if presiding over my judgment. He's planning something, I know it." She impatiently glanced out the window. "I wish this inundation would pass so we could get on with the ceremonies."

"Don't worry. I'll have the quickest coronation on record, after having waited the longest for it to begin." Moses sardonically eyed her then changed the subject. "However, I've an idea to help pass the time and to provide us both with improved standing with the gods."

He nodded to the tray and lifted the cloth covering it. Beneath the linen lay a miniature replica of the temple of Karnak with two spires lifting from within the open court. Moses' eyes softened. "My gift to you upon your jubilee for all you have done for me, Hatshepsut." For the first time in years he truly meant the words.

Hatshepsut pursed her brow. "I don't understand. It appears two obelisks are standing in the open–roofed court of Karnak."

"Memorials raised in Amon's temple as a tribute to your devotion to the god, and mine," Moses added.

Hatshepsut's mouth lifted. "What a wonderful idea! To have an obelisk within the god's house would be the same as if I prostrated myself continually before him."

"True enough. Only one obelisk dominates the outer courtyard now, but with your permission, two will stand within that holy place."

Hatshepsut quizzically studied him. "How could you possibly accomplish such a feat? Do you plan to dismantle the temple?"

Moses smiled. "I'll not remove a single stone, yet within the span of two months our obelisks will stand in the sanctuary. The quarrymen have already begun their work. The flood waters will allow easier transport to Thebes, and the cooler weather will offer respite for the workers."

Hatshepsut watched him in disbelief, tears brimming in her eyes. Was it possible? Had Moses suggested a way to bridge the gulf between her and her god? Might this provide their means of forgiveness? She gripped his hands. "You're more than a son, Moses, you're a savior."

He shook his head, a shadow passing over his countenance. "No, just a man in as much need of the god's blessing as you are, should Amon choose to bestow it."

Isis raised an eyebrow at the student Priest who polished the sanctuary floor directly in her path. Taking Puseneb's arm, she skirted the youth as if even he might be a spy in Hatshepsut's employ.

Out of earshot, she bent toward Puseneb. "Of course Thutmose is coming, I summoned him myself."

Puseneb reared. "You what? I commissioned Rekmire for the task. Gods! What if they both summoned him?"

Isis' face drained, her fingers digging into Puseneb's arm. "Why would you do such a thing?"

"Because it was necessary to bring that rebel home." Puseneb shook his arm free. "By the throne of Osiris, woman, why can't stay out of other people's affairs?"

"Other people's? He's my son."

Puseneb entered his office with Isis following, still arguing her point. Ignoring her, he threw aside the dusty drapes then slumped in his chair and haphazardly sorted through a pile of papyri.

Isis paced before him. "I tell you it's more my business than yours. We've only days until the crown passes to that traitor, and here you sit."

Puseneb looked up, his countenance flushed. "What is it you expect me to do? Halt the coronation till Thutmose arrives? Poison the royal family?" Isis' face lit and Puseneb's eyes widened, his jowls wobbling as he vigorously shook his head. "Oh no, I'll not have any part in your scandalous schemes. I'll not call damnation down on my own head. Hatshepsut may be in the way but she is still royal, if not divine."

"She's no more royal than Thutmose; and as to divine, I have my doubts. But it's not her I am concerned about," Isis put in.

Puseneb leaned forward. "You try anything and you'll likely mangle it. You'll have us both chopped to bits and fed as fish bait. No, there will be no plotting here. Now get out!" He threw an arm toward the door then wiped his forehead with a cloth, but Isis refused to budge.

"I can't believe you'd rather let a Semite rule than take matters into your own hands. By the gods, Puseneb, I thought you had more backbone."

"I do." He abruptly rose, striding to the door. "And I intend to preserve it as long as possible. I also have sense enough to know when not to listen to you. So help me, if the royal family falls ill, I'll —"

Isis lifted a well-groomed brow. "You'll what? Reveal the fact we are both involved? Because we are. I have witnesses enough to prove that, and it will be your head as well if I fall, for I'll not fall alone."

Puseneb blanched and glanced at the door, afraid someone might overhear. He swallowed. "Give Thutmose a few more days. I'm sure he'll show."

"And if he doesn't?"

Puseneb shook his head, stammering anything to appease her. "Then I'll — we'll — think of something."

Isis gloated. "Good. I'm glad you see it my way. I'll meet you here in two days to initiate a plan."

Puseneb snorted in protest but Isis whirled and vanished before he could form the words.

Closing the door in her wake as if shutting out an evil spirit, he leaned against it, his eyes closed and his breathing labored, trying to blot out the face that had begun to haunt him even in his waking hours.

Moses stood beneath the second spire as the workmen tugged on a network of ropes and pulleys, lifting the colossal granite obelisk from the ramp of sand toward the open roof where it would stand as a matched pair with the first he had just raised within the court of Karnak.

"Pull!" Moses commanded.

The workmen strained against the weight, their sinews bulging from their arms and their torsos sweating. Others quickly dug the sand from the base of the shaft, revealing the second frame Moses had built into the temple floor.

"Harder!" Moses fixed his eyes on the obelisk as the white knuckled grip of the workmen edged it higher and higher through the opening until it reached into the blue of Amon Ra's domain. Precariously teetering in that sunlit space, it thudded into the base as the sound reverberated throughout the sanctuary, momentarily swaying before standing perpendicular with the floor.

No one moved as all eyes fastened on the electrum tipped monument, as if expecting it to come crashing back to the ground again. But it did not, whereupon a thunderous cheer arose seeming to shake the very pillars themselves. There in Amon's sanctuary the two obelisks stood, gleaming like visions of the gods and lifting their engraved salutations toward the sun, while swarms of workmen scooped the sand at their bases into carts to transport it back to the desert from which it had come.

Moses let out his breath and wiped his hands on a cloth as if he himself had pulled it from the ground. He turned to Hatshepsut, his body shiny with sweat and his face beaming. "It is done. Now they will stand for eternity as a memorial to your reign and mine."

Hatshepsut clasped her hands together, her face aglow as if reflecting the light from their brilliant peaks. "We will begin the ceremonies at once: this evening the banquet; tomorrow, a day of celebration in honor of my Jubilee; and the following day," her eyes met his, "the coronation."

Moses wiped his neck and face with a towel. "Until evening then. In the meantime I think I'll do something unusual and rest."

"In the arms of a certain bride–to–be?" Hatshepsut smiled and Moses nodded.

They both knew of whom she spoke, though Hatshepsut must have thought his time better spent with Nefru.

"Then wile the rest of the day away if you choose. You deserve it." She gazed up at the obelisks. "As for me, I think I'll stay here awhile and pray." Admiration shone in her eyes as she continued to study the spires that now dominated the inner court, their sides inscribed with words of praise for her and Moses.

She sighed. "You know Moses, in spite of the minor difficulties during my reign, I believe the gods have blessed us."

Moses nodded, his face softening with pity. He wouldn't ruin the moment by disagreeing with her, but could foresee the ruin of Egypt if her reign continued. He scanned the court, the usual stillness broken by the buzz and hubbub of workmen gathering their supplies and cleaning up. "Then enjoy your solitude, such as it is," he murmured.

"Nothing can disturb me now, for our monuments will ever stand before the gods proclaiming our worthiness."

Moses clenched his jaw, thankful her statement did not require comment. His eyes swept to the top of the obelisks and into the blue beyond them. Beautiful though they were, he wondered how she could believe two pieces of granite raised within the court of Amon could eradicate all the sins of their pasts.

The banquet room bustled with activity as honored officials filed before the head table, their wives on their arms and the scented cones customarily worn on their heads melting over their wigs and making the air heavy with fragrance. Though the congratulating guests meant well, showering the royal family with gifts and bouquets, the banqueting room thickened with a mixture of sweat and perfume.

Moses turned to Tasha, noting her slender arms beneath the sleeves of her robe, her eyes luminous with expectancy. He glanced at the door, wishing he could find them a way of escape and a moment of solitude, but it was not feasible.

"We have only to endure until tomorrow," he whispered. He traced her cheek with his finger, caressing her with his eyes. If it weren't for those seated about him he would have taken her in his arms and expressed his love for her at that very moment.

Nefru looked their way, her features sharp and her eyes shrewd. Swirling the wine in her goblet, she glanced across the room at Isis who sat near the High Priest. As if on cue, the consort rose and crossed the floor to where a servant stood. The scantily clad maiden with a string of beads about her abdomen balanced the jug on her shoulder, preparing to serve the royal table.

Isis eyed the jug, the pounding drum and tambourine making it impossible to hear her own voice. She spoke as loudly as she dared, pointing to her table, but the girl shook her head, gesturing to the head table instead. Again Isis pointed, glaring at the girl. Setting the jug aside, the maid left the room.

Isis glanced about, seeing the royal family's attention focused on a nearly naked juggler who promenaded about the room tossing colored balls into the air to a lively tune. Pulling a vial from her sleeve, she leaned over the jug and was about to open it when the servant returned with a fresh jug of wine. Isis tucked the vial back into her sash.

"Here you are, my Lady." The girl caught the attention of an unoccupied servant who hoisted the fresh jug to her shoulder and sauntered back to Isis' table. With the frustration of a cat in heat, Isis followed the girl, her lips set and her brow furrowed as she seated herself once again beside Puseneb.

"What are you doing?" the High Priest asked, his eyes on his plate as he took another mouthful of roasted quail.

"You'll find out soon enough." Isis tossed Moses a glare. "See how he flaunts his position?"

"And how Nefru detests it," Puseneb put in. "The girl has almost as much venom in her veins as you do. Forget it and enjoy your meal. By tomorrow Thutmose will either be here and our worries ended, or the coronation will take place and Moses will be Pharaoh. Either way, wasting a good meal won't solve anything." Puseneb took another bite.

Isis scowled, lifting her goblet as a servant hurried to refill it. But the purple liquid reminded her too much of her aborted scheme and she set her goblet down again, having lost her thirst.

Puseneb grunted. "Finished already? The night is young and there is still much to enjoy."

"How can you eat at a time like this?" Isis hissed.

"Because there is little else we can do."

"Have you no imagination?" Isis pulled the vial from her sash. "I must think of another plan."

Puseneb nearly dropped his drumstick. "Are you mad?" Realizing he had drawn the attention of several at their table, he forced a smile then lowered his voice to a whispered string of curses. "Put that down! If you're caught —"

"If we're caught," Isis muttered.

Puseneb wildly looked about for another place to sit but all the seats were taken. "You'd be better off to poison your own jug," Puseneb rasped.

"That's it!" Isis' red lips lifted at the suggestion. "I'll drop the contents into our own jug then switch the two. I could take the jug back, summon the girl who serves the royal table and proclaim our wine unfit, asking her to search for another. Meanwhile, I will switch this jug for hers."

Puseneb attempted to swallow but the mouthful seemed to stick in his throat. "Forget it and save yourself an execution."

Isis frowned, darting a glance about her table, then, under cover of her sleeve, she tipped its contents into her own jug. Standing, she hailed a servant, demanding he carry it to the main area where she awaited the maiden who served the royal table. At last she caught the girl's eye.

"This wine is unfit. I want it traded for another jug."

Isis padded the comment with a smile but the girl frowned, craning her neck to see if another servant would come to their aid. Unable to summon anyone, she hoisted Isis' jug to her shoulder before Isis could protest, and hurried to the kitchen. If only Isis had a second vial, but she had brought only one. In less time than it took for the event to register in Isis' muddled mind, the slave returned with a fresh jug and resolutely set it at Isis' feet.

"Here, my Lady." The girl's eyes flashed. "I hope you are finally satisfied," whereupon the girl lifted her own jug and sauntered toward the royal table.

"What of the other wine?" Isis feebly called after her, suddenly feeling ill.

The girl glanced over her shoulder. "Given to the only ones apparently fit to consume it, poured into the pig slop."

Isis numbly nodded, turning with heavy steps back to her table. She seated herself beside Puseneb, cursing beneath her breath. "I've successfully plotted the murder of a herd of pigs."

Puseneb sighed with relief, peering at her over a crust of sweetbread. "Hopefully they won't trace the malady back to its source." Isis was about to comment on his own likeness to the beasts, when Puseneb stopped and tilted his head. "What was that?"

"What was what?" Isis asked with irritation.

The commotion in the banqueting room subsided as everyone paused to listen to the growing tumult outside.

"By Osiris' beard, a riot!" Puseneb attempted to stand, but his legs weakened and he sat down again. "It's those damned Syrian rebels! They must have broken free from the school in the compound. Now we'll all be killed!" His face drained as the noise swelled.

Moses protectively stood over Tasha, his eyes on the double doors. Other couples cringed about their tables while servants froze mid–step, platters hoisted above their heads or jugs on their shoulders. Hatshepsut commanded a servant to bolt the double doors but before he could do so they burst open and a guard raced into the room.

"Thutmose has returned with all the booty of Syria!"

The guests broke into relieved chatter as Puseneb jumped to his feet, his fear vanished.

Isis' eyes widened, her mouth open, and for the first time that Puseneb could recollect, she was too stunned to speak.

"Didn't I tell you he'd come?" Puseneb chided, the mixture of wine and elation making him giddy.

Hatshepsut sat statue–like, watching the space beyond the doors with fixed horror, while Nefru gloatingly turned to Moses as if daring him to react. Moses did not notice her, however, his eyes on Tasha as dread and determination stirred in their depths.

Yet Thutmose did not enter the banqueting hall that night, nor did he request an audience with the Pharaoh. Instead he proceeded to Karnak to deposit his booty, not even requesting a visit with Puseneb or his mother until he had rested.

Meanwhile those attending the banquet couldn't help but wonder how one hot–blooded royal upstart could so unnerve Her Majesty and the heir as to dismantle the coronation feast before it had hardly begun.

At first light Thutmose strode through the near empty sanctuary of Karnak and down the shadowed west corridor, the reliefs of long dead Pharaohs seeming to come to life as he passed beneath the flickering lamps along the wall. He felt tired after having spent the night depositing booty and captives, and had but a few minor matters to attend to before returning to the Delta.

Puseneb's door loomed ahead of him, and without so much as announcing himself, Thutmose stepped into the reception area and through the doors of the inner office where the High Priest sat at his cluttered desk.

Puseneb caught his breath, nearly choking. "Why Thutmose — I'm so glad you've come."

Thutmose's face appeared haggard in the dusty light filtering through the slatted windows. "What is the meaning of this?" He dropped a papyrus onto the Priest's desk.

"I, well —" Puseneb carefully unrolled the parchment, reading it for the first time. "Ah, yes," he chortled. "A celebration in your honor. I, er, that is, there certainly will be a celebration. We couldn't honor you without you being here." He attempted a laugh.

"A ploy to bring me to Thebes so I would join in your scheme against Moses?"

Isis appeared in the doorway standing so still she seemed as much a fixture as the other ornaments. Puseneb glanced at her for support, and Thutmose whirled. "On your death bed, are you?"

Isis attempted a laugh. "The gods must have heard your prayers for my health has returned."

"Do you think I would pray for you?" he retorted.

Isis clenched her teeth, not trusting herself to answer.

Puseneb took a deep breath. "I understand you have blessed us with the booty from two conquests. Sidon and —"

"Tyre."

"Yes, and more captives for our school. It is doing well, though there is always room for improvement," Puseneb noted.

The youth warily eyed him.

Puseneb rose, walking about his desk while attempting to form a plan and muster his confidence all in the same moment. "Because of your successes we thought a commemoration of your achievements in order."

"We?"

"That is, I wish to acknowledge your accomplishments, your conquests at Gaza, Joppa, and now Sidon and Tyre. You seem over modest, Thutmose." Puseneb smiled with effort. "Even the Pharaoh acknowledges your victories."

"It seems she absorbs herself more with her own honor than mine. I've seen the two obelisks in the sanctuary."

"Quite a feat." Puseneb looked down at the papyri on his desk, not wishing to bring Hatshepsut or Moses into the conversation. He cleared his throat. "I have felt for some time the gods wish to honor you for your generosity."

Thutmose watched him with hawk–like eyes. "I leave tomorrow for the Delta."

"But you can't!" Isis blurted. "I mean, wouldn't you like to attend the coronation?"

"And hear you harp about how you feel it should be me? If I know you, you're up to something, and I don't plan to be part of it. Ebny is dead because of your schemes, and now my own Officer plots with you." He shook his head. "I've had enough of your folly. The farther I am from the ceremony the better."

Puseneb folded his fat fingers beneath his chin, trying to devise a convincing argument. "Whatever Isis thought to be true is out of her hands now, as even you must realize. We know you are gifted and blessed, but wouldn't dream of suggesting you replace Moses as heir. The ceremony is scheduled for tomorrow, and what the gods have ordained will be. A decision of such magnitude is theirs alone."

Thutmose skeptically watched him, unconvinced.

Puseneb's own words had sparked a notion and his features brightened. "It is the gods who ultimately decide such matters, do they not? If they feel you deserve recognition for your conquests then accept it with thanksgiving." He shrewdly studied the lad. "Their blessings may prove the help you need to assure your success in future campaigns."

Thutmose pondered his words. True enough. Conquering the confederation at Megiddo would demand more than the usual blessing. "Perhaps. When is the ceremony?"

"Tomorrow morning." Puseneb glanced at Isis. "If you are present I am sure the gods will bestow their blessing. Merely attend the ceremony and accept their honor. Afterward you may leave."

Thutmose watched him with reservation. "If it means the gods' blessing I suppose I could attend, but I'll not stay a day longer."

Puseneb let out his breath with relief, nodding in agreement. A day was all he needed.

The temple of Karnak overflowed with onlookers who pressed into the outer court and spilled onto the streets of Thebes, each straining for a glimpse of the god's son and Pharaoh–to–be, and the brides he would then wed. The moment had arrived and Egypt's heir was about to take his rightful place.

The noise in the crowded sanctuary subsided as the Priests entered, filling their censors and circling the royal party who stood before the marble dais beneath Amon's temporarily empty shrine. Moses uncomfortably shifted in the stifling heat, yet his eyes were not on the Priests or even on Tasha who stood next to him, but on the two obelisks in the center of the sanctuary, their spires reaching through the open roof and into the sky as if pointing to the sun god himself.

Moses' face softened beneath the light that poured into the court, glancing off his oiled shoulders and causing the simple diadem on his head to shine like a hallowed sphere. In spite of his not being a god's son Amon had blessed him: allowing him life as an infant when all other Habiru his age had died; raising him to the status of a Prince within the royal house; seeing him through the terrors of war and political unrest; granting him the right to know his true family before their deaths; and allowing him to aspire to heights of unequalled accomplishment within Hatshepsut's administration, to the point of lifting two obelisks within Amon's very temple; then being crowned Regent, and now Pharaoh.

The truth seemed to expand within him as if by divine revelation, and he took a deep breath, swelling his chest with the realization. In spite of his parentage the gods had watched over him, setting him apart from even the most privileged Egyptian and honoring him above all other men.

Hatshepsut moved to his side, taking the double diadem from her own head and holding it toward Puseneb who spoke a blessing over it. At his pronouncement, four white robed Priests entered, carrying aloft the icon of Amon as they circled before the dais. Puseneb followed, taking the crown from Hatshepsut and raising it aloft.

Moses watched them parade before the royal party, their eyes unmoving as if in a trance. He glanced at Tasha who stood beside him, her expression reflecting rapturous anticipation. The space before the dais widened as the Priests promenaded in a growing circle, clearing the center of the court around the royal family as all watched.

"The god Amon blesses you. The god, Amon, chooses his successor, searching for one to fill the position left by his daughter, Maat Ka Re Hatshepsut."

Moses shot a questioning look to the High Priest but he did not seem to notice. Instead, Puseneb lifted his eyes heavenward, absorbed in the sacredness of the moment. Moses pursed his brow, his body tense, while Tasha reached from the folds of her robe and clasped his hand, her fingers warm and responsive. Hatshepsut seemed at once alert, while Nefru gloated at her side.

"It is for this reason the god chooses his successor," Puseneb reiterated. The Priests slowed their pace, circling in a soft shuffle of steps.

Moses glanced at Hatshepsut whose face remained fixed on the deity, while Nefru expectantly held her breath. The Priests stopped across the room from Moses.

"The god has chosen..."

Slowly rotating, they turned their backs to him.

"...the god's true son and successor...."

A hush fell over the crowd.

"...Men Khepru Re Thutmose."

Moses' eyes widened as Tasha's hand fell from his grasp. All movement ceased as each absorbed the meaning of the words. A low rumble began at the front of the court and gained momentum as if a huge wave crested above the temple threatening to wipe out the sanctuary.

Thutmose stared, unable to take his eyes from the god. Had he dreamt it? Gods, what had happened? He looked across the room at Moses who stood motionless with shock, his face as white as limestone; then at

Hatshepsut who appeared locked in a moment from which she could not escape.

Lifting the crown for all to see, Puseneb ceremoniously placed it on Thutmose's head. The youth dropped his jaw and turned to Isis, but she wisely lowered her eyes as if too absorbed in reverent worship to notice. He searched Puseneb's face but saw nothing in answer to his questions. How? Why?

As if on cue, Nefru stepped from her place from between Moses and Hatshepsut, and crossed the floor to where Thutmose stood. Positioning herself at his side, she lifted her head as Puseneb waved a censor about them, pronouncing his blessing on the marriage of the royal pair.

Nefru possessively wrapped her hand about Thutmose's arm, surprised at its firmness. She glanced up into his face but he stood immobile, having as much difficulty comprehending the moment as those about him.

Without warning Hatshepsut crumpled to the floor, weeping, while several attendants hurried to her side, leading her out of the sanctuary. Moses' mind whirled, lost in the tumult of the moment as darkness closed about him. Strange, but he felt no fear or pain, only a great numbing emptiness.

He moved as if in a dream, hearing the dull hum of noise about him but not comprehending it, and seeing a blur of bodies but not focusing on anyone in particular. Instead, he led Tasha from the temple and through the crowded court to the confines of their curtained litter. Once inside, though she cradled his hand in hers, he felt nothing at all, not regret, or hatred, or even love.

It was as if the gods had reached toward him with a hallowed treasure, and in a moment of twisted irony, wrenched it from his grasp, taking his soul as well.

CHAPTER 14

Thutmose stood with downcast eyes behind a desk littered with official documents in what would have been Moses' office. Though he had summoned his stepbrother, who now stood before him, he could not bring himself to look at the one whose place the gods had granted him.

Moses chose to break the silence. "You called for me?"

Thutmose lifted his gaze to search Moses' impassive countenance. "I never dreamed to be in this position, Moses."

"I don't need apologies." Moses flexed his jaw, his eyes hard.

Thutmose looked away. "I'm anxious to prepare for my campaign to Megiddo. Already Gaza and Joppa are ours, and well, you've heard the rest." He studied Moses from across his desk, and shook his head. "I had no part in this, Moses. You have to believe me."

"The gods have chosen and you have won," Moses stated. He could feel the color rising to his face, his pulse pounding in his ears. He wanted to slam back through the doors of the audience room, curse the gods, and never look back. Instead he stood immobile, facing the last person on earth he cared to see.

Thutmose cleared his throat. "Of course you'll want to marry Tasha, and you have my blessing." He paused while Moses aloofly studied him. "Marriage to Nefru certainly won't keep me in Egypt. I enjoy my campaigns more than I ever would a wife, especially Nefru. And I am at last to be named General." He stumbled over the words, realizing how they must sound.

"As Pharaoh you have the right."

"In the meantime someone has to oversee the Two Lands." Thutmose circled his desk and sat on the corner, attempting nonchalance. "I have decided to name you Vizier in my absence."

Moses' eyes shot up at him and Thutmose didn't know if surprise or anger crossed his face.

Moses straightened his posture, his back rigid. "I don't need platitudes. Give your position to another."

"But I need your help. I can't be both places at once."

Moses shook his head. "I won't accept a position merely to ease your conscience."

Thutmose slammed his fist onto the desk. "By the gods, Moses, I didn't ask for this. What more can I do but hand you the crown? I need you, Egypt needs you."

Moses' eyes narrowed.

Thutmose glanced at his hands and took a deep breath, rising and studying a map on the wall. "I plan to rebuild Avaris and move the capital north as soon as I return, restoring it as it was during our grandfather's reign. It only makes sense to rule within reach of our northern borders. You're a gifted architect, Moses, you've proven as much. Perhaps you could oversee the rebuilding."

Moses set his lips, his muscles taut. "Is this why you asked me here, to find a place for me within 'your kingdom'?" He emphasized the words as each watched the other.

Thutmose threw up his hands. "All right then, find your own position, though I can't imagine why the gods would waste your talent."

He eyed Moses as if attempting to decipher the answer. "There is a project needing attention, however." His eyes narrowed. "It concerns the Habiru."

Recognition flashed across Moses' face but Thutmose pretended not to notice.

"The more we oppress them the more they multiply. It's as if they thrive on abuse. If they were ever to join the Hyksos against us," he grunted, "I'd hate to imagine the outcome. But I don't intend to let that happen." The two studied each other. "I plan to reinstate my grandfather's death edict for all male Habiru infants."

Moses froze, hearing the words as if in a dream.

Thutmose's gaze intensified. "If I can't employ your talents elsewhere, perhaps you would help with the task."

Moses watched him with revulsion. "You're asking me to help murder innocent babies?"

"I know you have little stomach for bloodshed, but the Habiru are an abomination to begin with. Surely you don't object to 'controlling their numbers'?"

Moses willed his muscles to move, measuring his response. "You asked me to oversee the rebuilding of Avaris." He paused, his jaw tightening. "I accept your offer — under one condition," their eyes met, "that you withdraw the edict."

Thutmose allowed himself a low laugh, realization pounding in his brain. "Why should it matter?"

"Because the Habiru represent our best labor force, they live in Goshen within reach of Avaris, and could easily be recruited for the task. If we kill their young they would either turn on us or lose their will to work. Either way we cut our own throats."

"You would risk Egypt's welfare to spare several thousand slaves?"

"No. To build Egypt's future."

A question wrinkled Thutmose's brow but he attempted to control his response, and nodded. "Very well, you may supervise the rebuilding and I will withdraw the edict, for now. I will see how well these Habiru work and how hard you crack the whip over their backs."

Moses searched his face, wondering if he knew. Fear awakened every nerve in his body, his senses sharp. "I'll leave as soon as I can make ready a ship."

Thutmose warily watched him. "You might as well wait until my own ships can accompany you as my army is soon to leave for Megiddo. In the meantime I plan to keep a close watch on the Delta."

Hatshepsut attempted to sit up when Moses entered, her face gaunt in the brightness of her bedchamber. A breeze whispered through her curtains, making the heat bearable.

She reached out her arms. "Moses, I had hoped you would come."

He took her hands, wondering at her sudden illness and lack of strength. "Have the physicians determined what plagues you?"

She shook her head. "The gods have wreaked their vengeance at last, I am afraid. One can't battle them forever and win." A tear escaped in spite of her smile.

Moses squeezed her hands, glancing about to see who attended her. Had the gods truly done this or was there another explanation? He noted a tray of unfinished lunch. "You haven't eaten."

She waved her hand, turning her face from the food. "I don't have the stomach for it. It seems the cooks take less care with what they serve me now that I am less than Pharaoh."

He nodded, making a mental note to have a word with them. He took a seat near her bed. "I'm going north to Avaris with Thutmose to oversee the rebuilding of the new capital."

Her face momentarily lit then fell at the realization of his departure. "I'm afraid I've been too long at Thebes to consider such a notion myself," she said. "Someone has to look after the palace and Karnak." She sighed, looking up at him. "I'm just grateful to the gods we weren't all killed. I feared Thutmose would take his vengeance out on us, but he has been merciful." She gave a bitter laugh. "Who are we to question the gods, but Thutmose, of all people?"

Moses strode to her open balcony peering out at the view she had enjoyed these many years: at the ships languidly drifting up and down the Nile like white winged birds; at the city spread beneath them in a scatter of white blocks and spires; and at the sun burnishing the far reaches of the desert with a brilliance too bright to gaze upon.

"I wondered about relocating you to the palace at Pithom." Moses turned to watch her response. "I thought you might like to live there again. I could make the arrangements."

Hatshepsut's eyes darkened with a secret premonition, and she changed the subject. "Nefru seems happy. Have you seen her?"

Moses shook his head, glad he had not. He refrained from asking her the same question, somehow knowing what she would say. "I'm sure she is busy as Queen."

"Meryet says she has doubled her attendants and has all the dressmakers in a whirl." Hatshepsut chuckled. "Nefru always did insist on a flawless appearance, even as a child." She looked into Moses' face and sighed again. "It matters little now. Soon she also will leave."

Moses noted the dark circles beneath her eyes, her ghostlike pallor, and the loose hair frayed about her face. She looked old and spent, and he wondered how he could have thought her strong enough to make the journey north. "Perhaps you can join us once you are well."

He watched for some promise on her part but she shook her head, repositioning herself with effort and taking another sip from her goblet. "No, Moses. If Thutmose allows, I'll stay here for whatever time the gods grant me."

Moses started to argue but she lifted a hand in protest. "As much as I love my children, I love the gods more. Here at Thebes is where I belong, close to Amon until —" She avoided his eyes, taking another sip and leaving the thought unfinished.

Moses' face clouded with compassion and concern. "I sail tomorrow and may never see you again."

A tear slid down her cheek unheeded, and she nodded. "I know." She closed her eyes at the thought, leaning back against her cushions. "Perhaps in paradise when Osiris judges the actions of an impetuous Princess he will weigh them against the greater evil of ignoring the cries of an infant doomed for death." She looked into his face, a glimmer of purpose shining in her eyes. "Perhaps somewhere in the scheme of things mercy will be thought a virtue."

Moses watched her, struck by the irony of his own rescue mission, much the same. Yet his lay ahead of him while hers remained a memory. He bent and kissed her forehead, wishing he could see the same peace on her face he had seen on Jochebed's.

"Until paradise then.... Goodbye, mother." He left the thought unfinished, looking a last time at the frail form before walking from the room and quietly closing the door behind him.

Nefru held the cloth at arm's length then laid it against her cheek. "It pales me, don't you think?" She snatched up an embroidered linen piece and turned to the mirror. "Ah, this is better. I'll take a gown of this fabric for banqueting, something with sleeves. I hear the evenings are horribly cool in the Delta."

"My Lady," the dressmaker anxiously surveyed the pile already committed to become garments, summoning the courage to plead for more time, then thought better of it, "will there be anything else?"

"Did the merchant from Tyre bring any fabric besides those ghastly gaudy weaves? Something lighter, perhaps?"

"There's this purple length, Your Highness." The dressmaker lifted it from the pile just as an announcement sounded at the door.

"His Majesty to see the Queen."

Nefru put off answering Thutmose and glanced at the fabric's depth of color. "Yes, make me a cloak of it for the evenings. Now off with you, and see that I have the turquoise gown for my departure on the morrow."

The dressmaker's eyes widened and her jaw dropped but she said nothing as she hastily bowed toward the servant's exit, motioning her assistants to follow with the chosen fabrics.

No sooner had they closed the door than Thutmose entered by way of another, agitated at the delay. He nodded toward the heap of rejected cloth. "I see you are putting your vanity to use."

Nefru inspected the henna on her nails. "A Queen ought to dress the part, don't you agree? I've too long endured the sight of my mother in garments more suited to her attendants than royalty. A god's wife deserves the best."

"You flatter me." His words dripped with sarcasm though his face remained expressionless. "I've heard your mother is ill. If you wish to stay with her here in Thebes, you may."

"And miss the excitement of the move? Not by Osiris' beard."

"Then come if you like, but there won't be a palace to live in until Moses rebuilds it."

"Speaking of Moses," Nefru sauntered to her vanity, eyeing her reflection in the bronze mirror, "has he requested Tasha as his wife?"

"What if he has? I'm sure he would like to."

She whirled. "What does it matter what he would like?"

Thutmose grunted, covering his surprise at her outburst. "If I choose to grant the Overseer of All Royal Architecture the pleasure of a wife, I'll do so without asking you."

Nefru's nostrils flared. "Don't you even know? Hasn't it dawned on you yet who Moses really is? Will you propagate more Habiru at Egypt's expense?"

"This is foolishness." Thutmose's lip curled, seeing through her scheme. "You still want his blood, don't you? Isn't it enough that I've taken the crown and the kingdom?"

Nefru stepped toward him with the boldness of a lioness. "I want Tasha as my personal slave, to care for my wardrobe and see to my needs."

"She is no one's slave."

"But she ought to be."

"Why, to further wound Moses?" Thutmose's eyes narrowed over a grim smile. "That's what you really want, isn't it? Is it because losing you was what mattered least to him?"

Nefru's eyes flashed, but she had a ready weapon on her tongue. "Do you think I don't know about your 'conquests' in Syria, about the women you take captive for your pleasure?"

Thutmose studied her with a sneer, her words widening the gulf between them. He had chided himself more than once for not bringing the wench from Tyre. "I am Pharaoh and will do as I please without question. If I want a concubine I'll take one, and if you want to enjoy your life as Queen you'll not mention it again."

Nefru lifted her chin. "If our marriage means so little, perhaps I'll bear a son by a concubine of my own."

Before she could move Thutmose grabbed her wrist so tightly she cried out in pain. He clenched his teeth, his face close to hers. "If you so much as think of defiling my bed with the seed of some mortal pig I'll denounce you so quickly you'll not even remember what it was like to be Queen."

Nefru met his gaze with a challenge. "While denying yourself the privilege of a royal heir?"

He roughly unhanded her, disgust twisting his features. "You forget your sister, Meryet."

Nefru lifted a brow, attempting an answer but the comment toppled her confidence, knocking her arguments from her as surely as if he had struck her a physical blow.

Thutmose coldly eyed her. "If you care to remain at Thebes we'll both enjoy the reprieve, otherwise plan to live at Pithom. The needed renovations should occupy you."

Nefru massaged her wrist but said nothing.

"Be ready by sunrise or stay behind. It matters little to me." He threw her a last glance, wondering why fate had compelled the gods to give him a wife so like his mother.

Isis watched Thutmose's fleet disappear around the northern bend of the Nile, the dark earth on either side of the bank evidence that the season of Akhet was beginning to wane. She glanced at Hatshepsut's litter and smiled. The former Pharaoh, who had also come to watch, hadn't even the strength to stand, but sat within the confines of her carrier with her curtain drawn.

Puseneb noticed Isis' preoccupation and bent toward her. "I can't say I'll miss going north with the rest of Thutmose's administration, what with the Hyksos and Keftiu lurking about. Besides, Amon can always use a Priest at Thebes as surely as in the outposts of the Delta."

Isis' mouth curved upwards. "I'm sure the gods had you in mind when they created your profession. It's the only one where cowardice is lauded a virtue."

Puseneb glared. "I notice you weren't any too eager to join them."

Isis laughed, deep and throaty, but beneath her tone laid a viciousness that made him shudder. "I have a task to finish here at Thebes. Why leave to chance what I can bring about myself?"

Puseneb warily nodded, glancing at Hatshepsut's litter. "Just be sure you go about it slowly enough so as not to be detected."

Isis' dark eyes glittered like a serpent's. "Don't worry, Puseneb. Only the gods will know to thank me."

Thutmose's eyes narrowed on Moses' ship as it snaked ahead of his through the Wadi toward Pithom. The fleet had already passed Memphis, marked by lush vegetation as far as the eye could see and pyramids jutting skyward like gigantic prisms of light. Here at the apex of the Nile its tributaries stretched in every direction like the branches of a great bay tree. Thutmose had chosen the easternmost branch, the Wadi Tumilat, for good reason, for it held the secrets of Moses' birth and the means of either enticing him to full disclosure, or repulsing him enough to prove his innocence.

Thutmose leaned toward Rekmire. "I want Moses watched." His face hardened. "I don't fully trust him. There's something wrong."

Rekmire laughed. "And you're just now discovering it?"

"Even a condemned man deserves fair judgment."

Rekmire searched the verdant landscape ahead of the fleet. He would reserve comment until he had evidence of who Senmut Re Moses really was.

Thutmose nodded to a tiny cluster of rounded roofs that appeared more like bee hives in the distance than a village perched on the wadi. "On the other hand," he noted, "I don't want the masses of Habiru given opportunity to rebel. If Moses hands them mallets and chisels there's no telling where they'll aim them. As Vizier, I expect you to maintain order."

Rekmire met his gaze. "Believe me, no one will try anything as long as I'm in control, but I'll need more guards."

"You may have them. The Habiru mean nothing to me."

"And I'll need Overseers, the fiercest and most ruthless I can find."

"You may pick them from among my own troops."

A smile crept over Rekmire's face. "Then I have all I need: plenty of muscle and the freedom to use it."

Aaron studied the lines of Habiru marching along the northern highway to Avaris, conscripted for service in rebuilding Thutmose's capital. Dust billowed about them, defusing the sunlight but not lessening the heat that penetrated even in the shade. A burley Overseer cracked his whip across the back of an elderly Habiru who toppled at the blow.

Aaron turned to Moses. "What in Hades do they think they're doing? If the Overseers keep this up, they'll kill off the Habiru before they get to Avaris."

"Not if I can help it." Moses whipped his horse to a run, summoning the Overseer. "You there, your name."

The man's eyes narrowed. "Peku. Why?"

"Unless you want that whip across your own back you'd better go easy."

The Overseer's face hardened. "That's not what I was told."

Moses reined his mare, sidling closer. "And what was that?"

"If you want to know ask Rekmire. He's in charge of the work crews."

Moses looked northward where Rekmire had already taken the first group. A growing foreboding tightened in his chest as he rode back to Aaron. "I don't like the feel of this."

Aaron searched his face. "They're baiting you, aren't they?"

Moses nodded. "Why else would Thutmose force us to use the Habiru while allowing his Syrian captives to fatten themselves in our schools?"

"Next they'll be taking our women."

Moses shot him a wary glance. Both Tasha and Miriam had stayed behind at the village of Tju. He took a deep breath, sweat glistening on his brow. "I'm riding ahead to give Rekmire some company."

"Be careful," Aaron whispered, watching him go, "and may Yahovah go with you."

Moses rode until nearly noon before catching sight of Rekmire and the first party of slaves. He slowed his horse to a trot, nearing the group of Habiru who stood by the road in the sun while Rekmire and his Overseers sat in an almond grove, circulating a skin of water.

Moses dismounted, tying his mare to a branch while Rekmire rose to meet him, a sneer on his face. "Come to inspect our progress?"

"That's right. I'm in charge of this project start to finish, including the transport of slaves," Moses declared.

Rekmire crossed his arms, the gold bands about his biceps glinting. "Just what is it you question?"

Moses clenched his jaw, his expression impervious. "You'll get more work out them if you don't kill them first."

Rekmire's eyes danced, his brow raised in mock concern. "Well now, have we sympathy for slaves? If we lose one we'll merely replace it with another, as there are plenty to choose from, even if we have to supplement them with women."

Moses stood so near him Rekmire could feel his breath on his face. "If you intend to make this a butchery, think again."

Rekmire backed up a step, stifling a chuckle. He turned to a messenger who Moses recognized as having been in Isis' employ. "It's been brought to my attention that we need to treat our laborers with more care, which means more attendants. Ptamen, ride back to Tju and gather a group of women to disperse our water skins. A little beauty brightens even the ugliest task."

Fear and anger pounded in Moses' chest as he clenched his teeth. He wanted to grab Rekmire by the throat but refrained with effort. If he left now for Tju ahead of the messenger he could spare Miriam and Tasha, but if he rode to Avaris and confronted Thutmose he might be able to help more than just two. Ignoring Rekmire's insolence, he swung atop his steed, leaving the grove in a cloud of dust.

Daylight hung low in the western horizon by the time Moses entered Avaris. He slowed his horse to a trot, noting a bustle of activity evidencing the arrival of Thutmose and his army. Pharaoh had put his troops in charge of clearing the remains of the former palace and temple, which was reduced to heaps of rubble on either side of the avenue, ready for removal. Handfuls of soldiers strained to clear the debris, loading it onto carts and hauling it out of the city. Watching the Egyptians sweat at their own tasks seemed to ease the intensity of his burden.

Moses recognized Thutmose's chariot and slowed near the ruins of the former palace, dismounting. A wide marble terrace stretched across what was left of the palace grounds with two lone pillars reaching into the sky, having once supported a roof and walls. In a corner of the terrace a couch lay under the shade of an overhanging tree, partly hidden by a canopy of sheets.

"Greetings." Thutmose crossed the courtyard with a woman on his arm, her hair hanging to her waist.

At once Moses sensed a coolness in the Pharaoh's countenance and wondered if he had made the right choice. He nodded to the woman before addressing Thutmose. "So this is the site of the palace?"

"It is." Thutmose clasped the woman's hand and strolled to the edge of the terrace. Beyond the ruins of half walls and heaps of brick a cliff dropped to the sea creating a tantalizing view.

Thutmose nodded. "My grandfather, though he named Avaris his capital, never had the chance to properly rebuild the palace. I intend to complete the task."

Moses picked up a piece of broken pottery, and sardonically noted, "Looks like the Hyksos did a thorough job."

"They weren't as destructive as neglectful," Thutmose countered, "having no idea how to maintain the city. They were shepherds out of place in the splendor of Egypt." He watched Moses as if emphasizing the words. "What brings you here, other than surveying your future project?"

"Rekmire."

Thutmose chortled, motioning the girl to the couch and levelling his gaze on Moses. "You don't approve of his 'tactics'?"

"Since when does Egypt conscript the elderly and women?"

Thutmose glanced at his own woman. "It all depends on what you have in mind." A servant interrupted with a platter of fruit. Thutmose chose a fat fig, biting into the succulent pulp and nodding for Moses to help himself, though he refused. Thutmose continued, "As for the elderly, they've little left of this life anyway."

Moses flexed his jaw. He wanted to whirl Thutmose about and slam his fist into his supercilious face but he held himself back. "What about the daughter of a Kushite Chieftain, the Princess Tasha? Does she fall into the same category? It would be a shame to start a war over the indiscretion of an Overseer."

The silence lengthened between them and Thutmose hardened his visage. "What does Tasha have to do with this?"

"She chose to stay in Tju where Rekmire is gathering women to serve his crew."

"Then she has chosen her fate." Thutmose's eyes blazed. "She should be more careful with whom she associates."

Moses watched him with unmasked contempt. What had happened to the Egypt he once knew? Or was he just now seeing it for the first time? He stiffened. Perhaps he could save only one after all.

"You once asked if I would like to take Tasha as my wife." He crossed his arms. "I would, and have come to ask your favor on our union."

Thutmose studied him a long moment. "Why now?"

"Why not?" Moses didn't like playing games. They both knew he had more than one reason for making the request.

Thutmose peered into Moses' face as if looking into his soul. "All right then, marry her, but I can't guarantee your future."

Moses glared with equal fervor before dismissing himself. He would send for Tasha and Miriam at once. With Miriam serving as her maid perhaps he could save them both. He only hoped marrying Tasha would improve her position rather than worsen it.

The sky blushed with the sunset as Moses and Tasha stood under the boughs of a pomegranate tree near an acacia grove within sight of the slave camps. He covered her hands with his as if to shield her from what might come against them, while Aaron blessed their union as fervently and boldly as he dared. He spoke of their God, Yahovah, and of their hope for a future homeland where all Habiru could dwell in safety and freedom.

Moses hardly heard, however, his eyes full of Tasha. Miriam watched them, smiling, and when Aaron's words had ended she motioned him to her side. "I don't think they'll even notice we have gone." Aaron nodded.

Moses tugged Tasha toward him. He bent and kissed her as they melted into each other's embrace. "I should have done this years ago," he murmured, holding her close and reveling in the feel of her next to him. "Think of all we've missed."

She smiled with contentment. "Think of all we will share." She looked up into his eyes. "Oh Moses, I can hardly believe it is happening." She wrapped her arms around his neck, nestling her head against his chest and listening to his heartbeat.

They started back to camp, their arms entwined, listening to the sounds of lapwings that made their nests in the field, and watching the sky blaze as the sun dropped behind the hills in the west. They talked of their plans: how Moses hoped to settle closer to Pithom once he had overseen the rebuilding of the capital, acquiring a salaried position, while keeping as far from Avaris as possible.

"What of Thutmose?" Tasha asked.

Moses did not answer, hugging her tighter and shutting out the foreboding in his spirit at mention of the name. He purposefully skirted the camps of the laborers which Thutmose had ordered set up near Avaris, and steered Tasha toward his own encampment which consisted of the Overseers' tents, their attendants, and the few women who served them. Moses tried not to think about why the women were there, and kissed Tasha's fingers instead, grateful she would not be part of the scheme.

By the time they reached his tent darkness had fallen like a skirt. Neither spoke, thankful their love would be hidden from the eyes of passersby. Glancing down at her, Moses scooped her into his arms. "Remember our favorite spot in the garden?"

Tasha's cheeks burned at the memory. "How could I forget?"

Ducking beneath the tent flap, he closed it snugly behind her, enfolding her in his embrace. Even the uncertainty of what lay ahead of them seemed to lose itself in the hours of the night and the love they had longed to share.

Rekmire strode to Moses' tent just after dawn, jerking open the tent flap as light pierced the shadows, revealing the two huddled forms within. "A summons from Thutmose."

Moses abruptly rose, fastening his kilt and snatching the papyrus from Rekmire. He stepped into the morning light, scanning the parchment as his eyes narrowed to the thinness of a blade. "Why Tasha and why now?"

Rekmire hid his delight behind a smug exterior. "Thutmose needs another water–bearer."

"Then she'll work with me at the temple site."

Rekmire's face lit with a smile. "I wouldn't think of putting her anywhere else."

Tasha hurriedly dressed, leaving with the other girls ahead of the work crew while Moses followed, a knot in his stomach. At the building site hundreds of bodies moved in and out among the piles of brick, the Overseers' striped headdresses standing out amid the blur of activity. Yet Moses hardly noticed the workers or the temple wall that seemed to grow of its own accord. Instead his gaze followed Tasha as she slipped in and out among the Habiru, offering them water. It seemed she gladly tipped the water skin to their lips, heedless of her own discomfort.

Moses watched in wonderment. Didn't she regret coming with him to the Delta? Surely she wished to be anywhere but amid the rabble of slave crews at a building site.

A burly Overseer tugged at her arm and Moses snapped to attention. He recognized the man as Peku whom he had met earlier with Rekmire. The man's meaty hands dropped to the skin as he guzzled a drink.

Moses strode to Tasha's side, retrieving the skin. "Be sure you oversee the workers, Peku, and not the water bearers."

The man wiped an arm across his mouth, his face sullen.

"Now get to work." Moses glanced over his shoulder as a Habiru heralded Tasha, the Overseer following her with his eyes.

A muscle worked in Moses' jaw. If the Overseer so much as touched her....He glanced toward the sun, feeling his ire rise with the heat, and decided to let the thought rest, occupying himself instead with inspecting a plumb line hanging from a half built wall.

He wondered how Miriam had fared, as Thutmose had ordered her to an area just outside the city to serve near the brick pits. Though hardly desirable work, he knew her heart held a tender place for the men who labored there. Aaron had managed to receive a position as a Priest tending to the wounded and elderly, though he must also oversee burying the dead, which Moses feared would be the greater task. He wondered now at the wisdom in bringing them here, but better under his care than Rekmire's.

A commotion on the avenue diverted Moses' attention and he looked up to see a royal litter turn from the road and toward the work site. Nefru opened the curtain, her eyes disdainfully falling on Moses. The workmen moved out of her way as she peered down at him from the shaded recess.

"How does the building progress, Moses? It certainly looks as if you have enough help," she purred, picking Tasha out from the throng.

Moses ignored her, turning to a slate held by a scribe that recorded the progress of the wall.

Nefru continued, undaunted by Moses' rebuff, "Tell me, is this to be the palace? If so, where are my quarters?"

Moses scrawled on the slate and turned to her with obvious contempt. "This is the temple site. Thutmose ordered the palace built last." He watched her face fall. Satisfied, he walked away.

Nefru reddened but soon spied her intended target. "I've been travelling for hours." She fanned herself, eyeing Tasha. "Water girl, fetch me a drink."

Moses watched with annoyance as Tasha wound about the workmen while making her way to the litter, burdened with the weighty skin and nearly tripping over a loose brick.

"Faster or I'll have you flogged." Nefru threw Moses a glance, hiding a smile behind her fan.

Tasha arrived out of breath and dutifully tipped the liquid to Nefru's lips, but Nefru drew back, spilling water on her gown.

"Clumsy waif!" She struck Tasha across the face as the water skin tumbled from her grasp and onto the ground.

"There now, you've wasted it. Fetch me some more and hurry."

Tasha pressed her hand against her cheek, gathering the water skin and looking up in time to see Moses watching them, his expression grim.

He dismounted, walking to the carrier. "It seems you should have concentrated more on drinking and less on speaking." He crossed his arms. "We don't encourage onlookers as they tend to get in the way."

Nefru's nostrils flared. "I'll watch what I like where I like."

"Do so and you might end up a permanent part of this wall."

Nefru tossed her head, dropping the curtain and throwing an order to her servants to find Thutmose.

Tasha reappeared, struggling beneath the weight of the water skin, but Nefru no longer needed her.

Instead the two watched as the litter was carried from the temple site and up the avenue toward the ruins of the palace. If anger had not so consumed him Moses might have smiled, for he could almost feel the ground quake in anticipation of the coming eruption as Thutmose had not left the arms of the Syrian since his arrival.

Chapter 15

Thutmose watched Nefru's litter sway back down the avenue, its gentle movement giving no indication of the fury just unleashed between them. He strode to the edge of the patio, cursing beneath his breath and shaking off the advances of his concubine who had sparked the confrontation.

Summoning a messenger, he blurted, "Send for Amenhab at once. I want the army relocated at the garrison. I've had enough of Avaris." Thutmose motioned to the curtained couch where Nefru had just caught him and the Syrian unawares. "And take down that ridiculous canopy. I want walls, a roof, and a guard. By Amon, if Nefru comes near me again without announcing herself, so help me, I'll —" He sputtered a line of obscenities that made even his messenger blush.

"Yes, my Lord, right away," the man answered, hurrying toward the avenue where Amenhab still worked at directing the removal of rubble.

Thutmose walked to the couch and scowled at the woman whose breasts bulged from the robe she had hastily thrown about herself. Picking up her clothes, he threw them at her.

"Well don't just sit there gawking, get dressed. We're moving to the garrison today. Let Rekmire deal with the building and renovations, I've an army to prepare."

While the Syrian dressed she mumbled words in her own dialect Thutmose could not understand.

He shook his head. "Gods! My wife knows enough Egyptian to blister my ears while all this one can do is mutter in a foreign tongue. Still, if I had to choose between the two —"

Grabbing her arm, he barked an order to his servant to remove the couch and makeshift covering, and prepare the terrace for rebuilding.

The sun pierced the horizon east of the capital where piles of brick and clutter lay beside half-filled carts, void of the soldiers who had previously labored there. Were it not for the Habiru soon to amass at the various building sites, the capital would have seemed deserted.

South of Avaris, however, tents filled the landscape almost to the horizon, making it seem as if the entire city had relocated. In reality, only the slaves and Overseers occupied these temporary dwellings, required to rebuild what presently lay in ruins, which was most of the city. Before the rays of Ra had reached them, the slaves were positioned in rows according to their work crews, preparing for another day of labor, all but Moses. He had ridden out before sunrise to check on Miriam and Aaron, assuring Tasha he would meet her at the temple ruins.

The Overseers gathered around Rekmire who stood in their midst, a whip in his hand, the hefty Peku at his side. "Today we're dividing our efforts and quickening our pace. Thutmose wants the city cleared and the temple raised in equal time. That means fewer men for each task and longer hours. Half will accompany me while the rest serve with Peku."

The order spread from the Overseers down the long lines of slaves like the rumbling of thunder as word was passed among them. The news brought groans as their backs were already stiff and aching from work different than they were accustomed to, even as slaves.

Rekmire walked down the rows, cracking his whip over their heads, and quieting them. "I'm putting Peku in charge of the temple site while I oversee the removal of debris from the city." His face tightened with conviction. "If anyone thinks this an opportunity to ease up, think again, for you'll be the vultures' dinner by nightfall."

As the Habiru moved out along the highway they joined those of other camps who were added to their work force. Rekmire watched as if calculating a plan of his own then bent toward Peku, picking out Tasha from among the women.

The Overseer's face broadened with a grin. "Gladly," he muttered, eyeing Tasha as if about to devour a meal. Throwing Rekmire a knowing nod, he mounted and rode toward the temple site.

The sun had birthed full–bodied by the time Moses arrived at the work site, the slaves having already added a span to the temple's outer wall from its level of the previous day. The backs of the laborers glistened with sweat as they mixed mortar, setting the bricks in place at a furious pace.

Moses had just come from the brick pits, having assured himself of Miriam and Aaron's welfare. Aaron was now exclusively assigned to disposing of the bodies of those unable to keep pace with the rigors of slavery, the numbers of which were growing; and Miriam served water to the laborers. Moses was confident of nothing other than that they were still alive, though they fared better than others around them.

Moses alighted from his horse, searching for Tasha, and smiling with relief when he saw her. He could not find Rekmire, however, though the straining bodies of the Habiru seemed to move twice as fast as they had the day before.

He called to the brick layer nearest the wall. "You there! Take care or you'll have to build it again."

The slave glanced up in annoyance then looked over his shoulder at Peku who walked their way.

The Overseer wore a grin almost as wide as his face, making his bald head appear comical, though his tone was anything but humorous. "There'll be no mercy today, Moses. I'm in charge of the pace, you of the result."

Moses eyed him with contempt. "If the pace determines the result then I'll have a say in that as well."

"Not according to Rekmire who answers to Pharaoh." The Overseer purposefully cracked his whip across the back of an already laboring Habiru, causing him to cry out as the leather left a deep gash.

Moses' eyes narrowed. "Lift that again and you'll wear it around your neck."

The Overseer laughed in response, but Moses was concerned about the slave and called for water. Tasha hurried toward them, burdened with the water skin. Moses lifted it to the workman's back but Peku brought his whip down between them. "I'll mind the workers, architect, you see to the building."

Moses continued to pour but the Overseer knocked the water skin from his hands.

"You're so concerned about these slaves one is tempted to believe the rumor that you are one of them," Peku jeered.

Recognition shot across Moses' face as Peku assessed him, the eyes of the Habiru turning his way.

The Overseer's smile widened. "Water girl, fill that skin and bring me a drink in my quarters." He pointed to a small tent behind the work site, and turned to Moses, his eyes glittering with challenge. "A place where we can have some privacy."

Moses' face drained, followed by hatred as hot as the sun and as keen as his blade. The Habiru nearest him whispered among themselves but Moses did not notice, his attention fixed on Tasha who moved toward the well and filled the water skin as slowly as she dared. Following Peku with reluctant steps, she turned with a last pleading look at Moses before being pulled into the shadowy recess.

"Keep them moving," Moses shouted to the guards. "I have a question for the Overseer."

Moses forced his steps to a casual gait, though he could hear Tasha's screams and cries for help. Just outside the tent he turned and looked about, his hand on his sword, then ducked into the recess of darkness. Instantly the screams ceased, and sometime later Moses and Tasha reappeared as if nothing at all had happened.

The day progressed slowly, the golden orb seemingly fixed in the sky, until at last it began to slip near the western horizon. Moses wiped the sweat from his forehead, glancing at the tent that had remained strangely silent all day. He had told the others Peku had gone to the brick pits to see about increasing their tally to match the pace at the temple site. So far the other Overseers had not questioned him further, though Moses wondered if Rekmire would believe the tale.

Fear beat in his chest and quickened his pulse as he stood over the laborers, a whip in his hand. Tasha glanced at him, her brow etched with concern, but Moses could do little to ease her worries. If he could keep the project moving perhaps Peku's absence would not be immediately noticed.

Moses inspected the wall, checking and re–checking the level. As he scanned the rest of the project he saw two Habiru arguing among themselves, and recognized the first as the man he had aided.

"Quiet you two and get back to work."

Instead of complying, the first struck the second, wrenching a tool from his hand. The second struggled to retrieve it until Moses' whip sliced the air between them. "I said get to work!"

The first man's face twisted with anger. "Who made you our Overseer?"

The words broke a dam of fury and Moses brought his whip down across the man's back with the speed of a striking snake, widening the gash already there. "I should have let Peku have his way with you. Now back to work or you'll see what a whip can really do."

The man jeered with derision, "Will you kill me as you did the Overseer?"

Moses' eyes widened, his limbs, as heavy as stone, refusing to move. The others turned his way as if they also knew his secret. His heart thundered in his chest and his forehead instantly beaded with sweat. Slowly, as if in a dream, he turned and walked toward his horse as Tasha hurried to his side.

He mounted and looked down at her. "It is known."

Tasha gasped, her hand over her mouth. "What will we do? Where will we go?"

"Try to get word to Aaron. Tell him to meet me just after sundown south of the city in the grove of acacia outside our camp."

"What of us, Moses?"

He wiped a tear from her cheek, attempting to memorize the details of her face. "Right now the safest place for you is as far away from me as possible."

The slave stooped through the shadowed opening of Peku's tent as the moon cast a ghastly glow across his back where an open wound still oozed with blood and pus.

"Peku entered this very place and was never seen again," he stated.

Rekmire warily poked his head in and looked about before ducking in after him, his hand on his sword. The darkness was lit by a single torch carried by Rekmire's guard, yet the space was empty. Clearly the body the slave had promised they would find was nowhere in sight. Rekmire eyed the man.

"I tell you I saw Moses and the girl enter and then leave, but the Overseer never left this place," the Habiru insisted, his tone desperate.

"You hoped to buy your freedom with this? What do you think I am?" Rekmire reached for the man's throat, nearly tripping over a rug that covered the ground between them. Surveying the ornate carpet, Rekmire lifted a corner with his sword. "Here, see what lies beneath."

The man threw aside the heavy weave, frantically digging into the sand. Rekmire watched, his eyes narrowing and his pulse quickening. The cavity grew larger until at last a pale hand protruded.

Rekmire stared. The Habiru bent more vigorously, uncovering the face of the Overseer whose his eyes gaped as if horrified himself at the discovery, and whose blood still spilled from a slash across his throat, filling the shallow grave with a pool of red.

"There," the Habiru gasped.

They each stared at the grizzly sight, unable to move.

Finally Rekmire nodded, his face white in the lamplight. "So Moses has slit his own throat at last."

Moonlight shone through the tangled branches of the acacia grove, illuminating the ground in patches of light sliced with shadow. Moses stood so still he appeared to blend with the silhouette of trees and grass. Only the occasional movement of his horse gave him away.

He searched the northern field. Had Tasha managed to get word to Aaron? He only hoped, for Aaron's sake, fewer Habiru had died that day than in days past.

Moses tightened the straps of his packs to his horse, making sure of the water skins dangling on either side and ignoring the impulse to take a drink. He must save the precious liquid for what lay ahead.

Then he heard it, the pounding of hooves over the soft ground as every nerve awakened in his body. Instinctively he withdrew his sword, its edge glinting in the shadows as he watched two riders approach. He noted the slighter form of the second and relaxed his grip.

"It's us, Aaron and Tasha," Aaron called out.

The two dismounted and Moses walked from between the trees, sliding his sword in its sheath. Aaron hugged him in a fierce grip then held him at arm's length.

"Rekmire knows. We saw him on the highway heading toward the garrison. I'm sure a Habiru rode at his side."

Moses searched the distance. "Then I haven't much time."

"We haven't," Tasha corrected. "I'm going with you."

"You can't." Moses shook his head. "The way is treacherous and I have no guarantee of survival."

"I don't care about the risks, I care only about you."

Moses pressed her hand to his lips. "I'd die a thousand times over if anything ever happened to you. In spite of the difficulties, you're safest here. As long as I'm at large Thutmose will spare you, knowing you could eventually draw me back to Egypt."

Moses glanced at Aaron. "Once Thutmose leaves for Megiddo try to smuggle her and Miriam out of Egypt. Caravans leave regularly for the mines at Serabit. Follow the coast to Elath where we'll meet and make passage to Punt."

"You're not fleeing to Syria?"

Moses shook his head. "That's where Thutmose would expect to find me."

Aaron brightened. "Then you'll travel through the land of the Midianites, our distant kin. Their language is similar to ours. They will help if you have need." He pulled a scroll from under his cloak. "All the more reason to pass this treasure on to you. Sooner or later it will be discovered and destroyed anyway. It is the lineage of our family in the handwriting of our father. Guard it, for you will one day come to accept and appreciate it."

Moses nodded and tucked the parchment into his pack, too busy trying to comfort Tasha to focus on anything else. He wrapped his arms around her, gazing into her eyes. "You'll love Punt, it's a paradise unlike any other."

She nodded, blinking back her tears, unable to speak.

Aaron pursed his lips. "It's the desert between that worries me, but come, we don't increase your chances by delaying you."

Moses tipped Tasha's face to his, wishing the moment could last forever. "I love you, Tasha. I will always love you, and no amount of distance or time will change that."

Tasha reached up and pressed her lips against his, tears clinging to her lashes like dew, reflecting the moonlight. "I'll wait for you, Moses, if it takes a lifetime."

He hugged her to him. "In the spring as soon as Thutmose marches I'll look for you both at Elath, with Miriam, if you can manage it." He pulled a pouch from his sash. "This should help buy your way. Bury it until you need it." He handed it to Tasha, kissing her a last time.

Aaron pulled him aside. "Here, take my cloak. It will make you less noticeable in the darkness."

Moses unclasped his white cape and threw Aaron's roughly woven one about his shoulders then mounted. He gripped Aaron's arm. "Watch over her, Aaron, by the god you serve."

"I will, now go."

Moses turned in the opposite direction of Avaris, pulling back on the reins and looking a last time at Tasha, her face small in the moonlight. "I'll see you in the spring, my love. Until then you will be in my dreams."

Tears trickled down Tasha's face as she nodded, biting back the urge to cry out. Aaron wrapped an arm around her as together they watched him diminish into the night, the rhythm of his horse's hooves heard long after he had vanished, until even their steady beat faded into silence.

The face of the moon peeked through a high window, lighting a patch on the bed where Thutmose and his concubine lay when Rekmire burst through the door.

Thutmose sprang from the sheets, fumbling for his sword while the woman at his side attempted to cover her breasts.

Realizing it was Rekmire, Thutmose menacingly pointed his blade. "I'll have your head for this."

Rekmire whitened. "I knew you'd want to know, my Lord." He plunged ahead. "Moses has escaped after killing an Overseer."

Thutmose's jaw dropped. "He what? Who? Where?"

"Peku. We found him just now under his tent. More witnesses than I can count saw Moses enter, and now he's gone, left the temple site earlier today."

Thutmose adjusted his kilt, reaching for his scabbard and bolted to the door. "Guards, summon Amenhab and a detachment, now!" He strapped on his sandals and threw a cloak about his shoulders. "Which direction?"

"East, I'm sure of it."

A trumpet sounded as men poured from their quarters, securing their weapons and hurrying to the stables.

"I want action, now!" Thutmose jumped atop his steed. "Post a squad at every road leading from Avaris and send a detachment to Moses' camp."

Rekmire shook his head. "He's likely already gone and has probably taken his wife with him. She's the reason he killed the Overseer."

"He'll soon be ours and I want him alive. If you find nothing at Avaris, follow me to the border. He's headed for Syria, alright, but I'll not let him escape." Thutmose jabbed his heels into his horse, his limbs taut as together they lurched into the darkness toward the eastern highway.

Tasha stared out the opening of her tent and into the starry expanse while tears trickled down her face. She missed Moses more than she could bear, though they had known the joy of married love only briefly. Had Moses made it to the desert? She felt the need to pray, to petition her god. Yet if her god had not heard her at Thebes why would he hear her in the Delta? Perhaps she should pray to Amon. He had answered her once.

Realization bolted through her. No! Amon belonged to the Egyptians and they too would petition him.

Emptiness engulfed her. She had no one: no god, no husband, no family. She felt as if she stood in a vast wilderness, empty and alone. Kneeling, she bowed her head toward the earth, giving way to the grief that consumed her.

She thought of Aaron and Miriam. What would Thutmose do to them in his rage? If only a god existed big enough to reach across the starry expanse and help each of them in their separate places. She thought of Aaron's god. He had said somewhere above the sky Yahovah looked down on mankind as a father would his children. Still, he was not a god she could see or touch. Tasha felt a sinking sensation. A god she couldn't see? What kind of god was that?

A breeze tugged at the tent flap and caressed her cheek, and she wondered: could one see the wind? Or love? Or life itself? These were real though invisible forces. Might a god exist as real as the unseen elements of this world?

Hope surged through her as she lifted her tear streaked face to the sky. "Oh great Yahovah," she whispered, "if you are god and can hear my prayer, spare Moses. Keep him from danger, and if possible, bring us together again that we might renew the love we have known."

She closed her eyes, feeling no different than before, save for a tiny flame of hope kindled deep within her breast.

A full moon lit Thutmose's way as he neared the border, his men galloping at a furious pace behind him. He had seen no sign of Moses though he had ridden most of the night. Then, topping a hill, a rider sprang to the road ahead of him.

"There he is!" Thutmose shouted over his shoulder. "Amenhab, cut through that vineyard."

Amenhab and two of his Officers bounded off the road, though Thutmose's eyes never left the rider who raced through the moonlight as if being pursued by spirits of the nether world. Amenhab lunged back onto the highway behind the one whose cloak billowed like a ghostly pall. Yet when they neared the fork leading east to the desert and west to Goshen the rider veered west causing Amenhab and his horse to skid from the road. Thutmose passed him as Amenhab scrambled to remount.

Stretches of grassland, blue beneath the moon's glow, blurred past them while the pounding of horses' hooves beat a steady rhythm in the night. Here and there the all but abandoned villages of the Habiru bore silent witness of the recent rebuilding in Avaris, only the occasional moan of cattle could be heard.

They rode for what seemed hours in the direction of Pithom. Amenhab pulled in front of Thutmose, his arms lifting with each stride. "I'll try for him again."

A growing fear gnawed in Thutmose's stomach but he ignored it, intent on the chase. Suddenly the rider turned off the road toward the slave village of Tju. Why would Moses return to a slave village? There was nothing there for him. An unnamed apprehension tightened in Thutmose's chest as the rider leapt from his horse, his cape reflecting the moonlight. He disappeared into the village with Amenhab only a few steps behind.

Thutmose dismounted before the otherwise quiet village. "I want every hut searched," he barked. He started for the nearest hovel when Amenhab motioned to a nearby building, the only brick edifice in the village.

They cautiously entered the structure, swords drawn. Then they saw him. There in the dim shadows a man bowed on the floor as if imploring an unseen ruler.

Thutmose approached. "Rise Moses, you're as good as dead."

The man stood, his body bent and weary. He turned.

Thutmose's eyes widened, his jaw dropping. "By Amon, it's Aaron." Knotting his fists in rage, he cuffed the Habiru across the face, letting loose a tirade of curses. "Where's Moses, where did he go? Tell me or die."

Aaron stood his ground without flinching, his gaze fervent.

Thutmose clenched his teeth, turning from the man and throwing an order over his shoulder. "I want him tortured until he talks, and he will talk." He strode to the door. "Lower him to the status of a slave, and post extra guards around him and his family. I want no chance of their escape."

Amenhab wrinkled his brow. "Aaron serves as a Priest, my Lord."

"Who do you think he really worships? We're standing in a temple built to his god, Yahovah." Thutmose glared. "Come morning I want it levelled and everything in it burned."

Thutmose stepped outside, his fists knotted at his sides and his breathing ragged with rage. His eyes swept the village that seemed strangely serene in light of his presence. He heard a shuffle behind him as Amenhab joined him, but Thutmose did not turn around. Instead, he spoke into the night as if speaking to himself. "Where would you go if you were Moses?"

Amenhab paused. "To Syria, I suppose."

Thutmose nodded. "East to join with our enemies and the Hyksos coalition." He took a breath of the night air, attempting to cool his thoughts and refocus. "Any question as to where we'll be headed by morning?"

Sunrise crushed the sweetness from a bed of lilies just outside Hatshepsut's balcony, wafting its scent heavenward and into her room, yet she hardly noticed, lying so still and white upon her sheets.

A physician rose from a corner, searching for the steady rise and fall of her chest. Had it ceased? He lifted his brow as a second physician noiselessly tiptoed to her bed.

The first put an ear to her mouth then sighed with relief. "Thank Amon, she lives."

"Perhaps the potion the High Priest ordered has helped," the other offered.

The first nodded as they conferred about the suddenness of her illness and its implications. Had the gods truly cursed her, as was rumored? Or was this the result of Syrian foreigners in their midst? The gods only knew what plagues and curses they brought with them.

The physicians bent their heads in tragic agreement, looking a last time at the sleeping form before returning to their vigil.

Hatshepsut sensed their presence and willed her fingers to move but they merely trembled at the effort. She wanted to cry out, to escape the body holding her captive, to be free. The thought stunned her. Did she long for death? No, a thousand times no, but for life more vigorous and vibrant than she had ever known. Gods! She wanted to run, to skip as a child, to feel the breeze in her hair and smell the lilies of the field as they brushed against her skin.

She opened her eyelids a slit, seeing the room about her and the two physicians converged in the corner. She tried to call their names but no sound escaped her lips. Was this death? If so, why did she feel so alive, aware of everything around her, of every scent, sound, and detail? She smiled to herself. So the ancient inscriptions of life beyond the door were true. If this was death then she would fight it no longer.

She closed her eyes in submission, breathing air that seemed to buoy her up from her bed and beyond herself. The scent of lilies surrounded her, reminding her of that morning long ago when she had swam like a fish in the Nile, hearing the cries of a child and chancing upon a basket afloat among the reeds. She could almost hear it now, the river blending with the sounds of geese and the rustle of bulrushes in the wind.

"Moses." She breathed his name like a prayer, and wondered how he fared. Strange, but she felt closer to him now than when he had last stood by her bed. How she loved him, though he had never really been hers. She cringed at the thought. Why had Amon not accepted the child she so readily clutched to her bosom? Why had the gods rejected them both?

Surely Amon knew she had not meant to defy him. Instead, young and spirited, she had merely hoped for a higher ideal: the salvation of this child, and of her own right to rule. She half smiled. Willful? Yes. At last she would admit it, though she could not speak the word. 'Stubborn as a thorn,' her mother used to say. Now, too late, she realized its truth.

Yet, was mercy wrong? She had heard how the guards had plunged their blades through the soft bellies of the infants, tossing them to the wadi where crocodiles lunged to fatten themselves on the tender Habiru flesh. She could envision their bodies and remains even now as she had seen them near Pithom, hundreds sprawled in death about the villages and on the banks of the wadi, discarded like refuse.

Inwardly she had recoiled. She had hated her father for it, and as much as told him so. Perhaps that was why he had always suspected Moses.

Mercy, kindness, compassion...were these attributes she should only show Egyptians? Why not the Habiru?

No, she could not believe, even now, that she was wrong. How could the gods condemn her for the one redeemable act she had dared commit?

She felt her neck stiffen at the thought and slowly exhaled, letting go of all the anger and bitterness she had held inside.

In its place a surreal peace filled her and she took a deep breath as of new air, opening her eyes to an expanse of green as lush as any in the Delta. Geese called overhead and she looked up to watch their flight across the sky. A breeze whispered through the reeds on the riverbank, tousling her hair and moving like a presence among the trees. She lifted a hand and tucked a tendril of hair behind her ear, then laughed aloud and turned to see if the physicians had noticed.

Strange, but they weren't anywhere around, nor was the room in which she had lain. Only a faint strain of weeping could be heard, lost in the sudden beating of her heart and her own cries of joy.

PART II

"I will even make a way in the wilderness,
and rivers in the desert."
Isaiah 43:19b

CHAPTER 16

In the pre–dawn darkness Thutmose and his men rode like thunder toward the border, their prisoner in their midst. Thutmose could just make out the silhouette of a band of men at the border crossing. He squinted, recognizing them as the squad he had sent to Avaris with Rekmire.

Bridging the distance, he jerked his steed to a halt, eyeing his Vizier. "Find anything?"

"Nothing in camp but his wife and family. He apparently fled alone."

"We'll deal with them later." Thutmose pulled hard on the reins, causing his horse to rear. "What of Moses?"

Rekmire shook his head. "Only a caravan of miners left Egypt since our arrival. They were heading east through the desert to the mines at Serabit. I doubt Moses would take the desert route as there's nothing there but sand, heat, and death, but I told them to keep an eye out for him just the same. The promise of gold works wonders."

Thutmose peered toward the shadowed wasteland of dunes and desert and shook his head. "He's headed east, I'm sure of it." He cursed beneath his breath. "No doubt he plans to stir up a war against us. Why else would he leave his wife behind? If the Hyksos could manage an invasion centuries ago, think what they could do with an Egyptian Prince in their midst."

"Habiru," Rekmire corrected.

Thutmose nodded east toward the 'Way of the Sea.' "I want you and your men to start out for Syria and overtake him."

Rekmire snorted. "My Lord, we're not prepared. We've no provisions or water."

Thutmose clenched his teeth. "A man can live five days without water, I'm asking for three." He tossed him his own nearly empty water skin. "Take these men and ride like Hades. If you see anything, anything at all, pursue it."

Rekmire scanned the silhouetted wasteland. Soon the sun would crest over the subtle curve of the desert ushering in heat so intense it could snuff out life in a matter of hours.

The men watched Rekmire, hoping he would argue on their behalf but he did not. Instead he mounted his horse, nodding to the Habiru informant who had alerted them of Moses' escape and who had been all but lost amid the activity.

"What of him? Has he gained his freedom?"

A toothless grin stretched across the man's face, his eyes luminous with hope.

Frowning, Thutmose unsheathed his sword. "For telling us too late? I've too many Habiru on the loose as it is." Thrusting his sword through the man's belly, he left the Habiru slumped forward in the sand, spilling his blood in a darkening pool.

Isis stood amid the contradiction of clutter and splendor in what was once Hatshepsut's spacious bedchamber. Meryet had already picked over what was left of the valuables, choosing to stay in her own room rather than move into her mother's, preferring a sense of routine. The girl was boringly unassuming, but as such, was no threat to Isis as long as she kept her place.

Instead, Isis would occupy Hatshepsut's room. After all, the palace was as good as hers now that Thutmose had moved to Avaris.

Isis ran her fingers over the inlaid table, leaving behind a trail in the dust. It had obviously been weeks since a servant had ventured into the former Pharaoh's sanctum, likely because they feared to meet her Ka. Nonsense, Isis sneered. She strode to the balcony, looking out across the lawns and gardens that had occupied Hatshepsut's view these many years, across the river and harbor glistening beyond the city, and to the far western shore where Hatshepsut's temple rose amid the rubble and ruin of that sacred ground. Her gaze narrowed on the imposing edifice then she turned from the sight.

Though Isis wasn't Queen or even consort, as mother of the Pharaoh she had almost as many rights. Wives were, after all, disposable, their purpose merely to provide Egypt an heir. She, on the other hand, had borne Egypt a god whose domain reached throughout the Two Lands and beyond, to the Euphrates in the east and Ta–Seti in the south, whose name would live forever.

She scanned the room, picturing her own furniture in this space, her mementos from the past and all she might acquire in the future. With Thutmose in the Delta, Thebes was as much hers as it had been Hatshepsut's, and any conquests he added to Egypt's influence would merely swell her own coffers.

She thought of Puseneb with a strange twinge of appreciation, though her heart rarely stretched itself to include another. No matter how pompous and greedy he was, she felt a kinship with him. They had, after all, successfully collaborated in ridding Egypt of that cursed Queen and her impostor son, while encouraging Thutmose to fill Amon's coffers to such measure they were able to spill a substantial portion into their own.

Thutmose rode into Avaris like a Hamsin storm, his men at his heels. He reined to a stop near the temple site and jerked Aaron from his horse. Aaron stood with his head hung and his hands tied behind his back.

"I want everyone to see what happens to those who aid an escaping criminal." Thutmose's voice cut through the ping of hammers and clamor of the work site as all movement ceased and every eye turned his way.

"Rope him between those two poles." Thutmose nodded to the place where Peku's tent had stood. Several soldiers hustled Aaron to the protruding posts, stripping him to his loin cloth and cinching his arms so tightly they strained from their sockets.

Tasha watched in horror, clutching the water skin to her breast.

"In case anyone doesn't know what happens to traitors, I'll demonstrate." Thutmose scanned the faces at the site till he found Tasha's. "Let this be a lesson to any who hope to escape or who aid in another's. Aaron had the misfortune of serving as a decoy for the escaped murderer, Moses."

Thutmose nodded to a muscular soldier who stood behind Aaron, his whip raised. At Thutmose's signal the man flexed, bringing the leather across Aaron's back with a 'crack' while the onlookers gasped as with one voice. Aaron cried out, clenching his fists as the whip coiled about his body and was retracted, leaving a spiral of blood encircling him. Lifting it higher as if calculating the distance, the soldier sliced the air again, this time opening Aaron's flesh and causing his body to quiver uncontrollably.

Tasha groaned as if feeling the blow herself and fell to her knees, dropping the water skin.

Again the leather streaked through the air, ripping pieces of flesh as the soldier jerked it back, sending Aaron to the ground, suspended by his arms. He panted, lifting his face to the sky. "Oh great Yahovah...."

Aggravated at the mention of Aaron's god, the soldier raised the whip again, forcing it through the air with the power of a charging rhino. A wave of horror arose from the onlookers as it collided with Aaron's body, cutting another spiral across the already raw flesh as Aaron's head dropped forward in unconsciousness.

Thutmose lifted a hand and the whipping stopped, though the hefty soldier eyed Aaron as if contemplating whether or not to comply. At last he lowered his whip, perspiration beading his brow.

Tasha stifled her sobs, unable to conceal her fear. Had Aaron died, giving his life for his brother? Another thought caused her to press her hands to her bosom in anguish. Had she lost her only hope of escape? She bowed her head in shame, wondering how she could think of her own needs at such a moment. She covered her face, weeping.

Thutmose stared at the still form. "Does he live?"

The soldier grabbed a handful of hair and lifted Aaron's head, watching for the rise and fall of his chest then dropped it again. "Barely."

Thutmose let out his breath, yelling an order in the next. "A physician, and hurry!"

Several soldiers untied Aaron, dropping him onto a cloth and carrying him to a nearby cart. Though Thutmose could care less about the life of a slave, even a so called Priest, he did care about preserving every possibility of luring Moses back to Egypt.

His eyes, still broiling with unspent fury, sought out Tasha. Moses may have escaped but this one wouldn't. "You there!"

Tasha arose, her legs weak. Stumbling forward, she reluctantly bridged the distance between them.

Thutmose grabbed her arm, jerking her toward a horse. "You'll come when you're called, wench, or face the same treatment."

Amenhab watched, hesitant to even voice a question. "What should I do with her, my Lord?"

Thutmose mounted, reining back his horse, his features hard. "Send her under guard to Pithom to serve as Nefru's slave. I can't imagine a worse punishment than that."

Moses glanced behind him at the rolling dunes. Turning, he scanned the eastern horizon ahead of him as far as he could see, and noted the same, nothing but an endless sea of sand. The sun had risen only hours before yet he already felt uncomfortably hot. He knew he would need protection from the sun, but unclasped his homespun cape just the same and tucked it into his belongings. Except for that one item, all other apparel bespoke his position as an Egyptian: his kilt, whip, sword, and jewels. He took off his jeweled collar that identified him with royalty, and dropped it in the sand, rubbing his neck. Sand as bright as the sun stretched in every direction, an infinite desert of dips and mounds broken only by an occasional shadow beneath a dune. He felt lost in it, engulfed by its emptiness.

He forced his thoughts to the Delta and Tasha, but longing only deepened his despair. How he loved her. He wondered at her and Aaron's fate. Perhaps they should have come with him after all, but he was far from free. If Thutmose did not slay him this desert would. By now the Pharaoh would have sent out a search party, combing the camps and villages of the Habiru. Would he dare look in the desert? Moses grunted. Thutmose would likely picture him fleeing eastward to join Egypt's enemies. Such an assumption would at least buy him some time.

Moses looked over his shoulder just the same, digging his heels into his mare's flanks. The sun would soon rise high enough to make travel perilous. He would slow his pace then and try to rest in the shade of a dune.

Sweat trickled from beneath his headdress and into his eyes, blurring his vision. He longingly studied his water skin but left it alone, pulling his headdress lower instead. He must preserve every drop of the precious liquid if he hoped to survive.

The sun rose, dangling like a goggling globe, menacingly low. Moses shielded his eyes, throwing the weighty cloak about his shoulders again. Heat pounded on his head and rose in waves from the desert. He hadn't realized how much the heat had weakened him until he reached for his water skin and found its weight almost more than he could hold. He tipped the skin to his mouth with effort, trying to keep even a drop from spilling. As he swallowed the water sliced through his throat like a blade.

Alarm pounded in his brain. Would he ever find his way out of this desert? Ironically, the risk of travelling across Sinai was the one reason why Thutmose would not look for him here. In fact, he could die in this place and no one would know.

Moses' mare stumbled then righted itself, laboring through the sand with each step. Not until he reached the rocky soil near the Red Sea would he find solid ground and an occasional oasis providing water and shade, perhaps even dates and figs.

His mouth watered at the thought and he glanced at his pack. He would rest and refresh himself once the sun became unbearable. Sweat streamed down his face and into his mouth. He spat out the salty liquid, his eyes burning. Gods, would he even live through the day?

He thought he heard a noise and glanced behind him, but saw only the glare of the sun on sand. Wiping an arm across his forehead, he hurried his pace. Then he heard it again and turned, peering behind him across the distance. A blur of color arose from atop a dune revealing objects headed his way as if in slow motion.

"By Amon, Thutmose!" He kicked his horse to a run but the effort merely bogged the mare's steps, its hooves sinking deep in the sand. Moses kicked harder and the mare struggled then lurched as its knees buckled beneath its weight, hurtling him through space for what seemed an eternity before he landed on the softness of the sand, the brilliance of the desert swallowing him.

Amenhab dismounted near the garrison, sweat and dust streaking his face. He tied his horse to a tree and plunged his head into the water trough, greedily cupping the liquid to his mouth. His companions did the same.

Wiping an arm across his face, he leaned against a nearby tree, gulping for breath. "Tell Thutmose...the scouting party...has returned."

A guard called out the announcement and in the same moment Thutmose's door flung open. Thutmose searched his Officer's face, attempting to decipher the news before ushering him inside.

"No sign of him, my Lord, though several tradesmen from Syria passed our way."

"Had they seen anything, any trace of him?"

Amenhab shook his head. "I even offered to pay."

Thutmose cursed, peering out his window. "Moses must have hidden himself until they passed, knowing word would find its way back to me." He slammed his fist on the table. "Where in Hades has he gone? How could he have moved so quickly?" He paced like a caged leopard then looked up. "Where did that caravan come from?"

"From Tyre with purple cloth for trade. Surely they would have seen him," Amenhab reasoned.

Thutmose shook his head. "That's what he wants us to think. He's in Syria, alright. He has to be."

"Why not south through Sinai?"

Thutmose grunted. "Through that death–hole of a desert? We'd be rid of him for sure then."

"What about passage from Elath to another country, maybe Punt?"

Thutmose scrutinized Amenhab as if to read his thoughts. "If you were a runaway Prince with a wife and family still in Egypt would you travel to the desert to die, or seek an enemy strong enough to win back what you had lost?"

Amenhab sobered. "I see your point."

Thutmose resumed pacing. "He's headed for Syria alright, no doubt to lead a revolt against the Delta. It's the only move that will gain him what he wants."

"And what is that?"

Thutmose levelled his gaze at him. "This land for his people and the throne for himself."

Tasha's dark skin stood out against the white of Nefru's wall as she cringed, bracing herself for yet another blow, but instead Nefru dropped her hand, smiling.

"I feel thirsty — no hungry. Bring me something to eat."

Tasha hurried from the room to the kitchen, grateful for the reprieve. Her face stung from the blows already dealt her and her feet ached from having to stand for hours before her new mistress.

Nefru's slave! She had never thought it possible. If Yahovah had heard her prayer concerning Moses' welfare he must have looked the other way concerning hers. Then again, she thought with a measure of hope, perhaps this God could not watch over them both at the same time. If so, she would gladly suffer any number of blows if it would keep Moses from the fate awaiting him.

Tasha hurried back to the room with a tray, nearly dropping it in her haste, and set it before Nefru who reclined on a couch. Nefru purposefully chose a slice of succulent melon, biting into the sweet flesh with more than the usual relish, wanting to torment Tasha further since she had not yet eaten.

Nefru glanced at her feet, kicking off her sandals and twitching her painted toes. "I've suffered so from the dust of this place. Bring a basin and wash my feet. It gives me pleasure to have them cooled."

She looked at Tasha over her fruit, savoring the agony in the girl's eyes and the heaviness of her steps as she left to do her mistress's bidding. Tasha returned with a bowl of water, concentrating on not spilling it. Kneeling on the floor, she carefully set the bowl before her and reached for Nefru's foot.

Nefru winced as if from discomfort while Tasha dipped the cloth into the cool water and rubbed it over Nefru's soft flesh. Drying the first foot, Tasha reached for the other.

She had just finished the task when Nefru, her eyes on Tasha, flicked the rim of the bowl with her toe, toppling it onto Tasha's lap. Tasha arose, dripping and shaken amid Nefru's curses.

"Fool! You should have taken more care. Now clean up this mess or I'll have you flogged."

Tasha rushed from the room, returning with a clean towel. Tears trickled down her face as she soaked up the pool, wringing the water back into the basin. She scoured the spot on her hands and knees while Nefru watched, smirking with satisfaction.

Once finished, Tasha remained on her knees, her head bowed.

"There," Nefru gloated. "Remember that the next time you think you deserve better." She towered over Tasha as a victor would the conquered. "Now go eat your supper, but I'll expect you first thing in the morning, and see that you don't dawdle." Nefru eyed the henna on her nails. "I detest a servant who thinks herself above the summons of her mistress." Her eyes meaningfully fell on Tasha as the girl hastily bowed away.

The acrid scent of incense and medicinal herbs surrounded Aaron as he drifted in and out of consciousness. At first he thought himself in the temple of Apis lying prostrate before the bull god. He writhed, attempting to get up but pain shot through his back and shoulders, immobilizing him. He groaned, then heard the shuffle of feet and felt a cool cloth drop across his back.

"Oh great Yahovah," he mumbled into the sheet, "where am I, and what has happened?"

A picture of the village of Tju flashed before him and the brick temple built in honor of Yahovah. He winced, his memory blurred as another picture formed in his mind, that of a burly thug towering over him with a whip, cracking it across his back again and again. He moaned at the memory and instantly felt a hand on his head, hearing the mutter of a prayer from the Book of the Dead.

Aaron tried to protest but could not move, nor did any sound escape his lips. A guard muttered something in the corner, his sword clanking with his movements. The sound sharpened Aaron's senses, awakening him to the truth: Thutmose had placed him under guard while providing him with care. He had no idea what had happened to Tasha, but imagined her situation even more secure. They had little hope of escaping now.

"Moses," he whispered, imagining his brother as he had last seen him before he had disappeared into the darkness. "Thank Yahovah, you are free." He knew it must be true, for Thutmose would not have gone to the trouble of keeping him alive if Moses had been found.

A smile tugged at his lips in spite of his pain. At least Thutmose had spared their lives, and somewhere beyond Egypt's border Moses lived.

Thutmose inspected the reins of his chariot, giving them a final tug to assure their snugness. He patted his steed's coat as the animal pawed the ground in answer, its dark back glistening beneath the sun. Behind Thutmose a multitude of soldiers prepared for the journey, making ready their arms and provisions. Some secured pack horses for carrying supplies, while others doused their headdresses with water to gain an advantage over the heat. Still others rechecked their near–bursting water skins, guzzling last minute drinks while they had the opportunity.

Egypt's army would march many miles before reaching Syria, and if they found no trace of Moses at Gaza or Joppa, they would continue to Megiddo where he had likely taken refuge. Before they reached the city, however, they would battle elements of a different sort, for winter had not released its grip on Syria.

Thutmose made sure his bow and axe at the side of his chariot, scanning the highway ahead of them. "I can hardly wait to get out of here and across the desert. Megiddo's booty isn't the only prize I hope to return with."

Vizier Rekmire stood with a party of officials to see the Pharaoh off. "Just remember, Moses knows of your campaigns and will have a strategy of his own in place."

Thutmose eyed his longtime friend while taking the blue war helmet from his steward and setting it on his own head. "Don't underestimate my skill, Rekmire. Moses represents the best prize of the battle and I don't intend to let him escape a second time." His eyes narrowed. "Meanwhile, Vizier, take care to watch over the capital in my absence. I wouldn't want to return to find anything amiss."

Rekmire met Thutmose's gaze with one of determination. "You'll not be disappointed, my Lord, I promise you."

Thutmose nodded, scanning the desert and wondering how Hatshepsut would have reacted had she lived to hear of Moses' flight. Knowing he was being hunted would likely have sent her to the nether world even if illness hadn't. He stood a moment in contemplation then whipped the reins of his chariot. What did he care? According to Puseneb, Hatshepsut was damned anyway.

"Gone to the world of the dead," he whispered. "May she suffer an eternity worthy of her treason."

With a last look at Rekmire, he whipped his horse to a run, thankful the gods did not require him to mourn for the deceased any more than he would mourn the death of Moses.

Moses groaned and tried to move but his limbs were as heavy as stone, his body throbbing with pain. He attempted to sit up then dropped back again, feeling as if he had just awakened from the dead. He lifted his arm to shade his eyes and saw the blur of two faces bent over him.

He jerked to attention. Had Thutmose captured him and was he about to die? He forced himself onto one elbow, feeling the softness of a sheet beneath him and a cool cloth on his forehead. Surely Thutmose would not have treated him like this. But who were these men, and where was he? He squinted, making out a thin face and a wider one, conferring with each other with insistence.

"I tell you he's the one the Officer spoke of. We found the collar. Surely it was his. He'll bring us a good price in Egypt."

The second shook his head, unconvinced. "We can't go back. We have a schedule to keep."

"We don't have to go back, merely prolong the affair. We can send word to Pharaoh saying we have evidence but need more money to investigate, drag it out a bit. It will gain us more in the end, perhaps even a permanent income."

"Or a place with the dead. I hear Pharaoh has little patience with those who cross him." The wiry one scrutinized Moses. "I say we report him and move on."

"And I say we wait, strike a bargain and name our price. Let's make Pharaoh pay what this one is worth."

"We'll get paid alright, at the end of a rope for harboring a criminal."

"Ptah!" the largest cursed. "I doubt Thutmose even looks in this direction. He knows the risks of crossing the desert. No one in their right mind would attempt it," the broad man grinned, "except apparently this one. We could retire on the money he will bring us. In the meantime, he'll prove a sturdy addition to our work crew at the mines."

The other grimaced, muttering obscenities under his breath as he bent to give Moses a drink. The rows of Habiru stared at the newcomer with jealous longing, wishing they were privileged to suffer the attention paid one so near death.

Moses dropped back onto the sheet. Captured, sentenced to work the mines at Serabit until Thutmose found him. What kind of escape was that?

Gods! He closed his eyes, picturing himself roped among the rest, the sun searing his back and the sand blistering his feet. He should have fled to Syria after all. Anything would be better than this.

He forced his thoughts in another direction.

"Tasha," he whispered. She seemed so near he could almost feel her cool hand on his forehead, her warm breath against his cheek. Why had he left her? Yet she would never have lasted among these men even if she had survived the desert.

"Tasha." He breathed the name again, an ache knotting inside him so intense it sapped his strength and took away his breath. Gods, how he missed her! In spite of the risks, the only life for him was at her side. All other avenues represented a slow, bloodletting death such as even the living experience.

Egypt's standards flashed in the sun above a sea of soldiers, twenty abreast and seemingly miles deep. They marched like an encroaching wave, their swords and shields gleaming beneath the sun. The Great Sea, though invisible from across the hills, mingled its scent with the pungent odor of cedar as the army once again approached the rocky crags opposite Megiddo.

Thutmose reined his chariot to a stop at the crossroads, studying the snow–capped peaks. The mountains rose like a wall to their right, with patches of white clinging to the lower shelves and thickening to a continuous cap near the top where it lost itself in the clouds. Thutmose shivered under a lambskin cape, his sandals already exchanged for fur–lined boots.

Amenhab nosed his horse next to Thutmose's. "Which direction will we take to get around these mountains?"

Thutmose didn't answer, instead he studied the road that forked in either direction about the impasse, then lifted his eyes to the peaks and whipped his horse to a gallop as the army followed in his wake.

They made camp at the base of the mountains, a ring of fires once more marking their perimeter. Thutmose strode to a fallen log where Amenhab sat eating a bowl of stew. He accepted a bowl of his own and scooped a spoonful of the grub, savoring the taste as it spread its warmth to places the fire would never reach.

Amenhab smiled at him, more from the food than the company. "So we're taking the most northern route and surprising the enemy?"

Thutmose shook his head. Setting his bowl aside, he picked up a stick and drew a line in the dirt. Amenhab assumed the line to be the highway, branching out in either direction about the mountains.

"This is our position." Thutmose drew a circle on one side of the line. "Right now we sit directly across from Megiddo." He marked the city with an 'X'. "These are the mountains." He drew a series of peaks between the two points.

Amenhab laughed. "So which route do we take, the northern or southern?"

"Neither." Thutmose pushed the stick in a straight line from the circle through the peaks to the 'X' of Megiddo.

Amenhab's eyes widened and he nearly dropped his bowl, staring at Thutmose as if he were deranged. "You mean you're going to —"

Thutmose nodded. "Tomorrow we head for the mountain pass of Aruna," he jabbed the stick into the center of the 'X', "cutting off the confederation where they least expect it. We'll leave my chariot and our excess gear here with some servants and retrieve them on our return."

"True enough, as the mountain pass won't allow any more than a single rider through at a time, nor do we know where it opens up. If the confederation awaits us on the other side we'll be cut down one at a time with no chance of escape."

Thutmose tossed the stick into the fire atop a pile of embers where it sent a spray of sparks into the night. "It's our best chance at winning this war, and a move no one else under the circumstances would dare do."

"For good reason," Amenhab answered, staring at him a long moment before picking up his bowl again. He might never enjoy another sunset in the land of the living, but he could try to enjoy his last meal.

CHAPTER 17

Tasha reached into the thick branches of the olive tree, searching for nuggets of green behind the leaves. She glanced into her bag, finding it only half full, and fearfully looked at the palace from where Nefru would at any moment send a servant to demand her quota. Hastening her pace, she moved her hand in and out among the branches, grabbing whole clusters of olives and scratching her knuckles in the process. Blood oozed from her fingers but still she labored, dropping the olives into her bag.

"Losing skin?" Another servant, not much older than she, stuck her head between the branches. She held up her hands showing Tasha her bandaged palms with only her fingertips protruding. Her fingers looked gnarled and scarred and Tasha tried not to show her dismay.

"I wear rags every day," the girl matter–of–factly stated. "It helps keep my hands from bleeding."

Tasha stared at her own hands, horrified they might one day look the same. She rubbed her knuckles then glanced at the girl who had known many more hours of labor than she.

"Thank you, I'll try the bandages." Tasha untied her sash, ripping it in two and winding a piece about each hand.

The girl smiled. "My name is Nepthys after the goddess. And yours?"

"Tasha."

"From Avaris?" the girl asked.

Tasha absently nodded in agreement then shook her head. "No, from Ta–Seti, Kerma of Kush." She turned back to her work, avoiding the girl's searching gaze as she resumed rustling among the leaves.

Nepthys studied Tasha. "I don't know what you've done, but you're certainly on the Queen's dark side." Tasha worked more feverishly at mention of Nefru. The girl continued, "I also had to learn quickly, but she never had it out for me quite the same. How do you manage?"

Tasha paused, her brow pursed. How did she manage? She attempted to do her best to please Nefru, but under normal conditions the pressure would have broken her. Instead, somehow she had withstood the torment. Something always diverted Nefru's attention or nudged her twisted heart to allow a moment's reprieve.

A curious thought struck her, almost making her laugh aloud. Might Yahovah be answering her petitions after all? Was it He who was helping her? She realized her companion still awaited an answer.

"I — well, I suppose I pray."

Nepthys' brow lifted. "To which god?"

Tasha paused. Could she trust Nepthys with the truth? She didn't know, but felt the overwhelming desire to try, and decided to risk the details. "I pray to the Habiru God, Yahovah."

The girl's eyes widened like two full moons staring through the branches. The girls watched each other, perched atop their ladders, neither of them moving.

Tasha smiled. "Is it so strange to pray to a foreign God? Just because He is worshipped by the Habiru doesn't mean He is ineffective." She stopped, watching the girl's troubled expression at mention of the word. "Are you Habiru?"

Nepthys nodded. "Partly. My mother was Habiru; my father an Egyptian Overseer. Once she had me he —" Nepthys dropped her eyes, absorbing herself in her work. "I've been a slave since birth, first for my father's family, then here at the palace."

"For your father's family? That's odd. How did you come to serve at the palace?"

Nepthys took a deep breath. "My father sold me to a Royal steward who placed me under the Queen's care."

"Perhaps he hoped for a better life for you." Tasha swallowed her own distaste at the words. "Serving royalty is believed an honor."

Nepthys shook her head. "No, he didn't aim to better my life, only to profit from it, and he got a fair price."

Pity seeped through Tasha's eyes. "What of your mother?"

"I've never met her, though I've wondered if she might be the Habiru woman sometimes brought to my father's bedchamber. He has never allowed us to speak."

Tasha's throat tightened as an ache formed inside her. She knew how it felt to lose a loved one. "I am so sorry," she whispered, tears trickling from her eyes. She pictured her own family as she had last seen them, but somehow even that didn't seem as painful as parting from

Moses. She spoke with difficulty. "I too lost someone I love, and though I can't see him, I pray for him daily."

Nepthys watched her with wonder.

Tasha took a deep breath, conveying her thoughts as carefully as possible. "Yahovah hears our prayers, I am sure of it, for He has heard and answered mine." Her eyes misted as the girl held her gaze.

Just then the palace door swung open and a servant hurried out. Nefru's voice sounded shrilly behind her, "… And she'd better have a full bag or I'll have her hide."

Tasha glanced at her bag in alarm, her limbs trembling in anticipation of Nefru's punishment. But before the servant arrived, Nepthys reached through the branches, replacing Tasha's half empty bag with her own full one. Tasha didn't even have time to thank her as the servant ordered her down from the ladder and to the palace.

She dared a backward glance before entering, but could only see the leaves thick and rustling as Nepthys hurried to fill yet another bag.

Moses massaged his wrists where the ropes had cut into his flesh, and threw a glare at his captors, though they did not seem to notice. They were too busy chatting among themselves while jouncing atop their camels, keeping only an occasional watch over the slaves roped together below them. Moses gazed westward at the Red Sea stretching beyond the blue into infinity. He and Aaron had sailed those waters only a year ago, yet it seemed an eternity.

He looked away. The sight of water only made him thirsty. He glanced at his own nearly empty water skin dangling just out of reach at the side of his horse. If he had drank more he might have had the strength to escape his captors.

His feet ached as he pushed them over the rocky ground. Once more he cursed his luck, and searched the shore for signs of an oasis but saw none. His bitterness hardened to hatred as he studied the men who had shackled him. He thought of the Overseer in Avaris whose throat he had slit and prayed for an opportunity to repeat the act.

A slave ahead of him dropped to his knees, tangling the line, while another called out for water. Soon a chorus of cries erupted like a flock of gulls on a beach, whereupon a guard grudgingly passed a water skin down the line of eager hands, but Moses refused to plead. Instead, when his turn came he grabbed the skin and guzzled until his thirst had quenched, surprised the guards allowed him the privilege. His eyes narrowed in realization. As long as his captors could expect a hefty reward they would make sure he lived.

The line resumed its lumbering pace into the blinding daylight while Moses wondered about the slaves tethered to him. Why didn't they fight? Why not band together and overpower the few who held them captive? He felt disgust rise in him like bile.

He should have headed east to stir up the confederation against Thutmose. Together they could have invaded the Delta, freeing the Habiru and retaking the capital.

A picture of Tasha formed in his mind and he felt his heart ache with longing. Why had he left her? What evil had Thutmose subjected her to in his absence? By the gods, if he so much as touched her....

He clenched his jaw, his fists straining against his bonds, and glanced down to find his wrists bleeding.

He closed his eyes as he pushed one foot in front of the other, fear for Tasha weakening him. Would she have been any better off here? He glanced up at the men atop their camels and knew the answer.

He stiffened, their wild gestures rousing him from his thoughts. They reined their camels and pointed eastward, their eyes bulging. Moses turned, seeing horses and riders swooping toward them in a cloud of sand.

"Amalekites!"

The word hung in the air like a dark omen while the line of Habiru ceased to move, hoping, as did their captors, the vision would disappear. Someone shouted for them to form a circle but they only tangled about each other in their haste. The intruders topped a rocky knoll, their scimitars in their teeth, and the colors of their billowing robes now visible.

The largest Egyptian blanched. "Cut the slaves free, now!" He tossed a bundle of weapons to the ground, dropping from his camel.

The guards sliced through the tethers as one by one the slaves scrambled for swords, readying themselves for the fray.

"What of him?"

A guard pointed to Moses who stood with his hands outstretched, his eyes on the Amalekites as they rode like the wind toward them.

The Overseer hesitated only a moment. "Free him!"

The blade broke Moses' bonds as an Egyptian tossed him a sword. He caught the weapon and whirled to face an Amalekite who sprang from his horse. Moses lifted the blade with both hands and swung as the man leapt back. Seeing Moses' bleeding wrists, the warrior straightened with a confident jeer on his face. He was about to speak when Moses lunged, the sword slicing through the man's belly and out the other side. Moses shoved the weight aside and looked about, finding his horse roped between several camels and pawing as if it also wished to escape.

Moses stepped toward the animal but the Egyptian Overseer spied him and started to protest. An Amalekite, finishing a less experienced Habiru, grabbed the Overseer from behind. The man's eyes bulged as the Amalekite reached around and slit his throat. Opening his mouth to speak, the Overseer dropped face forward, spilling a pool of blood beneath him.

The warrior momentarily paused, savoring the victory then started toward Moses, but a young Habiru, blade in hand, stepped between them, eager to vent his fury. Jumping the Amalekite, he wrapped himself about the man as the two dropped to the dust, arms and legs flailing. The sinews of the Habiru strained as he fought to hold back the enemy. Moses raised his sword to finish the match when the Amalekite rolled, putting the Habiru between them.

The young man raised his knife but the Amalekite moved more quickly, his blade slicing through the Habiru's body. The young man's features froze as if unwilling to believe what had just happened. He looked at Moses, his eyes wide with realization before falling lifeless to the earth.

The Amalekite pushed the body aside, striding toward Moses, his bloodied blade lifted to strike again. Another Amalekite, seeing the two, moved in at Moses' left. Moses took a step back, nearly tripping over the body of the Overseer whose purse bulged at his side. Crouching, Moses sliced the bag free and tossed it between the two Amalekites. Gold coins scattered onto the ground like glittering pebbles. The second man stared, dropping to his knees to gather the find while the first barked an order.

Still the man dug in the dirt, stuffing coins into his shirt. The first turned on his comrade, lifting his sword with both hands and plunging it into the Amalakite's back.

Moses wasted no time. Cutting his horse loose, he swung atop it just as the first warrior pulled his blade free. Bridging the distance, the man lunged at Moses, falling into the space behind him as Moses' horse leapt to a run.

Moses glanced back to see him attempt to rally his comrades but they were occupied in battles of their own. Moses skirted the caravan, avoiding the dead strewn across the ground, most of them Habiru. A pitiful few still struggled against their invaders, but the Amalekites hopelessly outnumbered them. Moses wondered at the tug in his heart to go back but knew it was impossible. His only hope of escape was to put as much distance as possible between him and the battle. The Amalekites had won, and by some luck of the gods, he was free.

Aaron trudged into camp, his hands tied behind his back, a guard at his side. The guard untied him with as much care as he would have a corpse, and shoved him toward the mud pit.

"Now dance."

Aaron stumbled forward, massaging his wrists and looking about to see if he could find Miriam. Scanning the camp, he caught sight of her and she of him, her eyes filling with concern as she approached. Tears spilled down her cheeks as she handed him the water skin.

"Thank God you're alive," she whispered. "The guards had you and Moses tracked at every camp possible the night of his escape. When I heard you'd been captured

—" A sob quivered on her lips but she bit it back. "I've never prayed so hard in my life."

Aaron untied his sandals, glancing at the guards, his brow furrowed. "Then keep praying, we'll need it. As far as I know Moses is free. If he weren't I wouldn't be alive. I only hope he has the sense to stay that way."

Miriam's voice dropped. "It was our God who preserved you, and He will do the same for Moses. Yahovah can save him now as surely as when he was an infant."

Aaron studied her a long moment then tossed his sandals on the grass at his feet. "Any word of Tasha?"

Miriam caught her breath as the guard turned their way. "Given to Nefru as a slave."

"Yahovah help her,"Aaron breathed

"Yes."

The guard eyed them, hands on his hips. "You there, get moving or you'll find out what a flogging really feels like."

Aaron wearily turned toward the pit, looking a last time at his unblemished feet before stepping into the mud. He heard a gasp from behind him and realized Miriam had just seen his back for the first time.

He ignored her outcry, the muddy ooze rising to his knees as he attempted to balance himself. Groaning, she turned from his scars, her eyes brimming with tears, and continued to administer water to the others, though her gaze never left Aaron for long.

A young woman whose braids dangled over her shoulders approached and opened a cloth tied about her waist, spilling chopped straw in front of him. Aaron looked into her face and found irresistible warmth.

She attempted a smile then glanced back at the Overseers before motioning to the bank. "It's easier at the edge, shallower so you don't have to step as high."

Aaron gratefully nodded, his eyes following her as she walked back to the straw where the methodical thud of choppers hacked it to smaller lengths. He pushed the grass under his feet, stepping high again and again until the mud covered it.

As he worked an area, he moved forward to work another space while the brick makers scooped buckets of the mixture from behind him and still others poured it into molds. He scanned the fields southward where red-brown brick lay in geometrical rows as far as he could see, appearing like a gigantic courtyard as it dried beneath the sun.

The woman returned, her apron overflowing with straw. "They overfill us in their effort to increase the tally." She purposefully dropped some straw on the shore, shaking what was left onto the mud. "But we have ways of easing our burdens." She smiled and Aaron's heart lightened.

As she turned down the path Aaron noted the supple curves of her body beneath her sheath and he looked away. It only sharpened the pain of enslavement to long for a woman. He had best keep his eyes elsewhere or he would end up no better off than Moses.

A man his age sidled closer, stomping his own pile beneath his feet. "You married?"

Aaron shook his head.

The man nodded to the girl. "Hard to keep your eyes on your work when the only beauty in this place is the women who serve us. The Egyptians delight in such torment." He shook his head and sighed. "I have a wife and newborn son. The only mercy the Overseers show us is allowing new mothers to nurse their young, though they are sent back to the slave villages in Goshen where we don't hear from them for months, a torment of a different kind."

Aaron followed the man's hungry gaze as the woman approached again, and at once he wanted to protect her, to keep the eyes of even the Habiru from violating her. Diverting the man's attention, Aaron kept him talking of other matters while the woman poured straw in front of them.

The man told of his childhood and family, of parents whom he had lost years ago to a plague when dysentery struck the villages. He supposed the rotting corpses of the infants killed at Pharaoh's decree had caused the disease. He spoke of his years as an orphan and slave, of his eventual marriage, and of his hope to live in a free land with his wife and child, to farm and build for himself rather than for Egypt.

Aaron, in turn, told of his sister, Miriam, who served them here, and of his younger brother, Moses.

The man looked up sharply. "You mean the traitor, Moses: the Habiru turned Egyptian?"

Aaron stiffened. "Raised in Pharaoh's court through no fault of his own." His eyes bore into the man's soul. "You're fortunate Moses dissuaded Pharaoh from reviving the death decree, or we would have seen yet another blood bath of Habiru infants, perhaps your own."

The man's eyes softened. "Then I have him to thank for the life of my son."

Aaron nodded and took a deep breath, changing the subject. "What is your son's name?"

The man's countenance brightened. "Joshua, 'The Lord is our Salvation.'"

Aaron smiled, trying not to let the man see his disbelief at the words. He lifted his gaze to the young woman as she again ventured down the path toward them. "True enough," he muttered, "for only God can save us from this place."

Thutmose led his horse along the precipice, a cliff at his right and a rock wall on his left. Behind him his Officers struggled over the narrow path as they led their horses single file, followed by an unending line of foot soldiers.

Thutmose hugged his lambskin closer as the wind whistled through the gully, biting his flesh and tearing at his cape. He would have given anything to be out of these mountains and back in the desert, anything except the opportunity to capture Moses.

Behind him a horse stumbled, causing a cascade of rocks to skitter over the cliff and down into the narrow valley below them. The frightened Officer needed no reprimand as the possibility of falling threatened more than anything Thutmose could have said. They had been walking since early morning, having made camp in the mountains, and continued into the afternoon as they made their descent through the pass toward the base of the mountain.

By late afternoon Thutmose could see a gap of light far ahead between the rocky walls. He motioned his men to keep quiet, praying the enemy would not be waiting for them on the other side. Only the element of surprise would assure them victory.

Hours later Thutmose neared the opening, his feet numb and his body shivering. He unsheathed his sword in readiness, hoping for enough time to gain a foothold in the valley before being discovered. Stepping with his horse from the shadowy chasm, he mounted again, every nerve alert as he scanned his surroundings. The valley opened before him just as he had imagined it: a wide field with the hint of snow, and in the distance a scatter of tents beneath the imposing walls of Megiddo. There weren't nearly as many tents as he had expected, nor had the enemy anticipated his arrival.

Thutmose's horse impatiently danced while soldiers trickled from the opening onto the field. At last, when enough stood on the plain to draw attention, they heard a whoop of exclamation from across the valley followed by an eruption of activity appearing comical from a distance. Here and there men, seemingly as small as insects, scrambled toward their chariots and horses, attempting to ready themselves while the Egyptian army grew before their eyes. The confederation appeared chaotic and unorganized, as if unable to believe what was happening in their very midst.

Thutmose waited as long as he could, not wanting to give the enemy time to bridge the gap, yet needing to protect his men still pouring through the opening. When he could wait no longer, he held up his sword and let loose a war whoop of his own, charging with a portion of his army toward the disorganized confederate ranks.

A bearded bulk of a man, oversized compared to his horse, rushed toward him ahead of the rest, his sword brandished in readiness. Thutmose braced himself. He was tempted to look about for Moses but forced himself to focus on the battle at hand. The two groups met in a clash of metal and horses as various pairs broke away to struggle on their own. The Hyksos leader nosed toward Thutmose, his huge sword crashing against Thutmose's with a blow that sent him and his horse back a pace. Thutmose attempted to hold his ground and waited for the next blow, ducking as the blade whizzed overhead. Taking the opportunity, he lunged but the Hyksos turned out of his path.

Thutmose's horse pranced in a circle as his enemy's sword sliced the air where he had just been. Thutmose swallowed. This battle could prove more difficult than he had anticipated. Keeping his eyes on his foe, he nudged his horse backward, working about until the Hyksos, impatient for a fight, attacked first. More agile than his enemy, Thutmose dodged, lifting his sword and slicing the Hyksos' arm just below his fur cape.

The man swore, his face purpling and his eyes ablaze as blood spurted from the wound. He gritted his teeth and lifted his sword, hacking toward Thutmose as through dense brush, but Thutmose anticipated his moves and dodged the heavy blade. Sweat ran in rivulets down the Hyksos' face as he fought, lunging at Thutmose with scattered, cumbersome blows. Thutmose drew back and swung around, quickly plunging his blade through several layers of fur and clothing before meeting its mark.

The Hyksos reared, surprise on his face. He placed his hand over the wound as blood trickled between his fingers, his face white and his mouth agape. Turning about, he struggled through the fray, allowing his soldiers to close the gap behind him, and putting as much distance as he could between Thutmose and himself. Those he passed saw him retreating and followed, falling out of formation and creating a tangle of horses and humanity as the confederates retreated toward the city. Those ahead of the Hyksos leader entered first, whereupon the great wooden gates closed just as their leader had bridged the distance to the wall. The remaining confederates leapt from their horses and pounded on the gates.

Thutmose and his men pursued but became entrapped by an impasse of abandoned chariots and horses. The doors of Megiddo swung open again as the confederates shoved their way inside, then closed just as quickly. However the Hyksos leader had not moved swiftly enough. Holding his side, he and a handful of others backed against the gates, their eyes on the oncoming Egyptians.

Thutmose had almost reached him when several dozen ropes fell over the wall. The Hyksos leader grabbed hold, as did the others, and was lifted out of reach and over the wall just as the Egyptians arrived.

When the men at last stood atop the wall, relief on their faces, they surveyed the Egyptian army below them. Only an unfortunate few of the confederacy remained outside the gates.

"By Amon!" Thutmose expelled the curse through his teeth.

Amenhab rushed to his side, breathless with excitement. "We have routed the confederation!"

Behind him the Egyptian army let out a shout of victory which seemed to shake the entire valley as it echoed from the mountain wall and back again. Falling out of line, soldiers began searching the bodies of the fallen, taking what valuables they could find, while others ran inside the tents, coming out with armloads of goods and jugs of beer. Seeing the booty, the entire army followed until the whole valley echoed with the clamor and chaos of plundering.

Thutmose attempted to shout above the commotion, "Leave it and set a siege!" He motioned a group of soldiers already absorbed in looting and drinking. "To the back wall! Don't let any escape!"

The group reluctantly obeyed, leaving the goods and mounting their horses. Weaving between the rows of tents and celebrants, they disappeared around the wall and behind the city. Some moments later a rider raced back toward Thutmose, the hooves of his steed barely visible as he covered the ground between them.

The excited rider gasped for breath, reining the horse to a stop. "A band of them has already escaped, my Lord, by way of a back gate."

Thutmose's face constricted. "After them!"

Yet his words were lost amid the noise of revelry as he and the messenger surveyed what had become of Egypt's army. Men with jugs guzzled beer as if they had never tasted it before, while others gathered loot, so absorbed in the spoil they hadn't even heard the shout of their commander.

Thutmose threw his sword to the ground, shaking his head with fury. He had won the battle but lost the prize, having allowed the confederate leaders to escape, and in all likelihood, Moses with them.

Moses followed the path southward along the coast of the Red Sea. To the west the blue brought back the memory of his voyage to Punt. It seemed surreal, as if it had never happened, but it had. He had hardly known Aaron at the time, but after months at sea they had grown as close as if they had never been separated. Now he wondered if he would ever see his brother again.

Moses looked eastward, the desert diminishing in waves of sand as infinite as the sea, lost to the horizon.

He pictured Tasha, Aaron and Miriam attempting to find their way across that wasteland, but couldn't imagine them surviving a day let alone managing the journey to Elath. A deep loneliness filled him and with it the knowledge that he would likely never see his loved ones again. He forced his attention to the road, sweat running down his neck and under his cloak as the sun pounded above him from a brazen sky.

He reached for his water skin but found it empty. Snatching it up, he wrung the last drop into his mouth as panic seized him. He searched the distance for sign of an oasis. There must be one. Caravans regularly travelled this route for good reason. Wiping the sweat from his forehead, he squinted into the distance, attempting to clear his vision.

Was that an outcrop of rock ahead, or did those faint protrusions represent vegetation? He hurried his pace.

The smell of the sea buoyed him along as he fixed his eyes on the spot unfolding before him like a blossoming flower. An oasis! It seemed hours before he finally entered the overhanging boughs of palms and acacias as his horse eagerly followed the scent of water.

Moses looked for a well when a noise jolted him to attention. He heard the voices of men and a maiden, their heated words closely resembling the Habiru tongue. The volume swelled to a venomous torrent as he neared a clearing.

"I tell you it's ours," a woman insisted. "We arrived here first."

"We have travelled farthest and are more in number," a deeper voice countered.

Moses stepped from the foliage and saw several young women huddled near a well, their staves raised as they stood their ground against half a dozen Bedouin shepherds.

"It's ours," one of the women insisted, lifting her skirt to the knee and raising her staff in readiness for a fight.

A man stepped forward from the rest, hands on his hips and his feet askance. "What do you say, men? Shall we leave our flocks and have some fun with these maidens?"

No sooner had the words left his mouth than the girl's staff cracked across his skull, sending him reeling backward. His eyes flashed, and as she swung again he grabbed her rod before she could retrieve it, pulling her toward him. "And this is also how you use a staff."

He wrapped his meaty arms about her, pulling her against him and forcing her lips to his as she struggled to free herself, bending away from him. He dropped the staff, feeling for her sash, and in the same instant a whip snapped above his ear and he drew back, dropping the girl. The whip lashed out again, this time coiling about his arm.

"This is how you use a whip," Moses answered in Habiru, stepping between the two, his jaw clenched.

Another shepherd reached for his staff but Moses readied his sword in his other hand, pulling hard on the whip as he retrieved it from the man's arm. The Bedouin gasped in pain, his arm spiraled with red as he held it and cursed.

Another man stepped forward. "Who are you and what right have you to interfere?"

Moses ignored his question, nodding to the girls to fill their water troughs.

The first Bedouin still awaited an answer but his comrades had already turned away. Ruefully, he followed suit, standing at a distance with the others, their silence ominous. Eventually they left with their flocks to find another well, for there were several in the oasis.

Moses stepped to the trough and greedily cupped the water to his mouth, splashing it onto his face and filling his water skin. He nodded to the girl who had incited the argument.

"Do you always defend your rights with such relish?" he asked.

She tossed her head. "Only when the occasion demands it. Those men have trailed us for days. It wasn't only the water they wanted."

"True enough. Your father should know better than to send young maidens unaccompanied into the wilderness."

The girl's eyes sparked. "You would do no differently if you had only daughters."

Moses took another drink rather than comment.

The girls crowded about, watching him with wide, wondering eyes. "Are you travelling far? Where did you come from? Would you accompany us?"

Moses tended his horse, ignoring the barrage of questions. "I'm headed for Elath and the sea."

Their faces lit, the smallest exulting. "We live just this side of the port in the desert of Midian."

"Is that so?" Moses snugly tied his water skin.

The girls practically danced with joy, all but the first whom he had rescued.

She eyed him, hands on her hips. "Where are you from and what is your name?"

One of the girls noted his whip and pleated kilt, and pointed. "Look, Zipporah, he's Egyptian!"

The woman lifted a corner of his cape with her staff, studying the weave. "If so, how does he know our tongue and where did he come by this?"

Moses' eyes narrowed. If he admitted to being Habiru they would know he was a runaway. "I came upon a caravan ambushed by Amalekites and grabbed this cape for protection from the sun. As to the language, I've had

Habiru slaves in my keep." Moses turned his attention to his horse as it drank deep draughts of water, wishing he had not revealed so much of his travels.

The youngest jumped up and down. "A real Egyptian! I've always wanted to meet one."

Moses' jaw tightened. He, an Egyptian? If only it were true.

Zipporah turned to him. "It is unusual to meet an Egyptian this far east, but we could certainly use a hand in making our way home. Will you accompany us?"

Moses shrewdly eyed her. She seemed to demand rather than ask, but he would overlook the insult. The Midianites knew their way through the desert, including the location of other oases. It would be a fair exchange. "Alright, I will accompany you, but you must tell no one we met."

The younger girls emphatically nodded, while another ventured. "Are you running from someone? Have you committed a crime?"

Moses averted his gaze. "I'm a deserter from Pharaoh's army. If he finds me he'll kill me."

At this the girls excitedly whispered among themselves, and Zipporah's face softened. "Then we understand your plight. We have no sympathy for Egypt's armies. In exchange for seeing us home we will provide you with sanctuary as long as you need. Pharaoh would never suspect finding you among a family of desert Midianites."

"Of seven Midianite shepherdesses," the younger corrected, giggling.

The elder threw her a disapproving look then nodded to Moses. "We'll make camp here for the night and leave at first light."

Moses surveyed the circle of eager eyes and swallowed hard. He had the sinking feeling he had just been captured a second time.

CHAPTER 18

Moses stood in the shadows of the Midianite tent watching the shepherdesses herd their flock of sheep and goats toward the fenced enclosure for the night. He studied the women, their faces flushed and streaked with sweat, their clothes dusty, and their hair escaping their headdresses. He shook his head. How had he, who had walked the courts of Pharaoh, come to live in such a place, a camp of desert Bedouin? He chuckled at the absurdity.

"Something amuses you." Jethro, father of the girls, sat at the far side of the tent, studying him.

Moses avoided Jethro and looked out the door again. "No, just fascinated, that's all." He uncomfortably shifted, wondering how such a lowly nomad could leave him at a loss for words.

Jethro poured Moses a cup of strong tea. "God did not see fit to bless me with sons. The only two born to my wife, may she rest in peace, died in infancy." He nodded to the door, "My daughters have sacrificed much to fill the gap."

Moses cleared his throat, trying to think of something to say. He had the strange feeling this man could read his thoughts and it unnerved him. Instead, he absorbed himself in the foul brew and changed the subject. "How many cattle do you own?"

"Nearly a hundred sheep and twice as many goats." The man took a leisurely drink. "It's difficult to keep track as they breed and bear young this time of year."

Moses nodded, curiously watching the old man until he himself became the object of the elder's steady gaze. Moses scanned the dwelling that appeared bare except for a few ornate items. Otherwise, simplicity, even poverty evidenced itself in the near empty room and sparse furnishings.

Jethro broke the silence. "You are used to a life of affluence, perhaps as a nobleman."

Moses' eyes shot up at him then dropped to his cup again as he concentrated on swallowing a second mouthful. He set his cup aside. "I am tired after my journey and should retire to my tent."

"Understandable. It must have been difficult coming all the way from Egypt. Most men would not have survived alone." Jethro's eyes narrowed with the scrutiny of a wizard.

Moses ignored his probing and glanced out the door. "If it is all right with you, I think I'll —"

At that moment Zipporah and three of her sisters burst through the doorway, their eyes shining with excitement and their sun–baked complexions rosy.

"Our work is finished, father. Play for us and we will dance," Zipporah breathlessly stated.

Jethro laughed as Zipporah grabbed his hand, pulling his spindly, folded legs to a standing position. He momentarily reeled before steadying himself, then accepting the reed flute, he glanced at Moses. "Will you join us?"

Moses weakly smiled. "Of course." He threw an expression of masked disgust Zipporah's way but she merely beamed. Positioning her sisters in a circle at the center of the room, she lifted her skirt in anticipation, pointing her right foot.

Moses ruefully watched, comparing her crudeness to the experienced dancers who entertained at Egyptian feasts. The most glaring difference between the two was that these were fully clothed while Egyptian dancers wore hardly more than a string of beads about their abdomen.

A melody burst from the flute, filling the room as Jethro tapped his foot in rhythm. Moses hid a smirk behind his cup. These women both repulsed and fascinated him, not at all like the pampered women of the palace. He thought of Nefru, and the comparison made him chuckle.

He sobered. Surprisingly, the girls' movements appeared agile and their steps intricate. They concentrated on design and motion rather than hand springs and acrobatics such as Egyptian dancers perform.

Zipporah's skirts rose in an arc as she twirled past him and Moses found himself picking her out from the rest, following her and catching her eye as she turned his way. She possessed the spirit of an unbroken horse set free in the desert, and he felt drawn by her energy.

Moses glanced at Jethro, and seeing the elder's eyes on him, leaned against the tent post feigning aloofness. This family vaguely reminded him in dress and custom of the Habiru, a fact he would just as soon forget, for in truth they were related, as was he. The notion annoyed him. He didn't belong here. He closed his eyes and pictured Egypt as he had last seen it, envisioning Tasha in the moonlit grove his last night in Egypt.

Tasha. An ache formed in his throat and knotted in his stomach. He recalled their few nights together as man and wife, her love still alive in some secret place within him. He could almost feel her now in the crook of his arm, her head on his shoulder. Gods, how he missed her: her soft laughter, her eyes shining into his, her body warm and responsive.

The thought of her filled him with such longing he dared not open his eyes lest her nearness disappear. It was as if her scent wafted across the reaches of the desert, enticing him to her arms once again. The flute in the background reminded him of the lutenist who had accompanied him and Tasha in the garden after their first banquet together. He imagined them there again, the hum of activity lost in the darkness as the star studded body of Nut arched above them. Lotus blossoms wafted their scent on the warm night air, and in the distance the Nile reflected the lights of the city as if tiny candles floated in the dark at the edge of the sky. He could almost feel Tasha's breath on his chest as she raised her face to his, filling his soul with sweetness and igniting his body with desire.

He determined with his last waking thought to leave for the port of Elath once he had regained strength, and to pray to every god imaginable that she too would find a way of escape.

Tasha leaned over the cot vomiting into a slop bucket. Gagging at the sickening taste, she lay back panting on her bed. Perspiration beaded her brow and hair clung to her forehead in a wavy frame.

She slid a hand over her slightly rounded belly. She had suspected as much, her fears confirmed when her flow had ceased. She groaned. If only she had insisted ongoing with Moses. Whatever had befallen him could not possibly be worse than the fate awaiting her once Nefru discovered her secret.

Nepthys burst into the room, the echo of a shrill voice sounding behind her. "It's Nefru! Hurry, she calls for you." She took one look at the frail form and ran to Tasha's side. "What is it? What's wrong?"

Tasha half–smiled, patting her abdomen. "Both a curse and a blessing." Her lips quivered as she forced back the tears. "What can I do? Nefru will kill the child."

Nepthys' eyes bugged as she looked at Tasha's belly.

A scream pierced the silence behind them. "I want her now!" Footsteps neared.

Nepthys slid the coverlet up to Tasha's chin as Nefru burst into the room, and stood to face their mistress in Tasha's place.

"A fever, my Lady. I've seen it often in my years of service. Soon spots will appear and as the fever heightens, wild delusions will overtake her mind. Afterward, if she survives, scars will cover her body where the spots have been." Nefru took a step closer, skeptically peering down at Tasha.

"Don't get too near, Your Highness. It spreads quickly," Nepthys warned.

Nefru reared, taking a step back and studying the small, dark face above the sheet. She shook her head in disbelief. "That's ridiculous. I don't see any sign of sickness."

"It's early yet, my Lady, but during this stage the disease spreads most quickly." She turned and bent over Tasha, examining her eyes in search of symptoms then nodded. "Just as I thought, a plague."

Nefru gasped, covering her mouth.

"You have a lovely complexion, my Lady, smooth and unmarred. I beg you not to bring harm to yourself, for you are Pharaoh's wife."

Nefru lifted a hand to her smooth cheek, contemplating Nepthys' words. "And — you know how to care for this sickness so it does not spread?"

Nepthys nodded, not trusting her voice enough to speak.

The Queen scowled, her tone brusque. "Then I suppose I have little recourse. See that she is on her feet soon and catches up with her duties if she survives. I will be away for a while, thank Amon, as I have business in Avaris."

Nepthys nodded, turning to Tasha as the door closed. "There must be a god watching over you," she whispered. Rising, she glanced toward the door then made her way to a mending chest. Tasha raised her brow as Nepthys pulled a needle from a swatch of linen. "Just in case she puts a servant up to spying."

Nepthys pricked her finger and dabbed Tasha's face and arms with small red dots. "With any luck she'll stay in Avaris long enough to give us a welcomed reprieve. Perhaps even long enough for you to have your child."

"We will pray," Tasha managed.

Nepthys curiously watched her. "Yes, I suppose we could."

Thutmose reined to a stop before the newly completed palace, not taking time to admire its columned porches nor the marbled grandeur rising into the sky above the sea. Instead he stepped from his chariot, pushing past his concubine who had run out to meet him.

He said nothing to Rekmire who waited at one side for his attention.

"A scribe, now!" he commanded, whereupon a young man hurried forward, reed pen and scroll in hand. "Send a dispatch to Thebes with a message for Puseneb: he is to destroy all monuments bearing the names of Moses and Hatshepsut. He is to deface their statues, vandalize their tombs, desecrate Hatshepsut's temple, and erase the memory of them from Egypt forever. No one is to speak their names again except as a curse."

Rekmire's eyes widened. "What of the obelisks in the Temple of Karnak, my Lord?"

"Destroy them."

Rekmire gulped back his fear. "But they can't be removed without damaging the temple. To do so, my Lord, would incur Amon's wrath."

"Then cover them with something, I don't care, just so long as the gods and people can't read their inscriptions." He continued without stopping, "I want Hatshepsut's records destroyed and her administration exiled to Elephantine, all but Puseneb for whom I have something special in mind."

Rekmire hardly dared form the question foremost in his mind. "Then you did not find Moses?"

Thutmose's eyes blazed in answer but he said nothing, for Nefru had just arrived at that palace, interrupting their meeting. Her eyes disdainfully met his, her lip curled in a sneer, and Thutmose wondered how he had ever found her attractive.

"One thing more." He meaningfully turned to her. "I want the Princess Meryet brought to Avaris to become my second wife, one whom I can enjoy, who will give me a son and heir."

Nefru's eyes widened then intensified as the air crackled with tension between them. She turned in a huff and entered the palace.

Yet Rekmire had more than women on his mind and dared one more question. "About the fugitive, my Lord, might we send out a scouting party into Sinai just in case?"

Thutmose peered down the shadowed hall as if seeing the one of whom they spoke. He took an unsteady breath. "Go ahead, but you won't find anything." He turned to his Vizier, his expression hard and his fists knotted at his sides. "He has escaped with the confederate leaders deep into Syrian territory to stir up an even bigger army against us."

Rekmire's jaw dropped in response and he started to speak, but Thutmose continued more to himself than to his Vizier. "By the blood of my fathers, I'll hunt him down and bring him back to Egypt, whether in one piece or many."

Moses roused himself from his mat as the sun poured through the open tent flap. He rubbed his eyes and looked about for his sandals. It had been almost three months since he had fled the Delta. Surely by now Aaron and Tasha had arranged their escape. It would be an opportune time, for Thutmose would have left for Syria on another of his campaigns, hopefully still looking for him there.

Moses draped Aaron's rough–textured cape about his shoulders, ducking out of the tent and into the sunshine. The time had come for him to leave Midian.

A column of smoke lifted above the fire while the aroma of roasted lamb mingled with the pungent odor of sheep and goats in their pens. Leah, the youngest of the sisters, sat beside the fire, smiling up at him.

"Did you have a good sleep? Father says you will need lots of rest if you intend to take the herd to summer pasture." She pointed to a distant ridge of rock before a rugged range of mountains. "The herds like to graze there on the plain in the shadow of Mount Sinai during the hottest months after the sun has burnt everything here in the valley."

"I've stayed long enough. It is time I completed my journey." Moses looked as far west as he could. "I'm supposed to meet someone. Besides," he attempted a smile, "I'm no shepherd."

"Then what are you?"

He studied her a moment but did not answer, and the girl continued. "Father says —"

"Leah!" Zipporah's voice cut through the serene morning air as she stepped into view, a shepherd's crook in her hand. "Tend to the cooking and leave our guest to me."

The younger girl frowned, resentfully fastening her eyes on her older sister.

Zipporah threw Moses a glance then nodded. "Come, I'll show you what shepherding is really like." She motioned him toward the sheepfold.

"I can't," Moses protested, continuing in the direction of his horse, but Zipporah bridged the distance between them.

He handed her an empty water skin. "Here, fill this while I get my bedroll."

Zipporah's smile vanished and she stared at him. The thought struck Moses that her features seemed uncommonly beautiful when at rest, unmarred by her actions. A strand of hair fell across her face. Never before had he noticed, but she had eyes the color of the Great Sea, green and fathomless.

She frowned, breaking the magic of the moment and he turned back to his horse, retrieving his pack. "The water skin," he called over his shoulder. As he passed Leah, he handed her a piece of hide in which to wrap some meat. "Something for my journey."

Leah smiled up at him and obligingly sliced a generous portion, but Zipporah stopped her.

She stood halfway between the sheep pen and the fire and dropped the empty water skin at her feet, her hands on her hips. "It seems our guest has lost his manners. Since when do you order your hostesses to do your bidding?"

Moses flushed with anger. "I didn't think a shepherdess who draws water for sheep would mind filling the water skin for her guest."

He walked toward her and bent to retrieve the skin but she put her foot on it. "You didn't ask, you ordered."

Moses' eyes flashed. "If you won't comply, at least remove your foot and I'll fill it myself."

"I won't, and you will ask."

They faced each other like two well matched jackals, neither giving ground. Zipporah's nostrils flared. "Or are you so high born and mighty you refuse to ask? Do you think we haven't noticed your airs?"

Moses forced calmness into his tone. "I am used to servants and stewards doing my bidding."

He reached for the skin but she kicked it from him. "Servants and stewards? Who are you really?"

Moses' jaw firmed. "I told you, a soldier on a mission for Pharaoh."

She took his hand in hers and scrutinized his palm. "These are not the hands of a soldier."

Moses jerked away, but her eyes bore into his, their depths intensifying. "Who are you and where are you from?"

Moses snatched up the water skin. "It's time for me to go."

"Look!" Leah arose, dropping the meat she had prepared and pointing north where a patch of cloud grew about a band of approaching horsemen.

Moses hardly saw the sight before looking for a weapon. He snatched Leah's knife and started toward his horse but Zipporah moved into action.

"No!" She pointed to a shed in the sheepfold. "Hide here."

Moses glanced at his horse then back at Zipporah.

"Hurry or they'll see you!" Zipporah anxiously watched the riders.

Moses ducked beneath the fence and into the shadows of the shed, clutching the knife. The sheep momentarily objected but soon returned to their languid munching of straw. Zipporah ordered Leah back to the fire and strode to meet the men.

The foremost dismounted, his striped headdress setting him apart from other visitors to their camp. Jethro hobbled from his tent but Zipporah stepped in front of him, facing the men.

"Who are you and what do you want?" She raised her voice to a pitch even Moses could hear.

"We're looking for a fugitive who may have come this way." The stranger studied the young women who had gathered about the fire and raised a brow. "If he were in the vicinity I'm sure he would have stopped."

Another laughed. "More for the company than sustenance."

One of them spotted Moses' horse and rode toward it. He accusingly turned. "Where did this come from?" He scanned the camp as he spoke, the other Egyptian alighting from his horse and entering the tents.

Zipporah stammered, at a momentary loss for words. "We — we found it when it wandered into our camp."

The soldier took the reins of the mare, appraising it as he did so, and addressed his comrade. "It's from Egypt alright. Probably escaped when the caravan we passed was ambushed." He nodded to the shed, peering between the slats of the fence. "What's in there?"

"A sheepfold and shed where our cattle rest and bear their young."

Moses tightened his grip on the knife, his breathing quickening. The soldier started toward the fence but the other shook his head. "Come, we'll not find him among a family of desert Bedouin." He laughed. "Somehow I can't imagine a Prince of Egypt doing anything more than stopping for food and water." He pointed in the direction of the Red Sea. "It's more likely he took refuge in one of the oases along the way."

"We've been to most of them." The first watched Zipporah, his eyes hungrily roving over her body.

She met his gaze with a defiant glare.

The other turned toward his horse and mounted. "If he went anywhere he probably headed for Elath, perhaps seeking passage to another land, such as Punt. I hear he visited there several years ago while acquiring riches for the former Pharaoh."

Another reined in his horse. "Then we'll not find him here. Come."

The men glanced about the camp a last time, their lips curled in scorn. Without further comment they

turned their steeds southward toward Elath and the Red
Sea, kicking up a receding cloud of dust in their wake.

Moses stepped from the shadows of the pen,
watching the horses diminish, eventually lost in a blur
of sand. A lump formed in his throat. Once at Elath
they would set a watch over the port. Even if Tasha and
Aaron were to make it across the desert, which seemed
impossible, they would get no farther.

Zipporah broke the silence. "A Prince?"

Her words were lost in a realization as vast as the
desert surrounding him. He stared at the white–hot glare
spread as far and wide as he could see while the Midianite
women clustered about him. He would never escape now,
not with Thutmose's scouts watching for him. Worst of
all, the safest place for him was here in the desert with a
family of lowly Bedouin.

With as much pomp as Pharaoh himself, Puseneb
followed the steward down Karnak's western wing to the
treasured White House, a room so filled with Thutmose's
war trophies the pile barely fit into the room and reached
nearly to the ceiling. Puseneb was well acquainted with
the cache, for he had personally helped store the horde
and would have a hand in sorting and documenting it
when time allowed.

Lately, however, he had been so occupied with
Pharaoh's edict of destruction he had time for little else.
Just considering defacing another of the former Pharaoh's
statues made him sweat. He had overseen the ruin of
every monument erected to her and her impostor son,
chiseling off their names and images and replacing them
with Thutmose's own until not a trace of the former

administration was left in Egypt. He had ordered the obelisks in Karnak's court plastered over, and had helped banish an entire administration to exile, though they had pled and wept more sorrowfully than a funeral dirge as they filed onto the ships.

At last it appeared his service for the new Pharaoh would be recognized for the feat it was, for it had taken almost as much time to deface the monuments as it had to create them. After several months of toil, Puseneb and his servants had successfully erased the two cursed ones, may their names never be spoken, from Egypt's remembrance. No doubt he would now be rewarded.

The steward unlocked the double doors and the two stepped into the treasure house, Puseneb's eyes glittering like jewels as he studied the mountain of gold, electrum, and precious stones. Though the steward never said a word, Puseneb knew his thoughts and felt the heat of frustration at having to choose only one item. If he were blessed, the steward would offer him two. Who would know the difference?

He picked up an ornate gold and obsidian crown inlaid with a turquoise and silver Eye of Horus. He suddenly recognized the crown as having once belonged to Hatshepsut, and dropped it as if it were accursed. The eye seemed to stare up at him from among the litter of articles as if accusing him for his part in her downfall. Shaken, Puseneb turned away to another area of the pile.

He lifted a large shield once wielded by Thutmose I, surely the largest and thickest item of gold in the room. Holding it against his belly, he searched the maze of objects, his gaze alighting on various treasures from Syria, Kush, Wawat, Punt, and even the Isles of the Great Sea.

He was still studying the dazzling items when the flame from the lamp momentarily swayed, making the light and shadows dance on the wall, then all was still again. Puseneb was too busy to care, and continued to search through the horde, but the light seemed to dim so that he struggled to see. At last he had made up his mind. He would take the shield, and if allowed, would ask for the jeweled crown from the Governor of Tyre. Surely Thutmose wouldn't care for the discarded relic of a conquered foreigner. To be sure it fit, he set the weighty piece atop his head and turned to the steward, but the door was closed and he alone stood amidst that unimaginable heap of wealth.

Puseneb looked puzzled, then chuckled to himself and turned to the mound with renewed vigor, climbing atop it and frantically picking through the treasures as a starving child would a platter of sweet breads. At last he had time to search in earnest. He would find the biggest and best before the steward returned.

He admired a ruby studded necklace and stuffed it into his shirt, tucking an ankh into his sash as well. No one would miss these small articles among so many.

He clawed his way to the top of the pile, digging, tugging, and sweating with effort until the crown nearly toppled from his head, precariously tipping over one eye. Like a victor in battle, he pulled a sword from the tangled treasures and thrust it at an imaginary enemy. He laughed aloud, gathering an armload of objects and attempting to stumble down the mound, but found the weight more than he could carry.

The light from the lamp suddenly sputtered and died, and Puseneb dropped the treasures, unable to see anything at all. Falling to his knees, he gouged his flesh on the hard metal as he struggled from the heap, searching for the floor, the sword still in his hand.

Panting and sweating, he at last felt the smooth, cold marble beneath him and crawled to the door, trying the handle, but it was locked. Calling for the steward, he listened, hearing only the echo of his own voice within the empty chamber.

Turning to the blackness of the room he searched for a speck of light, anything to indicate an exit, a window, a way of escape, but saw nothing. His thoughts raced. Had the steward been called away? But why had he locked the door? Or had it locked of its own accord? Impossible, he knew the door well and had replaced the lock himself with a more secure one as he feared others might gain access to the treasure. It had a special bolt, and only he and a privileged few knew how to open it.

The thought left him numb with horror. Was this Thutmose's doing? Had the Pharaoh tricked him? His flesh turned cold and clammy, and his heart pounded as if to escape his chest. He stood and banged on the door, hearing only the frantic rhythm resounding in the hallway. He pounded until his fists ached, but still no one came. He hacked with his sword and clawed at the bolt, but it was no use. At last, realizing the futility of a struggle, he turned again to the blackness. The steward had left him alone and had purposefully locked the door behind him.

Puseneb sank to the floor before a scatter of unseen treasures, the heavy crown askew over one eye. He stared into the darkness. Thutmose had marked him as surely as he had the others and now there was no escape. He would have been better off to have been exiled, but that was no comfort to him now. Ironically, the horde of wealth he had so long coveted was his...for what little time he had left to enjoy it.

Nefru stood on the pillared porch overlooking the Great Sea and stared with indifference at the water as sunlight glanced off its crests in points of silver. She took a leisurely sip from her goblet. What was she doing in Avaris and why had she even bothered to come?

Since Meryet's arrival Thutmose had done nothing but taunt her with his absence, entertaining her sister instead. The usually compliant Meryet had, in the course of Nefru's stay, become aloof and unapproachable, remaining behind closed doors in Thutmose's apartment while servants came and went at her bidding. Nefru's features twisted with envy.

If only the Hyksos had finished him off on his last mission. Instead, he had won yet another battle, as if the gods had not blessed him above reason already. It appeared no enemy could stand against him, though many had tried. He had even triumphed over Hatshepsut and Moses, and rumor had it he had ordered the holy Puseneb snuffed out of existence as well. Nefru laughed with bitterness. She could no more win Thutmose's favor than she could hope to enjoy his defeat.

A breeze tugged at her robe, outlining the contours of her body. Perhaps she should return to Pithom and forget her marriage.

She stubbornly shook her head. Her presence represented the one discomfort she could assure the newly wedded pair and she intended to make it count.

She took another sip, her eyes fixed on a cluster of specks that seemed to materialize from the very sea. She stood transfixed, watching them grow until a voice broke the silence behind her. "Keftiu! The Keftiu are coming!"

With the announcement the palace flew into a flurry of excitement. Thutmose's voice rose above the rest as he ordered his soldiers to the quay. Footsteps hastened in all directions but Nefru remained rooted where she stood, sipping her wine and watching the fleet enlarge as it sailed toward her. As the ships glided toward port she noted the bulls brandished on their sails and the soldiers' armor gleaming in the afternoon sun.

"I hope they skewer Thutmose through his shriveled heart," she whispered. "At least then there'll be room for no other." She smiled to herself and finished her drink.

"My Lady!" Nefru's maid ran into the room, breathless. "I've looked for you everywhere. Come, we must flee!"

She grasped Nefru's arm, guiding her to the door, but Nefru resisted. "I'm not going anywhere. I've done nothing wrong. Let the Keftiu deal with me as they will."

Ignoring her demands, the maid wrapped a cloak about the Queen's shoulders, grabbing a few articles and stuffing them into a satchel.

She pulled Nefru to the door just as a servant burst into the room. "An envoy from Thera, and they come peaceably."

The maid dropped the bag as her hands flew to her breast. "Thank the gods!"

Nefru lifted a well–groomed brow. "An envoy?" Moses had travelled to the Isle of Thera years before, having quite a tale to tell when he had returned. She pushed thoughts of Moses aside and imagined instead the naked bull jumpers depicted on their artwork, their muscular bodies reflecting the sun. She smiled. At last she would see them in the flesh.

Sinking into a chair, she yielded to the hands of her servants as the women applied her make–up and rearranged her hair. Nefru accepted a refilled goblet to calm her nerves.

An envoy from Thera....They had threatened the port several years earlier when Thutmose had commanded the northern troops. Why come peaceably now? Instead of fear, however, she felt the thrill of excitement. What would they look like, and what would they think of her?

The steward of her wardrobe breezed into the room with a blue gown draped over one arm.

"No, the rose one," Nefru took another drink. "It will give me color."

Nefru let the attendants fuss about her, reveling in their attention. She had not realized, until the prospect of visitors, how she had come to depend on her servants to fill the emptiness in her hours. The thought surprised her, and she wondered if Thutmose had noticed, or even cared. Probably not, as Meryet occupied his every moment. Jealousy flamed through her but the wine dulled its impact. She would no longer pine in her room but would meet this envoy face to face, no matter what Thutmose thought of it.

A trumpet sounded and Nefru set her goblet aside, unsteadily rising. She allowed her entourage to lead her from her chamber to the audience room where she took her place next to Meryet in a reception line. She proudly lifted her head in spite of the fact she stood farthest of the two from Thutmose. They waited for what seemed hours before hearing the commotion of their guests' arrival.

All at once a face loomed over her, the visage of a god. His skin shone like bronze and his features rivalled those of Amon himself. Nefru gasped. The man's hair hung in ringlets about his face, his muscular arms extending toward her with an intricately painted urn.

"For you, my Lady." His eyes as blue as the sky held hers, raising her from the depths of despondency to heights such as only gods and goddesses experience.

She found her voice as she unashamedly stared at him. "How stunning. I have truly never seen anything like it." Realizing the eyes of those in the room rested on her, she blushed, her cheeks turning a complimentary rosy hue.

He lifted her hand to his lips. "I am sure you will have ample opportunity to convey your thanks."

Nefru smiled, acutely aware of his hand on hers and the touch of his lips on her skin. She glanced at Thutmose but found him occupied in other conversation.

Nefru reluctantly lowered her hand. "I hope to have many such opportunities. How long do you plan to stay in Avaris?"

"As long as we are welcome."

Nefru slipped her arm through his, the bulging muscle flexing at her touch. She smiled up at him and turned toward the patio. "Then we have much to discuss and can take as long as we like."

His arm brushed her breast and she felt her body tingle to life. He pressed his other hand over hers, turning to smile at his comrades. Though she wondered if his reaction had anything to do with her, she didn't care. All that mattered was that he stood at her side.

"What is your name?" She looked into his eyes, at once lost in their blueness as if adrift on a vast sea.

"Styrone, Commander of Thera's navy."

CHAPTER 19

Moses stopped midway up Mount Sinai and turned to look at the view. Below him the wasteland reached in muted hues to an infinite haze of blue at the horizon; behind him, in the opposite direction, stretched a rough and rugged terrain of seemingly endless mountains.

"Beautiful, isn't it?" Zipporah rested on her staff, studying the scene as the goats clambered on ahead of her. "I never tire of it. It's what I like best about coming here."

Moses watched her, allowing himself a low laugh. "You mean you actually find something beautiful in not seeing evidence of another living being? Don't you feel trapped in this wasteland?"

"You can't compare the desert to the Delta. This is peace and solitude, though the desert can take a life in a matter of hours. See there?" She lifted a slim dark arm and pointed south across the gentle contours of desert. "Our camp."

Moses squinted but could see nothing save a tiny wisp of smoke rising from the desert floor.

"And there?" She pointed west where an outline of turquoise marked the beginning of the Red Sea. She took a deep breath. "Sometimes I can even make out faint traces of ships. So you see, we are not alone." She smiled. "Besides, Yahweh is with us. Have you heard of Him?"

Moses stared at her. The last thing he wanted was a lecture on her religion. "Yes, the Habiru pronounce his name Yahovah, but worship the same god."

"The one and only God." Her statement gave no room for argument and she turned to resume her ascent. They had left the sheep with two of her younger sisters at the base of the mountain while they took the goats to a spring farther up to refill their water skins. "Father says Yahweh dwells in this mountain." She took a few more steps as a scuff of rock skittered down the precipice behind her. "Yet I've come here often and have never seen Him. Father says no man can see Him and live."

Moses smiled to himself. Zipporah had seen nothing because there was nothing to see, but even if Yahovah did exist, what kind of god would dwell in a mountain?

She turned, waiting for him to catch up with her. Moses ignored the affront. She obviously had never known the luxury of owning a horse. Still, her attitude grated him, and he reminded himself he had agreed to come not for her company but to hide from further scouts.

He stopped on a jutting ledge and scanned the view at his feet. Unclasping his cloak, he draped it over his arm, his chest shiny with sweat. He glanced farther up the trail, wondering when they would reach their destination where they could make camp for the night. He didn't care to flounder up the mountainside in the dark.

"It isn't far," Zipporah called out as if reading his thoughts. "There's a plateau just ahead where the goats can graze, and a spring to refresh ourselves."

Moses watched her with annoyance, wondering how much farther 'not far' was. He continued up the trail, concentrating on his steps and keeping careful watch on the sun's slow decline in the west. The horizon was set afire with the sunset when they finally came upon a grassy plateau where a spring gurgled. The water filled a natural basin near a rock wall where the goats eagerly gathered to drink.

"We'll sleep here," Zipporah stated, dropping her bundle. "The flock won't wander now that they have water."

Moses gladly dropped his belongings and grabbed his water skin. Kneeling by the pool, he scooped mouthfuls of the liquid then splashed it on his face and neck. After filling his water skin he reclined next to the pool, his energy spent.

Zipporah walked to where he lay and knelt beside him. Lifting her sleeves, she reached into the pool and washed the dust from her face and arms then drank a handful, letting the water dribble down her chin and into the neckline of her robe. Moses watched as she pulled off her headdress, shaking her hair free. It fell over her shoulders in a dark glistening wave, covering one breast, and Moses found himself watching her with more than indifference. She smiled at him, her green eyes searching.

Moses impatiently rose, leaving the water skin near his pack and rummaging through his belongings. He wondered now at Zipporah's motive in asking him to accompany her. Had she really hoped to keep him from being discovered, or did she have something else in mind?

He untied his bedroll and shook it free with a snap, laying it atop his mat, and looked about for wood to build a fire.

Zipporah walked to where he stood, bending over her own bundle and producing a pot and pan. "I'll make tea and fry up some salted meat."

As he walked past her his arm brushed hers and he cursed his luck at finding himself here in her company. In spite of his agitation, the air invigorated him and the darkness surrounded him like a comforting curtain. He scrounged for an armload of brush and started back to the campsite. As he arrived Zipporah met him and reached for the wood. Their eyes met and their fingers touched as she lifted it into her arms.

"I — I hope you didn't mind the climb up the mountain." She paused, an awkward silence between them. "I knew you would like it here once we arrived."

Moses nodded, irritated. "It doesn't matter if I like it or not. I am here."

They both fell silent as Zipporah built a fire, propping sticks against each other over shavings of wood and goats hair. She struck a piece of flint until sparks ignited in a tiny burst of light. At first the flame died, but she tried again and again until successful, blowing on the tiny tongue of fire until it grew. Pushing it beside the pile, she added leaves and twigs as it crackled to life.

Zipporah glanced up to find Moses watching her. "Come warm yourself," she invited. Her voice sounded soft and soothing in the darkness like the cooing of a dove, but Moses continued to stand.

She looked up at him, the flame reflected in her eyes.

He gazed into the darkness. His hope of ever seeing Tasha seemed as remote as the farthest horizon now lost from view. He had no future, and no past he cared to remember other than her. There was only the present.

He knelt before the fire, warming himself. At length he took the plate Zipporah offered him and a cup of steaming liquid. He slowly ate, watching her as she moved about the fire, her hair catching the light as if spun with copper, her movement and her shadow hypnotic. When she had finished eating she walked to the pool to wash, and though he could no longer see her, he could hear the pleasant splash of water and the steady trickle of liquid running over the rock.

Moses set his plate aside and stared into the fire. Why had the gods dealt with him so? Did they taunt him, taking pleasure in his suffering? He hated the desert and had no respect for those who spent their lives here, especially lowly shepherds. He glanced at Zipporah and grunted. The only thing a Bedouin could look forward to was a good meal and a willing woman.

As if reading his thoughts, Zipporah walked to the fire, squatting beside him. He could feel the warmth of her body next to his, lean and firm, her breathing shallow.

His voice broke the silence. "Do you usually come here alone, or with your sisters?"

She looked into his eyes. "I rarely come alone. Usually two of my younger sisters accompany me to the plateau while the others stay below."

He watched the flames twirl and gyrate, the colors merging then separating like a band of wild dancers, their shadows on the rock wall mimicking them.

He turned to Zipporah. "How old are you?" He took a sip of the warm liquid.

"Thirty years." She smiled.

"That's quite a feat, thirty and not yet married."

She shrugged. "I keep busy enough and haven't felt the need. Besides," she paused, carefully weighing her words, "men are scarce in the desert."

Their eyes met and Moses took another sip. "What about other Bedouin?"

Zipporah laughed. "It's difficult to marry someone with whom you usually quarrel." She stood and stretched, her arms appearing almost white in the firelight.

Moses set his cup aside and stood to face her. "Is that why you asked me here?"

Zipporah froze, her face revealing what she dared not admit. She looked down but he lifted her chin, forcing her eyes to his, their green depths intensifying as if peering into his very soul. He closed his eyes, not wanting to reveal the struggle within him.

Pulling her into his arms, he kissed her with more fierceness than he had intended as her body melted into his. Then taking her by the hand, he drew her to his bed where they warmed themselves by a fire that steadily burned until morning.

Meryet sat at her vanity while her maid fussed over her make–up. She picked up her bronze mirror and critically eyed the fine lines at the corners of her eyes. She mustn't appear to have aged or Thutmose might not find her attractive, in spite of the light in her eyes and her precious secret. If she didn't take care she would look no better than Nefru, and she could not tolerate that, for her sister had allowed herself to plummet to uncommonly low depths until her lifestyle had begun to show in her appearance.

An announcement sounded at the door and Thutmose entered before the servant had a chance to admit him. "You summoned me?"

Meryet gave a startled laugh and dismissed her maid, reluctantly laying aside the mirror.

Thutmose sat on her couch, frowning. "I wish Styrone and his bunch would leave. He's far too concerned about my military affairs, asking for a tour of the garrison and shipyards. He mocks me. He knows we haven't a navy let alone a shipyard."

Meryet picked up her mirror again. "Perhaps you should build one."

"I only have so much manpower, and need all I have for my army and for rebuilding the capital."

Meryet dipped her fingers in a jar of olive oil, dabbing it at the corners of her eyes. "The Habiru could build your ships."

Thutmose rose, his jaw clenched at the very mention of them. "My men are used to marching not sailing. I confiscated over seven hundred chariots at Megiddo and I aim to use them. There would be no room for chariots aboard ships."

Meryet shrugged. "What about an alliance? The Keftiu could provide the ships and we the men."

A picture of Styrone came to mind and Thutmose shook his head. "They're more likely to use their strength against us, not for us. No, there'll be no alliance with the likes of them." He paced the length of her room. "I wish they'd go back to their island. Their departure is long overdue."

Meryet scrutinized the corners of her eyes, already imagining an improvement after the oil. "If Nefru would leave Styrone alone they might want to leave."

Thutmose's eyes narrowed and she realized he didn't know. He strode to her side. "What's she doing and with whom?"

Meryet's throat tightened so she could hardly breathe. She had witnessed the extent of Thutmose's fury and did not relish it being unleashed even on her wayward sister. She swallowed, forcing a laugh. "Drinking. Nefru makes a fool of herself at every banquet."

Thutmose studied her. "What has that to do with the Keftiu?"

"I — well." Meryet glanced about the room as if for escape, her mind racing. She had little respect for her sister but would not be responsible for her destruction. Thutmose pulled her to her feet and Meryet glanced down at her abdomen, her features lifting. "She would be jealous if she knew."

Thutmose stopped, his brow wrinkling. "Knew what?"

Meryet clasped his rough hand in hers, moving it to her abdomen, and breathed a prayer of thanksgiving for the timing of her news. "About our child."

Thutmose's jaw dropped.

Meryet nodded. "A son and heir, Thutmose, I am sure. The gods are blessing us with a child."

Thutmose sat down and looked at her in astonishment. "You mean you're going to have a baby?"

Meryet nodded, her face brightening with pent–up laughter. She spilled it in a musical trill like the song of a bird. "Our baby, Thutmose, a son to sit on the throne after you," she smiled, "to follow in your steps, to rule the Two Lands, to build your navy."

Thutmose watched her, trying to picture it. His Syrian concubine had given him a daughter more than a year ago, yet he hardly knew the child. She toddled about the palace keeping her mother and half a dozen servants occupied, but a son and heir was what he truly wanted.

A grin spread across his face. He held Meryet at arm's length, looking her up and down as if to assess the change even now occurring within her. He beamed. All at once the long wait until next year's campaign didn't seem like such a bleak prospect after all.

Nefru sat beneath the trellis and stared out at a midnight sea awash with a silvery span under a full moon.

The lengthening glow stretched from the cliff's edge near where she sat to the unseen horizon, making it appear she had only to step out onto the sea and walk that moonlit path to oblivion.

She heard a noise behind her and started, turning to see Styrone stride across the yard. He approached her and smiled. She had never noticed before, but at night his features seemed too sharply cut, appearing even grotesque in the darkness, partly hidden by the shadows of his face.

Nefru rose, her hand on the gentle bulge of her abdomen. "Did anyone see you?"

"I don't think so." Styrone took a last glance behind him, touching his sword. "Only my men who keep watch," he turned back to her, a smile slitting his face, "and if we wait here any longer they'll have an eyeful." He pulled her toward the garden house. "Come, I haven't much time." He paused, catching himself before revealing too much. "I'm to meet with my Officers tonight to plan our departure."

Nefru clutched his arm. "Departure? Has Thutmose told you to leave?"

"No, but I sense his dissatisfaction."

She shivered at the mere mention of her husband. "As far as I know he doesn't suspect us." A frown tugged at her mouth. "He's far too busy with his army and Meryet."

Styrone opened the door of the garden house and closed it behind them, already unfastening his kilt. His eyes lit with anticipation. "If he doesn't suspect, all the better."

Nefru reluctantly dropped her robe as Styrone pulled her into his embrace. An unnamed fear pounded in her breasts. "Then why meet with your men?"

He ignored her, a question of his own on his mind. His voice dropped to a husky whisper as he kissed her neck. "The child, when is it to be born?"

She pulled away, all passion draining from her body, her senses alert. Her hand instinctively moved to her abdomen. "I — I'm not sure. Why?"

Styrone studied her then shook his head. "It doesn't matter. It will happen soon enough."

Nefru felt faint with realization, going through the motions of their lovemaking as if her mind were detached from her body. Styrone was leaving her. Had he merely used her? If so, why? Questions pelted her with dizzying speed. Had he designs on the throne through their child?

Once finished Nefru dressed and straightened her hair, her heart pounding and her head light. She felt ugly and used, as if a monster from the nether world had violated her, impregnating her with its child. As they stepped from the garden house a twig crackled, nearly making her heart stop. Her hand flew to her mouth. Styrone crouched like a lion, ready to spring, his thighs tense and his sword drawn.

A figure stepped from the shadows. "It's me, Archiles." The voice of Styrone's Officer cut through the silence. "I've come to warn you. Thutmose has set a watch over your apartment."

Styrone stepped under cover of darkness while Nefru hurried after him, feeling vulnerable and exposed. Another fear engulfed her: fear her husband would discover her dark secret.

Styrone's Officer continued, "We'll have to call off our meeting and figure out how to get you back inside without him seeing you, perhaps by way of the balcony."

Styrone's eyes narrowed. "Then he suspects."

"It's likely. At the least his friendly reception is waning. Besides, we might as well leave for Thera now that you have accomplished what you set out to, if you know what I mean."

Styrone glanced at Nefru. "Oh, I've left my mark all right."

The Keftiu turned their backs on Nefru as they hurried toward the palace, their voices dropping to a whisper as they left her to fend for herself.

The sting of betrayal flamed across Nefru's face as surely as if Styrone had struck her, her body convulsing with revulsion at the knowledge of what she carried and to whom it belonged.

Lifting her gown, she fled up the walkway toward a seldom used back entrance, vowing to never trust another man as long as she lived. Hastening down the royal wing, she turned in the direction of the physician's quarters, her feet pattering as softly as raindrops over the polished floor. The physician would vouch for her whereabouts this past hour as well as prescribe a remedy for the curse in her womb. She had heard of herbs used to expel an unwanted child, and would bribe the physician for his cooperation, or else silence him herself if he did not. She would do anything to rid herself of the memory of Styrone.

Aaron awoke with effort, rolling from his mat and attempting to shake the sleep from his head. His body ached and every joint felt stiff and unyielding. His feet were dry and cracked, caked with bits of mud he had not been able to wash off. He groaned as Miriam poked her head into his tent.

"Hurry! The Overseer approaches."

Aaron unsteadily arose and threw a worn cloak about his shoulders, one he had found near a dead Habiru. Fitting he should wear it. The way he felt, he could be next.

"Come!" Miriam called again before scurrying past his door.

Aaron lifted the tent flap, bracing himself for a confrontation, when lilting laughter met his ears.

Elisheba, the woman he had met at the brick pit, stepped into the Overseer's path. The man's eyes widened with surprise then interest as he followed her with his gaze.

Aaron hurried to his place in line, his heart pounding. Elisheba glanced his way before finding her own spot, though the Overseer continued to watch her. Had she risked herself for him? It appeared so, and of all reasons, because he had overslept. Aaron chided himself for his foolishness. He should have gone to bed as soon as he returned to camp, but instead he had led several Habiru in a time of worship about the well. Now he questioned the wisdom of it.

He glanced down the line at the Overseer who reluctantly moved on, keenly eyeing the row of laborers. A knot formed in Aaron's stomach and with it a desire to shield Elisheba from danger.

As the group trudged toward the brick pit Aaron agonized over what had happened, consumed with concern for Elisheba as he stepped once again into the mud. While he worked he kept watch over her, her movements awakening him, her glance quickening his pulse, and the Overseer's advances tightening the knot inside him. She bent over the pit where he stood and slowly dumped a load of straw.

He looked up at her, her braids dangling over her shoulders, and glanced toward the Overseer. "Thank you, but you shouldn't have risked yourself this morning."

Someone called her name and she looked at Aaron a last time before returning to her work, an unspoken understanding between them. The sun rose higher and crawled across the sky, replaced by an occasional cloud and a light afternoon rain that washed away his perspiration and cooled his skin. Elisheba bent over the pit again, wisps of hair framing her face, her thin, wet tunic clinging to the curves of her body. Aaron nervously eyed the Overseer, wondering if he would notice. He wanted to tell her of his concern, of his desire to protect her, but did not know how to form the words.

"Elisheba, I —" The words stuck in his throat and she prolonged the dumping of her straw, carefully brushing the strands from the folds of her apron. "Are you married?"

She shook her head as pain blurred her vision. "I — no, I can't." She glanced behind her at the Overseer and dropped her gaze.

Aaron watched the man with fury, her meaning understood in her silence. His throat felt so dry he could hardly speak. "I understand. It's not your fault. But would you, could you if you wanted to."

She studied his face, her eyes widening, and shook her head. "No one would want me this way."

Aaron's frame hardened. "I would, I do. I mean, it doesn't matter about the Overseer. We would manage somehow."

"I don't know." Elisheba glanced behind her, seeing the Overseer absorbed in conversation. "I could, but —"

"I would care for you and protect you as much as possible."

She nodded, unable to speak, biting back scalding tears. She slowly arose, turning up the path as the Overseer stepped in front of her. Aaron held his breath and clenched his teeth as the bulk of a man pulled her from the heap of straw toward a small tent just out of Aaron's view. The hour crept by as he awaited her return. When she finally arrived she kept her eyes lowered, avoiding his face.

Aaron felt weak with anguish, his head throbbing with hatred and his body numb. He plodded over the straw in the pit as if his limbs were made of stone, and when at last the day had ended he and Elisheba slowly and silently walked back to camp.

Aaron took her hand in his, her fingers cold and trembling as he enclosed them in his own. He gazed into her eyes, praying she would see strength in him instead of anger, and love in place of hatred and despair. He didn't want her to know that he, as well, wondered about the wisdom of such a union, nor did he care to admit he needed her comfort as much as she needed his.

She seemed to understand, however, without even speaking. A smile quivered on her lips as Aaron led her to his tent, where, in the simplest of ceremonies, they covenanted to love one another as much as Yahovah allowed. Then, too spent to think of anything else, they fell asleep in each other's arms, concerned only with surviving another day and avoiding the nightmare that stalked them.

Tasha paced before the open window, her belly tightening with another contraction. She caught her breath, gasping for air, and tried to will herself to relax, to focus on anything but the pain, but could hardly manage without crying out. Once the grip of childbirth had released its hold she leaned against the wall, panting, her strength spent.

The baby would soon be born. It was no small miracle that Nefru had stayed away these many months, but word had come she would soon return, and Tasha had watched with dismay as the servants busied themselves in preparation.

What of her and Moses' child? She pressed her hands over her belly, closing her eyes and groaning as the next contraction took hold, closely following on the heels of the last. She gasped for breath, her legs weakening as she eased herself onto her cot.

Nepthys abruptly entered, dropping a pile of bricks in the center of the room and stacking them in the form of a bottomless chair. "A birthing stool such as Habiru women use," she explained. "Come, sit on it, and with the next contraction push as hard as you can. We'll have this baby yet."

Tasha raised herself with effort, making her way to the stool and lifting her robe. Nepthys helped her onto the makeshift chair then waited below with a cloth to catch the child.

The clamor of hooves sounded outside the window as several chariots clattered to a stop. Tasha gasped with fear, but the next contraction tightened about her with such strength it took her breath away, her abdomen hard as she pushed with all her might. Panting as if having run a race, she gritted her teeth and waited for the next, groaning like a maimed animal as pain ripped through her body. A searing heat spread throughout her loins, burning as she pushed, and she cried out, fists clenched, as an immense pressure burst beneath her.

"Good! The head has come and he has hair as black as the night." Nepthys attempted a smile but the sound of Nefru's shrill voice pierced the air. Tasha's eyes widened, but Nepthys encouragingly nodded. "There, now the head is free. With this next contraction, press hard, really hard, and we'll have this baby."

Tasha gasped for breath, her eyes luminous with pain as sweat soaked her gown. A moment later the suffocating squeeze of childbirth took hold again. She grunted, clenching her fists till her palms bled and pushing with all her might as the pent–up pressure released from her body and the infant slipped free into the waiting arms of Nepthys. Tasha groaned, faint with exhaustion, her limbs glistening as the chord pulsed between her and her child. Nepthys quickly pinched and cut the fleshy rope uniting them, wrapping the babe in a blanket.

She looked into the wee face as Nepthys nodded. "A son, Tasha. You and Moses have a son."

Tasha reached out to touch him but Nefru's voice shrieked in the silence of the hall. Nepthys glanced at the back door. "I'm taking him to the village as you arranged."

"Let me see him first!" Tasha cried, but footsteps neared, and with a last frightened glance behind her, Nepthys hurried out the back way, closing the door just as Nefru entered the other.

Tasha dropped her head, weeping into the folds of her gown, her hair disheveled.

Nefru stepped into the room, her mouth dropping at sight of Tasha as rage ignited in her eyes. "So you thought to have this child without my knowledge, did you? Well I'm back and none too soon." Her lips tightened with fury. "Never again will I have a reminder of Moses or any other man in my house." She moved her hand over her own flat abdomen and watched with twisted wonder as another contraction wracked Tasha's body, reveling in the pain reflected on the delicate features. Tasha cried out, and Nefru squatted before her, transfixed with both fascination and revulsion. As Tasha pushed, Nefru reached beneath the folds of the garment to catch the child, but instead into Nefru's hands fell the bloody mass of afterbirth.

Nefru's face contorted with horror. Screaming she dropped the discarded flesh, staring as if haunted by demons of the Netherworld.

Shaking, she clenched her teeth and struck Tasha full across the face. "Where's the child? I demand to know!" She struck her again then steadied herself, as if the blow had required more energy than she had to give.

Instead of answering, Tasha hung her head and sobbed, her hair clinging to her damp face and her limbs so weak she could not stop from shaking. Darkness threatened to engulf her as she thought of the child she yearned to hold. Her body ached, and her breasts felt hard and ready to burst.

Yet in spite of her grief a spark of hope lit within her, lifting her thoughts above the torment of the moment. Hadn't Yahovah spared Moses as an infant, providing him a hiding place in this very palace? If Moses' God could accomplish such a feat, surely He could spare their son, assuring him refuge in the village of Moses' birth.

An eerie calm settled about the mountain as Moses and Zipporah broke camp. Winter would soon arrive, and with it more plentiful pasture in the valley. Moses looked around as he rolled up his belongings.

A sudden gust of wind stirred the brush and sand, rippling over the surface of the pool and making tiny waves on the water. Moses tied a rope about his pack, his eyes moving beyond the plateau to a path that wound around the mountain beyond them. He almost expected to see a form stroll from behind the rock wall and enter their camp.

Zipporah hurried toward him. "Come, we must be on our way. The Spirit of Yahweh moves in this place."

Moses glanced at the sky, giving the rope on his pack a hefty tug before hoisting it over his shoulder. "It's only the wind whistling through the canyons," he corrected. Still he warily looked about, listening as the storm moaned through the rocky crags. He and Zipporah hurried their pace down the mountain as if unseen fingers reached after them, the goats instinctively clamoring ahead.

"This god of yours," Moses called out to Zipporah, "tell me about him."

Zipporah paused, carefully choosing her words. "He is the God of creation. In the beginning He created man and woman, putting them in a beautiful garden. He walked with them, sharing His heart and His plans. But when they disobeyed He became angry, forcing them from the garden to a desert such as this where they learned to survive off the land."

She turned and looked back up the mountain. "Even though the world became so wicked Yahweh had to destroy mankind in a flood, one man and his family chose to worship Him still."

"A flood?" Moses had heard of the event in his own studies as a boy, for the Egyptians had also recorded a flood, as had the Syrians and others, but for a different purpose and with different deities. Might these stories stem from the same ancient source?

Zipporah tested the path with her staff. "You see, Yahweh is not all judgment, but kind and merciful as well. From what father understands of the ancient writings —"

"You mean you have written records?"

She appraised him, her green eyes vivid. "Of course, there is even a scroll referring to writings before the flood. Father has some of the scrolls hidden in urns in his sacred tent. The Habiru also have such scrolls, copied by the ancients and handed down from generation to generation."

Moses remembered the scroll Aaron had given him and wondered what it contained. "These writings, are they genealogies?"

Zipporah nodded. "Yes, and stories. They reveal Yahweh's desire to know mankind as He knew Adam and Eve."

A reverence he hadn't felt in years stirred within him. "Has Yahovah spoken to anyone since the garden?"

Zipporah laughed into the wind. "Of course. There was Seth, Enoch, and Abraham, who knew Yahweh best. We Midianites are also favored to have descended from Abraham."

"The Habiru are descendants of his as well. What do you know of these men?" Moses asked.

She shrugged. "We have many of the same customs. They came from Abraham's first wife, Sarah, while we descended from his second wife, Keturah." She lifted her chin. "Though we are close kin, the Habiru remain enslaved while we enjoy our freedom."

Zipporah shaded her eyes and studied the distant wisp of smoke marking her family's camp, but Moses could not take his thoughts from this god. His gods had never spoken to him, though he had prayed and pleaded for years. No doubt they saved their revelations for true Egyptians.

"Has your god ever spoken to you or your father?"

She looked at him aghast and shook her head. "Of course not. He hasn't spoken to our people in years."

"What of the Habiru? Might he have spoken to them?"

Zipporah incredulously studied him. "Why would Yahweh choose to speak to slaves?" She smiled with self–assurance, her eyes as clear and green as the Great Sea. "I don't know whether or not He speaks to anyone today, but I am certain He would never speak to a Habiru."

Chapter 20

Isis lay on her couch with a cool cloth on her forehead, her eyes red and swollen. She moaned and tried to sit up, but was too weak, and fell back in a dizzy stupor. How could it be?

She sniffed and dabbed at her eyes, taking care with her make–up, still haunted by images she could not rid herself of. After days of not hearing from Puseneb she herself conducted a search and had found him, much to her dismay, very dead. She sniffed again, still horrified at the memory. If she had not been Thutmose's own mother she might have been disposed of along with the High Priest. Instead, she had found her dear friend among the treasures of the god's house, his hands bloodied from pounding on the door, and his face fixed in perpetual agony. It appeared he had even tried to hack his way out with an ornate sword, but without success, not being used to physical exertion.

Poor Puseneb. She envisioned him now, a portly spirit roaming the halls of Karnak and quoting from the Book of the Dead, or, gods forbid, sentenced for eternity to serve as Hatshepsut's personal Priest.

She groaned at the thought, glancing at the crown she had garnered for her trouble, found near Puseneb's body. Poor man, he who loved the treasure house more than life itself, forced to die in it.

Puseneb wasn't the only spirit haunting Isis, however. Though the High Priest and his servants had labored to erase the names of Hatshepsut and her supposed son, her presence lingered still, whispering from the defaced walls of Karnak, and blowing like a hot breath through the halls of the palace and in this very room, forcing herself into even the thoughts of those who hated her.

Isis rose on one elbow and peered about as if expecting Hatshepsut and Puseneb to materialize before her, but instead she saw only the fluttering curtains before the balcony. She watched them a moment then dropped to her couch again, attempting to reason away her fears.

Since Puseneb's untimely death she had had numerous dreams and visions, seeing him strolling down Karnak's western wing with Hatshepsut at his arm, though the physicians had assured her it was merely the effect of too much wine.

Isis shuddered, reaching again for her goblet and emptying its contents. She felt a sudden breeze and wrapped her robe tighter about herself. Why would they bother her even if they did return? She trembled with unspoken knowledge, all too aware of the answer, and feeling suddenly nauseous as she peered into her empty goblet.

If the gods allowed, she would honor their memory by sending them each a gift from the treasure house to their tombs. After all, she had the wealth of Karnak at her disposal now that Puseneb was gone. Was she bribing the dead? Perhaps, but she must do something to placate them, especially Hatshepsut. If Puseneb disclosed the source of the former Pharaoh's death, Hatshepsut would have reason to vindicate herself, and she would.

Isis stood, attempting to steady herself, affected as much by the wine as by her throbbing headache. Life at Thebes was not at all what she had expected. In fact it seemed more of an exile than the prize she had hoped for. Though Thutmose had put her in charge of the palace, being here also kept her as far from him as possible. Perhaps that was his plan. She had just received word she was a grandmother again, though someone other than Thutmose had informed her. Nor had she been invited to see the baby. Thutmose obviously wanted nothing to do with her now that he had won the throne, conveniently forgetting who had helped him attain it. She steadied herself on her table.

Perhaps she was merely lonely. The palace seemed as quiet as a tomb with all those closest to her gone. When Hatshepsut had been present at least the festivals and holy days were maintained. Now it was all the servants could do to offer a semblance of decorum, let alone an atmosphere of festivity. Life at the palace had been reduced to that of a well-kept inn, while the world outside appeared unaffected. Everyone here seemed in a state of mourning. If that were to change it would be up to her.

Isis clapped for a servant, pointing to the jug as the girl entered. The maid poured her a drink and handed it to her.

Isis unsteadily straightened herself. "Summon the Steward of the Wardrobe and the head cooks and bakers. I wish to prepare a banquet for my Officers and their wives."

The girl's brow furrowed. "My Lady, which Officers shall I invite? All we have left are your personal stewards, the Governor, and the Priests of the temple, except the High Priest, of course."

Isis shuddered. "They will do. Summon them all and throw a banquet worthy of our company," she managed, with a wave of her hand.

"In whose honor, my Lady?" The girl bowed in order to hide the obvious bewilderment on her countenance.

Isis took another drink and hiccupped. "In honor of Hatshepsut and Puseneb, may their Kas rest in peace." She glanced about the room, fearing they might appear to thank her. Seeing they had not, she continued. "Perhaps if I honor them, even after their deaths, they will bless me from the nether world." She muttered beneath her breath, "Which would certainly be preferable to a personal visit." So saying she hiccupped and poured herself another drink.

Moses sat outside Zipporah's tent, remembering his return to Jethro's camp almost a year earlier. "Married?" The word had jarred him like a physical blow.

Jethro had nodded, quoting: 'A man who lies with a woman chooses her as his wife.' Unknowingly, according to Midianite custom, Moses had chosen Zipporah.

Moses made mental note of the women he had been intimate with since his youth. If he had married every woman he had lain with he would have had a harem by now. Besides, he was already married to Tasha, a fact he had chosen not to mention. He had tried to get out of the union with Zipporah but Jethro would not hear of it.

Squatting on his heels, Moses absently drew in the sand, outlining a crude map of the desert and Red Sea, marking the port of Elath and the land of Midian. He leaned against the tent post. If only he had left when given the chance. Now there was little hope of leaving Midian, or of ever seeing Tasha again.

Moses cursed his luck. He was no better than a prisoner. Now he would never be able to leave, not with Zipporah giving birth to their child. He felt revulsion twist in his stomach at the notion. He had married a Midianite shepherdess and soon his own children would scamper about this Bedouin camp, living in tents and feeding off the desert. He, who had once walked the halls of Karnak.

Moses started as the cries of an infant pierced the silence. A wave of joy flooded him, and on its heels, remorse. How could he contemplate leaving Zipporah alone with their child? He wearily stood, his shoulders heavy as he approached the tent.

Leah emerged smiling, wiping her hands on a cloth. "You have a son, Moses. Yahweh has blessed you with a boy."

Jethro's face lit. "Welcome news, indeed, to these weathered ears." He laid a hand on Moses' shoulder, his eyes twinkling. "I had seven times hoped to hear those words." He laughed, tightening his grip, though his eyes sobered. "Men are rare in Midian, Moses, and we don't lightly lose them."

Moses nodded, his brow creasing. He understood Jethro's meaning. "Don't worry, I'll not leave her."

The elder patted Moses' back. "Good. Then let us thank Yahweh for this child and celebrate his arrival."

The two momentarily turned from the tent of labor. Snatching a young lamb from the fold, they strode to the tent of worship marked by a crude rock altar outside the door. Placing the lamb atop the stones and tying its feet, Jethro laid a hand on the animal to hold it in place while lifting his other hand and muttering an inaudible prayer.

Taking his knife from its scabbard, he held it high above the beast and plunged it into its chest as blood spurted through the white wool, making a red seam that spilled onto the rocks beneath it. Jethro looked at the sacrifice a last time before ducking into the tent and kneeling in the shadows on the worn rug.

Moses followed and peered about, feeling ridiculous in the near empty room. No idol dominated this space nor awaited Jethro's petition. Instead, a simple table occupied the floor, and a wall of urns marked its library. Moses half chuckled. Was this all Yahovah required? What kind of god accepted a tent made of animal skins instead of a temple, and a few dozen urns rather than vast schools and libraries? These surroundings ought to insult rather than impress a deity.

Jethro bowed his head to the ground, his arms outstretched as words poured from his lips like water from a fountain. At first it sounded like the mumble of a foreign tongue, but as Moses listened he recognized the words as exclamations of praise, the same words to a song he had sometimes heard Zipporah sing. Then he asked Yahweh to bless Moses' and Zipporah's union and their child, asking that they would have a long and contented life with their son, prospering as they lived together in this land.

Moses squirmed at being the subject of prayer, and wondered if this god would hear a weathered, old nomad praying in a crude tent.

Soon the prayer ended and Jethro lifted his hands above him, and simply added, "In the name of Yahweh, so be it."

Rising on wobbly legs, he turned and grinned at Moses. "It's the same prayer I prayed seven times before." His eyes lit like lamps in the shadows. "Only this time I could change the gender."

Moses laughed in spite of his somber mood. "You prayed and still your god gave you only daughters?"

Jethro shrugged. "His wisdom is greater than mine. Perhaps He did so that my daughters might give me twice as many sons." Jethro motioned Moses ahead of him and out into the sunshine.

Moses thoughtfully returned to the tent where Zipporah lay, feeling guilty for having desired to escape.

"Go on in," Jethro urged. "Let's see this son of yours and that beautiful daughter of mine."

Moses ducked into the tent, squinting in the semidarkness. Lying on a mat near the wall he could see Zipporah holding a bundle to her breast. Leah pulled the cloth aside so they could see the child.

Jethro beamed. "There you are, a son as surely as I stand. What will you name him?"

Moses watched the nursing infant, its tiny fist curled in a knot as he concentrated on sucking, holding to his mother's nipple as if to never let go.

"Gershom," Moses whispered.

Zipporah looked up. "Gershom, isn't that Habiru?"

Jethro lifted a hand. "Wait daughter." Interceding with restrained concern, he looked to Moses. "Why Gershom?"

Moses studied the serene forms of his wife and child, trying with all he possessed to divorce himself from his past and embrace the present. His voice barely rose above the hum of activity outside the tent. "For I have been a stranger in a strange land."

Jethro's eyes dropped with unspoken knowledge, but Moses knew he understood. For Moses had yet to feel at home in Midian among those with whom he had inseparably joined himself.

Aaron held Elisheba against his chest, stroking her hair and soothing her sobs. Her tears soaked through his linen tunic and her body quaked. Though she had become his wife in every sense, still the Overseer violated her whenever he pleased, taunting Aaron and making a mockery of their marriage.

Aaron clenched his teeth, biting back the rage that pounded in his temples and pulsed through his veins. He had begged Yahovah to strike the man dead, but He had not. Instead, the Overseer seemed to feed on Aaron's anger, taking every opportunity to flaunt his power. At last in desperation Aaron had contrived a solution of his own.

He rubbed a thumb over the smooth hollow of Elisheba's cheek, her skin soft and alluring, and kissed her there. As the sky lit with sunrise and those about the camp began to stir, he rehearsed again what she must do.

When they finally pushed back the tent flap, the fires of the night had died to glowing embers with wisps of smoke lingering in the morning air, adding a pungent scent to the camp.

The Overseer turned as Elisheba and Aaron emerged, a smile breaking across his face. Aaron gripped her hand as if to hold her back then reluctantly let her go. She hesitated only a moment as the Overseer's eyes slid over her body. Then turning with purpose she walked toward what was left of the fire as if to warm herself.

Aaron held his breath. As Elisheba neared she tripped, falling face forward into the coals, turning her face as she fell. She did not scream or even cry out, and at first Aaron thought she had fainted.

Rushing to her side, he lifted her into his arms. The Overseer also hurried to where she lay, cursing beneath his breath. He accusingly glared at Aaron, noting the burn already blistering half her face.

"Call the physicians, and hurry!"

A servant scrambled to do his bidding while Aaron accepted a wet cloth to place over the wound.

The Overseer cursed again, pacing like a caged lion. "Damned wench! Why didn't she watch where she was going?"

He scrutinized the pair till Aaron almost squirmed. Then studying her raw flesh with one eye nearly swollen shut, he turned away in disgust. "What do I care? She is only a slave."

Aaron watched him, his face hard with hatred. If it weren't for him he would have his beautiful Elisheba to himself, still. He glanced down at her quaking body, warm to the touch as if with fever, her brow beaded with perspiration. A physician clambered toward them, pushing through the throng, but Elisheba hardly noticed.

Looking up at Aaron, she forced her lips to move. "We did it, Aaron."

Aaron nodded, tears blurring his vision. He held her tighter as she writhed with pain, her beauty of moments before marred and disfigured. He shook his head, his love for her overpowering all else. What did it matter? She would always be the most beautiful woman in his eyes.

Her body jerked with spasms as he held her, tears trickling down his cheeks. He bent to kiss her forehead and tenderly smiled at her. "Now I'll never have to share you again."

She attempted a crooked smile before succumbing to the pain, her body going limp in his arms as the physician worked to preserve what he could of the delicate flesh.

Thutmose sat on his throne, oblivious to the steady drizzle of rain in the courtyard outside. A smile tugged at the corners of his mouth as he watched the nurse pursue the toddling Prince. His son squealed with delight, his chubby feet pattering across the polished floor as he attempted to outrun her, but she easily caught up to him, whisking him into her arms and bowing toward the throne in apology.

The Pharaoh chuckled. "I've not watched anything so amusing in months. Leave him be." The nurse's eyes widened, but Thutmose insisted. "I'll watch him myself. See? Amenhotep merely wants to explore."

The child's curls bobbed about his face as he waddled toward the throne, crawling onto the first step.

The nurse raised a brow, her breath coming in gasps. "If you really think he is alright...." The child teetered and her hands lurched forward, but Amenhotep righted himself, taking another step before crawling atop the dais.

Thutmose waved the nurse from the room. "He's fine and I've nothing better to do, especially in this weather."

The nurse bowed again, backing toward the door, anxiously glancing at the toddler a last time.

Thutmose motioned her away and she disappeared beyond the double doors. Leaning back, he watched Amenhotep explore the gold fringe on the rug, the finely woven threads slipping through his fingers like liquid as he grabbed at it again and again, content to watch it shimmer and fall. Thutmose shook his head, wondering at a child who could occupy himself with so trivial a pastime. He had hoped Amenhotep had inherited his own drive rather than Meryet's complacency. Gods! A son content to sit in any one place for long couldn't possibly take after him.

The Pharaoh restlessly arose, his hands clasped behind him as he descended the dais and walked to the balcony. Outside a grey sky seethed and churned as if the gods themselves battled there, spewing bolts of lightning across the distant horizon as rain pelted the roof in a monotonous rhythm, running in rivulets onto the already soggy ground.

Thutmose hated winter, the only time of year when the elements forced him and his army to stay put. What of these chariots Amenhab had suggested they build? They had confiscated enough during their last battle to provide for his entire first regiment. Should he build enough for his whole army? He had no navy, though he couldn't transport chariots and horses by boat anyway. Outfitting his entire army with chariots would make travel through the desert bearable and their victories swift.

Did he have enough metal and smiths to complete the job? He thought a moment. Copper continued to fill their coffers from the mines at Sinai, with gold and silver still in store from his own conquests and tribute. He would have it brought from the treasure house at Karnak and melted down in Avaris. As to laborers, perhaps Meryet was right, he would have his metal smiths train the Habiru to build them. What harm would it do? If they could build cities they could build chariots.

In a flurry of conviction Thutmose strode to the double doors. His first Officer must give a count of the number of chariots needed. If they could outfit even half the army they could greatly improve their chances against the coalition.

"Scribe," he called to a man sitting cross–legged in the half–lit hall, waiting to serve him, "a message for Officer Amenhab."

The man scrambled to ready his pen and palette, eagerly anticipating the dictation.

"I want a count of the number of available chariots light enough for war; and the number needed to outfit my entire army. I want to know how many metal smith shops we have in Avaris, and the laborers needed to complete the task before spring. Amenhab is to conscript the laborers from among the Habiru."

The scribe frantically wrote, unaccustomed of late to any demands by the Pharaoh.

"Give the message to Officer Amenhab, and tell him to get back to me at once." The Pharaoh clasped his hands behind his back, the hint of a smile on his face. "Perhaps we can occupy ourselves this winter after all."

A cry erupted from behind him and Thutmose turned to see the Prince sprawled on the marble floor, having toppled from the dais, his face red as he drew a breath for an even louder wail.

Thutmose started for the child then turned back to the hall. "And fetch that damned nurse. She should never have left him to begin with."

Leaving the boy to fend for himself, Thutmose strode to the balcony, his mind on the coming battle, hardly noticing the diminishing cries of his son as the nurse whisked him from the room.

Thutmose stared at the sky, his eyes distant, picturing an army of charioteers racing across the wilderness to Syria. A smile spread across his face. He would meet with Amenhab on the morrow and discuss his plan. With his whole army outfitted, the coalition at Kadesh would be easy prey.

Nefru lay in bed, her flesh nearly transparent in the morning light and her once shiny locks dull and lifeless.

She moved a hand, motioning her servant from the room. "I want Tasha," she rasped.

The servant bowed away, intent on fetching the one her mistress insisted upon during such bouts. Within moments Tasha appeared in the doorway, wiping her hands on a cloth and attempting to divine her mistress's need.

"Have you left the palace today?" Nefru managed.

Tasha shook her head, attempting to conceal her fear at Nefru's knowledge of her visits to the village.

Nefru sneered. "I know what you're up to. You're visiting your child. Well I won't allow it." She raised herself up on one elbow, intending to emphasize her words when a fit of coughing overtook her, causing color to at last brush her cheeks.

Nefru lay down again. "I tell you I'll have you flogged if you leave." She looked at Tasha with as much determination as she could muster before her body sagged into the mound of cushions, having spent the sum of her strength. "Has the physician arrived? He was to see me today."

"No, my Lady." Tasha's eyes swept the pathetic form. Ever since Nefru's arrival her condition had worsened, and with it the determination to see everyone else suffer as she did.

"Have the clouds cleared?" Nefru's gaze lifted to her window and the ominous sky beyond it.

"Not yet, my Lady." Tasha kept her eyes on her mistress. She hoped she would dismiss her so she could return to the kitchen, as she awaited Nepthys' arrival and news of her son. Nepthys seemed able to slip away without Nefru knowing, whereas the Queen watched Tasha's every move.

Nefru lifted her hand, viewing her nails with effort. "I want my hands groomed in case Thutmose arrives. He is said to be in the vicinity gathering slaves for another of his projects. He plans to improve his army, I hear, by building chariots." Nefru meaningfully eyed Tasha. "The better to capture Moses with."

Tasha caught her breath, though she tried to maintain her composure. "I will do your nails, my Lady, in case — in case the Pharaoh arrives." She quickly turned to the table, fumbling through the baskets for the necessary articles, but the images blurred as tears spilled down her cheeks.

"What are you doing? Have you left me?" Nefru's voice echoed in the near empty palace.

Tasha took a deep breath, wiping her eyes on the hem of her gown as she gathered the utensils. Pulling up a stool to Nefru's bed, she took the thin hand in her own, keeping her eyes on the slender fingers and the all too white nails. Avoiding Nefru's face, she brushed and filed, tapering the ends to a pleasant curve and polishing them with henna.

Nefru curiously studied her. "Something beyond yourself strengthens you. What is it?"

Tasha stopped, looking at her mistress with surprise before resuming filing. She remained silent at length, unable to find the words to explain her experience. How could she tell an Egyptian about the Habiru God who had sustained her these past years; about the presence she often sensed even when alone; and about the thrill she felt deep inside her when worshipping with the Habiru.

Nefru peered from the dark hollows of her eyes as if demanding an answer.

Tasha cleared her throat. "You find me strong?"

Nefru nodded.

"And you think it due to some power outside myself?" Tasha reiterated.

Nefru nodded again, her cold fingers curling about Tasha's as she pulled Tasha toward her. "Perhaps it is due to a potion or magic spell. Give it to me that I may be well."

Tasha looked at the pitiful face, about to speak when a knock sounded at the door. She stood and opened it, and the physician from Avaris bustled into the room allowing no time for questions. He fumbled through his bag and found a vial, and without an explanation, walked to the Queen's couch and tipped it to her mouth, assuring her she would soon experience the sweetness of sleep. Nefru was at once taken with his presence, her eyes never leaving him as they conversed in low tones. Tasha softly walked to the door, feeling a twinge of guilt at the missed opportunity to complete her conversation. Then again, perhaps Yahovah had provided her a means of escape in order to visit her son.

Hurrying to the kitchen, she threw a cloak about her shoulders, filling a basket with sweet breads and slipping out the back door toward the village of Tju, trying to convince herself she had done the right thing in avoiding Nefru's question.

The sun rose clear and bright, slicing through the grey of past months as Thutmose stood at the open doors of his balcony, calculating the time it would take to arrive at Kadesh with his army of charioteers. He had even conscripted some of the Habiru to drive them so his archers would be free to fight as the chariots easily held two.

Thutmose turned as Meryet entered the room, Amenhotep at her side. The boy reached up to him but Thutmose kissed his forehead instead. "I must leave today for the garrison."

Meryet's expression clouded. "Why the garrison and why now?"

"You know of my preparations for this campaign. I have Kadesh to conquer, and a Syrian and Hyksos confederation to contend with." He walked to a nearby bust of his grandfather and set his crown on it, taking the blue war helmet from another.

"You can't leave yet. Spring hasn't even arrived, and you promised you wouldn't march as early as last year." Meryet bit her lip, trying to control her response. "Amenhotep hardly knows he has a father or me a husband."

Thutmose's eyes flashed. "I'll not delay this campaign for my son, or you, or any other reason. Moses must be captured and the confederation crushed."

"Moses!" Meryet spat the word as if it were poison. "You aren't even certain he lives. Have you seen him?"

"I've seen his handiwork. A confederation of armies even now awaits me at Kadesh."

Thutmose strode to the door but Meryet stepped into his path, Amenhotep in tow. The boy's eyes searched the faces above him as the two continued to argue.

"How long will this chase last? When will you stop pursuing Moses and admit the truth, that he is dead? Even the Priests have assured you, as have your Syrian captives, yet you continue to hunt a spirit."

Thutmose stormed out the door but Meryet scooped Amenhotep into her arms and hurried into the hall after him. The child began to cry and she had to raise her voice above his to be heard. "How long will you ignore your wife and son? All winter you prepared your army and built your chariots."

Thutmose continued down the hall as her voice echoed in the corridor after him.

"When will you be content to stay in Egypt?"

His torso firm and his steps determined, Thutmose threw the words over his shoulder without looking back. "When Moses is dead and I have his head in my hand as a trophy."

Moses entered the sacred tent which seemed to hold the dust of centuries. Reaching among the urns, he took down the one containing Aaron's scroll. He reverently unrolled the parchment, wondering if his father had truly written the words. He glanced it over then started reading from the beginning, tracing with a careful finger from right to left the names of his ancestors: Abraham, Isaac, Jacob, Levi, and eventually Amram, his father, and Aaron.

His throat tightened and blood pulsed in his temples with the knowledge of who he was and where he belonged. Aaron had not wanted him to forget.

Jethro entered and peered over Moses' shoulder. "Why is it an Egyptian Prince holds such a fascination for Habiru history?"

Moses re–rolled the papyri, forcing his voice to an even tone. "The Egyptians pride themselves in the knowledge of all people, why not the Habiru?"

"What is it you are interested in?"

The elder's eyes bore into Moses' but Moses avoided his gaze, tucking the scroll back into the urn. "I am curious about the worship of your god. Religion in general interests me."

Jethro nodded but did not look convinced. "The scroll appears to be one of the more ancient ones. Don't you want to read something recent?" Moses flexed his jaw, about to speak when Jethro added. "Midianite traditions are similar to those of the Habiru, except we have had more years to perfect our traditions, while the Habiru haven't practiced their worship since leaving Canaan."

"You are wrong," Moses corrected. "The previous Pharaoh erected a temple to their god in one of the Habiru villages. I saw it myself."

Jethro raised a brow and reached to the top shelf, pulling a scroll from another clay pot. "If you are truly interested in our worship, here are some Midianite rituals you will find helpful."

Moses obligingly nodded. Looking up he saw Gershom toddle through the open door, momentarily diverting their attention. His chubby legs propelled him faster than he had intended to go, and unable to stop, he sprawled face forward at Moses' feet. His face puckered and he was about to cry when Moses raised him to a standing position while the boy held out a scraped knee for his inspection.

Moses sympathetically examined the wound and was about to speak when Zipporah bustled into the tent, throwing Moses a turbulent look and whisking the child into her arms. "Have you nothing better to do than study these dusty old scrolls?"

"If he aims to serve Yahweh he must know something of our history and traditions," Jethro reasoned.

Zipporah threw Moses a glare, her beauty marred by a frown. "It is not Midianite tradition he is interested in but an ancient Habiru scroll he has packed around with him these many years. Why study the Habiru when the Egyptians far outdistance them in wealth and knowledge?" She pointedly eyed Moses, situating Gershom on her hip. "I didn't marry a Habiru or even a Midianite, but an Egyptian."

Whirling about, she strode from the tent while Gershom looked over her shoulder with a wide, confused gaze, a finger in his mouth.

Moses watched them go, concern etched on his brow. How could he bring himself to tell her the truth: that she had, in fact, married a Habiru, and carried one in her arms?

Nefru's eyes held those of the physician as he stood his full height.

"Your Highness," he took a deep breath, "you won't have to worry about having children. That part of your life is finished."

Nefru stared wide-eyed. Surely he didn't mean never. Her mind spun, taking her back to news of the birth of Meryet's son. She had seethed with envy, hoping to one day make peace with Thutmose by bearing Egypt's heir, but now this man was telling her it would never happen.

"Are you sure?" Her breathing came in shallow gasps, her face white above the sheet.

The physician nodded, softening his tone. "My Lady, you will never bear children again."

Nefru remembered the night she had approached the physician at Avaris, begging for herbs to expel the child...her only child.

She shuddered, her features twisting as she attempted to absorb the news which seemed all too fitting a curse for past wrongs. "You say it as if barrenness were a privilege. Do you forget who I am?"

The physician lowered his eyes, not sure how to answer. "Your Highness, barrenness is only one of the problems, and may have nothing to do with your illness. Barrenness strikes royalty and peasant alike, but this sickness is unlike anything I have ever seen, though while visiting Avaris I heard of several Keftiu with the same symptoms."

He shook his head, lifting his shoulders in a shrug. "Perhaps you contracted the disease after coming in contact with one of them." He avoided her face, feigning ignorance of her months at the capital in their company, and of her subsequent aborted pregnancy.

Nefru's eyes widened as a vision of Styrone flashed before her. Had he passed a disease onto her?

The room blurred and she felt light headed, her limbs weak. She glanced at the sunlight pouring through the open balcony and wondered how it dared shine when she must receive such news.

"Have you any idea the name of this disease? Is there a cure?"

The physician shook his head. "Though several with whom I conferred indicated they had seen the symptoms before, none knew of a remedy." He creased his brow. "Perhaps you should not come in contact with anyone else until we know what it is."

Nefru's lips whitened. No contact? No visitors? Must she even dispense with her servants?

"Tasha," her voice rose in desperation, "a drink." She sank back, exhausted from the effort.

The physician turned to the door but Nefru entreated him. "Have you no hope, no remedy of herbs, a potion, or anything?"

"I know of nothing, my Lady which would —"

"Imbecile!" Her shrill voice pierced the distance between them as if she had thrown a knife. "Thutmose is behind this, isn't he? It's his will I suffer this curse without aid."

The physician fumbled through his satchel, pulling out a small vial. "Here, my Lady." He set it on her table. "Instruct your servants to give you three droplets daily upon rising, and three more before going to bed."

"How in Hades will six drops help?" she shrieked.

"Make it three times daily," he hurriedly added, "and any other time you need relief. When you run out I will see to it you receive more."

Nefru looked up at him, her eyes dark hollows in her pale face. "Is there no cure at all? Is there nothing more you can do for me?"

Lifting his chin, the physician dared one last directive. "I would, if I were you, contact a Priest. It may be the gods can aid in this matter." So saying, he hurried from the room, fearing the realization of her future might jeopardize his own.

CHAPTER 21

Thutmose slowed his chariot as he entered the forest south of Kadesh. Trees larger than he had ever seen lifted their boughs entangling themselves in a canopy overhead, their gnarled trunks partly hidden by the dense brush.

"Seems like a good place to be ambushed," Amenhab muttered, looking about.

Thutmose nodded, tightening his fist about the reins, his sword readied in the other. His army had passed through Syria without incident, nor had they seen any sign of scouts or of the coalition. Surely the enemy anticipated his return and were waiting for him.

Thutmose yaahed his horse to a run, the chariots behind his matching his pace until the ground shook beneath them, yet they passed through the forest without incident. Eventually the trees lessened, giving way to open fields before a backdrop of mountains, and in the distance the sound of rushing water.

"The Orontes," Amenhab called out.

They passed an obscure village perched on the riverbank but Thutmose did not stop. He had a much bigger prize in mind than a few tumble–down huts and a handful of peasants. Since the enemy had not yet come to him, he would go to them. If the confederation had allowed him to penetrate this far into Syria without incident, there was only one other place they could possibly be: Kadesh.

Thutmose's army continued up–river like a swarm of encroaching locusts, the rumble of over fifteen hundred chariots making the earth tremble in anticipation of their arrival. They rounded a bend where the plain levelled and the river forked into two wide arms. At its center, on an almost invisible island, rose a megalith of walls and towers.

"Kadesh," Thutmose breathed. He slowed his chariot, searching for the army he had hoped to find ready and waiting, but saw only empty fields on either side of the river. Atop the walls the armor of innumerable soldiers glinted in the dying embers of sunset as they peered down at them from the rampart, the massive gates shut. Between them lay the Orontes.

Thutmose cursed beneath his breath. Of what use were chariots if he couldn't cross the river? Even rafts would prove ineffective against the strong current and would only allow several to cross at a time, giving the enemy opportunity for ambush.

Amenhab rode to his side surveying the fields of stubble, evidence of the city's preparation against a siege. Kadesh had already harvested everything edible, no doubt storing it within the city in anticipation of Thutmose's arrival. He could wait all summer and still leave in defeat as the city was well stocked, and he would never survive the winter without sustenance for his army.

Thutmose scanned the surrounding fields, the vineyards and groves picked clean. He turned to Amenhab, his voice a monotone. "I want the vines uprooted and all fruit trees chopped to the ground. Burn any huts you come across, and take whatever prisoners you find."

Amenhab nodded, awaiting the Pharaoh's final command. Thutmose clenched his teeth as if to keep from saying the words. "Once that is done we will return to Egypt."

Amenhab started to protest but Thutmose interjected, "...until next year when we return with Egypt's first armada."

Moses carefully moved the reed pen over the stretched parchment as the letters blended with seemingly endless rows of words already copied. He rubbed his eyes, the candlelight barely piercing the morning shadows. Outside the sun had just begun to warm the eastern horizon with a reddish glow, inflaming the sand and distant rock.

He felt a sacred awe rise within him, but the feeling seemed out of place under the circumstances. He brushed it aside, moving his pen over the parchment once more.

He scanned the document. Why did he feel driven to copy these records, to combine all he could of the Habiru's history with the information in Jethro's scrolls? True, the Habiru's records would then be complete, but would anyone ever read them? He pictured the nameless masses of Habiru still in Egypt. Didn't they deserve to know their past?

Moses had begun with the account of creation and of the first beings Yahovah had made, far different than the nine gods and goddesses of the Egyptian ennead. Yet there were similarities between the accounts, such as the more ancient god, Aton, the god of air and sunlight, the first creator who made Shu from his breath, and who made Tefnut, goddess of dew, from his saliva. The Hebrew texts also mentioned Yahovah's use of saliva in creating mankind, afterward breathing into him the breath of life. Might these two stories stem from the same original source, one being a distortion of the other? If so, which was the original?

Perhaps if he could hear Yahovah speak he would know.

"Still at work?"

Moses jumped as Jethro's voice broke the silence. Laying aside his pen, he took an unsteady breath. "Yes. Morning has come too soon."

"Zipporah will wonder at a man who prefers parchment and ink to a wife and warm bed." The elder smiled but Moses sensed a warning behind his words.

Moses stood and stretched, then dropped his hands as he studied his father–in–law. A beard tumbled down Jethro's chest, his hair falling in waves to his shoulders. Moses would have thought the appearance strange except he had come to look much the same, not having cut his hair since his arrival. He knew he appeared as much like a desert Bedouin as any other man, which would work to his advantage if their camp was ever visited again by Egyptian scouts.

Moses glanced outside the tent. "Is Zipporah ready to leave?"

Jethro nodded. "She and her sister have packed their bedrolls with enough belongings for the summer. Gershom wants to go as well, and the herd is anxious for pasture. Why don't you reconsider and accompany them?"

Moses stepped outside, lifting his eyes to the jutting mountain awash with red and gold. Even at a distance it seemed to possess an unearthly aura, but no, somehow the timing wasn't right. He shook his head. "Not this summer, Jethro. I'm not ready, maybe in another year."

Jethro grunted into his beard. "Not ready for what? You know more about shepherding this year than last."

Moses searched the elder's face. Jethro could teach him much about Habiru history, and more importantly, about their god. He turned his gaze to the mountain. "You believe Yahovah lives there?" He paused as if searching the distance for a sign. When the elder did not answer he continued, "If that is true, I want to be ready to meet him the next time I go."

Jethro sputtered. "But — but that's impossible." He snorted at the absurdity. "No one can see Yahweh and live."

"Then I won't look, but I want to hear his voice, to speak with him."

Jethro's eyes narrowed. He did not doubt Yahweh could speak, but today and to Moses? Yet a more important question persisted. "Are you ready for what He will say?"

Moses studied him, but instead of answering, he threw his cloak over his shoulders. "I'll tell Zipporah and the others to go on without me. Maybe next year."

Jethro warily nodded. "I'm glad it's you breaking the news to her and not me." So saying, the elder quickly hobbled between the two closest tents, not wanting to hear the outburst he knew would follow Moses' announcement.

In the first rays of dawn Aaron watched Elisheba sleep, studying the face of his beloved as her hair fanned about her head like a feathery crown. Though half of her face was badly scarred, when she lay next to him on her side she appeared as she had before the accident: beautiful and unmarred. He had never noticed before, but she had the most remarkable hair he had ever seen, almost transparent in the light. He felt its texture slip through his fingers like liquid, catching the sunlight as it filtered through the tent flap.

His lovely Elisheba. A knot tightened in his throat. At least they had won, of sorts, as the Overseer, may Yahovah curse his flesh, had not touched her since the incident.

Elisheba stirred and he wrapped his arms about her as if to shield her from further harm. He knew she would never again belong to anyone else, not now or ever.

Aaron clenched his jaw, his face grim. What had his people done to deserve such treatment? Had Yahovah abandoned them as some claimed? He had never before had to face the bitterness of bondage, having enjoyed preferred treatment at Hatshepsut's order. Yet it had sickened him to see the hardships inflicted on his people. Now he experienced it himself daily, and the more he saw the more enraged he became. How could Yahovah allow them to suffer so? What had they done to deserve this?

Elisheba, sensing his restlessness, stirred and opened her eyes, sleepily rising on one elbow. She looked into his face and Aaron tried to hide any expression of pity or regret, but she knew him too well.

Her eyes fell. "Perhaps we were wrong to take matters into our own hands."

"No." Aaron fiercely hugged her. "We were not wrong and have lost nothing. The fire has only made you sweeter and our love stronger." He held her out from him, forcing her eyes to his. "We have each other now more than ever."

She nodded and he pulled her into his embrace. He could feel her shoulders relax and her breasts rise and fall against his chest as she breathed more calmly. They sat a long moment in each other's arms, both wishing the reverie could continue, but such was not the reality of their existence.

Aaron kissed her forehead. "Come, my love, the sun rises and here we sit. What would Pharaoh say?"

He chuckled as he pulled her to her feet, but his smile faded to wonder, watching her as if viewing a being he did not deserve to touch. Even the elements seemed to confirm the fact, for a sudden burst of light shone through the tent flap so brightly he could see nothing of her scars, only an unearthly glow enveloping her, and if it were possible, shining through her.

A tear like a tiny gem worked its way down the scarred side of her cheek and she smiled, though one side of her mouth drooped. Her eyes held his, and she appeared angelic in the ethereal moments of morning, as if time stood still for them. If nothing else, they had their love, totally, irrevocably, and nothing, not even captivity, could change that.

She reached out and took his hand as together they stepped from the tent into the light of dawn, bathed in the brilliance of sunrise.

Tasha administered another dose of droplets to Nefru then carefully closed the door of her chamber. The physician had assured her the medication would help calm Nefru, and within moments his prediction had proven true. With her mistress sleeping Tasha could at last make the visit to the village she had missed several days earlier.

She tightened the veil about her face, lifting the basket filled with fruit and bread onto her arm. If she appeared on her way to market no one would question her leaving. Little Jesse loved fruit and seldom found it in the confines of the village.

Once out of sight of the palace Tasha fairly flew over the dusty road. The sun had dried the rain to a skiff of powder making a cloudy trail at her feet. Merchants, farmers, and tradesmen passed her by, their colorful headdresses appearing to blend to form a single moving tapestry as the throngs made their way to and from Pithom. Tasha felt caught up in the pace of it, buoyed by hope that lifted her spirits and quickened her steps. At last she would see her son.

Life at Pithom wasn't as dark as it had been before Nefru's illness. In fact, it seemed Yahovah continued to bless her even here. In the months since her son's birth and Nefru's return, her duties had lessened as Nefru had grown too weak to taunt her, allowing her more visits to the village.

Tasha shuddered, marveling at how she had withstood Nefru's hatred, and how Yahovah had sustained her these past few years. She slowed as she entered the village, turning toward the familiar hut where Jesse lived. Even before she reached the door she heard his exclamations as he stepped from the dark recess, his arms extended.

"Tasha!"

Her heart constricted at the word as she caught him to her bosom. Yet she dared not risk the luxury of disclosing her true identity, not when the discovery might harm them both.

"Yes I've come, and with another basket of surprises." Tasha stepped into the hut and glanced about, her eyes adjusting to the semidarkness.

"He's grown since you last saw him and speaks much clearer." Tasha heard the voice before she saw the

387

woman standing at the far side of the room, a pot in her hands. The woman set the object aside and stepped forward, gratefully accepting the basket. "The guards have heightened security since Pharaoh and his army left for Syria, but it has not greatly affected our village as we are too far from the border."

Tasha instinctively pulled Jesse closer. "What does Pharaoh fear? The Habiru build his chariots and even assist his army."

The woman reassuringly smiled. "Apparently he believes the confederation in Syria more of a threat than he is prepared for, especially with the Hyksos' involvement."

Tasha relaxed. She had heard rumors of the Hyksos and their confederation, but also remembered Moses explaining how they had ruled the Delta years earlier during the reign of a Habiru named Joseph Ben Jacob, Zapeth Peneah in Egyptian.

Thoughts of Moses brought a stab of pain deep inside her and she turned her attention to their child instead. "How is Jesse with the other children? Has anyone noticed his darker skin?"

"Not yet, though it hasn't darkened much because I don't allow him outside during the day." The woman dispensed with the rest of her answer as they both understood it would happen soon enough. Seeing the concern on Tasha's face, she added. "In summer most of the children end up as black as the earth anyway. He should blend in fine for now."

Tasha tried to mirror the woman's optimism but could not. Instead, she took Jesse's hand in hers, his flesh still light compared to her own. "When he must go out I want him rubbed with mud. After it dries it will temporarily lighten his skin. It is the only remedy I know of, and it may keep the others from questioning his identity for now."

The woman nodded, wondering how long such efforts would last. When the child reached a certain age he would have to leave the village and join the laborers in the fields near Avaris. He would not be able to hide in her hut then, but she did not voice her fears, not wanting to break the cherished tranquility between mother and child.

Turning to fill the pot with the meal she had prepared, she left them alone to enjoy the illusion that only the two of them occupied the room as mother and son.

Shouts of revelry lifted into the purple sky above the illumined walls of Kadesh as a low moon silhouetted the countryside in blues and silver. Beyond the river a rider approached the dock, dismounting and leading his horse to the waiting ferry. The guards along the wall stopped celebrating, squinting into the shadows before recognizing their own scout and opening the gates in anticipation of his arrival.

After ferrying across the river the man entered the fortress and nodded to the group of officials awaiting him, his message divined in his even breathing and tone. "It's true, the Egyptians have gone. I followed them as far south as Sidon."

"Did they take the city?" The Gorvernor's eyes fastened on the messenger, his pointed beard giving him a foreboding appearance in the darkness.

The scout grunted. "They never even stopped but fled like a herd of frightened gazelle. They'll likely not stop till they reach Egypt."

Cheers erupted, but still the Governor persisted. "Are you sure?"

"I spoke with Sidon's Governor myself. He put me up for the night." The messenger accepted a drink, taking a long draught before continuing. "He believes Thutmose's return without booty or captives represents his defeat, just as every other city–state will surmise."

The Governor smiled behind his beard. "True enough." He threw an order over his shoulder. "It's time the confederation celebrated its own victory. More wine for everyone!"

Ishmael, the Hyksos leader, stepped forward, his countenance grave. "Don't think you've gotten off so easily, Governor. If Thutmose is anything like his grandfather he'll return with an even larger force next year. I say we meet him at Gaza in the spring and stop him before he gets the chance."

The Governor raised a brow. "Would you have us risk our necks to defend all of Syria? We're safe enough here, this last episode proved as much." He took a drink. "Besides, most of the confederation has already disbanded, content to concentrate their efforts at home in their own cities." He grunted. "Forget it Ishmael. Find yourself a wench and be content in Syria."

Ishmael ignored him. "If we band together we can stop him. He would never have defeated us at Megiddo if every city–state had joined us. Next year we'll create an even more powerful army and drive him farther west than the Delta."

The Governor peered into the distance, his features sharp in the moonlight. "Who do you propose would lead this confederate army, or would the honor be yours?"

Ishmael shook his head. "What does it matter who leads us as long as we triumph? If enough armies join us we could win even on Egyptian soil."

The Gorvernor's lip curled as he eyed the unpopular Hyksos. "You Semites are all alike. What is a life so long as you gain an inch of ground?" He grunted. "No, your designs run deeper than freeing Syria. Your eye rests on the Delta and we all know it."

Ishmael bristled. "What if it does? Why should you care if the Hyksos were to reoccupy Egypt? You would never again have to share your land with us or worry about Pharaoh marching on Syrian soil."

The Governor shrewdly eyed him. "Instead we would worry about the Hyksos and Habiru, an unstoppable union."

Ishmael clenched his jaw. "All the Habiru want is their own land, and all we Hyksos need is pasture for our cattle. With our people content in the Delta you would have all of Syria to yourselves."

The Governor snorted. "Where do you propose the Habiru would live in this scheme of yours? With you in Egypt? For we'll not willingly make room for them here." He lifted his goblet in mock toast. "To the future conqueror of the Delta: Pharaoh Ishmael!"

Laughter bellowed from within the walls as the servants wove in and out among the Officers, refilling their goblets.

Ishmael whirled, leaving the celebrants to themselves, his men at his heels. "Come, we're visiting these southern city–states to see just how feasible an alliance truly is. Tyre and Sidon once joined us; perhaps they will do so again, if for no other reason than to gain the release of their loved ones still captive in Egypt."

A young Hyksos looked up into his leader's face, attempting to keep pace. "And if they don't?"

Ishmael's eyes burned like live coals. "Then, as the Governor hinted, we'll employ an even better ally, one within Egypt's own borders who has ample reason to join us."

The young man's brow arched in question but Ishmael continued, more to himself than to his comrades. "If nothing else, the bitterness of four hundred years of bondage will work to our advantage."

Moses carefully crawled out of his bed roll, glancing at Zipporah who lay with Gershom at her side. She had greeted him less than enthusiastically upon her return from Mount Sinai, but he was glad to have them back. The summer had seemed far too long without them, though he had accomplished much in the way of his studies. He ducked through the tent flap and stretched, squinting into the early light. His eyes sought the sun–gilded mountain. Perhaps next year he would accompany his family to summer pasture.

"Up so early?" Jethro hobbled toward the fire pit with an armload of brush, laying it beside a pile of dung.

Moses watched as he arranged the dung on the tinder, deftly starting the fire. The lines around Moses' mouth lifted. Who would have thought he would one day warm himself before a dung fire with a family of Bedouin? He grunted, turning his attention to the mountain.

Jethro followed his gaze. "There's nothing more beautiful than the mountains at sunrise."

"Except the colors at sunset," Moses interjected, squatting to warm himself.

Jethro smiled. "In between the two we battle the heat."

Moses nodded then looked to the tent of worship at the edge of camp where Jethro performed his Priestly duties. He mater–of–factly stated, "In Egypt we worship our gods at sunrise." Jethro stiffened at the comment, but Moses continued. "I thought, since I plan to learn the worship of your god, this morning would be a good time to begin."

Jethro furrowed his brow. "I'm glad you want to worship Yahweh, but this is not Egypt, and our ways are not theirs. We don't have nearly as many religious rites, nor do we have elaborate temples, as all our One God requires are clean hands and a pure heart."

Moses stood, frustration lining his face. "Just the same, I would like to use the tent of worship."

Jethro stared at the fire. "You may, but be sure to leave your Egyptian ways outside the door."

Moses took a deep breath and strode through camp to the tent of worship. Pushing aside the tent flap, he let it fall behind him. Once inside, he walked to the front of the room and knelt on the worn rug, listening in the silence. The darkness felt ominous, as if someone were watching, and he glanced about but saw no one. He attempted to focus on praying but felt distracted, and studied his surroundings instead as his eyes adjusted to the shadowy enclosure.

Actually, this tent was no different than any other. It contained a table, some urns, a lamp and utensils, flint, and an old rug; hardly a temple by Egyptian standards.

He smiled to himself, amused at his former reluctance to enter. What had he to fear in this place, he who had knelt in the holy of holies at Deir el Bahri and

Karnak, standing before Amon's shrine and kissing the god's feet?

Yet as he reached up to light the lamp his hand trembled, and the hairs on his flesh lifted.

Closing his eyes, he contemplated what to say, but his thoughts seemed muddled. Instead, Jethro's words re–echoed in the silence of the place as if he could audibly hear them: 'All our God requires are clean hands and a pure heart.'

A pure heart? At once the faces of the women he had lain with paraded before him, the woman from Punt rising from the rest to point at him in accusation.

Sweat beaded on Moses' brow, and he shook the memories from his head, but as soon as they vanished he saw instead the faces of the Habiru with whom he had scorned to associate. He heard the crack of the Overseer's whip as it lashed across their backs and then saw the whip raised in his own hand as the Habiru strained to make brick. Finally he saw the face of the Habiru who had pleaded for his help as the Amalekite's sword sliced through his body, the struggling few scattered among the carnage as Moses fled to safety.

Moses' eyes shot open, his chest heaving and his face glistening with sweat. He looked about then stood, struck by his own weight of shame, and backed toward the door and into the brilliant sunlight.

Jethro met him outside the door, a lamb slung over his shoulder. "Finished so soon?" He studied his son–in–law and smiled. "There is a certain ritual you overlooked."

Moses glanced at the struggling sheep, then at the heap of stones near the doorway.

"The sacrifice," Jethro said, smiling.

Moses nodded and took a deep breath, glancing back at the dark doorway, the walled enclosure seeming more than a mere tent after all. He peered into the distance at Mount Sinai ablaze with morning light. "Perhaps another day when I am better prepared and have learned more about your god."

Tasha announced herself at Nefru's room, pushing through the open door with a tray. She set it on the table and glanced at her mistress whose form seemed lost amid a mound of cushions.

"As Her Majesty requested," Tasha bowed her head.

"Well don't just stand there." The words sounded muffled, lost in the pillows as Nefru raised her tousled head from their midst.

Her hair seemed to reach in every direction, her eyes circled and glassy, and Tasha at once felt a stab of pity. She hurried to lift the plate from the tray and stepped toward the bed. "Curried fish and vegetables, prepared just as you like them."

Nefru gagged at the words and dropped back onto her pillows. "I don't feel like eating."

Tasha studied the ashen face, knowing Nefru had refused her last meal as well. "Would you like me to help you?"

Nefru curiously watched her as Tasha pulled up a stool, setting the tray on her lap. The Queen's brow knit in question. "I don't understand you, Tasha. I've tormented you, making your life as unbearable as possible, and as soon as I am too weak to inflict further injury, you offer more service than I require, treating me like a favored mistress."

Tasha took a deep breath, wondering how to respond and trying to sort out her own feelings. She cut a slice of fish, hardly noticing the food's aroma as it wafted about her. "I have no reason to hate you, for I have experienced love in spite of my treatment here."

Nefru's mouth fell open, heedless of the bite Tasha had placed in it. "Who dares? Another servant? An Officer? If anyone so much as touches one of my maids I'll —"

Tasha chuckled. "Not a man, not a person at all," she glanced down, stirring the food, "but a God."

Nefru's eyes widened.

Tasha studied her, wondering if she dared reveal the truth in her heart. She cleared her throat. "The Habiru God, Yahovah."

Nefru absently chewed, her eyes wide with disbelief. "How can anyone experience love from an object of stone?"

Tasha shook her head. "Our God, the Habiru God, is not made of stone. His hands formed us." She lifted another bite to Nefru's mouth. "He is the creator of everything and everyone, the Habiru and Egyptians alike."

Nefru's brow furrowed. "The gods and goddesses of the Underworld created all things: the sky, the sea, the land. There was no Habiru god named among them."

"The Habiru believe differently. They believe the One God, Yahovah, created the world and everything in it." Tasha glanced past the open balcony at the bright afternoon sky. "He is all powerful and needs no help from other gods."

Nefru half raised herself. "But you're not Habiru any more than I am. Just because you had a child by one —" She stopped herself, rephrasing her thoughts. "Just because you associate with the Habiru doesn't make you one of them."

Tasha shrugged. "I don't have to be one of them. Their God accepts anyone, not just the Habiru, as long as we worship Him for who He is; our love in exchange for His."

Nefru grunted. "Is that all?" She took a drink with difficulty. "How could any god be happy without gifts?"

"I have heard the Habiru offer Him sacrifices, but love and belief are sacrifices as well," Tasha answered. "In return, He hears and answers our prayers." Tasha stirred the vegetables, lifting another spoonful.

Nefru's lip curled in derision. "What god is there who answers prayer? Certainly not mine, though I've petitioned night and day, praying to every god imaginable. Still they do nothing. They are as impotent as the stones they are made of." She frowned. "You have placed your faith in a lie."

"Not a lie," Tasha spoke with conviction. "I know Yahovah has power, for He has helped me many times," she stumbled over the admittance, "when my own gods did not. I no longer worship them, for Yahovah alone hears and helps me." Tasha nudged a spoonful into Nefru's mouth, meeting her curious gaze.

Nefru swallowed with difficulty. "How can you say he answers? We've kept the Habiru in bondage these four hundred years and he does nothing to free them. You call that power?" She reached for her goblet with a trembling hand.

Tasha helped her drink. "He has a different power, providing us with love that reaches beyond our circumstances." Tasha felt her spirit lift at the admission and she smiled, unaware of a radiance shining from her face. "It is His presence that helps me."

Nefru laughed. "You, who are a slave, who lost your husband and had to give up your child?" She gave a grunt of triumph. "I hardly call that help."

Passion flamed through Tasha, a hint of victory shining in her eyes. "My strength did not come because Yahovah took away my troubles, but because He helped me in the midst of them."

Nefru quietly regarded her then chuckled. "What an odd way to look at one's captivity." She shook her head. "I pity you, Tasha. Slavery has done strange things to your mind."

"There is strength greater than the physical, Nefru. With Yahovah's help I have been able to withstand the deepest kind of sorrow." Her eyes swam with tears but she did not care. "He has provided me with comfort and encouragement in spite of my circumstances, and one day, if He chooses, He will make a way through them."

Nefru watched her, wondering at the surety in her tone and the conviction on her face.

Tasha continued, "He has the power to change bitterness to joy and hatred to peace; to change our hearts, which is the greatest miracle of all."

Nefru regarded her as if seeing a creature with whom she could not identify, but rather than refuting the words, she finished her supper in quiet contemplation.

Tasha rose almost reverently, leaving Nefru alone with her thoughts. Back in the kitchen she set the tray aside and reached for her veil. Excitement welled within her, not only because she could now visit her son, though longing burned in her breasts, but for the truth she had at last shared with Nefru.

Today when the Habiru met for prayer, as they often did in the village, she would suggest they pray for Nefru. Not because she deserved it or had even asked for it, but because Yahovah loved her as much as any of them.

CHAPTER 22

Thutmose entered the palace yard and reined his chariot to a stop before the stable erected where the terrace had once been. His eyes swept over the palace: its marble walls gleaming behind well–trimmed hedges; the lawns edged with lilies and narcissus; and the cypress he had planted his first year as Pharaoh already reaching past the upper balconies. Yet he could hardly celebrate the fact that Avaris had fared well in his absence, nor that Vizier Rekmire had flawlessly managed the affairs of state. What did anything matter as long as Kadesh was unconquered and Moses free?

Thutmose tossed the reins into his chariot and marched up the columned porch, ignoring Rekmire who stood outside the entryway to greet him. One look at Thutmose and the Vizier knew better than to ask, nor did Pharaoh offer comment.

Rekmire fell into step beside him, not daring to speak until they had walked the entire the length of the main hall. "We have continued our cleanup of the city, Your Highness, and have nearly completed the temple. The Priests agree worship can begin in a matter of weeks after the dedication ceremony."

"Good. I've another project needing your immediate attention," Thutmose stated as they turned up the corridor toward the official wing. They neared several Officers who bowed in exaggerated fashion as Pharaoh and his entourage passed by. "I want an order proclaimed immediately. A party is to leave at once for Syria to gather wood for building."

Rekmire raised a brow but did not voice his question.

"I want whole cedars brought back from Lebanon. The rest of the wood can be cut there. We'll gather our offensive weaponry while our enemies hold up in their cities celebrating."

The Vizier's brow furrowed. "Celebrating?"

"We encountered a temporary setback in Syria," Thutmose answered.

Rekmire nervously cleared his throat. "Most of the rebuilding has been done, my Lord. What purpose would we have for whole cedars?"

"Why, for ships, of course."

"But we have more than enough chariots, and there is little threat to Egypt now that the Keftiu are on friendly terms."

Thutmose's eyes flashed. "Did I mention the Keftiu? These are for those damned Syrians, the confederate dogs that hold up at Kadesh." Rekmire opened his mouth to answer but Thutmose interjected, "We'll sail up the coastline gathering tribute from the city–states already conquered, and once we reach the Orontes we'll surround it and capture those cocky confederates. Come next spring I'll give them a dose of Egyptian brutality they'll not soon forget."

Thutmose stepped into his audience room with Rekmire close behind him. Not waiting for his servant, he snatched up a goblet and filled it with wine. Tipping it to his mouth, he finished it in a single swallow and strode to the throne.

"Then you plan to send for lumber immediately?" Rekmire stood at a distance, his brow furrowed.

"Yes, and I expect you to oversee the project."

"Me? But that would mean travelling to Syria."

"See that the cedars reach our shipping docks before winter in time for building," Thutmose stated with finality, seating himself and regarding Rekmire with a cold glare.

The Vizier gulped, his mind racing.

Thutmose accepted a refilled goblet from a servant. Taking a drink he turned to the balcony, staring into the blue sky as if envisioning the ships. "I want Syrian builders from among our captives who are trained in curving the ribs of ships, and the Habiru used as hewers of wood. If the fleet isn't ready by next spring I'll finish it with human hide." He took a final gulp, setting his goblet aside.

Rekmire bowed in acknowledgement, attempting to cover his obvious anxiety at the news. He would have argued against his involvement altogether, but just then a messenger entered the room followed by Thutmose's advisor. The two approached the throne whereupon the messenger handed Thutmose a scroll.

Rekmire paused, backing toward the door, then turned and disappeared down the hall as if pursued by spirits of the dead.

Thutmose rubbed his hands over the gritty stubble on his face. He was tired and wished he had stayed at the garrison with the rest of his army instead of seeing to business his first day in Avaris. Pursing his lips in displeasure, he broke the seal on the scroll, glancing it over and was about to comment when he noted Meryet's steward standing in the doorway.

Thutmose grunted his acknowledgement.

"My Lord, the Queen and Pharaoh's son request an audience."

"Concerning what?" Thutmose barked, his visage hard.

The man paused then apologetically smiled. "My Lord, Amenhotep calls for his father."

Thutmose stared at him until the steward squirmed, his silence answer enough.

Taking a deep breath, the steward ventured, "A few moments, my Lord, would mean so much."

Pharaoh studied the scroll. "A good night's sleep in my own bed will mean more. I'll see them tomorrow."

His advisor cleared his throat and bent toward him. "My, Lord, if I may, on the morrow you have the council meeting, and have already scheduled to meet with your Officers afterward at the garrison."

Thutmose lifted a stony gaze at the steward as if in answer, and turned his attention back to the scroll, at last giving a flourish of signature before handing the parchment to the messenger. He dismissed the man with a nod, and after conferring briefly with his advisor, strode across the room and toward the doorway.

"Perhaps another time," Thutmose muttered as he passed the steward.

The man's mouth opened to reply, but thinking better of it, he closed it again. What could he possibly tell Her Highness? After all, what should matter more to Pharaoh than those he loved the most?

Ishmael craned his neck from his perch high in the rocky crags above the Highway to the Sea. Squinting behind shaggy brows, he motioned to the carts below them winding in a continuous caravan back toward Egypt.

"You really think the Egyptians have changed their agenda?" he mumbled from behind his beard. "You think they're taking all this lumber to the Delta to rebuild their cities?"

The Officer at his side nodded. "What else could it be? The Governor of Tyre says —"

"Who cares what the Governor of Tyre says," Ishmael retorted. "The Governor never met Thutmose in battle, nor felt the desperation of being driven farther and farther east." He scowled. "These city–states have handed Thutmose their wealth, their arms, even their children, and now this."

The two scrutinized the carts more closely. The younger Officer ventured, "With cartloads of lumber being transported from Syria, it certainly looks to me as if he's building. Maybe he has decided to quit campaigning and concentrate on Egypt."

Ishmael shook his head. "Do you think a General, so determined to take a city he would risk the mountain path of Aruna, would give up so easily on Kadesh?"

A scuff of rock skittered from the slope behind them and Ishmael ducked, turning to see one of his scouts drop behind a bush.

"Gods! If we're not careful we'll have no choice but to fight." Ishmael anxiously watched the road as the rubble tumbled down the hillside, catching the attention of several Egyptian soldiers who turned to scan the slope. After a few moments they resumed their task, ordering the Habiru, who accompanied them, to walk between the hills and carts as a human barrier in case trouble erupted.

"See there?" Ishmael whispered. "We'd have to go through the Habiru to get at them."

"Let's do it then," his Officer answered, moving his hand to his sword.

Ishmael shook his head, his eyes fastened on the cedars roped together over two cart lengths as the Egyptians continued past them. "What could they possibly want with whole cedars?" he muttered. "Why not cut them in lengths before transporting them?"

"Perhaps they are building columns of wood instead of stone," the other offered.

Ishmael's brow furrowed, his voice low. "No." He intently studied the scene, his eyes narrowing as if focused on a single thought. "Masts. Might Thutmose be building a navy?"

Styrone sauntered into the throne room at Thera's capital, the pastoral scenes depicted on its walls contrasted with the chaos of wind and rain that thrashed the sky outside. As he approached, several young women with bare breasts hastily rose from the king's side and left the room.

"You sent for me, Your Majesty?" Styrone bridged the silence with a slight bow and a hint of obeisance, though none registered on his face.

"Yes." Perseus set his goblet aside. "Have you heard of Thutmose's most recent campaign?"

Styrone nodded. "One of our ships brought word by way of a merchant from Gaza. Apparently his mission at Kadesh failed and he now directs his energies toward building in Egypt."

The king's brow lifted in question.

Styrone grunted. "The Syrians believe he has fought his last battle."

The wind rhythmically whipped a shutter against the window as the two studied each other. "Then unfortunately he'll be there to face us when we invade his shores." The king pinned Styrone in his glare. "We should have sailed in the spring like I suggested while he and his army were away."

Styrone shifted. "Your Majesty, we've lost hundreds to the disease plaguing us. I also feel its effects, as have many of my men." He rubbed his forearm as if willing the muscles to retain their vigor.

The king sneered. "All the while our island teeters at the brink of destruction." He arose, walking to the window where the storm bent a cypress nearly to the ground, the sky a churning mass of grey. "Each winter grows worse. At times our island quakes as if the very gods battle beneath it. We never know when another tremor will prove our last. It's as if we're destined to repeat the fate of Atlantis. In a matter of years we too may become a mere legend."

Styrone started to protest, but the king's eyes narrowed on him. "I've heard another rumor, of an Egyptian Queen who bears your child." Styrone sputtered in protest, but the king continued, "Could it be you delayed an attack on Avaris to save your offspring? Would you risk the lives of your people for one half–blooded whelp?"

Styrone swallowed, attempting a laugh. "It was a prolonged affair, my Lord, the degradation of the Pharaoh's bed, nothing more." He took a step closer, his teeth clenched. "Who dared accuse me?"

Perseus walked to a nearby table, but not without first noting whether Styrone's hand had moved to his sword. He refilled his goblet. "It doesn't matter who suggested it. My only concern is whether or not it is true."

Styrone's lip curled. "It isn't. What would I want with a half–breed son?"

"Who said anything about a son?" The king took a long draught of his drink while a shutter noisily banged against the window. "One only needs half royal blood to provide an acceptable heir, even in Egypt."

"I have no heir. Even if I did it would not be my son sitting on Egypt's throne but yours."

The king set his goblet aside, meeting Styrone's gaze with a glower. "See you remember that."

He had no sooner spoken the words than the floor began to roll, the walls swaying as if Minotaur himself moved beneath them. Stone ground against stone as bits of rock and rubble crumbled to the floor, filling the air with dust. The two pressed themselves flat against the walls, their eyes on the ceiling as if expecting it to topple onto them. Outside screams pierced the night, and a deafening crash caused their legs to buckle. Styrone closed his eyes until the ground stilled and the walls ceased to move.

Perseus gasped for breath, still pressed against the wall. Through a haze of dust his eyes met his commander's. "An attack, Styrone. We must occupy the Delta at the first opportunity."

Styrone slowly nodded, his visage hard.

"Set a watch near Avaris and another at the port of Gaza. Perhaps you are wrong and Thutmose will again march on Syria. If and when he does we will strike. Once you have taken Avaris, the rest of us will follow."

Styrone suppressed a smile. Of course the king would join him after the battle, as he would not think of risking his neck in the fray. Styrone bowed low enough, however, so the king would not detect his cynicism or his thoughts. If he ever won the Delta it would not be the king's son who sat on Egypt's throne. No son of a weak–kneed coward would rule the new capital of Santaurus, but the son of a warrior.

Elisheba held up their infant, softly cooing as she bounced him in the air, delighting in his smile.

"Our son, Aaron," she tenderly whispered, turning to her husband, her smile fading. "What's wrong?"

Aaron shook his head, unable to share her happiness. "It's the thought of bringing a child into this world," he breathed, his vision blurred with tears.

She gripped his hand. "Yahovah hears us, I know He does, I feel it. Some of the others do too. Many believe something wondrous is about to happen."

Aaron suppressed a laugh. "If you're speaking of the prophecy to Abraham, I'm afraid the four hundred years of bondage have nearly arrived, and nothing is happening. Though Yahovah is far greater than we are, His timing is apparently not the same as ours."

Elisheba cuddled their child to her breast. "Being greater, He is able to see what we cannot. He will answer in time."

Miriam ducked through the doorway, her face aglow. "I've secured permission! You're allowed to take the child to the village of Tju and nurse him there until he is weaned."

"There is a God in heaven!" Elisheba breathed.

Aaron's face twisted in dismay. "I won't see you or Nadab for two, maybe three years."

"But he will live, and I will have a chance to regain strength."

Aaron absently nodded, looking at his wife and son with a mixture of longing and regret. He slowly turned to his sister, though he already anticipated her answer. "Is a transfer possible for me?"

Miriam shook her head. "I'm sorry, Aaron. I could do nothing for you. The Overseers wouldn't hear of it." She brightened. "But I am able to go. During the day I will work in the fields, and in the evenings I will keep Elisheba and Nadab company."

Aaron looked at his wife, the unscarred side of her face turned toward him as she bent over their son. "Of course they wouldn't allow us both to relocate. That would be too kind. Instead, they separate us and delight in our torment."

Miriam watched him with pity, but could not contain her joy at being able to leave the labor site. "Come, Elisheba. I'll hold Nadab while you pack. Aaron, get her bedroll, will you?" She pressed the baby's cheek against her own, cooing in soft tones. "We're going to see you safely to the village and give your mother a much needed rest." She glanced at Elisheba who packed her satchel in silence. "Has the Overseer said anything about your leaving?"

Aaron's eyes shot toward his wife, fury darkening his countenance. "So help me, if he as much as touches her, I'll —"

"Don't worry. He hasn't touched me since the accident. And no, he has said nothing." Elisheba turned, the scarred side of her face appearing even more grotesque in the shadows.

"Butchers!" Aaron pushed the word through clenched teeth, tears spilling down his cheeks. He dropped the bedroll and reached for Elisheba, clutching her to his chest. "I can't let you go, I won't."

The desperation in his voice startled the baby and he started to cry. Miriam cradled him against her body and turned to the doorway, glancing back at the two of them. "We'll wait outside until you're ready."

Miriam slipped out the door as Aaron cradled Elisheba in his arms. "I'll not let you go, I can't. What will I do without you?" He fiercely hugged her, his shoulders quaking with the force of his sobs. "How long must we wait in this god–forsaken place? How many more years until Yahovah hears us?"

Elisheba gently pulled away, tears glistening on her cheeks and lashes. She bit her twisted lip. "I don't know, Aaron, but until He does we have no choice but to survive and hope." She reached up and planted a kiss on his forehead, holding her lips there until the cries of their infant reached her ears, causing her milk to let down.

She smoothed Aaron's hair from his face. "It won't be long, beloved, and once Nadab is weaned and I return, we will have a son safe at the village to carry on our name."

Scooping up the bedroll, she ducked through the tent flap and into the brightness of the day, leaving him alone in the shadows. Aaron wanted to run after her, to stand at the edge of camp as other men did and peer down the dusty road until they had disappeared from sight, but he refused to. He wouldn't give the Overseer the pleasure of watching.

Instead he crumpled to his knees in the empty tent, doubled over with silent sobs. Wrapping his arms about himself, he rocked back and forth, pleading with a God he could not see for a need too great to put into words.

Meryet held her son's hand as together they worked their way through the rubble and racket of the shipyard at Avaris. Everywhere the framework of unfinished vessels lifted into the sky like the skeletal rib cages of giant sea creatures, making the place look more like a graveyard than a construction dock.

Other ships, farther along, wore a tangled web of sails and rigging as workmen struggled to affix the ropes to the masts. The finished vessels lifted their brilliant sails like gigantic ibis, their great white wings flapping in the wind as if eager for flight. Everywhere they looked men worked, sawing and hoisting, hammering and daubing with pitch. A workman dangling from a high cedar mast hollered an order to those below who scurried to do his bidding.

Amenhotep peered up at them, shading his eyes against the sun, more taken with the activity than with finding his father, but Meryet would not allow the confusion to distract her nor to soften the lines of determination on her brow. Clutching her son's hand, she marched up the quay toward the offices where she presumed to find Thutmose.

Her heart beat in her breast like a caged bird as she entered the building, yet frightened as she was, she had determined to confront him. Her husband had all but avoided her these past months since his return from Syria, spending more time at the shipyards than at the palace, and too many hours with his newly recruited navy to even count. Spring neared again as did his departure for his next campaign, and still he labored.

An Officer met Meryet at the door, taken aback by her presence. "I — er, can I help you, My Lady?"

"Where can I find Pharaoh?"

The man bowed hastily, turning on his heel as he led the royal duo down a dusty corridor. Announcing their arrival at the door of Thutmose's office, he stepped aside and out of earshot.

Meryet entered the room, unable to keep from noticing the disarray of documents and official effects before allowing her eyes to fall on the stony expression of her husband.

She raised herself to her full height. "We thought since you didn't have time to visit us, we would visit you."

Thutmose's eyes narrowed. "It couldn't wait?"

"Until when?" She lifted a brow for emphasis.

Thutmose drew a breath and rose from behind his cluttered desk. Meryet avoided his scowl and studied the room instead. Sunlight sifted through the dust that appeared to float upward on beams of light toward a high slatted window, giving the room an aura of mystery as if something sacred occurred within. She shook off the notion, turning with resolve to her husband.

He spoke first, frowning. "This is no place for a woman and child, especially royalty. The men are busy and behind schedule, and accidents occur. I'll have you both escorted back to the palace at once."

Tears sprang to Meryet's eyes, her words muffled between sobs as she protested. Soon Thutmose joined the debate, forgetting Amenhotep as he vented his own frustrations.

Spying a miniature ship on his father's desk, the boy investigated the object while the voices of his parents blended with the general hubbub of the construction site outside. He picked up the tiny ship, turning it in his hands, and walked to a pan of drinking water. Setting the vessel afloat, he squatted on his heels, watching the ship bob and sail as if on a miniature lake. The din of voices softened to baffled whispers and then chuckles.

Meryet wiped her eyes and watched with wonder as a smile broke across Thutmose's face. He bent toward his son, grinning.

"So I have a little sailor, do I?" Thutmose picked up his son but the boy drew back, assessing him as he would have a stranger. An expression of dismay crossed Thutmose's face but he quickly disguised it, giving the child an awkward squeeze before setting him down again.

"Perhaps a tour of the shipyards would suffice, at a safe distance of course." He avoided Meryet's pleased expression and picked up the small boat, handing it to Amenhotep. "We can't have the son of Egypt's Naval Commander wondering what a war vessel looks like."

Amenhotep hugged his prize as Thutmose lead him down the corridor and into the sunlight. Meryet followed, drying the smudged kohl about her eyes and sniffing while putting on her most dignified posture. After all, the child belonged to her as much as Thutmose. A feeble smile found its way to her lips as she watched the two of them, listening to her husband's explanations of the various activities they passed.

Thutmose guided them around the quay to the far side of the bay where a cluster of finished vessels were bobbing in brilliant array, securely tied to the dock. The sides of the ships gleamed as their masts pointed heavenward, their sails wrapped as tightly as mummies until the day they would unfurl before the wind on their first voyage north to Kadesh.

Meryet took a deep breath of the pungent air, hearing the gulls overhead as if they too exclaimed aloud the wonder she felt within. She watched Thutmose lift Amenhotep into his arms, pointing to the finished ships and telling of the exploits he would soon accomplish with his fleet. It reminded her of how he had acted when she first arrived at Avaris, only this time instead of her being the object of his attention their son had won his heart.

Meryet lifted her chin, dignity shining in her eyes. What did it matter as long as she knew he cared? Somehow, watching him with Amenhotep gave her almost as much pleasure as being the object of Thutmose's affection herself.

Moses dipped his reed pen into the pigment beneath a sputtering lamp and scratched the last words onto the parchment. Leaning back he surveyed the finished scroll. He had just completed writing as much Habiru history as he could piece together from what he had learned in Midian and what Aaron and Miriam had told him. He had even added the genealogical information from the ancient scroll Aaron had given him.

More than anything, Moses was moved by a certain promise Yahovah had made to Abraham, of how his descendants would serve in Egypt four hundred years and afterward would be freed from bondage to inherit the promised land of Canaan.

Yahovah had said to Abraham: "Know for certain that your descendants will be strangers in a country not their own, and they will be enslaved and mistreated four hundred years. But I will punish the nation they serve as slaves, and afterward they will come out with great possessions."

Moses laid down his pen. What did this promise mean? Without a doubt it referred to the Habiru's enslavement in Egypt. But how could the Habiru hope to escape the mightiest nation on earth? If the genealogical records he had copied were correct, Abraham lived nearly four hundred years ago, which meant this feat, if it happened, would occur in his lifetime.

Moses shuddered at the thought and rolled up the scroll, placing it in the jar and on the shelf with the others. Though he may not understand all he had written, he had at least completed the task, but for what purpose? Was he only adding further scrolls to Jethro's already dusty archives? Or had he truly contributed to the Habiru's history?

He shrugged. Why had he bothered? Did his work merely represent the effort of a misplaced Habiru trying to discover his lineage? Yet he felt more pride in his heritage than ever before. And though he doubted any Habiru in Egypt would ever read the scrolls, he was no longer the only Habiru here, for he now had a son.

Moses ducked outside the tent where the pre–dawn darkness had begun to lift like a curtain, revealing the dips and curves of the horizon. He studied the shadowy protrusion of Mount Sinai, a citadel before a craggy range of mountains, serving as a barred gate to what lay beyond it. He had visited the mountain several times since Gershom's birth, yet all without incident. Perhaps his desire to speak with Yahovah was nothing more than the daydream of a mystic, the result of immersing himself in too much Habiru lore.

He started toward his tent where Zipporah and Gershom slept, wondering if he dared enter and enjoy a few hours of much needed sleep. If he stayed up and built a fire, Zipporah may believe he had gone to bed late and risen early rather than spending the entire night studying. He would never hear the end of it, however, if he awakened her.

He paused just outside the door and drew a deep breath, firming his torso with resolve. He had yet to cower before a woman and would not start now. The face of Tasha flashed before him and he felt a pang of loss. How he missed her gentle ways and loving words.

He entered the tent with a heavy heart, hearing Zipporah's soft breathing, and in an unseen corner, the hint of a snore from Gershom. The boy had grown so much of late Moses could hardly believe the time that had elapsed since his arrival in Midian. He crawled atop his pallet and glanced at Zipporah who stirred then continued sleeping. Folding his hands behind his head, he stared into the darkness above him.

The thought had never occurred to him before, but it presented itself now with strange insistence. What if he voluntarily returned to Egypt? The absurdity of the notion made him laugh aloud, and he held his breath, fearing he might have awakened Zipporah or Gershom. Instead they continued sleeping, and he considered the idea more carefully.

To return would mean certain death, sure and swift, and he dared not endanger Zipporah and Gershom. Should he go alone? Why go at all? Of course he longed to see Aaron, Miriam...and Tasha.

Tasha's face lingered in his mind and he pictured her again, their last night together so real it seemed to have occurred only days before. In reality, he now had two wives, one with whom he lived, the other only a memory.

Zipporah turned and rested her hand on his chest, and Moses closed his eyes as if to shut out the present. He wondered if Tasha had remained faithful, or if circumstances had forced her into the arms of another. He clenched his jaw, his breathing quickening. Why did she still evoke such passion in him? Would he ever see her again?

Her face faded and the slow moving masses of Habiru rose to take her place. The sights and sounds of the Habiru haunted him like spirits of the Underworld. He shifted, nearly forming the question out loud: what could he do for them? They were forced to serve Pharaoh, the most powerful man on earth: to build his cities, tend his fields and cattle, and care for his people. Didn't Yahovah hear their cries? Didn't he care? Why didn't he answer them?

He left the thought unfinished, concentrating on another. Why had Yahovah spared him at all, first as an infant, then as an adult?

In the darkness he could see a young man purposefully striding down the corridors of the palace, kneeling before Amon's shrine at Karnak, and facing Egypt's enemies as if favored with divine standing. He saw himself as he must have appeared: confident, poised, and full of his own intentions, carrying out with unyielding exactness the wishes of the Pharaoh and gods. How proud and righteous he must have seemed, a Prince and supposed god's son. Yet where had it gotten him? What had he accomplished during his forty years in Egypt, or in his entire life, for that matter?

He thought of the myriads of tasks he had performed: the building of temples; waging of wars; the voyages and wonders of those years...all wasted. Why had he not put his energy to greater use, perhaps toward freeing the Habiru? Hatshepsut might have listened. She had certainly heeded his request to free his family.

Instead he had managed to save a handful, and in the end, only one: himself. The admission made his pain more acute, but the fact remained: while he enjoyed freedom and safety, albeit at a price, the Habiru endured hardship unto death, and only Yahovah knew the fate of his loved ones.

Zipporah snuggled closer. "Moses?" She gave a wry chuckle. "I never expected to find you here."

Her words sliced the darkness with a sarcastic edge, and Moses grunted, wanting to respond in kind, but did not. Instead, he wondered at the strange direction of his thoughts. What could he possibly do for the Habiru?

Gershom stirred and arose from his palette, finding his way to his father. He crawled atop his chest and curled his arms around Moses' neck, his voice hoarse with sleep. "Have you been writing, father? Mother says you waste your time on those stories." He lifted his head and peered into Moses' face, his dark eyes searching. "Will you teach me to write?"

"Nonsense!" Zipporah spat the word and turned her back to them. "What should our son care about Habiru history, or what should you care, for that matter?"

The two ignored her, and Gershom once again laid his head on Moses' chest, listening to his steady heartbeat and even breathing.

"Tell me a story, father, the one about Abraham and his son. No." He nestled his head against Moses as if making himself more comfortable. "Tell me about Joseph, Pharaoh's helper, and the granaries, and how he saved Egypt. You know all about Egypt because you lived there."

"Alright, I'll tell you the story."

As Moses began, Zipporah got up in disgust, hastily dressing. She refused to listen to his words, her face twisted with resentment. If Moses spent half as much time with her as he did his writing she would have revealed the news sooner. Instead, she would save it for a time when she could make her point, for she carried in her womb their second child, miracle though it was, as Moses seldom shared their bed.

Zipporah glanced back at the two, the lines of her face hard in spite of Moses' and Gershom's blended forms. She ducked through the doorway, jerking the tent flap shut, and wondered how life would have differed had she married one of the Bedouin shepherds with whom her family usually quarreled. At least then she would have seen more of her husband, if merely to further an argument.

CHAPTER 23

Tasha set the tray aside as quietly as she could, reaching for her veil and draping it about her head. She peeked inside the basket she had prepared then glanced at Nefru's half–eaten tray. The Queen had not touched her sweetbread, or anything else for that matter. Reaching for the roll, she tucked it under the cloth. She now had Miriam, Elisheba, and little Nadab to think of, as well as her own son. Little did Nefru realize how many her table actually fed.

Turning to the door Tasha lifted the latch, cringing as the bolt creaked.

Nefru's voice cut through the silence. "Is that you, Tasha?"

Tasha's breath caught in her throat and she looked at the basket then back to the door. If she acted quickly she could still get away. Who would know or care? As it was, most of the servants left the palace in the afternoons, enjoying walks to town now that winter had passed.

"Tasha!" Nefru called out more urgently.

Tasha sighed and set her basket down, unwinding her veil. Lifting her shoulders, she walked to Nefru's door. Perhaps she only needed a drink or her coverlet straightened.

Tasha took a deep breath and announced herself. "What is it, Your Majesty? How can I help?"

Nefru did not want to talk through the door. "Come in, come in! Honestly, when I have to plead with my own servants to serve me is the day I should rid myself of all of you."

She looked into Tash's face, her eyes softening. "Come." She patted the side of her couch. "With the sun at last shining I too wish to be out of this bed and doing other things, but alas...." She sighed with resignation. "Let Nepthys go to market. I need you here today."

Tears sprang to Tasha's eyes but she turned to Nefru's vanity instead as if searching for something. She wiped a hand across her cheek lest her mistress see. She still could not chance the discovery of her son's hiding place. Suppressing the sting of sorrow at the change of plans, she fumbled for a comb, having assessed Nefru's greatest need.

"Don't bother with that. Who do I have to primp for?" Nefru attempted a smile, but Tasha could sense the hurt in her tone. "Come. I want to hear another story about the Habiru and their god. What is it you call him, Yahovah?"

Tasha took a deep breath and set the comb aside, reluctantly turning to the couch. She would have no visit to the village today, nor would she see the delight on Jesse or Elisheba's faces at the gifts she had brought. Instead, they would wait by the village gate until nightfall, wondering at her absence.

Tasha knelt beside the couch, avoiding Nefru's eyes. Her mistress did not seem to notice her disappointment, nor did she have anything else in mind but a continuance of the tale Tasha had begun.

"The flood you spoke of, a world–wide flood." Nefru's eyes brightened. "Egypt has such a tradition as well."

Tasha watched her with wonder. All Egyptians identified with a flood, for the Nile overflowed its banks each year, providing the richness of soil from the Southlands for their crops. Tasha would not be discussing Egyptian lore, however, nor did her stories focus on Egyptian gods and goddesses. Instead, she would tell of the power of Yahovah, marveling at Nefru's eagerness to learn in spite of the fact her illness worsened daily.

She picked up the tale where she had left off, with forty days and nights of tempest. Though the exact sequence of events escaped her, she carefully related what she knew while Nefru attentively listened as she would have to a web Priest. Occasionally Nefru asked a question, such as how Noah had collected the animals, why he had bothered with vipers and other harmful creatures, and what such a vessel could have possibly looked like.

Tasha answered as best she could: surmising Noah and his sons had many years to gather the creatures; wondering herself at the value of poisonous snakes; and drawing a rough sketch of what she thought the ship would have looked like, though she could not be sure. She had hardly finished when she glanced at her mistress and stopped midsentence. Nefru's lashes lay against her cheeks, her breathing shallow and even. Though her face seemed unusually pale, a serenity surrounded her Tasha would have thought impossible weeks earlier.

Tasha looked at her tormentor so peaceful and still, as white as a lotus petal on the sheet. It seemed Nefru could all too easily remain as she lay for eternity. Tasha felt a stab of fear and a strange sense of sorrow at the thought.

She glanced out the darkened view beyond the balcony and rose to close the doors. The sun had disappeared and rain once again pattered an uneven rhythm on the roof as Tasha softly tiptoed from the room. She would enjoy no visit at the village today or likely tomorrow either. Instead, Yahovah had required a higher purpose of her, for in spite of the seeming impossibility of the task, His presence had penetrated even in Nefru's bedchamber.

The Keftiu fleet approached the Delta, their sails taut against the wind. From a distance the ship's crew could make out the pinnacles and spires of Avaris, the sprawling megalith of a palace shining at the edge of the sea like a guiding star leading them to their destination. Spring had arrived and Styrone hoped the rumor would be proven false, and that Thutmose would once again campaign in Syria.

He clutched the arm of his Officer. "There in the harbor, are those vessels?"

The Officer squinted. "They can't be, my Lord. Thutmose doesn't own a navy."

"Then by the gods, someone has arrived before us."

"Perhaps it's merely a fleet of merchant trading vessels."

"Or an ally," Styrone interjected.

The Officer shook his head. "Impossible. Which of his Syrian neighbors would offer their ships, or even has a fleet of that size?"

Styrone's eyes narrowed. "Those aren't trading vessels but war ships built to carry soldiers by the hundreds."

Whirling, he ordered his fleet back to the sea but the Captain shook his head. "We can't turn back now. They will have spotted us and will question our intentions."

Styrone frowned as he studied the scene. "Then by Minotaur, we'll have to make this a peaceful mission." He threw an order over his shoulder. "Find something to offer as gifts!"

"We have brought nothing, my Lord." His Officer's voice broke beneath Styrone's glare, and he scattered the contents of a nearby basket to prove his point.

"Here." Styrone slipped off his armbands, reaching for his earring. "The rest of you do the same. With any luck these Egyptians will only think us poorly dressed." He shoved the basket toward a servant who began gathering the trinkets.

The crew watched in disbelief as they neared the Egyptian fleet whose sails brandished their gods and emblems, and whose gleaming hulls reflected the sun as if made of gold. There was no mistaking now who this fleet belonged to. An array of soldiers assembled at the dock to meet them.

Styrone shouted to his men who scrambled to make ready their arrival as his own vessels slid into port. "Hopefully they'll believe we come peaceably."

"Does that mean we leave our weapons behind?" an Officer anxiously asked.

Styrone nodded, his eyes on the shore. "But it doesn't mean we leave without accomplishing a task."

Turning to a wiry man at his side, he dropped his voice to a whisper. "I want you to steal away to the palace at Pithom and find out what you can about my child. We'll stay only as long as it takes for you to return." He focused on the port with narrowed gaze. "We may have to win Egypt by other means after all."

The Keftiu spy sped toward Pithom under cover of darkness, past fields white with moonlight and groves of trees lifting twisted limbs beneath a full moon. The night deepened as the moon dipped lower toward the west and a purple light emerged on the eastern horizon. Beyond the pungent fields and groves, he eventually passed numerous villages, strangely silhouetted clusters of huts with rounded roofs within walled enclosures. Still he and his steed continued toward Pithom. At daybreak he passed another village and heard a dog bark in the distance. Outside the village walls women and children bent to the task of gathering firewood, while others carried jugs on their heads. Just another slave village, according to the sketchy map an aide had given him.

Beyond the village he could hear the ripple of the Wadi Tumilat, and in the distance he could see the palace Styrone had spoken of.

He slowed his horse to a trot and dismounted within sight of the palace, tying his horse in the grove near a tumbled down cottage. Not sure what to do next, he squatted against the far wall of the cottage just out of sight of the palace and listened to the banter of servants as they shook rugs and tossed refuse. Closing his eyes, he attempted to form a plan as he basked beneath the sun that melted the chill of the previous night and warmed his weary bones. Resting his head on his knees, he waited.

Sometime later he heard a noise and started. He must have fallen asleep for the sun had already moved across the arch of sky and edged toward the western horizon. He cursed his folly, for he might have missed his opportunity altogether. Just then he saw a young woman approaching with a washing basket on her way to the river. She stepped onto the path near him and he reached out and jerked her into the shadows of the hut, cupping his hand over her mouth and laying a knife against her throat. He held her fast until she stopped struggling.

"The child," he rasped, "where is it?" He slowly peeled his fingers from her face, his breathing hard.

She trembled as the knife's edge grazed her flesh, her eyes widening. She shook her head. "He — he isn't here. We took him away months ago."

"Where?"

She waited as if calculating whether or not to speak. Irritated, the man tightened his grip and she caught her breath. "The child is at Tju, the nearby slave village."

The Keftiu pursed his brow. "A slave village? Why there?" As if deciphering her thoughts, he added, "Unless it was so Thutmose would not discover him."

Nepthys stared, her brow pursed, wondering at the admission. If Thutmose had not sent this man then who had, and how had he known of the child?

She cried out as the stranger dug his fingers into her arm, his teeth clenched and his voice fierce. "Does Thutmose know the child lives?"

Nepthys shook her head.

"Then take me to the boy so I can see him for myself." She hesitated, glancing at the palace. "Now," he ordered.

"I have a gift for him. May I fetch it?"

The Keftiu's eyes became slits of suspicion. He pulled her closer, her thin tunic ripping in his grip. "This time you won't come bearing gifts but a message. Now go." He shoved her ahead of him, taking the reins of his horse as together they walked down the dusty road toward Tju.

Nepthys stole an occasional backward glance at the palace, but no one seemed to notice she had gone. Who was this man and why did he care about Tasha's child? Her skin crawled with fear, her flesh bumping in spite of the heat. As they neared the village the man slowed his pace, hiding the blade in his cloak after noting a guard outside the gate.

"It's alright," Nepthys muttered. "The guard knows me. I come here often, as does the child's mother."

The man snorted. "A Queen coming to a slave village?"

Nepthys half turned in surprise but the man did not notice. She wound her way about the huts, the contented murmur of children and hum of activity filling the air. How could she betray Jesse?

As if reading her thoughts the man pricked her back with the knife point. "I don't want to hurt the child, only to be sure he lives. But I will kill you if you don't show me evidence of him."

Nepthys reluctantly stopped and pointed to a hut. The Keftiu approached it and peered into the dark recess beyond the open door. Soon a pair of eyes assessed him from the doorway then the face of a child appeared, solemnly regarding him. The boy stepped into the light and the Keftiu stood dumbfounded, staring at the dark skinned child whose black hair curled tightly about his face.

The Keftiu studied the boy then pulled Nepthys toward him, his eyes wild. "This couldn't be him!" He shook her as if to jar the truth from her lips. "What have you done with Nefru's child?"

Nepthys' jaw fell open. She shook her head. "My Lord, this isn't Nefru's child. The only child born at Pithom is the son of a slave."

He loosened his grip, taking a step back. "Slave? But Nefru had a child, I know it. Where is Styrone's child?"

At mention of the name both figures froze. Nepthys' eyes widened with recognition. Styrone! She had heard Nefru repeat the name as if a curse. This man must work for him. She glanced at the guard but thought better of alerting him, and took a deep breath. "Nefru has no child. She —" Nepthys hesitated, "She lost it after the Keftiu left, and has never quite recovered."

The man shook his head. "You're lying." He gripped her shoulders, his teeth barred. "You've hidden him. He lives, he must!"

Nepthys backed away. Why would Styrone, a foreigner, care about the child of a lover whom he had rejected? Nepthys shook her head, puzzled.

The guard noted the disturbance and started to approach but the Keftiu dropped his hands at his sides, staggering backward as if unable to comprehend the news. He stared with horror at the child who watched him with unmasked wonder. Then turning, he hurried through the gate toward his horse, disappearing back down the road to Avaris.

Ishmael and his men topped the last dune before the sunlit city of Gaza, the city's ships serenely anchored in the distant harbor. As they approached, the sound of friendly banter poured through the open gates while a party of tradesmen exited. The men curtly nodded then continued on their way, absorbed in admiring the armload of purple robes just acquired, cloth dyed with the excretion of the murex shellfish, a commodity the city was well known for.

Ishmael watched them go, dismounting inside the gates and handing the reins to his petty Officer. "I want you men to mingle, to get a feel for the attitude of the city while I approach the Governor."

A guard ushered him up a flight of stairs to a series of rooms atop the wall. After Ishmael announced himself, a servant opened the door, revealing a plush apartment of enormous size. Heavy drapes hung against a far wall behind a gold fringed couch with a purple throw. An array of foreign oddities gathered from profitable ventures abroad cluttered the room. Ishmael walked to a vase painted with delicate dancing girls, their aquiline noses and barred breasts giving way its origin.

He heard a noise behind him and turned with a question. "From Thera?"

"Yes." The Governor cleared his throat as Ishmael set the vase back in place.

The Governor, short and round with quick eyes and labored breathing, nodded to another room. "In here where we can talk privately." They stepped into a room where the sun shone through a wide open window, revealing a view of the highway and desert beyond the wall.

Ishmael smiled beneath his beard. "A convenient place to watch for one's enemies."

The Governor motioned him to a chair while the guard took his post just inside the door. "I have no enemies," the Governor answered.

"Your sons were carted off by the Egyptians and you say you have no enemies?"

"I gave Egypt what they wanted and they have left me alone."

Ishmael accepted a goblet. "You call the plunder of your city and the imprisonment of your children 'leaving you alone'?"

The Gorvernor's lips tightened. "Egypt receives regular payment and will bother us no more. They proved as much this last campaign."

Ishmael remained expressionless, his keen eyes absorbing the details of the room without appearing to focus on anything in particular. "I would call the payment of regular tribute a bother."

The Governor shrugged. "I have no quarrel with Thutmose and he has no further quarrel with me."

Ishmael lifted his brow. "Why do you say that?"

The Governor set his goblet aside. "He has conquered all he cares to. Haven't you heard? Egypt occupies him now."

"Such as building a navy?"

The words hung like an omen between the two.

The Governor allowed himself a low laugh. "I don't know where you received your information, but from what I've seen, I'd say your assumption is overstated and absurd. Thutmose has obviously decided to turn his attention inward, and well he should, for his capital needs rebuilding due to the Hyksos' last occupation," the Governor shrewdly added. Ishmael neither smiled nor moved, and the Governor, in a sudden gesture, reached for his goblet.

"Whole cedars from Lebanon? How about masts for ships and an armada to finish the job he didn't complete at Kadesh?" Ishmael retorted.

The Governor eyed him over the rim of his goblet. "He lost the battle at Kadesh."

"He never fought a battle, but I'm certain he plans to."

The Gorvernor's mouth fell open as if to speak, but he thought better of it and took a drink.

"Thutmose couldn't even get at the city. My guess is the next time he'll sail to its doors and force his way."

The Governor swallowed. "You have no proof. It's all conjecture."

"I know the man, his zeal and determination. He wants Syria to the Euphrates and won't stop until he gets it."

The Governor shook his head and rose, restlessly pacing before the open window. "How do you know he won't march on Canaan next as it also remains unconquered."

Ishmael laughed. "You know as well as I do no army would subject their men to the disease and filth of that place. It's accursed as surely as the abominations they practice. No, Thutmose wants Syria, the conquests of his grandfather, and he'll not rest until he gets it." Ishmael stood and faced the Governor, his shoulders squared. "But I aim to stop him, to retaliate in kind, so to speak. Gaza provides the perfect place to set watch, and as soon as Thutmose's ships sail east we will march on the Delta."

The Governor shook his head. "I don't know what you're talking about but I can assure you I am not interested."

"You're closest to Egypt's border and the first from whom they exact regular tribute."

"And the first to comply," the Governor answered, taking a deep breath. "I want nothing to do with you or your confederation." He strode to the door. "Nor do I want you spreading tales and swaying the minds of the citizens of this city. Gods! All I need is an uprising, or the Egyptians getting wind of this and paying me a visit."

He opened the door but Ishmael stood his ground. "Are you saying you won't help us, that you won't let us help you?"

"That's exactly what I'm saying. The kind of help you propose will get us killed." He nodded to the door. "Try Joppa, Tyre, or even Sidon. Surely one of them will agree to your scheme. While they don't give in to Egypt as readily, they also die in greater numbers."

Ishmael's brow furrowed. "Do you mean to say that if all of Syria met here to defend your city you wouldn't support it?"

"Support it?" The Governor chortled. "I wouldn't allow it. Good day."

Inside Zipporah struggled in childbirth as pain exacted its price from her body. Her sisters, like a flock of bustling geese, each offered a different service or advice in midwifery. One readied herself to catch the child, and another pressed a cool cloth to Zipporah's brow; a third held a cup of water to her lips, while the others coaxed and encouraged, keeping the men informed of their progress. With so much help Zipporah might have been frustrated and short–tempered, but she hardly noticed, so great was her pain.

Outside the tent Moses chided himself for worrying. After all, this was her second birth and women bore children every day. She obviously had all the help she needed. Still, her cries eroded his confidence and had long since sent Jethro to the farthest corner of camp. All Moses could do was pray as he walked back and forth in front of the tent.

Ironically, he could hardly remember Zipporah's labor with Gershom, so intent had he been on leaving. Nor had he appreciated the entanglement of marriage at the time.

All that had changed, however. He was now the doting father, the compliant husband, the studious Priest of Yahovah, and of all things, a shepherd. He shook his head at the absurdity. Strangest of all, he had even grown to appreciate life in the desert. The only part weighing upon him was his relationship with Zipporah, for it had never blossomed into the love he had hoped to experience, nor the sweetness of his love for Tasha. Perhaps one found the truest love only once in a lifetime.

Through the walls of the tent he could hear Zipporah gasping for breath and asking for more water, then groaning as another contraction took hold, the air rent again with the cries and curse of childbirth. Moses felt helpless, useless. He wanted to tear open the door and aid in the birth, to soothe his wife and show her their healthy son as promise of what would come. But the Midianites did not allow men to assist unless no other help presented itself, and with six sisters ready to give a hand, help was all too available.

Moses shook his head. If an Egyptian physician were only here the child might be born more quickly and with less pain. There were herbs and potions available to help ease the process. Why did the Midianites insist on living with outdated customs and methods? Egypt had advancements in medicine and apothecary the Midianites knew nothing of, boasting some of the world's greatest minds. Why discard such wisdom merely because it did not fit Bedouin tradition?

Moses glanced across camp at the tent of worship. While Jethro practiced his Priestly duties with exacting care, in the secrecy of his own worship Moses mingled Midianite and Egyptian custom with as much Habiru tradition as he knew. He did not believe it angered Yahovah to worship within the context of one's culture. Rather, he felt more closely akin to Him, as if the Habiru God would accept anyone, as long as they worshipped with reverence.

He sighed. If Zipporah only knew of his Habiru heritage she would recoil with revulsion; and if Jethro knew he practiced anything but Midianite tradition in that sacred tent Moses would promptly hear of it. It seemed Yahovah tolerated more than the mortals He created.

Moses looked at Gershom, the lad's unruly curls and lithe body much like his own at that age. Did he not owe it to his son to tell him the truth of his past, to share with Gershom his Habiru as well as his Egyptian heritage?

Another groan pierced the walls of the tent followed by the lusty cry of an infant. Moses and Gershom hurried to the door. After what seemed an eternity, Leah pushed aside the tent flap, a tiny bundle in her arms.

She smiled up at Moses, her own forehead damp with perspiration. "You are blessed again, Moses, with another son."

Gershom raised on tiptoe to see the wee purple face while Moses glanced past them, wondering how Zipporah fared.

"Weak but resting," Anna put in.

Moses let out his breath and looked again at his newborn son. Reaching for him as carefully as he would have an exquisite vase, he cradled the infant in the crook of his arm.

Gershom struggled for a closer look. "What shall we call him, father?"

Moses studied the child, a tiny fist curled next to his mouth where he already attempted to suckle, his eyelids drooping in sleep. Moses thought of his years in the wilderness and of all he had learned in this place. More importantly, he acknowledged his awareness of the Habiru God. He no longer felt alienated or abandoned. Instead, he sensed God's presence even amid the drudgery of daily existence, as if He watched over them all with fatherly love.

Moses smiled into the tiny face. "Eliezer."

"Eliezer? What does it mean?" Gershom looked up, his brow creased, for every name had meaning.

"'God is my helper,'" Moses breathed with reverence. "For truly I would never have survived these years or even my own infancy without Yahovah's... Yahweh's help."

Gershom watched his baby brother with wonder as Moses cuddled him against his chest.

Moses smiled at his sons, not just for the significance of the moment, but for the resolve in his own heart. Tonight while resting beside the fire he would tell Gershom the story of an infant's rescue by a beautiful Princess, of a slave child who grew up in a palace, and of a Prince who came to know his people and his God.

More than thirty of Egypt's ships pulled from harbor, their sails flapping in the wind, causing the emblems on them to leap and soar as if they had come to life. Thutmose watched the shore diminish without regret, his eyes flitting over the royal party: Meryet and Amenhotep clung to each other in the foreground as if watching him for the last time; behind them stood his Syrian concubine and their daughter, Sarena, their faces solemn. He remembered his relief at hearing that his concubine had provided him a daughter, as he had wanted no rival for his future heir. He could abide a half royal sister as a bride for his son, but not a contender for the throne. He clenched his jaw at the thought, remembering his own years of struggle in Moses' shadow.

Even the thought of the name set him on edge and he forced it from his mind, waving at his son as the blue–green water stretched between them, the white capped waves tossing the ships in a lolling motion. Thutmose firmly planted his feet, yet still his stomach rolled and lurched, and he gripped his middle to keep from getting sick. He would have to remember next time not to enjoy a banquet before setting sail.

As the capital and shoreline diminished, Thutmose glanced northwest to the edge of the sea where the Keftiu had appeared the previous year. He still didn't know what to make of their visit, unannounced and by all appearances, without purpose. Their pathetic array of gifts had only made him all the more suspicious.

He fixed his eyes on the horizon as if to scrutinize their motive but shook his head, taking a deep breath, glad the number of recruits this past winter had allowed him to leave an army behind. Everyone knew when he and his fleet would sail as surely as they knew his army marched in the spring. Such knowledge was troubling as it could invite an invasion, which is why he had left Rekmire with extra troops in his absence.

He turned to study the east and thought of Kadesh. At last he could take that fortress. By now, several years after his trek to the city, they may have thought him disinterested, perhaps even believing that building rather than campaigning consumed his energies.

A smile tugged at his mouth. Conquering the coastal cities had hardly proven a challenge as some had offered him tribute before he even had a chance to demand it, but after two years they owed him again. He would collect on his way east and assure their submission before continuing to Kadesh.

After several days and nights of travel Thutmose neared the city of Gaza, its white walls rising in the distance. He sent a party ashore, instructing them to gather tribute. Almost as soon as they had entered the gates they returned laden with baskets the Governor had given them. Thutmose smiled. These city–states were a compliant lot.

Hoisting the smaller boats back onto the sides of his ships, he continued up the coast to Joppa to repeat the process. Joppa appeared ethereal in the waning light and unaffected by the change in their status from an independent city–state to one of Egypt's tributaries. But before Thutmose's skiffs reached the shore the gates closed tightly and a row of archers formed atop the wall. Thutmose stared in disbelief.

"They must not recognize us. Perhaps they think the Keftiu are invading. Take another skiff ashore and announce our arrival," he ordered.

A handful of soldiers hurried to the task, rowing toward the towering walls and shouting their intentions while waving a flag emblazoned with the eye of Horus, but still the doors remained shut, a volley of arrows their only reply. Frustrated, Thutmose paced on deck while the smaller boats fought the waves back to his fleet.

"What do we do now?" Amenhab's face reflected the anxiety mirrored in his commander's.

"By Amon!" Thutmose slammed his fist against the hull, tightening his jaw. "We'll never make Kadesh at this rate. How can Joppa think they are strong enough to withstand us?"

Amenhab started to answer when Thutmose shook his head, eyeing the fortress. "Tell the Officers to prepare for battle. If Tyre and Sidon hear of this they may also resist and we'll have to retake them as well. We dare not risk word of rebellion spreading farther east. It appears we'll have to show these Governors the strength of Egypt's armada after all."

Amenhab swallowed hard. "And Kadesh, my Lord?"

Thutmose's eyes narrowed as he studied the city, "— will have to wait."

Meryet slid the filmy robe over her shoulders, tying it loosely. She studied herself in the bronze mirror, cocking her head in appraisal then applied a touch more ochre to her lips. She had dismissed her servants long ago, preferring silence to their stares and nods. She knew why they whispered and gossiped. Thutmose and his fleet had returned from Syria over a week ago and he had yet to call for her.

Meryet turned the mirror this way and that, attempting to view herself from every angle. Satisfied, she touched her fingers to a vial of myrrh, daubing it behind her ears, wrists, and ankles. She hoped the aroma would precede her, enticing Thutmose as she approached his bedchamber, drawing his heart to hers as she longed for it to be.

She stepped out of her door and glanced down the hall. Only a servant arranging a bouquet of flowers stood in the space between her and Thutmose's apartment. According to her steward, Pharaoh had spent most of the past week at the shipyards and his nights anywhere but at the palace, though tonight, she had heard, he planned to remain in his chamber.

The servant girl questioningly looked up as Meryet left, but the Queen fixed her eyes straight ahead, her footsteps echoing in the near empty hall as if she walked through a cavern. Her heart pounded in her ears and beat in her breast until she could hear nothing else, and she had to force herself to a slow gait and even breathing as she neared Pharaoh's apartment where a single guard stood watch. Seeing her, he nodded and stepped aside.

Meryet paused before the door, glancing back in the direction of Amenhotep's room where, only an hour before, a nurse had put him to bed. A hint of a smile tugged at her lips. Though just a boy, he was such a little man. Today with his miniature bow he had killed a bird, insisting the cooks fix it for his supper. They had, though Meryet grimaced at the thought, but not Amenhotep. Like a true warrior, he had eaten the bird with relish, telling everyone of his conquest. Meryet's eyes softened. How like his father.

She frowned. Surely not so much like Thutmose. Her legs weakened and she felt her resolve wane as she prepared to announce her presence. Perhaps she should wait for her husband to call for her.

Tears threatened the kohl carefully applied about her eyes, and she stiffened. No, she would not wait but would see him tonight, and would settle the question burning in her heart. She would know whether or not he truly loved her, if passion still flamed in his breast, or if love of soldiering had robbed him of it.

Her voice seemed too dry to announce herself effectively. Instead she pressed her fingers against the door causing it to creak, though it hardly budged.

"Who's there?" a voice demanded. Quick footsteps sounded in the room and Meryet felt the urge to flee, panic coloring her cheeks and taking away her breath as Thutmose flung open the door.

The anger on his brow softened to surprise at sight of her as he assessed her from head to foot. A smile crept over his countenance. "Why Meryet, what are you doing here?"

Tears started to spill but she held them back, her chin quivering. "I've come — that is, I thought —"

He cocked a brow, opening the door further. "Come in." She apprehensively entered as if stepping into a land she had never been to before, and looked about. She scanned the room in wonder, though Thutmose's eyes never left her. A huge map dominated one side of the wall and she recognized it as Syria.

"Even a conqueror needs time for," he studied the contours of her body, "diversion."

She nodded unenthusiastically, eyeing the map as one would the discovery of a rival. She noted the curve of the coastline, the cities he had just conquered marked in red. Farther up the coast, past Megiddo, Tyre, and Sidon, lay Kadesh, drawn in bold, dark letters, and encircled by the blue vein of the Orontes. The city stood out as if pulsating with life, smugly glaring down at her from its height on the wall like a secret lover whom she had intruded upon.

Thutmose followed her eyes to the map. "Kadesh," he reverently whispered. "I would have already taken it if it weren't for those cursed coastal cities. It took me the entire season just to subdue them."

Meryet saw his jaw flex and wondered if the subject had ended their activities for the evening.

He turned to her, setting his goblet on the table. "However, I've several months before I begin preparations for my next campaign."

"Oh." Meryet winced at the word while Thutmose watched her with growing interest, his unaccustomed attention making her feel uncomfortable, conscious of her every move. She looked into his face and found his gaze soft but penetrating. She was now the prize to be conquered.

He took her hand, pulling her toward him. "I've missed you."

"And I you," she whispered, the truth of the words painful for her to speak.

Kissing her tenderly, he untied her robe as it slipped like a whisper to the floor. Passion began to pulse through her body in spite of her doubt and confusion, and she felt herself sinking into it as she would have a bed of feathers. Pulling her against him, he mumbled something into her hair, but Meryet, lost in a haze of desire, did not hear.

He touched her hair, her shoulders, breathing deeply as her fragrance encircled them. She closed her eyes, her anxiety melting as the flame of desire engulfed her.

Thutmose pressed his mouth against hers, moving his lips to her breast, her neck, her ear, lighting a fire in her loins. It had been so long.

He opened his mouth to speak and she expectantly awaited his words.

Breathing heavily, he brushed her earlobe with his lips. "Next year, Kadesh."

CHAPTER 24

Styrone and his spy strode toward King Perseus' throne as confidently as possible. They could not help but notice the grit lying on the floor, evidence of the Island's most recent quake, and the cracks in the ceiling that branched out in every direction like an encroaching vine. Styrone forced his gaze to the throne and to the anxious countenance of the king.

"Just when do you plan to conquer the Delta?" Perseus demanded, his voice edged with impatience at his commander's bumbled schemes.

Styrone bowed, his expression impassive. "If it pleases my Lord, I will convey the details." His gaze met the king's. "I am sure Thutmose plans to conquer Kadesh with his newly built armada."

"Let him have it and all of Syria, if he so desires. It's the Delta I want."

Styrone curtly nodded, forcing calmness into his tone. "When Thutmose sails east with his navy he leaves a portion of his army behind. We met them our last visit. If we are to conquer the Delta we will need help."

The king searched Styrone's face as if attempting to divine his thoughts. "Meaning?"

"There are others in Egypt, Semites they have enslaved for four hundred years. Thutmose leaves them in his Officers' care every spring while he campaigns. If we can convince these slaves to join us we will have more than enough strength to subdue the Delta and meet Thutmose upon his return."

The king pursed his lips. "Just how do you plan to persuade them?"

"By killing the Officers and Overseers who afflict them. It will not be difficult to convince the Habiru that freedom with us is better than slavery under Egypt."

"When do you plan your move?"

Styrone took a deep breath. "In the spring as soon as Thutmose sails. If he is headed for Kadesh, the city he has yet to conquer, his voyage will be long and will give us the time we need. When he and his navy return, if they do, with the help of the Habiru we will force him back into the sea."

"Or into Syria," the king muttered, "where he can muster an even greater army from his conquests there, perhaps by way of an alliance."

Styrone shook his head. "The confederation is strong and likely awaits him at Kadesh. If we are fortunate, they will finish him first. I can't see them joining him against us. If they do, Egypt's schools are filled with their choicest sons and could be used as bargaining power to keep them at bay."

The king warily watched him, wondering what his commander would gain from the scheme. But rather than answer, he nodded, dismissing Styrone to set his plan in action. Though he didn't trust the man, he was the only one qualified to accomplish the task. Once completed, Perseus would rid himself of Styrone and command his people in their new land as he saw fit.

Styrone bowed low and left the room, his manner confident and unaffected. Once out of earshot, he bent toward his companion, his voice as low as the rumble of an earthquake. "You said my son is hidden away at the village of Tju?"

The spy nervously nodded.

"Then I want that village freed first and my son taken to safety in Pithom in case the Habiru give us any trouble."

"Certainly, my Lord." The man's voice lifted with a forced lilt. "I'll see to it myself so you can concentrate on —"

"Rubbish," Styrone interrupted. "I want to see him as soon as we arrive. Once I've laid eyes on the future heir of Santaurus I'll have reason to spill my own blood, if necessary, for our cause."

The man nodded less enthusiastically, his temples throbbing at the words. Before the ordeal ended it might well be his own blood spilled on Egypt's soil. Risking his neck in the future, however, seemed preferable to risking the truth now.

Nefru coughed, the spasm jerking her body as she lay amid the cushions on her couch. She lifted a frail hand and the physician reached for it, the coldness of it startling him. He held it tightly as if to warm her flesh with his own.

"Nefru?" he whispered, anxiously bending over her.

She stirred, her lips parting with effort. "Tasha."

Tasha moved from her post at the vanity, mixing the drink as the physician had instructed her. He nodded her toward the bed and Tasha pressed the cup to her mistress's lips.

Nefru shook her head. "No," she rasped, "I want to talk."

"Drink, please."

Nefru took a sip of the bitter herbs then grimaced, shaking her head. "No more. If nothing else kills me, that will." She relaxed, her dark eyes seeking Tasha's. "Alone," she whispered. "I must speak with you alone."

Tasha looked at the physician who sighed and reluctantly nodded. "Very well, I'll leave you two, but as soon as this 'conference' has ended I expect to oversee the drinking of your medicine myself." He spoke the words as if teasing, but Tasha caught the gravity in his tone.

Hesitantly Tasha pulled a stool close to the bed and sat next to her. Setting the cup aside, she took Nefru's thin hand in her own. and studied the pale countenance of her mistress.

A winsome smile crossed Nefru's face. "I would never have thought to spend my last moments with the one I had despised." Tasha started to protest but Nefru tightened her grip on her hand as if fearing she would pull away. "I was wrong, Tasha. You have been the one true friend —" Her eyes misted and she could not finish the words.

Tasha's face softened and she smiled. "Only the One God could have brought together such an unlikely pair."

Nefru nodded then sobered. "I am dying, aren't I?"

Tasha could not answer, and Nefru looked past her out the open window. "I remember my last view of my mother with physicians and attendants hovering about." Nefru coughed, her frail body thrown into a spasm. When quieted she looked up at Tasha. "How could I have been so cold? The only thing I cared about was the size of my wardrobe." She searched Tasha's face.

Tasha took a quavering breath. "Those years are behind you now. Yahovah does not hold us responsible for what we cannot change. The past is out of reach, as is our future. We can only grasp the present."

Nefru nodded, closing her eyes as if experiencing a soothing balm. She breathed deeply and evenly, and Tasha thought her asleep, but her eyelids lifted again. "If there is a paradise, do you think mother will be there? She had no room for any god but Amon, let alone the God of slaves."

"Only Yahovah knows what is in our hearts, Nefru," Tasha answered. "But I know she once loved a slave and saved him from certain death. Surely such sacrifice is worth something."

Nefru nodded, the words confirming what she already believed. "I wonder if Moses has come to know Him?"

Tasha winced at the name, and marveled Nefru could speak it without bitterness. It seemed nothing could separate the bond they shared, not even the man they had both loved. Tasha smiled. "How could anyone hear of this God and not wish to know Him better?"

They were quiet a long moment, united by more than the clasp of their hands.

Nefru stirred, her eyes bright with a feverish glaze. "Truly He has power for He has changed my heart from stone to flesh."

Tears slid down Tasha's cheeks in silent exultation. She tried to speak but could not.

Nefru closed her eyes, her lips barely moving. "And who would have thought I would come to care so deeply for a Kushite Princess?"

The hint of a smile remained on her lips, her hand falling limp in Tasha's. Tears streaked Tasha's face as she watched her mistress as if on any other afternoon, marveling at the peaceful expression on Nefru's countenance, the warmth of her words lingering in the room.

At length Tasha laid Nefru's hand atop her breast and walked to the door, her eyes glistening but her face radiant. She would inform the physician that Nefru no longer needed him.

Ishmael's scout lay against the dune, his eyes on the liquid horizon where he could just make out the sails of Egypt's fleet as it moved eastward up the coast of the Great Sea toward the city of Joppa.

Scrambling from his perch, he mounted his horse, kicking up a cloud of dust as he sped in the direction of the Hyksos' camp. Swinging to the ground, he approached Ishmael with the news.

"The Egyptians just left, a whole fleet of them, and they're sailing east."

"Kadesh." Ishmael spoke with the certainty of a prophet. He tightened the strap about his waist, his scabbard at his side. The scout anxiously watched him as did the others who had gathered about, waiting for his command.

Ishmael studied the band of men with his hands on his hips, and with the force of lighting he thrust his fist into the air. "To the Delta!"

At the words a scramble of activity ensued with tents falling in unison and several hundred Hyksos strapping on their scimitars and making sure their weapons. Within minutes only empty fire pits and a clutter of broken pottery remained of their camp.

Mounting his horse, Ishmael turned to the Delta, his breathing matching the pounding of his heart. He scanned the western desert as if divining the outcome of his plan. Once he got past the border guards and Overseers he would free the Habiru and turn his attention to the capital, releasing the Syrians and Hyksos imprisoned in Egypt's schools, including his own sons. With a combined Hyksos and Habiru army he could then take the capital.

He had heard of a century's old prophecy regarding the Habiru, words written by their forefather, Abraham, also the forefather of the Hyksos. The prophecy not only foretold their enslavement in Egypt, but of their release from bondage four hundred years later. According to his calculations, the time had come. He smiled behind his beard. Obviously he was the one destined to free them.

Ishmael whipped his horse to a run, the Delta beckoning as if the very soil the Hyksos had once claimed called to him again. Two of his sons, captured at Meggido, were doubtless praying for his appearance as well. However, winning back the Delta was the true prize worthy of the risk; freeing his sons merely a bonus.

The winds changed direction as Thutmose left the vastness of the Great Sea and moved into the narrower span of the Orontes. Trees lined the way, while here and there an open field displayed the efforts of farming.

He had already offered incense to Amon whose shrine graced his ship, and prayed he would be able to take Kadesh unawares, though he knew the unlikelihood of the notion. By now the confederation had heard of his retaking the coastal cities the year before and would be ready for him.

His chest heaved with conviction. Resist as they may, he had waited too long for this moment to balk at a volley of arrows and a bolted gate. As far as he was concerned, a confederate army held up behind its walls and Moses with it. The chance of finding him outweighed any amount of blood he might have to spill to accomplish the feat. Even if it took the lives of his choicest men, capturing Moses would be worth the cost.

By sundown the fleet rounded a bend in the river and Thutmose caught sight of the fortress of Kadesh at the apex of the Orontes, rising in the distance like a miniature mountain atop the island, reflecting the last rays of Ra.

"Shall we make camp and attack tomorrow?" Amenhab peered at the city, noting the soldiers already gathering atop the wall as the fleet neared.

Thutmose shook his head, feasting on the sight. "We'll have fewer casualties if we attack in the dark. Our aim isn't to strike them down from the wall but to set fire to the gates. By morning we should be able to take the city."

Amenhab watched him a moment before directing a ship to the far shore to collect brush for a fire and wood for a battering ram. Thutmose may not prove the most merciful of commanders but he was certainly the most relentless.

In the shadows of dusk, the soldiers did as they were commanded, then took their positions on the vessels. Upon touching the shore of the island they were met by a volley of arrows, and crouched behind their armor bearers, returning in kind, and making sure of their aim. Occasionally their arrows met their mark and an enemy toppled from the wall with a cry, or fell backward into oblivion, but most often the arrows soared above the wall and fell unseen into the city.

As darkness dropped Amenhab ordered the pile of brush pushed to the gates behind the protection of a wooden shield. A handful of Egyptians complied, several falling in the attempt, while the rest left the brush at the wooden gates and scrambled for cover as arrows whistled about them. At Pharaoh's command, flaming arrows arched into the night sky and imbedded in the brush where it slowly crackled to life, lighting a patch of the city gates against a backdrop of darkness. The blaze revealed several fallen Egyptians lying on the shore, seemingly staring up at the stars as if oblivious to the battle that raged about them. A throng gathered above the fire, watching in horror, while the Egyptians let loose a battery of arrows, causing several of the enemy fell to their deaths.

Desperate voices lifted within the city and atop the wall as flames leapt into the night, the size of the fire growing to match the flurry of activity. The blaze sent a glowing plume of smoke into the sky, an alarm to the surrounding countryside that Pharaoh and his navy had arrived. Throughout the night the Egyptians continued to feed the flames, and as dawn began to break only shouldering ruins remained where the gates had once been, while bodies lay indiscriminately scattered on the soil.

Thutmose peered at the sight. "As soon as the smoke clears we'll take the city."

A voice called out in Akkadian from atop the wall. "What is it you wish, Pharaoh? Gold? Jewels? We have plenty! We will even give you regular tribute in payment if you leave us alone."

Thutmose lifted his eyes to the man whose pointed beard made his features appear less than servile in the semidarkness. Thutmose cupped his hands in answer. "I want the fugitive, Senmut Re Moses."

The Governor stood motionless as if calculating his answer. "Do you speak of the impostor Prince who escaped Egypt years ago? He is not here. We have not seen or heard from him."

Thutmose's nostrils flared. "Give me Moses or I'll exact more than tribute from you. I'll take your city and your sons."

The Governor waited a long moment then disappeared from the wall as a sheet of arrows rained down on the Egyptians in answer.

Thutmose grunted. "He just signed his death decree. Amenhab, prepare the troops to batter the gates. He'll wish he had thrown Moses over the wall by the time we're finished with him."

Amenhab nodded, ordering his men to ready the battering ram. Transporting the beam ashore, the Egyptians situated themselves beneath a makeshift roof of shields and charged toward the city under a shower of arrows. The battering ram struck the charred gates with a thud, causing sparks to spray in the shadows of morning as the Egyptians ran back for another thrust.

"Again!" Amenhab ordered. The men flew at the remains of the gate a second time, knocking a hole in its center. Chunks of blackened wood dropped to the ground in a spray of sparks as they prepared to repeat the blow.

"Again!" Amenhab called, as several soldiers took the places of those who had fallen. The arrows ceased from atop the wall and the clatter of armor could be heard as the Syrians prepared to meet the Egyptians on level ground. Moments lengthened as the Egyptians chipped away at the gates, enlarging the hole with each thrust of the ram until little remained of the original wood but chunks of blackened board affixed to the hinges. Thutmose took a deep breath as both armies prepared for the fray.

The sun lifted its golden brow above a distant knoll, sending a beam of light toward him and reflecting on his armor as he raised his sword, ready for the charge. His army moved into position, and as he lowered his arm, his advancing foot soldiers ran ahead toward the city, disappearing through the opening.

The rest of his men followed as army met army in a clash of metal and voices, the cries of the dying and screams of women eventually lessening as the sun rose full–bodied in the morning sky.

Within an hour the battle had ended and Kadesh joined Thutmose's list of conquests. A scribe made note of the fray, listing the dead and wounded, while another tallied the booty being gathered aboard the appointed vessels.

Yet Thutmose remained in the city, sending search parties in every direction and overturning any possible hiding place. But search as he may, he did not find the fugitive Moses, nor was there any sign he had ever been there. *Perhaps the Governor has spoken truthfully after all.* In a few days he and his army would sail back up the Orontes River with gold and captives in tow, having won a decided victory. Yet it left a bittersweet taste in his mouth. *How could he enjoy even the triumph of Kadesh with Moses still at large?*

Sensing his mood, Amenhab attempted a lighter topic. He grinned. "Remember our years of playing in the desert? We always dreamed of fighting such a battle. Who would have thought all of Syria would fall before us?"

"All but Moses," Thutmose morosely answered.

Amenhab inhaled the fresh morning air, surveying the landscape north and south of the river. "What beasts are usually hunted here?"

Thutmose shrugged, but Amenhab persisted. "Ever been on an elephant hunt?"

"Can't say that I have."

"Beer, booty, and an elephant hunt. I can't think of a better combination than that, unless you add women." Amenhab smiled.

Thutmose remained unaffected.

"But I suppose it depends on the women," Amenhab added with a chuckle.

Thutmose peered into the distance, wondering where he should search next. He would accept Amenhab's offer, but not for the purpose of recreation so much as to release the pent–up rage he felt within. He would as easily give up hope of finding Moses as he would give up his own life, and he made a silent oath it would be one or the other.

A breeze moved through Meryet's hair and gown as she stood as still as an ivory statue on her balcony, her eyes on the Great Sea.

"What is it, mother? What's the matter?" Amenhotep joined her, studying the specks that seemed to materialize before them on the seascape.

"I'm not sure." Meryet did not move for a long moment, intently watching. She heard movement behind her, the pounding of footsteps and anxious voices.

"Our troops are gathering at the quay," someone called out.

Amenhotep's eyes widened. "Is it the Keftiu, mother?"

The ships drew nearer but Meryet could not make out the emblems on their sails. How she longed for them to be Thutmose's, but even from a distance she knew better, for they approached from the north, the direction of Thera, not from the east. All she could think of at mention of the Keftiu was their horrid leader, Styrone, and her sister's premature death. If fear did not hammer so loudly in her breast, hatred would have beat stronger.

Amenhotep tugged at her robe. "Everyone is leaving."

Meryet's expression remained unchanged. She could see them clearly now, able to make out the insignia of bulls leaping and swaying on their sails. "The Keftiu must know Thutmose and his navy are gone."

"Will they harm us?" her son asked.

Meryet turned from the sight, snatching up her satchel. "I don't know and I don't intend to find out."

Clutching her son's hand, she ran from the room and into the hall. Her steward met them on his way to her apartment, his face white. "My Lady, I fear an invasion."

"Prepare a chariot. We must flee!"

"Where will you go? What if they come peaceably?"

"It seems unlikely, considering Thutmose's absence. He warned us of this possibility." Meryet sought an exit as a tumult of exclamations rang throughout the palace, the name 'Keftiu' discernable above the uproar.

The steward moved into action. "Hurry, we haven't much time."

Grasping her son's hand, they raced down the hall toward the outer door. Realization awakened her senses, her son's flesh warm in her grasp. The Keftiu had met her and her son on an earlier visit. If they planned to take the Delta, his life more than hers, lay in jeopardy.

The steward rushed out the door and into the sunlight, and in that instant Meryet knew where she would go. They would hide in the one place the Keftiu would have no reason to look.

Within moments the steward led a pair of mares into the sunlight, a chariot in tow. He helped her and Amenhotep in, then stepped ahead of them and grabbed the reins.

"Where to, Your Majesty?"

Meryet's lips parted, her breathing uneven. "To the summer palace at Pithom near the villages of the Habiru." She gripped the side of the chariot as it lurched forward, clattering over the palace grounds and toward the city.

"If for some reason the Keftiu move as far south as Pithom, we'll hide among the Habiru themselves if we have to. They would never think to look for us there."

"My Lady," the steward eyed her attire, "even slaves would recognize you as royalty."

Meryet tore the jeweled collar from her neck and slid the polished bracelets from her arms, dropping the metal at his feet. "There, payment for our safe delivery."

The servant said nothing as they flew past the temple and down the avenue into the commotion of the city. Several troops of guards marched in quick rhythm toward the port as buildings blurred on either side. Still the chariot sped, turning southeast as they left the city for the outlying suburbs and villas that eventually lessened to the fields and orchards of the countryside.

Even at this distance the sound of battle could be heard behind them. The steward lashed the horses to a frenzied pace, glancing over his shoulder.

"Once Thutmose arrives I'll try to get word to him of your whereabouts."

Meryet's body tensed as she gripped the chariot and Amenhotep's hand. The wind whipped her gown about her slight form, threatening to snatch her reply as soon as she opened her mouth. "Get word to him as quickly as you can!"

"Any idea when he will return?"

Meryet anxiously set her face in the direction of Pithom, her body rigid and her eyes dark in the delicate features of her face. "Not nearly soon enough, I'm afraid, not nearly soon enough."

The Egyptian border patrol stood about the dying embers of the fire, packing away their belongings as they prepared to change shifts. They made a merry silhouette against the pre–dawn darkness, drinking beer and guffawing over the tale of the most portly member of their group. Their horses pulled restlessly on the tethers, pawing the earth, but still the guards made no move to investigate, too absorbed in conversation to question.

Then, like a tidal wave crashing over the dune, a blur of horses and riders swooped toward them as the guards fumbled for their bows and swords. In a whirlwind of confusion the intruders fell on them, piercing them through before the Egyptians knew what or who had attacked them. In a matter of moments they lay sprawled in a chaotic tangle of bodies and weaponry, left for the vultures and beasts of prey.

Ishmael, leader of the invading party, towered atop his steed, surveying the scene. He wrapped his reins around a meaty palm. "I want a few of our men here in hiding when the next patrol arrives. The rest of you follow me."

"We should go first to Avaris to free our sons," his Officer put in, wiping the blood from his sword.

Ishmael shook his head. "We'll free the Habiru first then take the capital. We don't have enough men to guarantee a victory in Avaris, and we don't want the army alerted." He cursed beneath his breath at the truth of his own words, for the Syrians had refused to join them.

Due to his limited numbers, his future and that of his men clearly rested in the hands of the Habiru. Yet if anyone had reason for revenge it was the Habiru who had been in bondage these four hundred years.

Pointing his arm, he motioned his men across the border, leaving the carnage as easily as he would have the debris at a camp site. As daylight filtered through the dusty haze Ishmael and his men continued westward toward Pithom without incident, anxiously searching for the villages of the Habiru. Sunlight burst above the horizon as he neared a cluster of huts where several Overseers cracked their whips above the heads of slaves as they trudged toward a nearby field.

With their backs to the oncoming troop, the Egyptians barked their commands, not even noticing the Hyksos who rushed toward them like an impending storm. Feeling the earth pounding beneath them, they turned, staring dumbfounded at the sight, unable to respond.

The Habiru watched the attackers slice the Egyptians to the ground until they lay sprawled in death, their whips tossed uselessly aside.

Ishmael turned to the Habiru who huddled in clusters, their faces gaunt and their emaciated bodies stooped from years of service as if they readily offered their backs to the Overseer's whip. He sneered. "Don't just stand there — move!" His voice rumbled with the intensity of thunder, but the Habiru drew back, raising their hands in defense.

Ishmael's features twisted with fury. "Is this the army we hoped for? Gods! We'll never win with this lot." He nodded to his Officer. "Throw them swords, daggers, anything. Maybe the feel of metal in their hands will awaken their need to defend themselves."

Still the men refused the weapons, fearfully looking about as if expecting the Egyptians to rise from the dead and punish them.

Ishmael dismounted and strode toward one elderly man who stood at the fringe of the group. Picking up a sword, he forced it into his palm. "Here, take it or I'll kill you myself."

The man quaked, holding the blade as if the weight proved more than he could manage. Ishmael shook his head, his teeth barred. "Use it, or die!" He forced a sword into the hand of another, and a blade to the next until each held weapons, though they appeared unable to wield them.

The Hyksos watched in dismay. The captives they had freed appeared to have no will to fight.

"I'm afraid these are hopeless, my Lord," his Officer stated. "Perhaps they're the worst of the lot, simpler than most." He touched his temple to convey his meaning.

Ishmael's brow wrinkled with worry. "If they are all this way we'll never leave this soil alive."

"They can't be," another breathed. "Surely we'll find men somewhere willing to fight for their freedom."

Ishmael grunted. "In the meantime, I'll not waste my weapons on these. Gather their swords. We'll make soldiers of those willing to use them."

A Hyksos dismounted, gathering the weapons as effortlessly as if he collected dirty bowls. He looked into the faces of the Habiru, hoping for a spark of life or courage, even anger, but saw only fear.

"Pathetic," he muttered as he wrapped up the weapons and rode away at the side of his commander. "You almost get the feeling they prefer it this way."

Styrone overturned a vanity, scattering jewelry and jars of fragrance across the polished floor. Clothes lay in chaotic heaps amid the clutter of broken pottery and half–hung curtains, the contents of baskets haphazardly spilled about. A bronze mirror lay against the far wall reflecting his towering form.

"I want them found, now!" he roared.

The Officer at his side surveyed the room–full of servants, his nostrils flared under the pressure of Styrone's demands. He approached a cowering maid. "Where are they? Where did they go?"

The rotund woman shook her head, fearfully wringing her hands. "I — I don't know. They fled the palace with the Queen's steward hours ago. I heard the chariot leave but —"

"Which direction?"

The woman lifted a quaking finger. "Eastward, perhaps."

Styrone's face reddened with unrestrained rage. "Perhaps?" He turned to his Officer. "They know nothing. Get rid of them."

The woman screamed as Styrone strode from the room, but her cries instantly died as did the others', the silence ominous. Styrone took no notice. He had hoped to first do away with Egypt's heir before proclaiming the title for his own son.

Thrusting his sword into its scabbard, he left the palace by way of the eastern door. Glancing past the stables, he cursed his luck at not finding the heir, yet he dared not waste any more time in the effort. Avaris was nearly his.

Egypt's patrol had met him upon his arrival and stood their ground for several hours until their commander had ordered them to retreat, perhaps hoping to gather reinforcements. Styrone had not seen them since, nor had he anticipated taking the capital so easily.

A Keftiu in his command stepped from the stables, shaking his head. "Nothing here but a few horses and chariots. The maid may have been right. We could send a party out after them."

Styrone peered westward and shook his head. "We haven't time. Besides, finding Pharaoh's son matters less than finding my own."

His spy cautiously exited from the palace, joining them in the waning light. "We found nothing in the servant's quarters or gardens, my Lord. Perhaps we should search the temple."

"Not now. I have something more important to attend to," Styrone snapped. "If we start now we should arrive in Goshen sometime tomorrow. I want to find the Habiru village you spoke of and see my son."

"Surely you would like to find Egypt's heir first. What if they escape to the border?" the spy insisted.

"Into that deathbed of a desert? I doubt they would even try, they're far too pampered. If they do try, they deserve to die." Styrone's body glistened with sweat. "Once I've made sure of my own son's safety I'll search the Delta to find Pharaoh's. In the meantime, I need to enlist the help of the Habiru."

He ordered his men to the stables to scrounge for horses and chariots. Stepping into the foremost chariot, he motioned his spy to join him.

The man's eyes shifted to the eastern highway then back to Styrone. "I'll wait here in case Thutmose and his army return."

"No, I've already left half of my men to guard the city and welcome Thutmose. That's enough. I'll need your help in finding my son."

"But —"

Styrone frowned. "What are you hiding?"

"Nothing, my Lord." The man gulped.

"Then get into this chariot." Styrone watched him with a scowl. "I wouldn't want you to miss this event."

The man opened his mouth but made no audible reply. Instead, he vigorously nodded, staring with fixed gaze as they sped out of the yard and down the avenue toward the eastern highway. Behind them a scatter of chariots followed while the rest of the Keftiu continued to scour the city, leaving death and destruction in their wake.

The wind whistled past Styrone's chariot, sweeping his hair behind him as if caught by an unseen hand. His thighs rippled with strength, his chest high and broad as he gripped the reins in one hand, the other instinctively on the hilt of his sword.

The spy watched him, wondering at his own fate. Why had the gods cursed him with the privilege of riding at his commander's side, and why had he the misfortune of discovering that Styrone's heir didn't exist? If he lived long enough to find Styrone's former lover he would thrust a sword through the Queen's cursed breast himself.

CHAPTER 25

As Meryet neared the village of Tju she thought she recognized a woman and child outside the gates and ordered her steward to stop.

"What is it, my Lady?"

Meryet ignored him. Alighting from the chariot, she approached the woman. "Tasha?" she asked, touching her arm.

Tasha turned, recognition widening her eyes. The others about them curiously glanced in their direction before continuing their duties.

It had been years since Meryet had seen the dark skinned Princess, although meeting her here seemed awkward and strained in spite of the news she had to share.

Meryet swallowed, her lips waxen. "The Keftiu have invaded the Delta and have taken Avaris."

Tasha gasped. "My Lady! How? When?"

"Yesterday. My son and I barely escaped. Only the gods know where they will go next."

"What of Pharaoh?"

"He's gone, left early this spring for Kadesh." Tears welled in Meryet's eyes. "They've taken the capital, I'm sure of it, and will kill my son and me if they find us."

Tasha shook her head in dismay. "It's not possible! How can they hope to win against Pharaoh?"

"I don't know, but there'll be a battle and bloodshed on our own soil, I'm sure of it." Meryet searched Tasha's face, about to continue when a commotion sounded behind them. She blanched, clutching Tasha's arm. "The Keftiu!"

The word sent a shiver up Tasha's spine as she hurried Meryet and her son through the gates and into a nearby hut. "Quickly, hide in here!"

The royal pair had no sooner ducked out of sight than Tasha turned and found herself staring into the face of the largest man she had ever seen. She froze. Could this be the Keftiu? However, their dress and demeanor differed from what she would have expected to see. Someone called the name 'Ishmael' and he turned and answered in Akkadian. She understood the words from what Ineni had taught her. These were not Keftiu at all, but Hyksos!

The huge man started toward the hut the Queen and her son had entered but Tasha stepped in his path. He lifted an arm to knock her out of his way then looked at her more closely.

"So the Egyptians enslave women from Ta–Seti, do they? They obviously believe anything breathing ought to lay face down in the dust and grovel at their feet." He glanced about then spat on the ground and called out over his shoulder. "Nothing here but women and children. We'll not find any recruits among these."

Jesse ran to aid his mother but she shielded him with her body, apprehensively watching the intruder.

Another warrior stepped into the space framed by the open gate, his sword drawn. "Then unless we're stopping for recreation, I suggest we move on. It's the men we want, not women and children, and we've already gathered men from the other villages. This one must be for women and children only."

The hefty man took a last look at Tasha. "They certainly know how to pick their women, but come, we need to organize. We'll camp here for the night and ride for Avaris in the morning." Replacing his sword, he turned back and disappeared through the gate.

Meryet cautiously stepped from the hut, her eyes large as she searched the village. "I don't think they were Keftiu at all."

"They seemed more like Habiru," Tasha answered. The two women stole to the gate and looked out at the men on horseback, their bearded faces and rough– spun cloaks giving them away as Semites. Beneath them moved a sea of restless Habiru, weapons in their hands, their bodies gaunt and haggard.

Tasha leaned against the wall, her face radiant with joy. "I don't know who they are or where they're from, but it appears they are freeing the Habiru. Our day of deliverance has come!" She hugged Jesse to her, tears trickling down her cheeks. "Thanks be to Yahovah!"

Meryet's eyes widened as if suddenly aware she didn't belong, but Tasha did not notice. Instead she lifted a tear stained face to the sky, a prayer of thanksgiving on her lips as she held Jesse.

When she had finished she looked about, but the Queen and her son had vanished.

Styrone and his men topped the hill just beyond the village of Tju, their horses and chariots lost in a cloud of dust and confusion. The sun reflected from their swords and shields as if set afire, and beat upon their bodies until they were streaked with sweat and dirt.

The spy pointed ahead outside the village where a sea of men stood as if awaiting them. Styrone reined to a halt, dust lifting about his chariot. His eyes shot to his spy.

"Who are they and what do they want?"

The man shook his head. "I don't know, but it appears the Habiru have already been freed."

Styrone frowned, assessing his numbers. "They have weapons and are accompanied by —"

"The Hyksos!" his Officer put in.

Styrone glared at them then barred his teeth and lashed his horse to a run, speeding headlong toward the throng ahead of his men. "By Minotaur, we'll fight the lot of them!"

The Hyksos mounted their horses, the foremost shouting out in a booming voice, "By the god of your fathers, fight!"

Like two herds of charging rhinos, the Keftiu chariots met the swords of the Hyksos in a clash of metal and a tangle of horses and bodies. Styrone picked Ishmael out as the leader and drove his chariot toward him. Ishmael saw him from the corner of his eye and struck down a soldier in his path until only he and the opposing commander faced each other.

Styrone swelled his chest, challenging the Hyksos in Akkadian. "So you want to free the Habiru, do you? To what end?"

Ishmael clenched his teeth in his fury. "I'll tell you when you lay in the dust at my feet begging for mercy."

Styrone dealt him a blow, throwing the Semite off–balance and sending his horse back a step.

The Keftiu leader smiled. "How do you know it won't be you lying in the dirt? Have you taken a look around? The Habiru aren't even fighting." He met Ishmael's sword with a ringing blow that clanged above the general clamor of battle.

The Semite didn't take his eyes from his foe but had the sinking feeling he spoke truthfully.

Styrone lunged but Ishmael dodged, catching the Keftiu on his shoulder. Blood spurted from the wound and Styrone's eyes flashed. "You'll die for that, barbarian."

At first Ishmael had not been sure exactly who he fought. Did this army represent part of Thutmose's defense? The men had arrived in Egyptian chariots, but their dress and appearance differed. He remembered the earthen vessels he had seen at Syrian city–states, and it came to him at once. "The Keftiu," he whispered.

Styrone grinned. "At least you know who will put an end to you."

"No, you'll be the one to die, you and your curly haired lot. I've heard your people don't know the difference between a man and a wench. Well this is the difference."

He thrust his arm forward but Styrone blocked it, throwing his sword against Ishmael's and forcing the metal into the air where it somersaulted in a high arc. Ishmael watched in disbelief as his sword landed on the ground with a thud.

Styrone smiled, showing an even row of teeth. "Wench, am I?"

Ishmael grabbed for his war axe, swinging it with deadly force, but the Keftiu turned out of its path, the blade just missing him, imbedding itself in Styrone's chariot.

The Keftiu's lip curled, his nostrils flared. "Did you hope to claim the Delta for yourself? Think again, Semite. Avaris is ours, the port, the garrison, the capital. You're two days too late."

He was about to strike when several Habiru stumbled between them, attempting to defend a Hyksos.

Ishmael leapt from his horse and retrieved his sword. "You speak too soon, Keftiu."

Styrone joined him on the ground as the two crouched like a pair of panthers, circling and eyeing each another with fixed gaze, their muscles taut. Styrone struck out with his sword but Ishmael dodged it, lifting his own in defense. They crouched again, their eyes furtive, their bodies ready to spring. In a single stroke Ishmael slashed Styrone across the chest causing blood to spurt as the Keftiu screamed with rage.

Without even surveying his wound, the Keftiu flew at his enemy, his hair streaming behind him. Ishmael stared, his bulk too massive to move quickly enough. Unable to avoid Styrone's blow, the Keftiu's blade plunged to its hilt in his stomach as Ishmael's eyes widened, his lips stammering something incomprehensible. Falling backward onto the ground, he clawed at the earth, clutching a handful of black soil and holding it long after his body had ceased to move.

Ishmael's comrades gaped in horror as if his end mirrored their own. Turning, they fled on horseback toward the border, leaving their wounded and the Habiru behind. Seeing the turn of battle, the Habiru dropped their swords and awaited their fate, but Styrone said nothing regarding them.

Instead he turned to the village, his spy in tow. The bloody gash across his chest oozed a streak of red but he did not seem to notice. Shoving the spy ahead of him through the gate, he looked about, surveying the huddle of huts.

"Now where's that son of mine and the wench who cares for him?" he gasped, his chest heaving.

The spy gulped, glancing about for means of escape but finding none.

"You there!" Styrone shouted to a woman who hid in the shadows. "Where's the royal child born at Pithom?"

The woman pointed to Tasha and her son who stood pressed against the village wall as if hoping to disappear into it.

Styrone shook his head. "It can't be. I want the Queen's child. Where's Nefru and her son?"

Tasha caught her breath, her hands trembling as she groped for Jesse. She emphatically shook her head, attempting an answer, "Nefru had no son. She never had the child. This is my son born at Pithom."

Styrone stared at her, then at his spy who apologetically lifted his shoulders. "Perhaps if you looked at the palace...," he lamely offered.

Styrone towered over the girl. "Who are you and how do you know this?"

Tasha met his gaze. "I served as her slave," she paused, "until her death."

Styrone's face constricted as if refusing to believe. Turning, he gripped his spy by the shoulders.

"She lies!" the spy insisted.

But before he could speak further Styrone shoved his blade into his belly. "Take this and join the rest of our enemies," Styrone said between gritted teeth.

The man's mouth gaped as if to continue in his defense, then his eyes widened and he slumped from the sword, his blood spilling in a pool at Styrone's feet.

Styrone turned to Tasha and her son, his fury unspent. "As for you, for knowing of it and not stopping her —"

A rider sped through the gate on horseback, skidding to a stop in a swirl of dust. "Thutmose has returned," he shouted, gulping air as if having run the distance himself, "and is retaking Avaris!"

Styrone's jaw dropped. "It's not possible."

"I tell you he's back and I barely escaped with my life."

Styrone bolted for the gate. With his men divided or dead there was no hope of winning the Delta, and with his ships moored in the port of Avaris he was cornered. He glanced about like a caged lion then grabbed a cowering Habiru. "Where are your ships, your dock?"

Not sure if he understood, the man feebly pointed to the wadi. There in the distance three rickety ships lifted their masts amid the bulrushes.

Styrone grunted. "You call those ships?"

"Probably an abandoned fleet," his Officer offered, "but at the moment our only means of escape. If we leave by way of the wadi and follow the channel north —"

"We may be able to find our own ships and head out to sea," Styrone finished. Leaping into his chariot, he led his men in a frantic race to the wadi. He passed the tumble–down palace at Pithom and glanced back at the darkened recess, cursing the Queen who had lived there. But he had no time to verify the story or to avenge himself.

Leaving the chariots at the makeshift dock, he and his men boarded the vessels, hacking loose the worn moorings and shoving out into the wadi. He watched the palace and village recede in the distance, his eyes narrowed and his jaw clenched. He would be fortunate to make it out of the Delta with his life, considering the condition of these vessels. However, more than his own fate occupied his thoughts. For not only had he lost his future home, but the son he had hoped to share it with didn't even exist.

Thutmose tore through the palace at Avaris calling the names of his wife and son. His heart pounded as he picked through the bodies and ruin but could find no clue as to what had become of them. His sword was stained with blood from the battle at the quay, having beaten back the Keftiu who remained in the city, forcing them into the streets and killing them as he went. Even now his men scoured the capital, finding them hiding in the apartments and villas of those they had murdered only days previously.

Thutmose rummaged among the rubble of Meryet's sitting room, noting the contents of a spilled table. He righted it, lifting her mirror from the floor and setting it in its place.

Frustration welled within him and tears blurred his vision. Where were they? Had the Keftiu imprisoned them, or worse, killed them before he arrived?

He tried to calm himself...to think. If they had time to flee they might have taken a few articles with them. He frantically searched the room, looking under baskets and among piles of clothing but could not find her satchel, which meant one thing: she and Amenhotep must have escaped before the Keftiu arrived. But where? Might they have tried to reach Bubastis where Rekmire and his army had retreated? But the Vizier had seen nothing of them. Could they be in hiding at the garrison?

Thutmose stopped, concentrating on the blue outside Meryet's balcony, and then rushed from the room and down the hall, calling for a band of men to join him. If his family had not attempted to meet Rekmire and were not to be found at the garrison, there was only one other place they might be.

Jumping into his chariot, he led a squadron through the city, past the occasional villa and vineyard scattered on the outskirts. Trees and fields blended into a continuous blur on either side as he sped toward the garrison. He stopped but found nothing, and continued at the same frantic pace toward Goshen, hardly noticing as the sun slipped behind the horizon and the moon lifted like a great silver face to take its place.

The hours of the night gave him time to think, and he relived the events of past weeks and his unwelcomed discovery at Kadesh, for Moses had, in fact, escaped farther east. That left Mitanni, the last unconquered city between Egypt and the Euphrates, as the final stronghold of his grandfather's conquests. He had heard that a remnant of confederates had taken residence there. It would require a longer campaign still to reach the city that lay on the bank of the Euphrates River, but after the ease with which he had taken Kadesh, nothing seemed impossible. A victory at Mitanni would mean the capture of Moses, but did he dare leave Egypt again?

The Keftiu had been routed and their ships burned, though a remnant may have escaped as Styrone had never been found. The only other possible threat to Egypt was the Hyksos and their supposed confederation, what was left of it.

As the hours passed Thutmose focused on the far horizon as if attempting to divine an answer, watching the sun rise in the east and wash the fields with light. He passed several Habiru villages as the road turned toward

Tju and Pithom. The orchards and fields were unusually quiet, in fact, alarmingly empty.

Thutmose grew uneasy. What if more Keftiu awaited him here? Or, cursed thought, what if they had freed the Habiru? He would have to turn back to Avaris for the rest of his army.

He came upon the village of Tju and stopped. Bodies lay strewn across the ground in chaotic abandon, their eyes staring and their limbs sprawled in death. He stepped from his chariot, the stench suffocating. These were not just Habiru, but Keftiu as well. In fact — he looked closer — there were Hyksos among them! He studied the largest and recognized the man at once, the beard and bulk giving him away as the Hyksos leader he had fought at Megiddo. What were they doing here?

Had they been in alliance with the Keftiu, or had they also taken opportunity in his absence, chancing upon the Keftiu at the same time? Whatever had happened, a battle was fought and it appeared both sides had lost to some degree. Still, Styrone didn't appear to be among the fallen, though strangely, Meryet's steward was.

Thutmose shook his head, trying to piece the mishap together. He glanced back at his Officer. "It appears the Keftiu have fought the Hyksos for us, and one or the other must have attempted to use the Habiru to their advantage."

Thutmose ordered his men to bury the bodies and secure the slaves, making sure they returned to their allotted villages. The bodies of guards and Overseers also lay among the lot, making it necessary for Thutmose to replace them with his own men until reinforcements could be found.

With several of his men accompanying him, he continued to the palace at Pithom, clattering to a stop just outside the entrance. Chariots lay scattered along the path to the wadi as if hastily abandoned, and horses meandered about munching on the tall grass. He recognized the chariots as his own from Avaris, obviously used by the Keftiu.

He glanced at the wadi. The three rickety vessels usually moored there were not to be seen. Had Styrone taken them? Thutmose half smiled at the thought, imagining Styrone trying to man oeuvre those sorry ships. It would prove a miracle if they made it up the wadi, let alone safely across the Great Sea. It appeared justice had prevailed after all.

While his men searched the grounds, Thutmose took the steps of the palace two at a time, pushing through the open door and into the seemingly empty hall, his sword in his hand. Though it appeared the enemy had all escaped, he must take care lest he happen upon one in hiding.

Thutmose stealthily made his way through the hall, his men at his heels. The shadows sharpened as he entered the reception room, his footsteps echoing in the silence. It appeared even the servants had abandoned the palace upon Nefru's death. It was just as well, as he didn't care to face her memory any more than he cared to face an enemy.

He looked about, seeing a door at the far end of the hall. Pressing on it, it creaked open, sounding like the cry of a child in the darkness. The hair on the back of his neck rose as he entered the room, standing in a slice of light from the open doorway.

He heard a noise, but before he could raise his sword two figures rushed at him from the darkness throwing their arms about his neck and smothering him with kisses.

"Father!"

Startled, Thutmose laughed aloud, his voice echoing throughout the empty palace. "Thank the gods, you're alive!"

Meryet pressed her moist cheek against his. "I never thought I'd see you again. The Keftiu and Hyksos both tried to take the Delta, and fought each other just outside the village of Tju. I don't know how many Habiru escaped. They had swords and chariots, and when we heard you enter the palace we thought they had returned for us."

He tried to quiet her but she shook her head, tears spilling down her cheeks. "Egypt is ruined, the palace is plundered, and our servants are all dead. There is nothing left for us!"

Thutmose hugged her to him, stroking her hair and speaking as softly as he would have to a child. "But there is, Meryet: there is the rebuilding of our capital and preparation for years of rule at home."

Meryet looked into his eyes, her face bright with hope. "Then you won't leave us again? You'll stay in Egypt and forget those horrid campaigns?"

Thutmose fell silent, his gaze fixed on a point in the distant darkness. "After Mitanni."

Moses stirred the fire as the flames reflected in the eyes of his sons, Gershom and Eliezer, who sat on either side of him in the darkness.

"Tell us another story father, the one about Abraham and his son. Tell us how Yahweh rescued his son from being killed."

Moses glanced at Zipporah. He knew she had heard the request though she continued cleaning the pot as vigorously as if she had not. Revulsion twisted her face of late to a constant grimace. Only in her sleep did she seem at peace.

Moses longed for her to understand, to share his past as well as his present, but since the discovery of his identity as a Habiru she had kept her distance. He no longer represented the Egypt she admired but a horde of slaves she despised. Her disgust resulted in part from generations of Midianite jealousy over Abraham's favored son, Isaac, father of the Habiru. Her other argument focused on believing that people content to remain slaves for four hundred years deserved nothing better.

Content? The word grated him beyond expression, but rather than argue, Moses had maintained a silence of his own, allowing it to stretch between them like a widening gulf.

His sons stared up at him as if he had, all this time, been formulating the tale in his mind. Gershom shifted, snuggling against his father in preparation for the story he knew would follow.

Moses began, "There was, in the distant land of Canaan, a wealthy Overlord named Abraham who had a son named Isaac from his beloved wife, Sarah. Abraham, who worshipped Yahweh as his God, had waited nearly a hundred years for this special son to be born. He loved Isaac and wanted only the best for him. He made the boy tiny sandals of the softest leather, and wove a little coat of camel hair to warm him when the fires went out at night and to cover him as he slept."

Eliezer smiled and hugged his own robe closer, his eyes dancing with delight.

"Then one day Yahweh, who had promised Abraham this son, spoke to him in a dream. 'Abraham.' The voice startled the old man, causing him to sit up on his pallet, but the voice persisted. 'I want you to take your son, your only son, Isaac, to Mount Moriah....'"

Moses turned his gaze in the direction of Mount Sinai as if seeing the mountain of which he spoke. The boys looked in the same direction, picturing the mountain as they often saw it, a distant fortress of rock jutting from the plain. "Offer him there to me as a sacrifice."

Though the boys had heard the story before from Jethro and Moses, their faces reflected wonderment and their eyes shone like four full moons as if they also travelled up that mountain to be sacrificed.

Gershom gulped. "Did he go willingly, father? Did he want to die?"

Zipporah sloshed a bowl of water, the sound breaking the stillness of the moment as surely as if she had hissed. Her scowl deepened and her eyes burned. "Fables! Why would Yahweh require the death of a promised son? Obviously Isaac wasn't the son of promise."

Moses ignored her, turning back to the fire as if drawing the story from the flames, his voice soft and low. "Yes, he went willingly, for his father had asked it of him, and he loved and obeyed his father."

"So he carried the knife," Gershom eagerly offered, "and packed the wood up the side of the mountain."

"Yes." Moses could feel the tension building as the story progressed while his sons pressed closer to him in the darkness. He continued, "It must have been hot and tiring as they climbed the mountain, and they were glad they had brought their water skin and lunch."

"Did they eat their lunch first?" Eliezer clasped his hands in anticipation.

Moses smiled and nodded. "I'm sure they did, there on the slopes overlooking the valley, sitting together as you and I are sitting here now, perhaps even telling a story as we are tonight."

"What story did he tell him, father?" Eliezer's eyes brightened.

Moses took a deep breath, looking far into the night. "He probably told him about the time Yahweh had promised him a son, and of His assurance that their descendants would become as numerous as the stars in the sky and the sand of the desert."

"It came true, didn't it?" Gershom sat upright. "You said there are more Habiru in Egypt than anyone can number."

Moses nodded, his face solemn.

"Why do you think Abraham told Isaac that story, father?" Eliezer asked.

"Probably because He wanted him to believe, as Abraham did, that God would take care of them, and that Isaac would survive even this, their greatest test."

Gershom smiled and Eliezer nestled under his father's arm. Moses stared in the direction of the unseen mountain, finishing the tale as the last flames faded to embers in the glowing pit.

"...And just as Abraham was ready to plunge the knife into his son an angel from God called out to him, 'Abraham, don't do this thing. Now I know you love the Lord your God more than anything or anyone, even more than your son.' Then Yahweh provided a ram caught in a nearby bush, and together they sacrificed it in Isaac's place with great joy and thanksgiving."

Gershom hugged his father with delight, but Eliezer remained silent, his head propped against Moses' arm in sleep. Without speaking, Zipporah lifted him to bed while Gershom reluctantly followed her. But Moses remained by the fire watching the embers die and wondering about another promise God had made to Abraham nearly four hundred years before: that after four hundred years of captivity his seed would leave the land of bondage and return to Canaan.

Moses peered west in the direction of Egypt. The rest of the story had yet to be written, and he couldn't help but wonder how Yahweh planned to accomplish it.

Meryet stood at the forefront of the crowd gathered at the quay, her face constricted in anguish and her eyes red and swollen. For ten years she had managed to keep Thutmose from another of his campaigns, content to collect tribute from the city–states already conquered. But he had not forgotten Mitanni, and at last the moment she feared had arrived. Thutmose was sailing east on what he claimed would be his last campaign, only this time he was taking their son, Amenhotep.

At the sound of the trumpets the crowd parted, allowing the Pharaoh and his army to march through their midst toward the polished and waiting fleet. Amenhotep, tall for fifteen years, walked at his father's side with as much pride as Pharaoh.

Thutmose beamed. He had reason to be happy. He had spent more than enough years in Egypt appeasing Meryet's uneasiness. It was time to finish what he had begun: the conquest of Syria to the Euphrates River. Only Mitanni stood in his way.

The event would be more than memorable with Amenhotep present, for on this, his son's first campaign, he would witness the placement of his father's boundary stele near his grandfather's on the banks of the Euphrates. Thutmose had waited long for this moment.

As the pair brushed past Meryet, Amenhotep paused to bid her farewell, but his mother could not speak and broke into a fit of weeping.

She clutched his arm. "Please don't leave me!" The youth started to answer but his father urged him on, hesitating only a moment himself before continuing past her toward the foremost ship. Thutmose turned back at the ramp, and though he never looked his wife's way, he addressed his Vizier loudly enough for her to hear.

"Rekmire, see that my edict is carried out exactly as ordered. Double the patrol at the capital and along our borders, and place extra guards at the palace. I wouldn't want anything unforeseen happening while I am away." He eyed his Vizier as an eagle would a mouse.

Rekmire exuberantly nodded. "As you command, my Lord."

"I especially want the Queen well protected."

"Certainly."

Ignoring her cries, Thutmose and Amenhotep continued up the ramp and onto the electrum plated ship, taking care not to look Meryet's way. Instead Thutmose scanned the sea for signs of oncoming vessels, then turned to search the throng for his Syrian concubine and their daughter, Sarena. The girl had grown into a delicate beauty, and though he had seen little of her and her mother in recent years, as Meryet insisted they reside far from the royal apartments, he made a mental note to move their residence closer upon his return. After all, the girl would one day become Amenhotep's wife.

Meryet followed his gaze, and as if divining his thoughts, wailed all the louder. As the last soldier marched up the ramp she lifted her gown and ran toward the foremost vessel in an attempt to steal aboard, but Thutmose ordered the plank pulled onto the ship.

Pharaoh's face hardened as she crumpled to the ground, crying and reaching toward him and their son as if pleading with him to break his resolve and call off his campaign. Forego his final conquest because of a woman's fears? He sneered, looking down on her with disdain as the gulf of blue widened between them. He now wondered what he had ever seen in her to begin with.

Amenhotep forlornly watched the shore, and Thutmose put an arm around him, steering him instead toward the open sea where they watched a gull swoop low, nearly touching the mast. The sun shone like a beckoning orb while the waves gently lapped against the hull.

As the fleet pushed out into the breadth of the Great Sea Thutmose realized the only thing Meryet had provided him no other woman could was this, their son and heir. He shook his head. Such a marriage, though necessary, seemed burdensome at times.

He searched the water northward where the Keftiu had fled years before, and seeing nothing, turned his attention to the east as the ships veered in the direction of Syria. He doubted the Keftiu would have the man– power to invade his shores a second time, but in spite of this confidence, he had taken no chances, building his reserve forces until he could leave an army in Avaris nearly the size of the navy accompanying him.

Thutmose filled his lungs as the wind caught in the sail above him, the all–seeing eye of Horus painted there staring eastward as if obsessed with the same determination he had. If he were to keep his promise to Meryet, after this campaign he would never again sail with his fleet or march in Syria.

He swelled his chest with the scent of the sea, a pang of regret overshadowing his thoughts. If this was truly to be his final campaign, he intended to make it count.

Styrone entered the bathhouse where steam from an ancient fissure filled the room, making the air uncomfortably thick as water bubbled from the heated pool. He glanced about the room, ignoring the advances of a man who reclined on a couch, and passing several couples entwined in each other's arms. He recognized both as belonging to someone else in the bathhouse, each of whom was occupied with another.

Finding a lover did not interest him today, however. Instead, he continued to brood over past events, especially the discovery of his nonexistent son. He who had once hoped to father a Prince!

A young woman entered the room and looked about, continuing to a bench where she preceded to disrobe, stepping into the bath. She did not appear particularly pretty and so Styrone ignored her.

What had happened to his hopes and plans? All he had worked for had gone awry. Why had the Hyksos moved into the Delta the very day of his conquest, and why had Thutmose arrived on their heels? And those sorry ships, if they could even be called by the name! Styrone cursed them beneath his breath. Merely making their way back across the sea to Thera had nearly cost them their lives.

Styrone sauntered to the pool and sat on the edge, studying his reflection in the water. His face appeared gaunt and emaciated, and his eyes lifeless hollows. What had happened to the strength he had once possessed?

He accepted a drink from a servant, feeling the liquid burn his throat as it spread warmth throughout his body. He was dying. Like most of the populous of Thera, a slow, sapping death was leaching the life from him until soon no breath would remain in him at all.

Styrone sighed, the drink numbing him from the horror of the thought. He had seen others die, had heard their whimpering cries and had watched their suffering as they wasted away to mere shadows, but he had ignored them, for the most part.

Had fate, in some sordid twist of terrestrial revenge, destined him to experience the same? He knew he deserved to die. His life had proven anything but gentle. In fact, he hardly knew the meaning of the word. But if he were to die he at least wanted a son to carry on his name and his purpose.

He shook his head, sensing the futility of the notion. He had hoped and planned, but his schemes had aborted as surely as had his child. Nefru! The name had become a curse.

Styrone glanced around the room, his gaze lingering on the wench who pulled herself up from the water, self–consciously wrapping her robe about her body. At last he was drawn to her by more than casual curiosity. Who was she and why had she come?

Rising, he strode to her, his smile revealing nothing of his thoughts. She had a shy, almost virgin manner about her, rare in Thera. He looked her up and down, her brown hair hanging to her shoulders, her face plain, but her deep brown eyes pensive. What did he care of royalty or even beauty? He needed only a woman, any woman, and this one would do just fine.

Moses tugged on the leather strap around his belongings while the herd of sheep and goats bleated under foot, stirring the dust as he and his family gathered outside their camp. His teenaged sons kissed their mother goodbye, and Moses also turned to Zipporah, but she refused to soften when he looked her way. Instead, her expression evidenced the contempt she had felt for him these many years at discovering the truth of his birth.

Moses turned his attention to his pack. "We won't be back until after summer as we have plenty of work at the mountain to keep us busy." He glanced at Jethro, attempting a smile. "With the herds at summer pasture you will have more time for study."

"Not if we plan to have a garden," Zipporah put in. "We'll need all the help we can get hauling water. Yahweh knows we have little enough help as it is." She meaningfully glared at Moses.

Moses took a deep breath, an answer ready on his tongue, but he threw the pack over his shoulder instead. "I would like to build some sheep pens while we're up there, and perhaps a permanent shelter, if I can scrounge enough wood."

Jethro shook his head. "It's not been done before, Moses. I don't know if Yahweh would approve."

Moses firmly planted his staff. "If it hasn't been done, how can you be certain He wouldn't approve?"

"I can't, but —"

Moses nodded toward the mountain. "Someday I would like to build a temple there as well."

Jethro's lips tightened. "I won't have you polluting our mountain with your Egyptian ways. Remember, it's the Egyptians who keep your people in bondage and defy Yahweh with their idols and temples."

Zipporah smiled, a smug triumph in her eyes.

Moses avoided her, addressing Jethro instead. "Don't worry, I'll take care not to anger our God." He paused, nodding to his sons. "But come, we have a long journey ahead of us before nightfall."

Gershom strode ahead of his father, a pack on his back and a staff in his hand, eager to start, but Eliezer lagged behind. He turned and waved at his mother. "We'll return soon, mother, I promise, and we'll bring back sheep and goats fatter than any you've ever seen."

Zipporah nodded, her mouth stretching to a smile but her eyes held anything but mirth.

Moses looked at his wife a last time. What did he see in her expression? Contempt? Regret? Did she wish to accompany them after all, or merely to add to his pain?

Moses winced at the irony. It was on Mount Sinai they had first initiated their love. Love? Was this the kind of love he had hoped to share with a woman? His thoughts roamed to Egypt and Tasha, but he would not allow himself to dwell on what he could not have. He had weightier matters on his mind.

Instead, he set his steps in the direction of Mount Sinai, not so much out of eagerness to provide pasture for his flocks, or even to escape Zipporah's barbs, but to initiate a relationship with the One God such as his forefathers had known, and to speak with Him, if possible, face to face.

Chapter 26

Tasha fearfully watched the gate as she and Jesse walked across the village compound toward the hut where the Habiru worshipped. A pair of guards passed, glancing into the village square before continuing their watch. Before his departure Pharaoh had posted extra guards at all the Habiru villages, and had doubled the number of Overseers, making the Habiru serve more vigorously than ever. Did he fear another uprising? The last had occurred more than ten years ago, and wouldn't have happened at all without the Hyksos' involvement.

Tasha continued toward the hut as quickly as she dared so as not to draw attention, keeping her eyes on the door where several Habiru had entered. One of the guards turned her way, eyeing her with suspicion but Tasha maintained a steady pace, her throat tight and dry.

"Mother," Jesse anxiously asked, glancing back at the guard, "are we going to Joshua's hut?" He knew the young man well, for he was about his age, raised by a grandmother who had willingly risked her life to gather the few in the village who wished to pray.

Tasha nodded, her breathing shallow as they crossed the dusty ground.

"Joshua says his father used to work in the brick pits near the capital, but he is dead now." The youth dropped his gaze. "I wish I had known my father."

Tasha studied him with concern. He had not mentioned his father in years. Why would he think of Moses now?

A movement at the gate caught her attention as a soldier entered the square, dressed in full armor and carrying a scroll.

"A message from Pharaoh Thutmose III, god of Egypt," the man brusquely announced. "In order to quell any notion of rebellion in his absence, Pharaoh has ordered a 'purging.'"

Tasha stopped, her pulse pounding in her ears.

"A purging?" one of the guards asked, echoing her thoughts. Grabbing the document, he scanned it. "What in the name of Amon?"

"The death of all male Habiru infants," the soldier explained.

Tasha pressed her hand against her mouth to keep from crying out, her mind racing as she pictured those in the village who had babies. Without looking back, she and Jesse hurried into Joshua's hut.

"It's come," Tasha blurted, panting and peering into the darkness of the hut. The heads of those bent in prayer lifted, their words silenced on their lips.

"What's come?" Joshua's grandmother snapped, her tone sharp at the intrusion.

"An edict from Pharaoh, I just overheard it." Tasha's voice dropped to a strangled whisper. "The death of all male Habiru infants!"

A woman gasped and another cried out, while a third scrambled to her feet, hurrying outside where the sounds of footsteps and clanking of metal could already be heard.

Joshua's grandmother stood to her feet, tears streaming down her face. "Yahovah, help us! Deliver us from this evil, and save us and our children."

As footsteps neared, several others hurried out the door, determined to save their infants. The rest remained on their knees, their faces stark in the darkness as they prayed amid the screams and wails that echoed outside their walls. A guard glanced in their hut, and seeing no infants, he left as quickly as he had come. It was as if time had turned back to an edict years earlier in this same village when the cries of infants and their parents had once before rent the heavens in despair.

The grizzly nightmare seemed to last for hours, and when the soldiers' footsteps finally receded and the carnage had ended, an unnatural stillness lay over the village, void of the cries of infants and the chatter of children. Instead, only the sounds of mourning could be heard, interspersed with a silence borne of the deepest sort of sorrow.

Aaron raked his fingers through his hair, rising from the floor to pace the confines of his tent. Elisheba lay on a nearby mat, her shoulders quaking with sobs.

"They're alright, Elisheba," Aaron soothed, more out of obligation than conviction. "We would have heard by now if they had been killed. They were too old. Even Pharaoh, heartless as he is, would not kill grown children." His face paled at the thought, but he continued for her benefit. "The deaths were of those two years and younger," he reiterated. He glanced out the tent westward where the sky flamed with color and resumed his pacing, muttering beneath his breath.

Still Elisheba sobbed. "Suppose they mistook little Ithamar for two years instead of three."

Aaron shook his head, steadying himself against the tent pole as the face of their fourth son formed in his mind. Weak at the possibility, he sank to the floor beside his wife. "At three years he can talk and run, he could even tell them his age if they asked."

Elisheba wept all the louder, picturing their son at the mercy of such butchers. "I hate this life! I would rather die than continue to live without him."

Aaron's eyes shot toward her, fear widening them as he pulled her into his embrace. "Don't speak so. Our children need you, and I need you."

She lifted her scarred face, her lip twisted at one corner. "If they're dead I'll never forgive myself for coming back, for not staying at the village and protecting them."

Aaron folded her body against his, smoothing her hair. "What could you have done, my love?"

She firmed her chin though her lip quivered with emotion. "I could have taken the blade myself, if need be. Perhaps that would satisfy them. Isn't that what they really want? Why stop at infants when you can murder the women who bore them?"

Aaron shook his head, tears trickling from the corners of his eyes in spite of his resolve. "I'll not lose you too, Elisheba." He clutched her tighter, burying his face in her hair. "I love our sons, but I'll not lose you again, no matter what happens."

They huddled together in the waning light as darkness fell. Elisheba had only just returned after weaning their youngest son, Ithamar, leaving him and his three older brothers at the village with Miriam. How she missed them.

She relaxed in Aaron's arms as he smoothed her hair, her robe falling from her shoulder and revealing the softness of her flesh beneath it. Aaron kissed her neck, the scent of her skin needing no perfume. Her pulse aroused him. How he wanted her. His body ached with desire, but he would not allow himself to take what was rightfully his, knowing the price they might have to pay.

"Elisheba." Just whispering her name comforted him. He eased her to the mat where they continued to hold each other even in sleep: Aaron dreaming of the day he could love his wife as Yahovah had intended; and Elisheba picturing their family of six about a fire, undivided, talking and laughing as they shared a meal.

A breeze stirred through the tent, caressing Aaron's face and drying his tears to salty streaks. He dreamed he heard a voice whisper his name, a voice carried by the wind that grew louder and louder until he could hear nothing else.

Startled, he sat upright, every nerve awakened, his torso glistening with sweat. He could feel the presence of someone in the tent and peered into the shadows, but saw no one. Still, he had heard it just as clearly as if someone had bent over him and called his name. He strained in the stillness, hearing only the pounding of silence in his ears and Elisheba's even breathing.

A breeze continued to stir the tent flap. Perhaps he had imagined it. He lowered himself to his mat again, glancing at the outline of Elisheba's body. Maybe she had called him in her sleep; but no, the voice had been a man's.

Aaron's flesh rose in bumps as he slipped the coverlet over his shoulders. It had been years since he had heard the stories written on ancient parchments and buried in dusty archives, but he remembered them as if having just read them the night before: how Yahovah had spoken to

Noah when the world fell into sin too great to overlook; when He had called Abraham at Ur, beckoning him to a new land; and when He had spoken to Jacob in a dream, providing for him in his years of sojourn.

Aaron hardly dared breathe as he stared into the darkness. Might Yahovah have called him? Absurd. Lately he had even questioned the existence of their God, so burdened was he with hopelessness and anger.

A vision of Moses flashed before him and he closed his eyes to keep it from vanishing. How he longed to see his brother again, to leave this place and claim the land of Canaan as Yahovah had promised them.

He shook his head at the absurdity, carefully pulling the coverlet over Elisheba and lying in the silence beside her. Surely Yahovah would choose to speak to someone more significant than him.

He watched his wife as she slept, then slowly and deliberately turned his back to her, determined to dream of something other than what he longed for most: freedom to live and love, and to finish his days in happiness. An impossible task, even for a God.

Meryet leaned over the rail of her balcony, her gown billowing above the waves that slapped against the rocks below her. She laughed with bitterness, peering eastward beyond the distant glistening surface as she had often done in days past. As far as she could see, water stretched to the horizon until it touched the sun without the slightest break in the blue, or hint of ships or sails.

She laughed again, though her face reflected anything but joy.

A voice interrupted her thoughts. "Come mistress, your hairdresser wishes to fit you with a wig. You will need it for the festival of our goddess." Her Steward of the Royal Wardrobe stood in the spacious room awaiting an answer, but Meryet did not feel like following the whims of her steward, even though she had served her these past ten years.

Meryet drew a deep breath. "Leave me this morning. I need solitude."

The steward looked distressed. The physicians had warned her to keep an eye on the Queen as she may be depressed, even hysterical, in the delayed absence of her husband and son.

"Are you sure there is nothing I can do for you, my Lady?"

Meryet petulantly shook her head. "Just go and leave me alone."

"Very well, my Lady. I will check in on you later," the steward answered, quietly closing the door.

Meryet stared out at the sea. Solitude? What she really wanted was her husband and son back. She could not believe even Amenhotep had deserted her. She had given him everything, sacrificing for his every whim, and like the others, he had taken without giving in return, even as her husband had done.

Husband? Her face twisted to a grimace. What had he ever done for her? He had 'blessed' her with his seed to provide Egypt an heir then had whisked him away from her on another of his campaigns, hoping to teach him about war.

Tears threatened to spill. Neither her husband nor her son wanted to be with her. Now they would both be preoccupied with his campaigns, for Amenhotep, young as he was, had interests in the navy. Would she even see them again? Perhaps their love, like everything else, was only an illusion.

She turned her gaze northward where the Keftiu had intruded upon their shore years earlier. She remembered her fear at the invasion. Was death also an illusion? The thought struck her as intriguing and she glanced back at her room, picturing the blood caked on her floor years earlier as she and her husband had found it upon their return from Pithom, spilled from the bodies of her former servants. No, surely death was real enough.

She thought of her father's death, of the overwhelming size of his coffin. The gold had dazzled her even as a child, and she remembered the constant parade of articles as the Priests carried object after object into the darkness of his tomb to be used in the afterlife. Was there any truth to the myths of life after death? She had visited his tomb years later and his belongings still appeared untouched, the food they had left for him dried and moldy.

Her mother's death had been much different, having experienced such a slow unclasping of life she seemed to have died long before breath actually left her body. She had lost everything meaningful to her: the throne, her certainty of eternity, and Moses. Surely she had died as much from a broken spirit as from illness, though it seemed far too timely, now that she truly examined it.

Nefru also was gone, prematurely. Meryet had never known her well, nor cared to, over pampered and supercilious as she was. Even as a girl the servants had cringed whenever Nefru called, though they had gladly served when she had beckoned.

Meryet turned to the room with a cynical smile. At least she had her servants, though she knew none of them well. She had lost the best of them when the Keftiu had invaded ten years ago. She shrugged. What did it matter?

Though she lived in a palace high above the Great Sea and held the coveted title of Queen, still she felt empty and alone, and nothing in life interested her.

Meryet thought of Thutmose and the dam of tears burst. Of all people, she had hoped he cared. She had thought his prolonged stay in Egypt and the absence of his campaigns were evidence of his love, but she had been wrong. For he loved only what he could conquer, and once he had conquered her, exacting a son from her womb, he had wanted nothing more to do with her.

She looked at her hands, thin and translucent in the morning light. The oversized ruby studded ankh on her finger glared up at her, a present from Thutmose upon his return from Kadesh.

She pulled it from her finger and flung it out into the space before her where it dropped to the rocks below, bouncing and glinting until lost in the tumult of waves. She smiled. What would Thutmose say at its absence? Her smile faded. Would he even notice?

Anger flared through her like an erupting volcano. "Well I'll not wait any longer. I'll not stand idly by and let them both reject me."

She peered over her balcony and almost lost her footing, catching herself on the railing. No, as much as she wanted to cast herself onto the rocks, she could not bring herself to do so. She desperately glanced about her room, her eyes falling on an exquisite vase from Tyre, a present from Thutmose after one of his campaigns, as if a piece of pottery could make up for his absence. What did she care about gifts? Thutmose's concubine had come from Tyre, all the more reason to destroy it.

Snatching it up, she lifted the vase high above her head and hurled it to the floor, watching fragments scatter to the far corners of the room. She anxiously awaited lest a servant interrupt her fury, but no one came, no doubt used, of late, to hearing pottery break in her room amid her rages. She grabbed a jagged shard and studied the milk white flesh of her forearm.

Stepping to her balcony, she lifted her chin and peered in the direction of the eastern horizon. With a sure, unwavering slice she opened her wrist, standing over the rail and watching her blood mingle with the waves. She dropped to her knees as the red oozed through her white linen gown, draining life from her face and limbs, and widening in a dark pool about her.

She eased herself onto the floor, feeling strangely comforted by the coolness of marble against her cheek as her body grew numb and her mind fogged with the dimness of death. She heard the waves below as if on a distant shore, and the banter of voices in the hall sounded muddled and out of reach. Only then did she contemplate what lay beyond life's door and the eternity she faced.

She heard a faraway scream, followed by the faint pounding of feet, but it was too late. For death like a cavernous tomb seemed to swallow her whole, and she wondered with her last thought, if life, such as it was, might have been better than what she would face after it.

The ships rhythmically rocked over the sea as the sun dropped low on the horizon, lighting the waves as if afire. Thutmose closed his eyes, the picture of Mitanni's final struggle all too fresh in his memory. More enemy had fallen in that battle than in any other he had fought. In fact, the Syrians seemed to topple over each other in their eagerness to get to his sword.

He frowned. He had not wanted to spill so much blood, but merely to find the one who had eluded him these many years. He had hardly believed it when the final soldier had fallen and he had still not found Moses. He had destroyed every hovel, levelled every edifice, leaving more dead than he intended, but had never come across even a shadow of evidence leading to the escaped fugitive.

He forced his thoughts to his supposed moment of triumph when he had planted his stele in the soil on the far side of the Euphrates across from his grandfather's. Yet in spite of his accomplishment he felt a sense of failure. Moses had escaped him, and even victory, such as it was, left a bitter taste in his mouth.

Amenhotep stood at his side, his face aglow with the headiness of battle and his cheeks ruddy in the wind. He stood taller than his father, his torso more muscular and his limbs promising the sturdiness of a warrior.

"Once we are home, father, I want to be in charge of the ships as you promised, and one day to lead a campaign of my own," he matter-of-factly stated.

Thutmose solemnly watched him, the wind having snatched his enthusiasm and carried it to the far reaches of the sea. "There is nothing glorious about war, son."

The faces of those he had slaughtered forced their way into his thoughts as if demanding recognition and Thutmose clenched his jaw, staring out at sea. He longed to surround himself with living things instead, with birds, plants, and exotic animals, anything growing and moving of its own accord. He had spilled the blood of countless Syrians for nothing, and when at last he had discovered the truth, he had vented his fury further on those he might have taken captive. He felt engulfed by it, as if the sea itself had turned to blood, reminding him of his senseless carnage.

He sighed, turning to the shore, the pleasant sights and sounds of gulls mingling with the lapping waves. "I want to send a party throughout Syria."

"May I go, father? I can shoot a bow as apt as any man. I proved myself at Mitanni, didn't I? Fourteen fell by my arrows alone."

Thutmose shook his head. "This will not be a party of war, son, but of peace."

The boy's face fell. "Father, this was my first battle. I want to be a warrior like you."

Pharaoh studied him: the squareness of his jaw much like his grandfather's, and the eagerness in his eyes like his own at fifteen years. Yet his shoulders and torso promised even greater strength than either he or his grandfather had possessed. Still an unnamed fear gnawed at him, a fear that his son would come to the end of his days as he had, empty and spent, burdened with bloodshed.

"There are better things than war, Amenhotep. I will show you."

"You have shown me, father. I want to be a General like you: to lead an army and command a fleet; to crush the heads of my enemies; to make women swoon with fear and old men grovel as they pay tribute; to win wars and build an empire."

Thutmose bit his lip. Whirling on his heel he directed a command to his Officer. "I want three ships to break away immediately. They are to land at the closest coastal city."

Amenhotep's eyes brightened, but the Officer cocked a brow in Pharaoh's direction. "To collect tribute, my Lord?"

"No. Plants and animals, Syrian specimens for a botanical garden and zoo," the Pharaoh stated.

"A zoo, my Lord?" The Officer stood transfixed as if having never heard the word.

Thutmose raised his voice to match the color of his face. "Yes, a zoo!" His eyes flashed. "And when we have returned to Avaris I want the captives we hold, who have completed their schooling, returned to Syria to serve as Overlords of their city–states."

Amenhotep's jaw dropped in disbelief. "But father, they might use their knowledge against us. We can't trust them. Why would you order such a thing?"

Thutmose reared, his words rumbling from deep within him as if a volcano were erupting. "Because I am Pharaoh and I command it!"

Turning on his heel, Thutmose marched the length of his ship, preparing to enforce the order while his son stared after him as if watching someone he did not know. Within minutes three of the largest ships pulled away from the fleet, heading toward the coastline.

Pharaoh stood transfixed, his chest heaving. No more would he shed the blood of these Syrians or leave the shores of the Delta for war and plunder. Instead, he would govern the Two Lands as those before him, enjoying the fruit of his labor and refreshing himself with what blessings the gods granted him.

He looked west where he would soon see the capital rise from the Great Sea, the hills and valleys falling about it like a verdant robe. How he longed for home, for the familiar surroundings of the palace, and for his wives. He thought of Nefru with a stab of guilt, remembering his complacency at the news of her death. Instead, he pictured Meryet waiting for him at the port where he had left her. He would make it up to her now that he had time, now that he realized how much life meant to him.

He breathed deeply of the pungent air, watching with satisfaction as the three ships diminished toward the Syrian shoreline. Amenhotep stood next to him, his eyes also on the ships. If he thought his father foolish, he did not say so, yet the set of his jaw and the determination on his face revealed a different future for Egypt, one which Pharaoh could attest profited nothing, but which his son would have to discover for himself.

Moses stood on the mountain precipice overlooking the scope of desert that seemed to stretch into infinity under an endless arch of blue. To the south lay Jethro's camp, though he could see nothing save a thin strand of smoke in the distance.

The wind whipped up the side of the mountain, rustling the leaves of an acacia tree clinging to the cliff, its gnarled limbs the result of years of battling the elements. Rooted deep in the earth, it tenaciously held its place on the mountainside, appearing twisted and misshapen, yet strangely beautiful.

Moses smiled. His destiny was much like that tree, seemingly out of place in the desert, tested and torn by unforeseen trials, yet clinging to the hope that good would come of it. Was there a purpose in all he had experienced? He looked at his sons who languidly lounged near the pool while the herd drank, and wondered at his role as a father. Even more of a contradiction was his role as a shepherd. He chuckled. Who would have thought, after years of education and training such only royalty receive, he would end up in the desert tending sheep? He laughed aloud, his laughter echoing against the mountain and back again.

Still, he had learned much while shepherding: such as how to survive in the desert, living off the date palm and the sap of the terebinth tree; how to tap underground streams in the sand and reservoirs in certain rocks after rainfall; he had also learned patience, a virtue he had never naturally known. Raising his boys had been much like tending sheep, as he had to learn to love and care for those too vulnerable to fend for themselves. But sheep and goats were even more headstrong than his sons and liked to wander, so he had devised easier ways of shepherding them, leading them through confining paths between clefts in the mountains, and building a sheep pen so he could rest while they gained strength to continue their course.

He chuckled. He had actually grown to like them, allowing his sons to name them and thinking of them as friends, though they were only dumb beasts. During his years in Egypt he could not remember caring for anything or anyone, unless it benefited him — except Tasha. A picture of her formed in his mind, and even after all these years, the thought of her brought such longing he felt overcome by it.

He gazed across the desert. Yet he had learned to sacrifice, to survive in spite of his losses. He studied the peaks lifting beyond him into the sky. Perhaps it was because he had come to sense a power greater than himself, a God who not only existed but had somehow guided him to this place. His heart lightened at the thought.

"Gershom and Eliezer," he announced as his sons looked his way, "I am going farther up the mountain."

Gershom's eyes widened. "Father, it will soon be dark and you may not find your way back."

"Then I will stay there until daybreak. If I haven't returned by sundown, eat your supper and bed down by the flock. Stay here and care for them until I return."

Moses bent over his pack, gathering a small portion of food for his evening meal and flint for building a fire. Picking up his staff, he walked across the plateau and behind a jutting wall of rock while his sons stared after him with unspoken concern.

Moses prodded the earth, testing his way along the rocky ledge that provided just enough room for his footing. He searched the path with wonder. Here was an outcrop, a pathway just wide enough for his feet, reaching around the mountainside as if the One God had carved it out for this very moment. He forced his eyes from the bottomless precipice, looking ahead and continuing one step at a time as the sun's light waned in the distance. A scuff of stone loosened beneath him and he slipped, grabbing hold of a terebinth root while he regained his footing. Trying not to tremble, he stepped more carefully until the path widened beneath him.

As the horizon lit with the sunset he came upon a level plateau covered with acacia trees. The last of the sun's rays shone around him, setting the landscape afire with color, glancing off the mountain in golds and pinks as if he had entered an ethereal realm.

He stood in awe, feeling party to something too sacred to witness. He hardly dared breathe, waiting and listening for the One God to speak, but hearing only the stirring of wind in the leaves. He searched the area for stones large enough to build an altar and found seven, stacking them atop one another. Gathering an armload of brush, he laid it on top of the altar and struck the flint over a pile of tender until it sparked to life with the gentle coaxing of his breath. He had no animal to offer as a sacrifice, nothing but his supper. Reverently he placed the cakes atop the fire and watched them burn.

The wind whistled about him and the darkness deepened as he waited. He added more brush to the blaze until the night seemed alive with its brilliance. If his sons saw the smoke they would know he had safely reached his destination. He warmed his hands over the fire, smelling the consumed cakes and feeling suddenly hungry. He waited but nothing happened. He smiled to himself. Had he thought the earth would quake or lightning bolt from the sky?

At last, weary of waiting, he lay down beside the altar with his head on his arm, and covered himself with his cloak. Closing his eyes, he breathed deeply and evenly until the steady movement of his own body began to lull him to sleep. Perhaps he should not have come. He certainly should have eaten his supper instead of burning it. He felt foolish as well as hungry, and was glad his sons had not witnessed the event, for they would not have understood.

His breathing grew shallow and unhurried, and soon a soft snore rumbled in his chest as the night cooled and a spray of stars lit the sky above him.

"Moses." The voice jarred him from his sleep and he roused on one elbow, staring into the darkness. The fire on the altar had died long ago, and he could see nothing. He listened, hearing only the strumming of wind in the trees, whistling through the rocks about him. He lay down and waited, then reluctantly closed his eyes.

"Moses." A chill swept over him. He had not imagined it this time, but had clearly heard his name. Quaking, he arose, leaning on his staff for support. Had one of his sons followed him, or was someone else here?

"Who is it?" Moses waited, peering into the darkness. Reluctantly he formed the words, "H–here I am, my LORD."

Beyond him a bush burst into flame and light leapt into the darkness. He had seen it happen often in the desert, a bush combusting of its own accord beneath the blazing sun, but never at night after the sun had fallen. There was no reasonable explanation.

Moses approached the bush with faltering steps, feeling warmth radiate from it as surely as if he had lit it himself. Yet as he watched, the branches remained intact, not consumed or changed by the fire. His eyes widened and he took another step forward.

"Do not come any closer," a voice called out.

Moses drew back, seeing the outline of a figure in the flames. Gasping, he shielded his eyes with his cloak, his limbs quaking.

"Take off your shoes for the ground you are standing on is holy."

In a desperate gesture, Moses flung his sandals aside, his limbs weak and his body trembling.

"I am the GOD of your fathers, of Abraham, Isaac, and Jacob....I have seen the affliction of my people and am come to deliver them."

Moses' eyes widened, hearing the words as if in a dream. He tried to speak but his lips refused to move.

"Come now and I will send you to Pharaoh so you may bring the children of Israel out of Egypt."

Pharaoh? The words tumbled out before he could stop them. "But who am I, my LORD, that I should go to Pharaoh?"

"Certainly I will be with you, and this will be a sign...for you will bring the people to this mountain again to worship Me."

Moses' mind whirled. Was this really happening? He had waited a lifetime to hear a god speak and now fear so consumed him at the prospect he could hardly stand. He wanted to run and hide but his legs would not carry him. Worse, this God had asked of him the one thing he could never do: return to Egypt and confront the Pharaoh.

Moses studied the figure. Was this a trick? Perhaps this was not the Habiru God at all but another deity enticing him to his death.

"But my LORD, when I come to the Israelites and tell them 'The God of your fathers has sent me to you,' and they ask me Your name, what shall I tell them?"

The voice thundered, the ground rumbling with the force of His words. "I Am that I Am. Tell them 'I Am' has sent me to you. Yahweh, GOD of your fathers, the GOD of Abraham, Isaac, and Jacob, has sent me to you.... Now go, and gather the elders."

Moses swallowed. Yahweh did dwell in this mountain! A lump formed in his throat, his voice barely a whisper, "What if they don't believe me?"

"What is in your hand?"

Moses looked at the rod as if wondering himself what he held.

"Cast it to the ground."

He dropped the stick and in an instant a viper writhed in its place. Moses leapt back into the darkness.

"Now pick it up by the tail."

Moses hesitated. To do so would mean certain death as the snake could coil about and strike his hand, yet he dared not question this Deity. His head felt light and his face glistened with sweat as he reached out a trembling hand, but as soon as he touched the tail the snake stiffened, becoming a rod again.

Moses' mouth gaped, his eyes reflecting the firelight.

"Now put your hand in your cloak and withdraw it."

Moses looked at his hand, hesitantly slipping it into his robe. Taking it out, he held it up to the light, gasping with horror at the white splotches covering his flesh, evidence of leprosy.

"Put it in again."

This time when he withdrew it, his hand was whole like the other. He stared at it, then at the bush still aflame, and dropped to his knees. How could he even look on a God so powerful? Yet even with such miracles, would Pharaoh listen? Moses thought of Thutmose as he had last seen him, a merciless warrior, conqueror of all the earth, ravaging whole cities that dared to defy him.

"But Yahweh, my LORD, I — I can't speak eloquently. I am not persuasive. Send another, I beg of you."

Light from the bush flared out into the darkness as if reaching for him, the voice as fierce as the flame, and Moses drew back, shielding his face.

"I know you can speak, but behold, your brother already comes to meet you....I will be with your mouth, and he will be your spokesman to the people."

Moses had waited long for this moment. As the voice and the fire faded, Moses realized the truth: Not only did Yahweh exist, but He inhabited this mountain and had personally spoken to him. What he hadn't anticipated was what Yahweh had asked of him: that he free the Habiru, a feat he doubted he could accomplish even with the help of such a God as this.

Tasha arose from the cot and stepped from her hut. Above her darkness lifted as infinite as time itself, scattered with stars too numerous to count. She stared at the jeweled expanse wishing she could escape into it.

Escape. If only it were possible. Though the village seemed quiet and serene, she shuddered as she remembered it only months earlier, strewn with the bodies of infants and the parents who had tried to protect them. When she and Jesse had finally made their way through the bloodshed and bodies to Miriam's hut they had miraculously found Aaron's four sons safe, the youngest in Miriam's arms. Once united, they had wept with both relief and sorrow, but what of the myriads of others?

Tasha hugged Jesse closer, blinking back the tears. She remembered news of Pharaoh's return and of the booty onlookers boasted could fill the Great Sea itself. Soon afterward Thutmose had freed his Syrian captives, sending them back to their homes, and the following spring had permanently moored his ships in Egypt's harbor. Some hoped the mercy he had shown the Syrians would extend to the Habiru, but it had not. Instead he seemed even more intent on making them suffer, and Tasha believed she knew why: for he had never found the one he had searched for.

"Moses." She murmured his name, gazing above her as if hoping to find him there.

Then she glimpsed it, the constellation of Orion and Pleiades, unchanging in their endless pursuit across the sky. A moan erupted from her lips, her eyes swimming with tears as the stars blurred in a dazzle of muted light above her.

"Why did you leave me, and why won't you return and help us?" she whispered to Moses in the darkness.

But even as she spoke the words she realized the futility of such a notion. For if he did live, to return to

Egypt would mean certain death, as Pharaoh had still not forgotten him.

Lifting her arms to the sky, her cheeks moist with tears, she prayed, "Oh Great Yahovah, watcher of all the earth, guide him, keep him in Your care. And if possible, if he lives, unite us once again and deliver us from this land."

Her gaze swept the star studded expanse before resting on the lovers locked in time and space. Then she ducked back into the shadows of her hut.

Moses awakened the next morning, still gripped with an unshakeable fear. Gradually he remembered what had happened the night before as if it were a dream. Yahweh had spoken to him, summoning him to Egypt to free His people!

His limbs weakened at the thought, nearly giving way beneath him as he struggled to his feet. Surely Pharaoh would kill him if he ever found him again, and for good reason. Had he not fled Egypt as a murderer, eluding punishment these many years? Thutmose would not have forgotten.

He looked for the bush that had burned the night before and found it, realizing it now appeared as ordinary as any other. He chuckled to himself. Perhaps it was only a dream after all. He would leave this place and seek pasture for his flock at some other mountain.

Searching the ground around him, he found his sandals flung to one side as if hastily discarded. Slowly he bent and picked them up, putting them on his feet and fastening the leather thongs. It had to have been a dream.

Moses looked for his staff and found it lying in the dirt not far from where he had slept. He started to reach for it then stopped, seeing the spiraled track of a viper.

Recognition coursed through him like flood waters through a ravine. He looked at the bush, at the altar topped with ashes, at the staff surrounded by markings in the sand. Then fearfully and reverently he picked up his rod, knowing what he must do.

Epilogue

In the palace yard and in the streets of Avaris thousands awaited the announcement of Pharaoh's death and Amenhotep's coronation. The din and confusion outside the palace directly contrasted with the quiet weeping and rustling of robes within the royal bedchamber as Thutmose's loved ones hovered about him like doting doves.

Pharaoh's form seemed frail and insignificant compared to the oversized bed inlaid with turquoise and obsidian beneath the curtained canopy. The formal wig, which he had insisted upon wearing for the occasion, precariously tipped on his head giving him an almost comical appearance, and the kohl about his eyes appeared hastily applied. He had wanted to wait until the last possible moment to lay aside his authority and crown his son, so there had, as yet, been no formal coronation.

The High Priest anxiously glanced outside the balcony but Thutmose shook his head. "The masses will have Amenhotep to themselves soon enough; I have only this moment. Let them hear of the coronation once it is done." His eyes moved about the room as he studied the faces around him.

It was not so much age as sorrow that had overtaken him: first with the death of Meryet, who even now enticed him to his grave; then with the loss of his prized ambition, the hope of capturing Moses. He sometimes thought he could hear the laughter of his escaped foe echoing throughout the halls of the palace, ever eluding him and making a mockery of his efforts.

Finally war itself, so glorious an achievement at the start, had sapped his strength as if the blood he had shed had been a slow letting of his own. Not even the zoo or botanical gardens, filled with innumerable oddities from faraway places and attracting thousands to the capital, could fill the void war had left in his soul. Spent and weary, the Pharaoh had faded into near non–existence until even his closest advisors looked to the day when Amenhotep would take his place.

The royal family stood about him: the Pharaoh's concubine on his left; his son and heir, Amenhotep, on his right; and next to his son, his Syrian daughter, Sarena, lean and beautiful like her mother but with the added softness life at the palace had lent her. At his feet hovered three others: the High Priest, a physician, and his closest friend, Amenhab, each present in these final moments for reasons of their own.

The High Priest wished to administer the final rite of passage to the Underworld; the physician hoped to prolong his life; and his friend, loyal to the end, wished to preserve the moment, taking in each detail and communicating to Pharaoh by his very presence his unwavering devotion. Yet it was Pharaoh's concubine who broke the silence, crumpling in a fit of weeping beside his bed and making even the Pharaoh uneasy.

"Gods, woman," Thutmose coughed as he expelled the words, rasping the last with such effort his countenance purpled, "stop that wailing and save all such nonsense my burial."

The High Priest looked at the double crown perched on a nearby bust as if to ask if the moment had arrived, but again Pharaoh shook his head. He had a more important matter to settle.

Moving his gaze to his children, he studied the pair. Amenhotep, whom he had named 'Commander of the Navy,' had taken the title in stride, seeing to the war ships with particular care, though Pharaoh had allowed no campaigns since Mitanni. He shuddered to think what would happen in his absence.

"Amenhotep?" His voice barely lifted above the silence.

The youth held out a thick hand and Thutmose took it in his own feeble one.

"You will reign after me, A Khepru Re Amenhotep, a tribute to the gods, your mother and I." He sobered at mention of his dead wife, and reached for his daughter, who appeared youthful and vulnerable as she leaned over his bed.

He smiled. "Sarena, you will possess a coveted title for one so young, and half Syrian at that." He quickly said the words, almost as an apology, but squeezed her hand just the same.

Pulling their hands together, he placed Sarena's under Amenhotep's, holding them there while he pronounced a blessing. "May the gods prosper you and your seed," he paused, catching his breath, "making your years as fruitful as the Two Lands over which you will rule."

Sarena dropped her gaze, avoiding Amenhotep's eyes. His frame dominated the bedside, his shoulders massive compared to her lithe stature and their father's emaciated body. As a girl she had watched him practice with his bow in the palace yards, and had admired the way he had whipped his stallions to a run when entering or leaving the grounds. Lately his duties had kept him away for days, a schedule he himself had imposed. Sarena had watched for his arrival just the same, knowing the youth whose hair mingled with the wind and whose form was fashioned by the gods would one day be her husband.

The moment had arrived then passed with such simplicity Sarena was unsure whether it had actually occurred. Yet the Pharaoh's simple words were all they needed to begin their union as husband and wife.

Amenhotep neither flinched nor softened as Thutmose finished his blessing, but straightened the arch of his back, hardening his torso as if to prove his virility.

Pharaoh moved his eyes up the stolid form to his son's face. "Remember, Amenhotep, make peace, not bloodshed, your goal." He paused, his breathing shallow as he anxiously watched his son. "I have paved the way for your reign. All you have left is to maintain the kingdom in my absence, to enjoy your years at the capital, and oversee the lands paying tribute."

Amenhotep flexed his jaw, not allowing himself to answer, for his thoughts differed too much from his father's to voice them now.

"You will stay at home then with Sarena?" Thutmose searched his son's stony countenance with concern. "Your mother, the gods bless her Ka, would have liked it very much if I had done so. In fact, she might still be alive if —" He stopped himself, not allowing guilt nor regret to darken the moment, for all too soon he would join Meryet in the afterlife where he would be hers for eternity.

Amenhotep shifted, retrieving his hand and crossing his arms, his feet firmly planted. He flexed and his muscles bulged from beneath his armbands. "I will do my best to rule as you have before me, with strength and power."

Pharaoh watched him a moment then whispered to Sarena, a glint in his eyes. "See that you make it worth his while to stay in Egypt."

Sarena blushed, hiding her smile behind a trembling hand, but she obligingly nodded.

Pharaoh moved his fingers with effort over the sheets, fumbling for the hand of his concubine to whom he had paid so little attention until the absence of Meryet. He covered her hand with his own then nodded to the High Priest, son of his beloved Vizier Rekmire who had served him until his recent death. Only Amenhab, faithful comrade from youth, stood at his bedside as if standing at attention before his General, his expression revealing the sorrow he would soon experience at his friend's passing.

Thutmose smiled at him ever so slightly then nodded to the High Priest who stepped to the ornate table on which the double crown rested.

All eyes in the room watched as the Priest lifted the crown of Upper and Lower Egypt from the bust and walked about the bedside to where Amenhotep stood. The Pharaoh paused long enough to draw his son's attention, letting Amenhotep know he could rob him of the honor as well as bestow it, if he chose, but even the heir knew that would never happen. Instead, Pharaoh nodded a final time and the double crown was lifted to Amenhotep's head.

Everyone smiled, including Thutmose, as the High Priest fitted the cumbersome crown in place. Pharaoh's concubine momentarily lifted a tear–streaked face to observe the youth before turning to weep again, more vigorously than ever, into Pharaoh's bed sheets.

Amenhotep stiffened his neck beneath the weight, his eyes bright as if he could feel himself becoming a god, sensing the power of immortality as it coursed through his body, strengthening his limbs. He would now be numbered among Egypt's deities and worshipped by the masses. His eyes disdainfully fell on his father as he held his head high and proud above the bed.

Thutmose looked first at the High Priest and then at Amenhab to see if they had noticed. They had, and exchanged glances, unable to hide their mistrust of the youth. But neither could change the moment already passed, nor could they go back in time to straighten what had twisted in the boy's spirit. The gods would have to deal with him now.

Thutmose closed his eyes. From this moment on whatever happened to Egypt no longer concerned him. He wanted only to pass peacefully to the afterlife and reap the eternity inherited by Pharaohs, gods, and other favored beings.

He thought of his mother at Thebes enjoying the riches Hatshepsut had left. Isis would no doubt have liked to have been here, standing over his bed wailing and fretting with everyone doing her bidding. But the gods had blessed him in that regard as well, for she would not receive news until after his passing. A smile tugged at his mouth. Once again he would leave without her permission.

His smile remained even after his body relaxed, feeling himself encompassed by warmth as if wrapped about by someone's arms, and he imagined them to be Meryet's. He could feel the heat of her breath on his cheek as he allowed his own to escape for the last time, succumbing to her presence as if embracing death.

The physician stood after having bent over the bed to cover Thutmose with the ceremonial cloth. The former Pharaoh's body would now be sent to the embalmers, and seventy days later, after a last journey up the Nile, he would enjoy the sleep of the honored with other Pharaohs west of Thebes.

Amenhotep towered over his father's form, watching to be sure all movement had ceased, then dry–eyed and impassive he turned from the bedside, the wails of the women echoing behind him as if haunting him with the memory of one he would just as soon forget.

As he stepped onto the balcony a thunderous cheer reverberated throughout the palace grounds and city as the multitudes viewed their Pharaoh and god for the first time. Amenhotep lifted a muscular arm in response, a smile of triumph on his face.

Why should he mourn? What did he care that his father had passed to the afterlife?

Egypt was his.

About the Author

The author has been a writer, journalist and columnist for over twenty years, and has a Bachelor of Arts in writing and Christian ministries. She pastored two churches for approximately fifteen years, and is currently in education.

The writer enjoys history, collecting fossils, and has a growing library on ancient Egypt and Israel. Visiting the Middle East provided first-hand insight into the people and places that inspired this book.

Besides *Two Sons from Egypt,* look for the sequels *Escape from Paradise* and *The Crimson Cord*, books II – III of *The Lion Awakes* fiction series.

The author's non-fiction *Discovering Truth* series provides valuable background information: *Discovering Moses and the Exodus: A Faith Building Adventure*, and book II, *Discovering the Promised Land: Conquering and Occupying Until He Comes*. Finally, chronicle your own spiritual journey in: *Discovering a Way through the Wilderness: Finding God in the Journey*.

Your comments are welcome at smithruth198@gmail.com.

Lightning Source UK Ltd.
Milton Keynes UK
UKHW010841070223
416609UK00003B/1074

9 781647 531997